不求人文化
Diy Culture Publishing

文化
Diy Culture Publishing

不求人文化
Diy Culture Publishing

不求人文化
Diy Culture Publishing

# NEW TOEIC Listening

## 50次新多益滿分的怪物講師

# 新多益聽力

# 答案＋解析本

# 自我檢測考試

| | | | | | | | | | |
|---|---|---|---|---|---|---|---|---|---|
| 001 (A) | 002 (C) | 003 (C) | 004 (B) | 005 (B) | 006 (B) | 007 (B) | 008 (B) | 009 (B) | 010 (A) |
| 011 (B) | 012 (B) | 013 (C) | 014 (D) | 015 (D) | 016 (A) | 017 (C) | 018 (D) | 019 (D) | 020 (C) |
| 021 (A) | 022 (B) | 023 (B) | 024 (D) | 025 (C) | 026 (A) | 027 (A) | 028 (A) | 029 (C) | 030 (B) |
| 031 (A) | 032 (B) | 033 (A) | 034 (D) | 035 (A) | 036 (B) | | | | |

# 自我檢測考試

## Part 1

**1.**

(A) He's pouring water into a glass.
(B) He's setting a plate on a table.
(C) He's putting away some cups.
(D) He's drinking from a bowl.

（A）他正把水倒入玻璃杯。
（B）他正把盤子放在桌上。
（C）他正把一些杯子收起。
（D）他正從碗裡喝東西。

**2.**

(A) The men are making a copy.
(B) The men are stocking books on a shelf.
(C) The men are looking at a computer screen.
(D) The men are filing some papers.

（A）男士們正在影印。
（B）男士們正在把書存放在書架上。
（C）男士們正看著電腦螢幕。
（D）男士們正在整理一些文件。

**3.**

(A) The men are assembling a rack.
(B) Paint is being applied to a wall.
(C) Containers have been set on shelves.
(D) Flower pots are being piled in a corner.

（A）男士們正在組裝架子。
（B）油漆被塗在牆上。
（C）容器已經放在貨架上。
（D）花瓶被堆在角落。

**4.**

(A) They've placed their shoes on the sand.
(B) They're strolling along the shore.
(C) Seaweed has been left along the water's edge.
(D) The rock is casting a shadow.

（A）他們已經把鞋子放在沙灘上。
（B）他們沿著海邊散步。
（C）海藻被留在水的邊緣。
（D）石頭正在產生影子。

## Part 2

**5.**

Who has the test results?
(A) That's what I thought.
(B) The secretary should have them.
(C) No, he hasn't.

誰有測驗的結果？
（A）那就是我所想的。
（B）秘書應該有。
（C）不，他沒有。

**6.**

Why weren't you at the party this afternoon?
(A) Yes, I wrote part of it.
(B) I thought it was tomorrow.
(C) I'll bring it later tonight.

為什麼你今天下午不在宴會中？
（A）是，我寫了其中一部分。
（B）我以為是明天。
（C）我今夜晚點會帶去。

**7.**

How do you like the new director?
(A) He's out of the office today.
(B) He's very demanding.
(C) No, that's not the right direction.

你的新主管怎麼樣呢？
（A）他今天不在辦公室。
（B）他要求很高。
（C）不，那不是對的方向。

**8.**

Could you come by my office before you leave?
(A) I don't know if the bill came this month.
(B) Sure. I'm on my way out now.
(C) No, she lives far away.

在你離開前，能到我辦公室來嗎？
（A）我不知道這個月帳單來了沒。
（B）當然，我正在下班當中。
（C）不，她住得很遠。

**9.**

Have you contacted the travel agency or do you want me to call them?
(A) Is that your phone number?

(B) I don't have time. Do you?
(C) No, I haven't had much yet.

你和旅行社聯繫了沒？還是由我來打電話給他們？
（A）那是你的電話號碼嗎？
（B）我沒有時間。你有嗎？
（C）不，我目前沒有很多。

**10.**

Did you make it to the new exhibit at the science museum?
(A) No, but I plan to next week.
(B) That's good news.
(C) Yes, to build a new museum.

你去過在科學博物館的新展覽會嗎?
（A）不，但我打算下週去。
（B）這真是個好消息。
（C）是的，為了蓋新的博物館。

**11.**

The marketing associate wasn't very helpful, was he?
(A) No, in the accounting department.
(B) I didn't think he was either.
(C) Thanks for your help.

行銷合夥人不太能幫忙，是吧？
（A）不，在會計部門。
（B）我也不認為他很會幫忙。
（C）謝謝你的幫忙。

**12.**

The microphones in the auditorium aren't working.
(A) Sometime this morning.
(B) I'll get the technician.
(C) The desk is next to the computer.

禮堂的麥克風壞掉了。
（A）今天上午某個時候。
（B）我會去找技師。
（C）那張桌子在電腦旁。

## Part 3

**問題13~15請參考以下對話。**

W : Excuse me. Can you tell me where a dry cleaner is here in the hotel? I spilt coffee on my shirt this morning, and need to have it cleaned within today.

M : Yes, there is one place located on the second floor. However I don't think they offer express service. You'd better go to the one across from the hotel. I'm sure they can do the service.

W : What a relief! I'll go there right away. I need the shirt for a job interview tomorrow afternoon.

女：抱歉。可以告訴我這間飯店的乾洗店在哪嗎？今天早上我打翻咖啡在我的襯衫上，今日之內要清洗乾淨。

男：是，在二樓有。但我想他們不提供快速服務。您最好去飯店對面那家。我相信他們在幾個小時之內做得到。

女：真幸運！我要馬上去。我明天下午的求職面試需要這件襯衫。

**13.**

Where are the speakers?
(A) In a bank
(B) In a shopping center
(C) In a hotel
(D) In a restaurant

說話者在哪裡？
（A）在銀行
（B）在購物中心
（C）在旅館
（D）在餐廳

**14.**

What does the woman want to do?
(A) Place an order
(B) Make a deposit
(C) Change her room
(D) Clean some clothes

這位女士想做什麼？
（A）下訂單
（B）存款
（C）換房間
（D）清洗衣物

**15.**

When is the interview?
(A) This morning

(B) This afternoon
(C) Tomorrow morning
(D) Tomorrow afternoon

什麼時候面試？
（A）今天上午
（B）今天下午
（C）明天早上
（D）明天下午

**問題16~18請參考以下對話。**

M : Hello, I'd like two tickets for Thursday night's theater performance.
W : I'm afraid all of the tickets are sold out for that performance.
M : Oh then, what about next week? Do you have tickets for next Saturday's performance?
W : Yes, we have. There are tickets for 7 p.m. and 9 p.m. Which would you like?

男：哈囉，我想要兩張週四晚上表演的門票。
女：那場表演所有的門票恐怕都賣完了。
男：哦，那麼下週的呢？有下週六表演的門票嗎？
女：是，有的。有晚上7點和晚上9點的。您想要哪一場的？

### 16.

Who most likely is the woman?
(A) A salesperson
(B) An athlete
(C) A security manager
(D) A museum curator

這位女士最有可能是什麼身分？
（A）一位售貨員
（B）一位運動員
（C）一位保全經理
（D）一位博物館館長

### 17.

What does the man want to do?
(A) Purchase a musical instrument
(B) Visit a museum
(C) Attend a performance
(D) Make a travel itinerary

這位男士想做什麼？
（A）購買樂器
（B）參觀博物館
（C）看表演
（D）安排旅遊行程

### 18.

What will the man probably do next?
(A) Complete a form
(B) Talk to the manager
(C) Listen to the music
(D) Purchase tickets

這個男士接著可能會做什麼？
（A）填寫表格
（B）與經理交談
（C）聽音樂
（D）購買門票

**問題19~21請參考以下對話。**

W : Becker, how's the marketing manager search going? Did you find anyone who is a good fit?
M : No. Personnel Department narrowed down the applications to two, but neither seems to be qualified. We're targeting young consumers in the clothing market. We need someone who has much experience in the related field.
W : I have a friend who is really qualified for the job. He's been with a clothing company for decades. Why don't you contact him to see if he's interested?

女：貝克，徵求行銷經理的事情進行得如何？你有找到任何不錯合適的人嗎？
男：沒有。人事部門縮小應徵者範圍到兩位，但似乎沒有人符合資格。我們的目標是服裝市場的年輕消費者，我們需要一位在相關領域有豐富經驗的人。
女：我有一個朋友相當有資格來做這個工作。他在一家服裝公司幾十年了。你何不聯絡他，看看他有沒有興趣？

### 19.

Which department needs a new manager?
(A) Personnel
(B) Customer service
(C) Accounting
(D) Marketing

哪個部門需要新的經理？
（A）人事部門
（B）客戶服務部門
（C）會計部門
（D）行銷部門

### 20.

What qualification does the man mention?
(A) Willingness to travel
(B) Strong references
(C) Relevant experience

(D) A university degree

這位男士論及什麼資格？
（A）願意出差
（B）有力的推薦
（C）相關工作經驗
（D）大學學位

### 21.

What does the woman recommend?
(A) Contacting a possible candidate
(B) Transferring to another branch
(C) Placing an advertisement on the Internet
(D) Rescheduling some interviews

這位女士建議了什麼？
（A）聯繫一位可能的候選人
（B）轉換到另一家分公司
（C）在網路上登廣告
（D）重新安排一些面試

**問題22~24請參考以下對話。**

M : Hi, Susan. I was a little late for the meeting and I missed some parts of the meeting. Could you tell me what the sales manager said about the Hong Kong office?

W : He said the Hong Kong group's doing great. They've boosted their sales this quarter by focusing on teenage consumers in their advertisement.

M : Great! So the manager suggests that we target younger people so our branch may raise our sales too, right?

W : You're right. And he said another meeting is scheduled for next week to deal with all the details.

男：嗨，蘇珊。我開會有點晚到，錯過了會議裡某些部分。你能告訴我關於香港辦公室銷售經理說了些什麼嗎？

女：他說，香港團隊做得非常好。他們在本季廣告中對準青少年消費者大力宣傳，快速提高了銷售量。

男：太棒了！所以經理建議我們將目標放在更年輕的人，而我們的分部也就更能提高我們的銷售，對嗎？

女：你說得對。他說下週要開另一次會議來討論細節。

### 22.

What does the man ask the woman for?
(A) How to get to another office
(B) Details about a meeting
(C) A list of advertisers
(D) Assistance with a sales proposal

這位男士向這位女士要求什麼？
（A）如何去另一間辦公室
（B）有關會議的詳情
（C）廣告主名單
（D）協助銷售的建議

### 23.

What have employees at the Hong Kong office done?
(A) Designed a new product
(B) Increased their sales
(C) Analyzed sales reports
(D) Finished their training

香港辦事處的員工做了什麼？
（A）設計一個新產品
（B）增加他們的銷售量
（C）分析銷售報告
（D）完成他們的培訓

### 24.

According to the man, what will occur next week?
(A) A manager will retire.
(B) A customer will arrive.
(C) A company will be acquired.
(D) A meeting will be held.

依據這位男士所言，下週將發生什麼事？
（A）一位經理將退休
（B）一位顧客將抵達
（C）一家公司將被收購
（D）將舉行會議

## Part 4

**問題25~27請參考以下電話留言。**

Hi, Erica. This is Madison Morton calling from Westwood Furniture store, and I'm a sales manager. I'm calling about the dress hanger you ordered from us last week. Unfortunately, the second type model you selected is not in stock. We can place a special order for it but I don't think we can get it in less than two months. However, we have the third type model available now. So I'd like to know whether you want to order the third type model or would rather wait for the second type model. I will leave for the day around six, so please call me back as soon as you get this message. Thank you.

嗨，艾瑞卡。這裡是西木傢俱店麥迪森摩頓，我是銷售經理。我是有關上週您和我們訂購的衣架來電的。很不巧的，您選的第二款沒有庫存。我們可以下特別訂單，但我不認為我們能在兩個月之內拿到。然而，我們目前有第三款可提供。所以我想知道您是否要訂購第三款，或願意等第二款。我今天六點左右會離開，所以當您聽到這個留言，請儘快回電給我。謝謝！

### 25.

Who is the caller?
(A) An accountant
(B) A clothing maker
(C) A sales manager
(D) A fashion designer

來電者是誰？
（A）一位會計師
（B）一位服裝製造商
（C）一位銷售經理
（D）一位時裝設計師

### 26.

What might be the problem?
(A) An item is not available.
(B) Some documents are missing.
(C) Some products were damaged.
(D) The delivery is late.

有可能是什麼問題？
（A）有個項目不能提供。
（B）有些文件遺失了。
（C）有些產品被損壞了。
（D）延遲交貨。

### 27.

What does the caller need to know from Erica?
(A) The type of model she wants
(B) The time she will return to the office
(C) The cost of a specially ordered item
(D) The expected arrival time of delivery

留言者需要從艾瑞卡得知什麼？
（A）她想要的款式
（B）她會回到辦公室的時間
（C）特別訂購的金額
（D）預計配送抵達的時間

**問題28~30請參考以下內容。**

As you all know, our network equipment sales on the capital area have gone up. We expect the sales will continue to increase, so we're planning to start a new branch in Busan in early August. I'm appointed to head the sales department in Busan, so I will be leaving my position as sales manager in July. Several new employees will be hired to deal with the increased business, but of course, the same chance will be given to the experienced sales representatives within our company. All of you are invited to consider the possibility of transferring to Busan. Please give us some feedback within next few weeks if you're interested in making this move.

如同大家所知道的，我們在首都地區的網絡設備銷售量上升了。我們期待銷售量將繼續增加，所以我們計劃在八月初開始在釜山開設新的分公司。我被安排帶領釜山銷售部門，所以我在七月離開銷售經理的職位。將有幾位新員工被雇用來處理增加的業務，當然，同樣的機會也會給予公司內經驗豐富的銷售代表們。請大家考慮轉換到釜山的可能性。若您有興趣此一變動，請在未來幾週之內給我們回應。

### 28.

Who is the speaker?
(A) A sales manager
(B) A maintenance worker
(C) A software designer
(D) A repair technician

誰是說話者？
（A）一位銷售經理
（B）一位維修工人
（C）一位軟體設計師
（D）一位維修技師

**29.**

What will happen in July?

(A) A company will stop its operation.

(B) Renovations on a new building will begin.

(C) The speaker will transfer to a new city.

(D) A presentation will be made at a meeting.

在七月會發生什麼

（A）一個公司將停止其運作。

（B）一個新建築的裝修將開始。

（C）說話者將到新的城市。

（D）將在會議上有一場報告。

**30.**

What does the speaker ask the listeners to consider?

(A) Meeting a project deadline

(B) Moving to a different office

(C) Recruiting more employees

(D) Modifying a building design

30.

說話者要求聽眾考慮什麼？

（A）遵守一個案子的最後期限

（B）轉換到不同的辦公室

（C）招募更多的員工

（D）修改建築設計

**問題31~33請參考以下內容。**

Welcome everyone to today's lecture series. Our featured speaker today is Mr. John Park, once the chairman of Stock Analyst Association. He is also an award-winning author of "Secret of Millionaire". Mr. Park will read excerpts from his book and answer questions from audience. Following that, he will be available to sign copies of his book. You can purchase the book at the back of the auditorium for twenty-five dollars. To get more information on his other books, you may refer to the brochures available there to anyone. Now, let's give a warm welcome to Mr. John Park.

歡迎大家來到今天的系列講座。我們今天的特別演講者，是曾為股票分析協會主席的約翰帕爾可先生。他也是百萬富翁先生的秘密的獲獎作者。帕爾可先生將讀出他書中的摘要和回答聽眾的問題。之後，他將會為他的書簽名。您可於觀眾席後面以二十五美元購買這本書。若想知道有關於他其他書籍的更多資訊，您可以參考這邊提供的小冊子。現在，請給予約翰帕爾可先生熱烈的歡迎。

**31.**

Who is Mr. Park?

(A) An author

(B) A conference organizer

(C) A bookstore owner

(D) A hotel receptionist

誰是帕爾可先生？

（A）一位作家

（B）一位會議舉辦人

（C）一位書店老闆

（D）一位旅館接待員

**32.**

What will Mr. Park talk about?

(A) His experience

(B) His book

(C) His heath

(D) His role as an analyst

帕爾可先生將談些什麼？

（A）他的經驗

（B）他的書

（C）他的健康

（D）他作為一位分析師的角色

**33.**

What can the listeners do at the back of the auditorium?

(A) Buy a book

(B) Read some signs

(C) Take a coffee break

(D) Register for future lectures

聽者可以在觀眾席後面做什麼？

（A）買書

（B）看一些告示

（C）小歇一下

（D）登記之後的演講

**問題34~36請參考以下內容。**

The following is a public service announcement, brought you by Radio ABC. Because of the drought, government officials are asking all city residents to conserve water. Residents are asked not to fill their swimming pools or water their gardens until further notice. Right now, the government is asking residents to do this on a voluntary basis, although if the situation becomes severe, it is possible that fines will be imposed. For more information, find energy conservation tips at our web site at www.energytips.or.uk.

以下由ABC電台為您帶來一則公共服務公告。由於乾旱，政府官員要求各城市的居民節省用水。直到進一步通知前，居民必須停止游泳池注水或花園澆水。此刻，政府要求居民主動來做這些措施，但如果情況變嚴重，有可能會加以罰款。相關訊息，請在我們網站www.enrgytips.or.uk搜尋節能小建議。

### 34.

Who is this talk directed to?
(A) Radio station employees
(B) Public servants
(C) Government officials
(D) Residents

這個談話是要指示什麼人？
（A）廣播電台員工
（B）公務員
（C）政府官員
（D）居民

### 35.

What are the listeners asked to avoid?
(A) Water plants
(B) Swim in the pool
(C) Take a walk
(D) Throw garbage

聽者被要求要避免做什麼？
（A）給植物澆水
（B）在游泳池游泳
（C）散步
（D）丟垃圾

### 36.

What can be found at web site mentioned by the speaker?
(A) A map of current weather information
(B) A list of ways to conserve energy
(C) Addresses of government officials
(D) A price list for gardening tools

在說話者提到的網站上可以發現什麼？
（A）目前氣象資訊的地圖
（B）節約能源的方式列表
（C）政府官員的地址
（D）園藝工具的價格表

# 答案&解析

Chapter 01 一人獨照相片

Quiz |

Q1. (A) reading some materials
(B) drinking a glass of wine
Q2. (A) working at a warehouse
(B) carrying a bucket
Q3. (A) examining some documents
(B) wearing a wristwatch
Q4. (A) resting on a bench
(B) tying his shoelace

**Q1**

(A) **She is reading some materials.**
她正在讀一些資料。

(B) She is drinking a glass of wine.
她正在喝一杯葡萄酒。

**Q2**

(A) He is working at a warehouse.
他正在一間倉庫工作。

(B) **He is carrying a bucket.**
他正在搬運一個水桶。

**Q3**

(A) **He is examining some documents.**
他正在審查一些文件。

(B) He is wearing a wristwatch.
他正戴著手錶。

**Q4**

(A) **A man is resting on a bench.**
一個男人正在長椅上休息。

(B) A man is tying his shoelace.
一個男人正在綁他的鞋帶。

**STEP 01** 若沒答對會後悔的考題

例子 (A)　1. (B)　2. (B)　3. (B)　4. (C)

例子 美W

| | |
|---|---|
| 1 主詞 | He, The man, A worker |
| 2 大動作 | working, using |
| 3 小動作 | wearing a helmet |
| 4 背景／場所／其他 | brick wall, bricks, a construction site |

(A) A worker's using a tool.
(B) A worker's wearing a tool belt.
(C) A worker's loading bricks onto a cart.

（A）工人正使用工具。
（B）工人正戴著工具腰帶。
（C）工人正把磚頭裝到手推車上。

**解說** 照片裡的男生正在拿著工具作業當中，所以（A）為答案。（B）不是答案，因為他沒有戴工具腰帶而是戴著安全帽的狀態。（C）也不是答案，因為該男生雖然是正在拿磚石做事情，但不是裝載當中，且照片裡也看不到手推車。 答案 (A)

**詞彙** tool 工具　tool belt 裝載　load 裝載　cart 手推車

**1.** 英M

| | |
|---|---|
| 1 主詞 | He, The(A) man, A shopper |
| 2 大動作 | shopping |
| 3 小動作 | reaching for |
| 4 背景／場所／其他 | foods, groceries, a store |

(A) The man is eating a meal.
(B) The man is shopping for groceries.
(C) The man is trying on a jacket.

（A）這個男人正在吃飯。
（B）這個男人正在購買食品雜貨。
（C）這個男人正試穿夾克。

**解說** 根據該男生在超市向陳列的食品伸手的動作可以知道他可能在購物當中，所以（B）為答案。（A）是故意誤導與用餐混淆的選項。（C）描述正在穿夾克的動作，而照片是穿著夾克的狀態，所以不是答案。 答案 (B)

**詞彙** meal 餐飯　shop for 購買…　grocery 食品雜貨　try on 試穿

**2.** 澳W

| | |
|---|---|
| 1 主詞 | She, The(A) woman |
| 2 大動作 | wearing glasses |
| 3 小動作 | sitting |
| 4 背景／場所／其他 | a sofa, a table, plants, a room |

(A) She's watching television.
(B) She's sitting on a sofa.
(C) She's reading a newspaper.

（A）她正看電視。
（B）她正坐在沙發上。
（C）她正在閱讀報紙。

**解說** 該女生在沙發上坐著休息，所以（B）為答案。（A）論及照片裡沒有的名詞television，所以不是答案。（C）是故意誤導與照片裡出現的書混淆的選項，而且照片裡沒有出現報紙，也沒有正在閱讀的狀況。 答案 (B)

**詞彙** **watch** 看 **sit** 坐 **sofa** 沙發 **newspaper** 報紙

**3.** 美M

| | |
|---|---|
| 1 主詞 | He, The(A) man |
| 2 小動作 | looking at |
| 3 背景 | wearing a suit and a tie |
| 4 背景／場所／其他 | a watch, a wristwatch, a road |

(A) The man is watching a game.
(B) The man is wearing a wristwatch.
(C) The man is adjusting his tie.

（A）這個男人正在觀看比賽。
（B）這個男人戴著手錶。
（C）這個男人正在調整他的領帶。

**解說** 該男生正在看著自己手腕上戴著的手錶，所以（B）為答案。（A）不是答案，因為該男生看著手錶，而不是看著比賽。（C）不是答案，因為沒有描述戴著領帶的狀態，而是描述了調整領帶的動作。 答案 (B)

**詞彙** **wear** 穿戴 **wristwatch** 腕錶 **adjust** 調整 **tie** 領帶

**4.** 美W

| | |
|---|---|
| 1 主詞 | She, The(A) woman, A girl |
| 2 大動作 | talking |
| 3 小動作 | sitting, holding |
| 4 背景／場所／其他 | a phone, a desk, a laptop, an office |

(A) She's looking at a computer screen.
(B) She's sitting on a bench.
(C) She's talking over the phone.

（A）她正注視著電腦螢幕。
（B）她正坐在長椅上。
（C）她正在打電話。

**解說** 該女生正在打電話當中，所以（C）為答案。（A）不是答案，因為照片裡女生的視線沒有對著電腦，而是往別的方向。（B）不是答案，因為她不是在長椅上坐著。 答案 (C)

**詞彙** **look at** 注視 **bench** 長椅 **over the phone** 在電話上

## STEP 02 考題實戰練習

| | | | |
|---|---|---|---|
| 1. (C) | 2. (D) | 3. (B) | 4. (A) |
| 5. (A) | 6. (D) | 7. (A) | 8. (C) |

**1.** 美W
(A) A man is climbing up a ladder.
(B) A man is piloting a plane.
(C) A man is boarding an airplane.
(D) A man is entering a house.

（A）一個男人正在爬梯子。
（B）一個男人正駕駛飛機。
（C）一個男人正登上飛機。
（D）一個男人正進入一棟房子。

**解說** 該男生正在登上飛機當中，所以（C）為答案。（A）不是答案，因為他不是在踏上梯子而是走上飛機的階梯。（B）不是答案，因為照片裡的男生正在登上飛機當中，而不是操作飛機。（D）不是答案，因為不是進屋而是進飛機當中。 答案 (C)

**詞彙** **climb up** 向上爬 **ladder** 梯子 **pilot** 操作 **board** 登乘

**2.** 美M
(A) He is opening a car door.
(B) He is unlocking a metal gate.
(C) He is carrying a suitcase.

(D) He is wearing a suit and a tie.

（A）他正在開車門。
（B）他正將一道鐵門解鎖。
（C）他正提著一個手提旅行箱。
（D）他正穿著西裝和領帶。

**解說** 該男生穿著西裝，且戴著領帶，所以（D）為答案。（A）不是答案，因為他不是在開車門，而是在開房子的門。選項（B）我們無法知道是否為鐵門。（C）不是答案，因為他拿著的不是旅行包而是公事包。 答案 (D)

**詞彙** unlock 解鎖 metal gate 鐵門 carry 提 suitcase 手提旅行箱 a suit and a tie 西裝和領帶

**3.** 英M
(A) She's writing a letter.
(B) She's placing a file folder on the desk.
(C) She's putting some luggage on the floor.
(D) She's opening up a file cabinet.

（A）她正在寫一封信。
（B）她正把文件夾放在辦公桌上。
（C）她正把一些行李放在地板上。
（D）她正在開一個文件櫃。

**解說** 該女生正在將文件夾放在桌子上，所以（B）為答案。（A）不是答案，因為該女生不是在寫信。（C）不是答案，因為這不是放置包包的動作，而是將檔案夾放在桌子上的動作。（D）不是答案，因為論及了照片裡沒有的名詞file cabinet。 答案 (B)

**詞彙** write 寫 place 放置 file folder 文件夾 put 放下 luggage 行李箱 cabinet 櫃子

**4.** 澳W
(A) She's using the sink.
(B) She's washing her hands.
(C) She's eating dessert.
(D) She's opening a drawer.

（A）她正在使用水槽。
（B）她正在洗手。
（C）她正在吃甜點。
（D）她正打開抽屜。

**解說** 該女生正在水槽洗碗當中，所以（A）為答案。（B）不是答案，因為不是洗手，而是洗碗當中。（C）不是答案，因為不是吃東西，而是洗碗。（D）不是答案，因為論及了照片裡沒有的名詞drawer。 答案 (A)

**詞彙** sink 水槽 wash 洗 dessert 點心 drawer 點心

**5.** 美W
(A) A man is dragging some luggage.
(B) A man is filling a bag with some tools.
(C) A man is walking up the stairs.
(D) A man is paving the road.

（A）一個男人正拖著一些行李。
（B）一個男人正把一些工具裝進袋子裡。
（C）一個男人正在走上樓梯。
（D）一個男人正在鋪馬路。

**解說** 該男生雙手拉著旅行包，所以（A）為答案。（B）不是答案，因為論及了照片裡沒有的名詞tools，而且照片裡沒有出現裝載東西的動作。（C）不是答案，因為不是走階梯，而是在馬路上走路。（D）不是答案，因為不是鋪馬路，只是在馬路上走路的畫面。 答案 (A)

**詞彙** drag 拖曳 luggage 行李 fill 裝滿 walk up 向上走 stairs 樓梯 pave 鋪平 road 道路

**6.** 美M
(A) The man is storing some tools.
(B) The man is sweeping the floor.
(C) The man is removing his hat.
(D) The man is working outdoors.

（A）一個男人正存放一些工具。
（B）一個男人正在掃地。
（C）一個男人正拿掉他的帽子。
（D）一個男人正在戶外工作。

**解說** 該男生正在戶外工作中，所以（D）為答案。（A）不是答案，因為不是收拾工具的動作，而是拿著工具做事的畫面。（B）不是答案，因為不是掃地的畫面。（C）不是答案，因為該男生是戴著帽子，而不是在脫帽。 答案 (D)

**詞彙** store 存放 sweep 掃 remove 掃 outdoors 戶外

**7.** 英M
(A) A man is standing on the ladder.
(B) A man is installing a shelf.
(C) A man is writing a letter.
(D) A man is hammering a nail.

（A）一個男人正站在梯子上。
（B）一個男人正在安裝架子。
（C）一個男人正在寫信。
（D）一個男人正在槌釘子。

**解說** 該男生正站在梯子上做事，所以（A）為答案。（B）論及了照片裡沒有的名詞shelf，所以不是答案。（C）是故意用與ladder相近的發音letter來誤導的選項。（D）不是答案，因為他不是在用榔頭。 答案 (A)

**詞彙** stand 站立 ladder 梯子 install 安裝 shelf 架子 write 寫 hammer 用榔頭槌 nail 釘子

8. 澳W

(A) She's looking at some plants.
(B) She's picking flowers in the garden.
(C) She's examining some documents.
(D) She's making a cup of coffee.

(A) 她正在看一些植物。
(B) 她正在花園裡摘花。
(C) 她正在查閱一些文件。
(D) 她正在做一杯咖啡。

**解說** 該女生正在看著一些文件，所以（C）為答案。（A）不是答案，因為她不是在看花草，而在看文件。（B）不是答案，因為花是已經插在花瓶裡的。（D）不是答案，因為她拿著咖啡杯。 答案 (C)

**詞彙** plant 花草、植物 pick 摘採

## Chapter 02 包含兩個以上人物的照片

### Quiz |

Q1. (A) playing musical instruments
(B) clapping their hands

Q2. (A) wearing ties
(B) holding bags

Q3. (A) trying on shoes
(B) paying for goods

Q4. (A) holding a cup
(B) wearing a hat

### Q1

(A) **They are playing musical instruments.**
他們正在演奏樂器。

(B) They are clapping their hands.
他們正在拍手。

### Q2

(A) **The men are wearing ties.**
男人們打著領帶。

(B) The men are holding bags.
男人們正抱著袋子。

### Q3

(A) Some shoppers are trying on shoes.
一些購物者正在試鞋子。

(B) **A man is paying for goods.**
一個男人正在付錢。

### Q4

(A) **A woman is holding a glass.**
一個女人正拿著杯子。

(B) A man is wearing a hat.
一個男人戴著帽子。

### STEP 01 若沒答對會後悔的考題

例子 (C) 1. (C) 2. (A) 3. (C) 4. (C)

例子 美W

| | |
|---|---|
| 1 主詞 | They |
| 2 概括性／群體性描述1 | having a meal |
| 3 概括性／群體性描述2 | looking at each other |
| 4 背景／場所／其他 | food, dishes, table |

(A) They're cooking some food.
(B) They're picking up some dishes.
(C) They're having a meal.

（A）他們正在烹調一些食物。
（B）他們正收拾一些碗盤。
（C）他們正在用餐。

**解說** 該男生和女生正在用餐當中，所以（C）為答案。（A）不是答案，因為不是在做菜，而是在吃著東西。（B）不是答案，因為雖然出現盤子，但不是在收拾的。 答案 (C)

**詞彙** **cook** 烹調 **pick up** 拿起來 **have a meal** 吃飯

**1.** 英M

| | |
|---|---|
| 1 主詞 | Some people, A woman |
| 2 概括性／群體性描述 | reading |
| 3 個別描述 | carrying a bag |
| 4 背景／場所／其他 | reading materials, train, suits and ties |

(A) Some people are boarding a train.
(B) A woman is pointing at a distance.
(C) Some people are reading.

（A）有些人正在登上火車。
（B）一個女人正指著遠處。
（C）有些人正在閱讀。

**解說** 這些人正在閱讀某個東西，所以（C）為答案。（A）不是答案，因為他們不是在登上火車，而是已經在火車上。（B）不是答案，因為該女生是在看著東西，而不是指著。 答案 (C)

**詞彙** **board** 登乘 **point at** 指向 **distance** 距離 **read** 閱讀

**2.** 澳W

| | |
|---|---|
| 1 主詞 | They |
| 2 概括性／群體性描述1 | facing each other |
| 3 概括性／群體性描述2 | sitting at the table |
| 4 背景／場所／其他 | cup, table |

(A) They are looking at each other.
(B) They are holding cups.
(C) They are ordering a meal.

（A）他們正互相注視著。
（B）他們都拿著杯子。
（C）他們正在點餐。

**解說** 該男生和女生正在坐著互相注視，所以（A）為答案。（B）不是答案，因為杯子是在桌上擺著，而不是這些人拿著的。（C）是為了故意誤導而將照片裡坐在餐桌的人描述為點餐的選項 答案 (A)

**詞彙** **look at each other** 互相注視 **hold** 握 **order** 訂購 **meal** 餐飯

**3.** 英M

| | |
|---|---|
| 1 主詞 | The people, Some people |
| 2 概括性／群體性描述 | waiting in line |
| 3 個別描述 | standing apart from others |
| 4 背景／場所／其他 | stairs, vehicles, equipment |

(A) They are driving up a hill.
(B) They are climbing over a wall.
(C) They are waiting in a line.

（A）他們在駕駛開越一座小山。
（B）他們正爬過一堵牆。
（C）他們正在排隊等待。

**解說** 這些人正在排隊等著要坐纜車，所以（C）為答案。選項（A）會聽見照片裡沒有的名詞hill，所以不是答案。（B）也是聽見照片裡沒有的名詞wall，所以不是答案。 答案 (C)

**詞彙** **drive up** 開車爬越 **climb over a wall** 攀爬越牆 **wait** 等待 **in a line** 排隊

**4.** 美W

| | |
|---|---|
| 1 主詞 | Some people, A woman |
| 2 概括性／群體性描述 | walking, strolling |
| 3 個別描述 | riding, talking, wearing |
| 4 背景／場所／其他 | bicycle, phone, bag, street |

(A) A bus is stopping for passengers.
(B) A woman is picking up her bag.
(C) A woman is talking on the phone.

（A）公車正在停車載客。
（B）一個女人正拿起她的背袋。

（C）一個女人正在講電話。

**解說** 該女生正在打電話，所以（C）為答案。（A）裡聽見照片裡沒有的名詞bus，所以不是答案。（B）不是答案，因為她是將包包背著，而不是拿起來的。
答案 (C)

**詞彙** stop 停車 passenger 乘客 pick up 拿起
on the phone 在電話上

## STEP 02 考題實戰練習

| | | | |
|---|---|---|---|
| 1. (B) | 2. (A) | 3. (D) | 4. (A) |
| 5. (D) | 6. (B) | 7. (A) | 8. (B) |

**1.** 美W
(A) They're writing on a chalkboard.
(B) They're working at a table.
(C) They're putting files in the cabinet.
(D) They're giving a presentation.

（A）他們正在寫黑板。
（B）他們正在桌邊工作。
（C）他們正在把文件放在櫃子裡。
（D）他們正在報告。

**解說** （B）較接近描述這些人在桌上看文件，所以為答案。（A）不是答案，因為聽到照片裡沒有的名詞chalkboard。（C）不是答案，因為出現了照片裡沒有的名詞cabinet。（D）不是答案，因為這些人正在看著文件工作，而不是在發表當中。
答案 (B)

**詞彙** write on 寫在…上 chalkboard 黑板 put 放
give a presentation 發表；報告

**2.** 美M
(A) A man is kicking a ball up in the air.
(B) Gardeners are trimming trees in a field.
(C) They're mowing a lawn in front of the house.
(D) Some plants in the park are being watered.

（A）一個男人正將球踢到空中。
（B）園丁正在田地修剪樹木。
（C）他們在屋前的草坪割草。
（D）公園一些植物正在被澆灌。

**解說** 該男生正在踢球，所以（A）為答案。（B）是故意用照片裡出現的trees來誤導的選項。（C）也是故意用照片裡看到的lawn來誤導的選項。（D）也是照片裡的plants來誤導的選項。
答案 (A)

**詞彙** kick 踢 in the air 在空中 trim a tree 修剪樹木
field 田地 mow a lawn 除草 plant 植物

**3.** 英M
(A) Some people are resting in a park.
(B) Some people are eating in a restaurant.
(C) Some people are sweeping the floor.
(D) Some people are wearing coats and hats.

（A）有些人正在公園休息。
（B）有些人正在餐廳吃飯。
（C）有些人正在掃地。
（D）有些人正穿著大衣和帽子。

**解說** 該男生和女生正穿著大衣且戴著帽子，所以（D）為答案。（A）是聽到照片裡沒有的名詞park，所以不是答案。（B）不是答案，因為無法判定照片裡的地點是否為餐廳。（C）不是答案，因為這些人只是站著，而不是掃地當中。
答案 (D)

**詞彙** rest 休息 sweep 掃 wear 穿戴

**4.** 澳W
(A) They are examining some papers.
(B) They are adjusting their glasses.
(C) They are taking some measurements.
(D) They are looking out the window.

（A）他們正在審閱一些文件。
（B）他們正在調整他們的眼鏡。
（C）他們正在進行一些測量。
（D）他們正看著窗外。

**解說** 這些人正在看著文件，所以（A）為答案。（B）不是答案，因為他們戴著眼鏡，而不是在調整當中。（C）不是答案，因為他們不是在測量，而是在看著文件。（D）是故意用照片裡出現的windows來誤導的選項。
答案 (A)

**詞彙** examine 審閱 paper 資料；報告 adjust 調整
take a measurement 調整 look out the window
看著窗外

**5.** 美W
(A) The people are greeting each other.
(B) The woman is driving a car.
(C) The woman is opening a car door.
(D) The man is handing a key to the woman.

（A）人們正在互相打招呼。
（B）這個女人正在開車。
（C）這個女人正在打開車門。
（D）這個男人正在將鑰匙交給這個女人。

**解說** 該男生將鑰匙給該女生，所以（D）為答案。（A）不是答案，因為他們只是互相面對，並不是在打招呼。（B）是故意用照片裡出現的car來誤導的選項。（C）也是故意用照片裡的car door來誤導的選項。
答案 (D)

**詞彙** **greet each other** 互相問候 **hand A to B** 將A交給B

**6.** 美M

(A) The men are boarding a train.
(B) The men are walking on the railroad.
(C) The men are fixing a machine.
(D) The men are waiting at the railroad crossing.

（A）男人們正在登上列車。
（B）男人們正走在鐵道上。
（C）男人們正在修理機器。
（D）男人們正在等著穿過鐵路。

**解說** 該兩個男生正在鐵路上走著，所以（B）為答案。（A）是故意用train來誤導的選項。（C）是用照片裡沒有的名詞machine，所以不是答案。（D）不是答案，因為這些人是在鐵路上走著，而不是在平交道口上等待。 答案 (B)

**詞彙** **board** 登乘 **railroad** 鐵路 **fix** 修理 **machine** 機器 **wait** 等候 **railroad crossing** 鐵路平交道

**7.** 英M

(A) Some people are shaking hands.
(B) A man is presenting his business card.
(C) A door is being checked by a repairman.
(D) One woman is closing the door behind her.

（A）有些人正在握手。
（B）有個男人正拿出他的名片。
（C）一扇門正由修理工人檢查中。
（D）一個女人正關上她身後的門。

**解說** 有兩個男生正在握手，所以（A）為答案。（B）裡聽到照片裡沒有的名詞business card，所以不是答案。（C）不是答案，因為無法知道該女生是否為修理工人。（D）不是答案，因為這扇門是已經關著的狀態。 答案 (A)

**詞彙** **shake hands** 握手 **present** 展示 **business card** 名片 **repairman** 修理工人 **close** 關

**8.** 澳W

(A) Some people are screening some products.
(B) Some people are looking at a computer screen.
(C) Some people are helping each other move a computer.
(D) Some people are putting away some equipment.

（A）有些人正在檢查一些產品。
（B）有些人正在注視著電腦螢幕。
（C）有些人正在互相幫助搬動電腦。
（D）有些人正在收拾一些設備。

**解說** 有兩個女生正在看著電腦螢幕，所以（B）為答案。（A）是故意將當作名詞的screen改成動詞用以誤導的選項。（C）是用照片裡出現的單字computer來誤導的選項。（D）不是答案，因為這些人是看著電腦螢幕，而不是收拾設備。 答案 (B)

**詞彙** **screen** 檢查 **look at** 注視 **each other** 互相 **move** 移動 **put away** 收拾 **equipment** 設備

Chapter 03 對照片裡的物件與背景的描述

Quiz |

Q1. (A) casting shadows (B) being planted
Q2. (A) A table (B) Diners
Q3. (A) being examined (B) being assembled
Q4. (A) fountain, spraying
(B) trees, being trimmed

Q1
(A) **Trees are casting shadows.**
樹木正投影著。

(B) Trees are being planted.
樹木正在被種植。

Q2
(A) **A table has been set for a meal.**
為了用餐，餐桌被擺設了。

(B) Diners are having their meals.
用餐者正在吃飯。

Q3
(A) **A map is being examined.**
地圖正在被查看中。

(B) A telescope is being assembled.
望遠鏡正被組裝中。

Q4
(A) **The fountain is spraying into the air.**
噴泉噴灑到空中。

(B) Some trees are being trimmed in the garden.
在花園的一些樹木正被修剪。

## STEP 01 若沒答對會後悔的考題

例子 (B) 1. (C) 2. (A) 3. (A) 4. (B)

例子 美W

| | |
|---|---|
| 1 主要物件 | lights |
| 2 靜態性狀況1 | (be/have been) turned on |
| 3 靜態性狀況2 | (be/have been) lined up |
| 4 背景／場所／其他 | wall, corridor, pedestrians |

(A) A worker is fixing a lamp.
(B) Some lights have been turned on.
(C) A painting is hanging on the wall.

（A）一名工人正在修理一盞燈。
（B）有些燈被打開了。
（C）一幅畫正在被掛在牆上。

**解說** 有一些燈正亮著，所以（B）為答案。（A）是故意用lamp來造成混淆的選項。（C）不是答案，因為並非有一幅畫掛在牆壁上，而是全部的牆壁上都有塗鴉。

答案 (B)

**詞彙** **worker** 工人 **fix** 修理 **lights** 燈具 **turn on** 開 **painting** 畫作 **hang** 等待 **wall** 牆壁

1. 英M

| | |
|---|---|
| 1 人物的動作 | A woman is watering some plants. |
| 2 物件的立場 | Plants are being watered. |
| 3 背景／場所／其他 | garden, plants, flowers |

(A) Flowers are being planted.
(B) Bushes are being trimmed by the woman.
(C) Some plants are being watered.

（A）花草正在被種植。
（B）灌木叢正被一個女人修剪。
（C）一些植物正在被澆水。

**解說** 該女生正給花草澆水當中，所以（C）為答案。（A）是故意誤導而讓你聯想到種花的選項。（B）裡聽到照片裡沒有的名詞bushes，所以不是答案。

答案 (C)

**詞彙** **plant** 種植 **bush** 灌木叢 **trim** 修剪 **water** 澆水

2. 澳W

| | |
|---|---|
| 1 主要物件 | bed, lamps |
| 2 靜態性狀況1 | (be/have been) between the lamps |
| 3 靜態性狀況2 | (be/have been) turned on |
| 4 背景／場所／其他 | room, floor |

(A) A bed is between the lamps.
(B) A maid is making the bed.
(C) Lamps are being turned on.

（A）一張床介於在檯燈之間。
（B）女傭正在整理床鋪。

（C）燈正被打開。

**解說** 這張床在檯燈之間，所以（A）為答案。照片裡沒有人，所以出現與人相關說法的（B）或聽到being的（C）不是答案。 答案 (A)

**詞彙** **maid** 女侍；女傭 **make the bed** 整理床鋪 **turn on** 開

**3.** 美M

| | |
|---|---|
| 1 人物的動作 | A worker is measuring a piece of wood. |
| 2 物件的立場 | A piece of wood is being measured. |
| 3 背景／場所／其他 | ruler |

(A) A piece of wood is being measured.
(B) There are machines at a construction site.
(C) A man is cutting down some trees.

（A）一塊木頭正在被測量。
（B）在工地有一些機器。
（C）一個男人正在砍一些樹木。

**解說** 有個人正測量一塊木頭，所以（A）為答案。（B）裡聽到照片裡沒有的名詞machines，所以不是答案。（C）不是答案，因為不是將樹木砍下來，而是在測量木頭。 答案 (A)

**詞彙** **a piece of** 一塊的… **measure** 測量 **machine** 機器 **construction site** 工地 **cut down** 砍伐

**4.** 美W

| | |
|---|---|
| 1 主要物件 | painting, bed, dressers |
| 2 靜態性狀況1 | (be/have been) above the bed |
| 3 靜態性狀況2 | (be/have been) between the dressers |
| 4 背景／場所／其他 | room, window, curtain |

(A) The curtain is covering the window.
(B) A painting is hanging above the bed.
(C) The floor is being cleaned.

（A）窗簾遮蓋著窗戶。
（B）一幅畫正掛在床的上方。
（C）地板正在被清掃。

**解說** 床鋪的上方掛著一幅畫，所以（B）為答案。（A）不是答案，因為窗簾並非遮住窗戶，而是拉開的。（C）不是答案，因為照片裡沒有人卻聽到being。 答案 (B)

**詞彙** **cover** 覆蓋 **painting** 畫作 **above** 上方 **floor** 地板 **clean** 清掃

## STEP 02 考題實戰練習

| | | | |
|---|---|---|---|
| 1. (D) | 2. (B) | 3. (B) | 4. (A) |
| 5. (C) | 6. (D) | 7. (C) | 8. (C) |

**1.** 美W
(A) Storage tanks are being assembled.
(B) Industrial equipment is being inspected.
(C) Construction materials are burning.
(D) Smoke is rising into the air.

（A）儲存槽正在被組裝。
（B）工業設備正在被檢查。
（C）建築材料正在燃燒。
（D）煙霧正在上升到空中。

**解說** 煙霧正上升到空中，所以（D）為答案。（A）和（B）不是答案，因為照片裡沒有人卻聽到being。（C）不是答案，因為出現了照片裡沒有的名詞construction materials。 答案 (D)

**詞彙** **storage tank** 儲存槽 **assemble** 組裝 **industrial equipment** 工業設備 **inspect** 檢查 **construction materials** 建築材料 **burn** 燃燒 **smoke** 煙 **into the air** 向空中

**2.** 美M
(A) Passengers are stepping onto a platform.
(B) The train is near the platform.
(C) People are purchasing tickets from machines.
(D) A train station is closed for repairs.

（A）乘客們正踏上月台。
（B）火車在月台處附近。
（C）人們正在機器購買票。
（D）火車站被關閉以維修。

**解說** 火車正在接近月台當中，所以（B）為答案。選項（A）和（C）因為照片裡看不到人，所以不是答案。（D）是故意用train station來誤導的選項。 答案 (B)

**詞彙** **step onto** 踏上… **near** 近處 **platform** 月台 **purchase** 購買 **train station** 火車站 **closed** 被關閉 **repair** 修理

3. 英M

(A) Groceries are being put in a bag.
(B) A purchase is being made.
(C) An assortment of items sits on a counter.
(D) A customer is removing an item from a shelf.

（A）雜貨正被放進一個袋子。
（B）一件採購正被進行中。
（C）在櫃檯上有各式各樣的物品。
（D）客人正從貨架上把一個品項移開。

**解說** 照片裡看得到付錢的畫面，所以（B）為答案。（A）裡聽到照片裡沒有的名詞bag，所以不是答案。（C）不是答案，因為商品不是擺在收銀台上面，而是陳列在收銀台後面。（D）不是答案，因為這個客人正在付錢當中，而不是移開商品。 答案(B)

**詞彙** **grocery** 雜貨 **put** 放 **make a purchase** 採購 **an assortment of** 各式各樣的 **item** 項目 **sit** 有 **customer** 顧客 **remove** 移除 **shelf** 架子

4. 澳W

(A) Boxes are stacked in a warehouse.
(B) Some boxes are laid down on the floor.
(C) The floor is being swept.
(D) Supplies are being unloaded in the warehouse.

（A）箱子被堆放在倉庫。
（B）一些箱子被放下於地板。
（C）地板正被打掃。
（D）備用品正在倉庫被卸貨中。

**解說** 這些箱子都堆放在倉庫裡，所以（A）為答案。（B）不是答案，因為這些箱子不在地板上，而在架子上。（C）和（D）不是答案，因為沒有人卻聽到being。 答案(A)

**詞彙** **stack** 堆置 **lay down** 放下 **sweep** 掃 **supplies** 備品；供應品 **unload** 卸貨 **warehouse** 倉庫

5. 美W

(A) Some sailors are standing on a deck.
(B) Some ducks are swimming near a boat.
(C) Some boats are floating by the dock.
(D) Some boats are being tied up at the pier.

（A）一些船員正站立在甲板上。
（B）一些鴨子正游在一艘小船附近。
（C）一些船隻正在船塢旁浮著。
（D）一些船隻正被綁在碼頭。

**解說** 這些船隻都被綁在碼頭，所以（C）為答案。（A）不是答案，因為聽到照片裡沒有的名詞sailors。（B）不是答案，因為出現照片裡沒有的名詞ducks。（D）不是答案，因為照片裡沒有人卻聽到being。 答案(C)

**詞彙** **sailor** 船員 **deck** 甲板 **float** 浮在（水面上） **dock** 船塢 **be tied up** 被綁 **pier** 碼頭

6. 美M

(A) A vehicle is being parked.
(B) A vehicle is being repaired.
(C) A vehicle is being driven.
(D) A vehicle is being washed.

（A）一輛車子正被停放中。
（B）一輛車子正在被修理。
（C）一輛車子正在被駕駛。
（D）一輛車子正在被清洗。

**解說** 這些人正在洗車當中，所以（D）為答案。（A）不是答案，因為這輛車子不是被停車當中。（B）不是答案，因為這輛車子不是被修理當中。（C）不是答案因為不是開車當中。 答案(D)

**詞彙** **vehicle** 車輛 **park** 泊車 **repair** 修理 **drive** 駕駛 **wash** 洗

7. 英M

(A) Diners are eating sandwiches at a table.
(B) A table is covered with a newspaper.
(C) Chairs are around the table.
(D) Some chairs are occupied.

（A）用餐者正在桌上吃三明治。
（B）餐桌被用報紙蓋著。
（C）椅子圍著桌子。
（D）有些椅子還沒有人坐。

**解說** 餐桌的周圍擺著一些椅子，所以（C）為答案。（A）不是答案，因為照片裡沒有人，而且也聽到照片裡沒有的名詞sandwiches。（B）不是答案，因為照片裡沒有報紙。（D）不是答案，因為不只是一些椅子沒人坐，而是全部的椅子都沒人坐。 答案(C)

**詞彙** **diner** 用餐者 **cover** 覆蓋 **newspaper** 報紙 **occupied**（座位）無人佔用

8. 澳W

(A) The woman is next to the hotel.
(B) The woman is putting her shoes in the drawer.
(C) The suitcase is full of clothes.
(D) The suitcase is being assembled.

（A）這個女人正在旅館旁邊。
（B）這個女人正把她的鞋子放進抽屜。
（C）這個手提箱裝滿了衣服。
（D）這個手提箱正在被組裝。

**解說** 該手提箱裝滿著衣服，所以（C）為答案。（A）不是答案，因為無法知道該女生在哪兒，只有看到她在室內而已。（B）不是答案，因為該女生雖然正在收鞋子，但不是放在抽屜裡而是放在手提箱裡。（D）不是答案因為該女生不是在組裝東西。 答案(C)

**詞彙** next to 在…旁邊 put 放 suitcase 旅行手提箱 full of 充滿… clothes 衣服 assemble 組裝

Chapter 04 出現特殊狀況的照片

## Quiz |

Q1. (A) eating in a restaurant
(B) being served in a restaurant

Q2. (A) working outdoors
(B) climbing down the ladder

Q3. (A) leaving the stage
(B) playing musical instruments

Q4. (A) using a mouse
(B) typing on a keyboard

### Q1

(A) **People are eating in a restaurant.**
人們正在餐廳吃飯。.

(B) The food is being served in a restaurant.
這食物正被餐廳供應中。

### Q2

(A) **Workers are working outdoors.**
工人正在戶外工作。

(B) The men are climbing down the ladder.
這個男人正在爬下梯子。

### Q3

(A) Some musicians are leaving the stage.
一些音樂家正在離開舞台。

(B) **People are playing musical instruments.**
人們正在演奏樂器。

### Q4

(A) She's using a mouse.
她正在使用滑鼠。

(B) **She's typing on a keyboard.**
她正在使用滑鼠。

## STEP 01 若沒答對會後悔的考題

例子 (B) 1. (C) 2. (B) 3. (B) 4. (A)

例子 美W

| 1 狀況 | 餐廳 |
|---|---|
| 2 對人物的描述 | X |
| 3 對物件的描述 | be unoccupied |
| 4 背景／場所／其他 | table, outdoors, shadows |

(A) A waiter is taking an order.
(B) The tables are unoccupied in a restaurant.
(C) People are helping themselves to the food.

（A）一個侍者正在接受客人點餐。
（B）餐廳的桌子還未被佔用。
（C）人們自助取用食物。

**解說** 餐桌和椅子都空著，所以（B）為答案。（A）不是答案，因為出現照片裡沒有的名詞waiter。（C）不是答案，因為照片裡沒有人出現。. 答案 (B)

**詞彙** **take an order** 服務點餐 **unoccupied** 無人佔用 **help oneself to** 自助食用⋯

## 1. 英M

| 1 狀況 | 交通 |
|---|---|
| 2 對人物的描述 | getting in the car |
| 3 對物件的描述 | be open |
| 4 背景／場所／其他 | car, door, tire |

(A) A girl is checking the tire.
(B) A girl is driving a car.
(C) A girl is entering the car.

（A）一個女孩正在檢查輪胎。
（B）一個女孩正在開車。
（C）一個女孩正進入汽車。

**解說** 該女孩正在進入車子裡，所以（C）為答案。（A）是故意用tire來誤導的選項。（B）是故意用car來誤導的選項。 答案 (C)

**詞彙** **check** 檢查 **tire** 輪胎

## 2. 澳W

| 1 狀況 | 工作場所 |
|---|---|
| 2 對人物的描述 | carrying a box |
| 3 對物件的描述 | be stacked |
| 4 背景／場所／其他 | warehouse, corner |

(A) A man is standing in a warehouse.
(B) A man is carrying a box.
(C) Some boxes are being loaded.

（A）一個男人正站在倉庫裡。
（B）一個男人正提著一個箱子。
（C）一些箱子正被裝載。

**解說** 該男生正拿著箱子移動當中，所以（B）為答案。（A）不是答案，因為該男生不是站著，而是在移動當中。（C）不是答案，因為有一些箱子堆著，但不是在被堆放當中。 答案 (B)

**詞彙** **warehouse** 倉庫 **carry** 攜提 **load** 承裝

## 3. 美M

| 1 狀況 | 公司 |
|---|---|
| 2 對人物的描述 | examining papers |
| 3 對物件的描述 | be seated |
| 4 背景／場所／其他 | office, table, chair |

(A) The seats are unoccupied.
(B) Some people are examining papers.
(C) A man is placing a file in the cabinet.

（A）座位沒有人坐。
（B）有些人正在查閱文件。
（C）一個男人正把文件夾放在櫃子。

**解說** 這些人看著文件並且對話當中，所以（B）為答案。（A）不是答案，因為這些座位坐著人，而不是空著的。（C）是故意用cabinet來誤導的選項。 答案 (B)

**詞彙** **unoccupied**（座位）無人佔用的 **examine** 查閱 **papers** 文件 **place** 置放

## 4. 美W

| 1 狀況 | 戶外／其他 |
|---|---|
| 2 對人物的描述 | X |
| 3 對物件的描述 | floating, in the water |
| 4 背景／場所／其他 | shadow, clouds, sky |

(A) Some boats are floating in the water.
(B) Some boats are tied up at the dock.
(C) People are rowing a boat.

（A）一些船隻正浮在水上。
（B）一些小船被綁在碼頭。
（C）人們正在划船。

**解說** 這些船隻正浮在水上，所以（A）為答案。（B）不是答案因為出現了照片裡沒有的名詞dock。（C）不是答案，因為照片裡沒有人。 答案 (A)

**詞彙** **float** 浮在（水面上） **tied up** 被綁著 **dock** 碼頭 **row**（用槳）划

## STEP 02 考題實戰練習

| | | | |
|---|---|---|---|
| 1. (C) | 2. (B) | 3. (B) | 4. (B) |
| 5. (C) | 6. (A) | 7. (D) | 8. (B) |

**1.** 美W

(A) Wine bottles have fallen on the ground.
(B) A shopper is paying for the purchase.
(C) Some bottles are lined up on the shelves.
(D) A woman is lifting up a crate.

（A）紅酒瓶掉到地上。
（B）一位購物者正在為採購付費。
（C）一些瓶子在貨架上排成一列。
（D）一個女人正舉起一個箱子

**解說** 架子上陳列著瓶子，所以（C）為答案。（A）不是答案，因為照片裡看不到ground。（B）不是答案，因為照片裡看不到錢，卻聽到paying for。（D）不是答案，因為照片裡看不到crate。 答案 (C)

**詞彙** **fall** 掉落 **shopper** 購物者 **pay for** 付費 **shelf** 架子 **lift up** 舉起

**2.** 美M

(A) A waitress is taking an order.
(B) There's some food on the serving dishes.
(C) People are eating a meal.
(D) There are some empty seats.

（A）一位女侍正在接受客人點餐。
（B）分菜盤上有一些食物。
（C）人們正在吃飯。
（D）有一些空座位。

**解說** 盤子上有食物，所以（B）為答案。（A）不是答案，因為無法知道將食物拿過來的人是男的還是女的，而且也不是正在幫客人點菜。（C）不是答案，因為照片裡沒有用餐的人。（D）不是答案，因為出現了照片裡沒有的名詞seats。 答案 (B)

**詞彙** **take an order** 服務點餐 **serving dish** 分菜盤 **eat a meal** 用餐 **empty** 空的

**3.** 英M

(A) He's setting the timer.
(B) He's checking the tire.
(C) He's pushing the cart.
(D) He's repairing the helmet.

（A）他正在設定計時器。
（B）他正在檢查輪胎。
（C）他正在推車。
（D）他正在的修理頭盔。

**解說** 該男生正在檢查輪胎當中，所以（B）為答案。（A）是故意用tire的相似音timer來誤導的選項。（C）也是故意用car的相似音cart來誤導的選項。（D）不是答案，因為該男生在修理車子，而不是修理安全帽。 答案 (B)

**詞彙** **set** 設定 **push** 推 **repair** 修理

**4.** 澳W

(A) He's filling a bag with dirt.
(B) He's digging a hole with a shovel.
(C) He's tying plants to a frame.
(D) He's planting flowers.

（A）他正在把土裝在袋子裡。
（B）他正在用鏟子挖一個洞。
（C）他把植物綑綁於框架。
（D）他正在種花。

**解說** 該男生正在用鏟子挖土當中，所以（B）為答案。（A）不是答案，因為出現了照片裡沒有的名詞bag。（C）是故意用plants來誤導的選項。（D）不是答案，因為出現了照片裡沒有的名詞flowers。 答案 (B)

**詞彙** **fill** 裝 **dirt** 土 **dig a hole** 挖洞 **shovel** 鏟子 **tie** 綁 **plant** 種植；植物

**5.** 美W

(A) They are writing in their notebooks.
(B) A woman is pointing to a building.
(C) They are looking at a laptop.
(D) A woman is passing paper to her co-worker.

（A）他們正寫在筆記本上。
（B）一個女人正指著一棟樓。
（C）他們正在看著筆記型電腦。
（D）一個女人正將報告交給她的同事。

**解說** 這些人正在看著laptop而說話當中，所以（C）為答案。（A）是故意用notebook來誤導的選項。（B）不是答案，因為不是女生而是男生指著東西，而且其所指著的對象也不是大樓而是laptop。（D）不是答案，因為照片裡看不到拿東西給別人的動作。 答案 (C)

**詞彙** **notebook** 筆記本 **point to** 指向… **pass** 傳遞 **co-worker** 同事

**6.** 美M

(A) The conference room is unoccupied.

(B) The office furniture is being moved.
(C) The desk is being cleaned.
(D) The table has been set for a meal.

（A）會議室沒人使用。
（B）辦公傢俱正被搬動中。
（C）桌子正清理中。
（D）餐桌為著一餐飯被擺設。

**解說** 該會議室是空著的，所以（A）為答案。（B）和（C）不是答案，因為照片裡沒人卻聽到being。（D）是故意用table來誤導的選項。 答案 (A)

**詞彙** **conference room** 會議室 **unoccupied** 無人佔用 **furniture** 傢俱 **move** 搬動 **clean** 清掃 **set the table** 擺設餐桌 **meal** 餐

**7.** 英M
(A) A cake is being sliced.
(B) A lamp is being turned off.
(C) Customers are being served.
(D) Candles are being lit.

（A）一塊蛋糕正被切下。
（B）一盞燈正被關掉。
（C）客人正在被服務。
（D）蠟燭正被點亮。

**解說** 蛋糕上的蠟燭正被點亮，所以（D）為答案。（A）是故意用cake來誤導的選項。（B）不是答案，因為出現了照片裡沒有的名詞lamp。（C）不是答案，因為無法知道照片裡的人是否為客人，且也不知道是否在接受服務。 答案 (D)

**詞彙** **slice** 把…切成薄片 **turn off** 關 **serve** 服務 **candle** 蠟燭 **light** 光亮；點亮

**8.** 澳W
(A) Plants are being watered in the garden.
(B) The women are sitting on a bench.
(C) The women are watching a game.
(D) A woman is wandering about in a forest.

（A）花園裡的植物正在被澆灌。
（B）這些女人正坐在長椅上。
（C）這些女人正在觀看比賽。
（D）一個女人正在森林中徘徊。

**解說** 這些女生正在長椅上坐著聊天當中，所以（B）為答案。（A）是故意用周遭背景的單字plants來誤導的選項。（C）不是答案，因為她們不是在看著比賽。（D）不是答案，因為她們不是在森林裡徘徊當中。 答案 (B)

**詞彙** **wander about** 徘徊；四處走 **forest** 森林

# Chapter 05 Who、Where 疑問句

## Quiz |

Q1. (1) Who's going to (2) Who handles
(3) Who should I (4) Who's in charge

Q2. (1) ⓐ (2) ⓑ (3) ⓐ

Q3. (1) Where should I (2) Where do you
(3) Where is (4) Where does

Q4. (1) ⓐ (2) ⓑ (3) ⓐ

## Q1

(1) Who's going to speak at the meeting after work?
誰將會在下班後的會議上演講？

(2) Who handles complaints regarding our products?
誰處理對我們產品的投訴？

(3) Who should I contact for the meeting?
有關這場會議我應該與誰聯繫？

(4) Who's in charge of safety inspections for your plant?
誰負責你們工廠的安全檢查？

## Q2

(1) Who's going to be in charge of the project?
ⓐ **John, our vice president.**
ⓑ I meet him quite often.

誰將要負責這個專案？
ⓐ 我們的副總裁約翰。
ⓑ 我經常見到他。

(2) Who will be responsible for taking notes for the meeting?
ⓐ They are Mr. Parks.
ⓑ **I think Jackson will.**

誰將負責在會議中做記錄？
ⓐ 他們是帕克先生們。
ⓑ 我認為是傑克森。

(3) Who can help this customer?
ⓐ **I have some time right now.**
ⓑ It's our custom.

誰能幫忙這位客人？
ⓐ 我現在有一點時間。
ⓑ 這是我們的習慣。

## Q3

(1) Where should I sign my name on these forms?
我應該在這些表格的哪裡簽署我的名字？

(2) Where do you plan to visit this weekend?
你計劃本週末拜訪哪裡？

(3) Where is the nearest pharmacy?
哪裡是最近的藥店？

(4) Where does the company have its main office?
公司的總辦公室在哪裡呢？

## Q4

(1) Where was his article published?
ⓐ **On page 12 in the newspaper.**
ⓑ Yes, last Thursday.

他的文章被刊登在哪兒？
ⓐ 在報紙的第十二頁上。
ⓑ 是的，上週四。

(2) Where is the copy machine?
ⓐ I like coffee.
ⓑ **We don't have one.**

影印機在哪兒？
ⓐ 我喜歡咖啡。
ⓑ 我們沒有。

(3) Where can I get directions to the city hall?
ⓐ **I can give them to you.**
ⓑ He's a new director.

我能在哪兒得知去市政府的方向？
ⓐ 我可以告訴你。
ⓑ 他是一位新的主任。

## STEP 01 若沒答對會後悔的考題

1. (B)　2. (A)　3. (B)　4. (A)　5. (B)

### 1. 美M 美W

| | |
|---|---|
| 1 疑問詞 | Where |
| 2 動詞（動作） | is |
| 3 對象／場所／其他狀況 | the conference room |

Where's the conference room?
(A) There's room in the cabinet.
(B) It's down the hall.

會議室在哪裡？
（A）在櫃子裡有空間。
（B）它在走廊盡頭。

**解說** 聽到了where，就知道答案要選包含場所說法（down the hall）的選項，因此（B）為答案。雖然（A）用了同音字room，但這裡的意思為「空間」。
答案 (B)

**詞彙** conference room 會議室　room 房間；空間　cabinet 櫃子

### 2. 英M 澳W

| | |
|---|---|
| 1 疑問詞 | Who |
| 2 動詞（動作） | is going to be working on |
| 3 對象／場所／其他狀況 | the renovation project |

Who's going to be working on the renovation project?
(A) The facilities department will.
(B) The projector isn't working.

誰將會去做修繕計畫？
（A）設施部門會。
（B）投影機不運轉。

**解說** 聽到了who，就知道答案要選包含部門名稱（facilities department）的選項，因此（A）為答案。（B）不是答案，且只用了同音字working，而這裡的意思為「運轉」，所以與考題裡的意思「做；做事」有差異。
答案 (A)

**詞彙** work on... 從事於…　renovation 修繕　working 運轉

### 3. 美W 美M

| | |
|---|---|
| 1 疑問詞 | Where |
| 2 主詞動詞（動作） | is he going |
| 3 對象／場所／其他狀況 | this afternoon |

Where's he going this afternoon?
(A) At the store.
(B) To the post office.

他今天下午將去哪裡？
（A）在商店。
（B）到郵局。

**解說** 聽到了where，就知道答案要選包含地點說法（to the post office）的選項，因此（B）為答案。雖然（A）也是地點說法，但該考題需要的答案，需要包含表達方向性或動作性的介系詞。（A）用了沒有動作性的at，所以不能作為答案。
答案 (B)

**詞彙** **this afternoon** 今天下午 **post office** 郵局

4. 美M 英M

| | |
|---|---|
| 1 疑問詞 | Who |
| 2 動詞（動作） | wrote |
| 3 對象／場所／其他狀況 | today's meeting agenda |

Who wrote the today's meeting agenda?
(A) I think Miyumi did.
(B) No, we're out of paper.

今天的會議議程是誰寫的？
（A）我想是米友美。
（B）不，我們的紙用完了。

**解說** 聽到了who，就知道答案要選包含人名（Miyumi）的選項，因此（A）為答案。（B）不是答案，因為對於疑問詞疑問句，不可以用Yes或No來回答。 答案 (A)

**詞彙** **write** 寫 **meeting agenda** 會議議程 **out of paper** 把紙用完了

5. 美W 澳W

| | |
|---|---|
| 1 疑問詞 | Where |
| 2 主詞動詞（動作） | can I buy |
| 3 對象／場所／其他狀況 | tickets for tonight's play |

Where can I buy tickets for tonight's play?
(A) I feel like playing tennis after work.
(B) At the theater.

我能在哪買到今晚舞台劇的門票？
（A）我想在下班後打網球。
（B）在劇院。

**解說** 聽到了where，就知道答案要選包含地點說法（at the theater）的選項，因此（B）為答案。（A）是故意用類似發音playing來誤導的選項。 答案 (B)

**詞彙** **buy** 買 **play** 舞台劇；玩…（遊戲／運動） **feel like -ing** 想要做… **after work** 下班後 **theater** 劇院

## STEP 02 考題實戰練習

1. (A) 2. (B) 3. (B) 4. (B) 5. (C) 6. (B)
7. (B) 8. (B) 9. (B) 10. (A) 11. (C) 12. (C)

1. 美M 美W

Where's the sales department?
(A) Next to the payroll office.
(B) No, I didn't sell all of them.
(C) Miss Jefferson from the marketing department.

銷售部門在哪裡？
（A）在發薪辦公室的旁邊。
（B）不，我沒有把全部賣掉。
（C）行銷部門的傑弗森小姐。

**解說** 聽到了where，就知道答案要選包含地點說法（next to the payroll office）的選項，因此（A）為答案。（B）不是答案，因為對於疑問詞疑問句，是用No來回答的。（C）是對who疑問句的回答，而且故意用了department來誤導的，所以不是答案。 答案 (A)

**詞彙** **sales department** 銷售部門 **payroll office** 薪資辦公室 **sell** 賣 **marketing department** 行銷部門

2. 美W 英M
Who's going to take the CEO to the hotel?
(A) Tomorrow morning.
(B) His secretary will.
(C) Thanks for the directions.

誰將帶CEO去飯店？
（A）明天早上。
（B）他的秘書。
（C）謝謝您告訴我方向。

**解說** 聽到了who，就知道答案要選包含職稱（secretary）的選項，因此（B）為答案。（A）是對於when疑問句的回答。（C）是對「我幫你的忙」等說法回答的方式。在該考題裡若沒有聽到疑問詞，有可能會被「帶去飯店」誤導。 答案 (B)

**詞彙** **take** 某人 **to** 某個場所 帶某人去某處 **secretary** 秘書 **directions** 方向；指示

3. 美M 澳W
Where are the vegetables stored after they've been picked?
(A) He'll go to the store tomorrow.
(B) In refrigerated storage containers.
(C) Because it might spoil.

蔬菜被摘完後儲存在哪裡？
（A）他明天將去商店。
（B）在冷藏保管容器裡。
（C）因為它可能會腐壞。

**解說** 聽到了where，就知道答案要選包含地點說法的選項，因此（B）為答案。（A）是故意用stored的類似發音store來誤導的選項。（C）是對於why疑問句的回答方式。 答案 (B)

**詞彙** **vegetable** 蔬菜 **store** 商店 **pick** 摘取
**refrigerated storage container** 冷藏保管容器 **spoil**（食物）腐壞

**4.** 美M 美W
Where can I find the factory manager?
(A) At 10 p.m.
(B) Go to the second door on the left.
(C) They're on the top shelf.

我在哪裡可以找到廠長？
（A）晚上十點。
（B）往左邊第二道門去。
（C）它們在貨架最上層。

**解說** 聽到了where，就知道答案要選包含地點說法（to the second floor）的選項，因此（B）為答案。（A）是對於when疑問句的回答方式，所以不是答案。（C）是包含地點說法的陷阱。該考題的工廠長是單數名詞，所以不可以用they來說。 答案 (B)

**詞彙** **factory manager** 廠長 **shelf** 架子

**5.** 英W 英M
Who will be interviewing the applicants?
(A) 5 applicants so far.
(B) Yes, I have a job interview today.
(C) I'll ask Ms. Shimamura to do it.

誰即將和申請者面談？
（A）到目前為止五位申請者。
（B）是，今天我有求職面試。
（C）我會請島村女士來做。

**解說** 聽到了who，就知道答案要選包含人名（Ms. Shimamura）的選項，因此（C）為答案。（A）是故意用同音字applicants來誤導的選項。（B）不是答案，因為對疑問詞疑問句用Yes來回答的。 答案 (C)

**詞彙** **applicant** 申請者 **so far** 到目前 **job interview** 求職面試 **ask** 某人 **to** 動詞原型 要求某人作某事

**6.** 美M 美W
Who should I ask if I need more paper for the copier?
(A) Yes, he asked me to.
(B) Speak to the department administrator.
(C) The newspaper's delivered every morning.

若我需要更多影印紙，我該向誰詢問？
（A）是的，是他要求我的。
（B）和該部門管理者說。
（C）報紙在每天早上遞送。

**解說** 聽到了who，就知道答案要選包含職稱（department administrator）的選項，因此（B）為答案。（A）是對於疑問詞疑問句用Yes來回答，所以不是答案。（C）是故意用paper的類似發音newspaper來誤導的選項。 答案 (B)

**詞彙** **copier** 影印機 **department administrator** 部門管理者 **newspaper** 報紙 **deliver** 配送

**7.** 英M 澳W
Where did you put the shipment of machine parts that arrived yesterday?
(A) It's a fact.
(B) They're in the store room.
(C) They're made of metal.

你把昨天送達的機器零件貨運放在哪？
（A）這是事實。
（B）它們在儲藏室。
（C）它們以金屬製成。

**解說** 聽到了where，就知道答案要選包含地點說法（in the store room）的選項，因此（B）為答案。（A）是用了完全無關的回答方式，所以不是答案。選項（C）要看machine parts來判斷，這應該是對於what疑問句的回答方式。 答案 (B)

**詞彙** **put** 放 **shipment** 貨運 **machine parts** 機械零件 **arrive** 抵達 **fact** 事實 **store room** 儲藏室 **metal** 儲藏室

**8.** 美M 美W
Who's available to give the closing speech?
(A) It closes at five.
(B) Dr. Sheppard can do it.
(C) I love peaches.

誰能為閉幕演講？
（A）它在五點關閉。
（B）雪帕德博士可以。
（C）我愛桃子。

**解說** 聽到了who，就知道答案要選包含人名（Dr. Sheppard）的選項，因此（B）為答案。（A）是用closing的類似發音closes來誤導的選項。（C）是用speech的類似發音peaches來誤導的選項。 答案 (B)

**詞彙** **available** 可用的；有空的
**give the closing speech** 做閉幕演講 **peach** 水蜜桃

**9.** 美W 英M
Who has the test results?
(A) That's what I thought.
(B) The secretary should have them.
(C) No, he hasn't.

誰有測驗結果？
（A）那就是我所想的。
（B）秘書應該有。
（C）不，他沒有。

**解說** 聽到了who，就知道答案要選包含職稱（secretary）

的選項，因此（B）為答案。（A）是對於陳述句或否定、附加、一般疑問句的回答方式。（C）不是答案，因為對於疑問詞疑問句，是用No來回答的。 答案 (B)

**詞彙** **result** 結果 **secretary** 秘書

**10.** 澳W 美W

Where do you file the meeting records?

(A) In the cabinet over there.
(B) Every Friday afternoon.
(C) Our past records are no longer available.

你把會議記錄歸檔在哪？
（A）在那邊的櫃子。
（B）每個星期五下午。
（C）我們之前的記錄已不能用了。

**解說** 聽到了where，就知道答案要選包含地點說法的選項，因此（A）為答案。（B）是對於How often疑問句的回答方式。（C）是故意用同音字records來誤導的選項。 答案 (A)

**詞彙** **file** 歸整檔案 **record** 記錄 **every** 每個…
**no longer available** 不再能使用

**11.** 英M 澳W

To whom should I address this package?

(A) He should do it.
(B) A suit and a tie.
(C) Dr. Kun Tao.

包裹的收件地址該寫誰？
（A）他應該做的。
（B）西裝和領帶。
（C）康陶博士。

**解說** To whom也是與who疑問句同類的考題，因此以人名來回答的（C）為答案。選項（A）無法知道he是指誰，所以不是答案。（B）是故意用address的類似發音dress來誤導的選項。 答案 (C)

**詞彙** **address** 寫收件人姓名地址 **package** 包裹
**a suit and a tie** 西裝和領帶

**12.** 美W 美M

Where should I go to buy some presents for our customers?

(A) They were impressed by the presentation.
(B) About twenty dollars.
(C) Try the department store near the ABC Bank.

我該去哪買給我們客戶的禮物？
（A）他們介紹讓人印象深刻。
（B）約二十元。
（C）試試去ABC銀行附近的百貨公司。

**解說** 聽到了where，就知道答案要選包含地點說法（near the ABC Bank）的選項，因此（C）為答案。（A）是故意用presents的類似發音presentation來誤導的選項。（B）是對於How much的回答方式，但也是可以和presents（禮物）做聯想來回答，所以得小心。 答案 (C)

**詞彙** **present** 禮物 **impressed** 印象深刻的 **department store** 百貨公司 **near** 在…附近

Chapter 06 When、Why 疑問句

Quiz |

Q1. (1) When does (2) When did
(3) When will (4) When were
Q2. (1) ⓑ (2) ⓐ (3) ⓑ
Q3. (1) Why are (2) Why was
(3) Why hasn't (4) Why don't
Q4. (1) ⓑ (2) ⓑ (3) ⓐ

## Q1

(1) When does your ight leave?
您的航班什麼時候離開？

(2) When did you sign up for the conference?
你什麼時候登錄這個會議的？

(3) When will the new manager start?
新的經理將於什麼時候開始？

(4) When were those articles written?
那些文章是什麼時候寫的？

## Q2

(1) When is the new product going to be released?
ⓐ At least twice a week.
ⓑ **In October, I believe.**

新產品將於什麼時候上市？
ⓐ 至少一週兩次。
ⓑ 我想是在十月。

(2) When will the factory begin production?
ⓐ **In less than two months.**
ⓑ At the new plant.

工廠什麼時候將開始生產？
ⓐ 不會在兩個月內。
ⓑ 在新工廠。

(3) When did Mr. Tanaka call?
ⓐ At her of ce.
ⓑ **About three hours ago.**

田中先生什麼時候打電話的？
ⓐ 在她的辦公室。
ⓑ 約三小時前。

## Q3

(1) Why are you walking so fast?
你為什麼走這麼快？

(2) Why was that company so profitable last year?
為什麼那間公司去年這麼獲利？

(3) Why hasn't the meeting started yet?
會議為什麼還不開始呢？

(4) Why don't we meet after lunch to discuss the budget?
我們何不在午餐後見面討論預算呢？

## Q4

(1) Why can't we take the highway?
ⓐ By train.
ⓑ **It's closed for road repairs.**

我們為什麼不走高速公路？
ⓐ 乘火車。
ⓑ 它因為道路維修而封閉。

(2) Why are so many people standing near the park?
ⓐ Have a seat.
ⓑ **That's a bus stop.**

為什麼很多人站在公園附近？
ⓐ 請坐。
ⓑ 那是一個巴士站。

(3) Why don't we take a quick break?
ⓐ **I can't. I've got too much to do.**
ⓑ Sorry, I didn't mean to break it.

我們何不小歇一下？
ⓐ 我不能。我有太多事要做。
ⓑ 對不起，我不是故意打破它的。

## STEP 01 若沒答對會後悔的考題

1. (A) 2. (B) 3. (B) 4. (A) 5. (B)

**1.** 美M 美W

| | |
|---|---|
| 1 疑問詞＋時間點 | When are |
| 2 主詞/動詞（動作） | you going |
| 3 對象／場所／其他狀況 | to Shanghai |

When are you going to Shanghai?
(A) Not until December.
(B) To see some potential clients.

這個研究的下一步預計什麼時候開始？
（A）我將每天學習。

（B）它將會在下月之內開始。

**解說** 聽到了when are，就可以知道要選以未來時間說法（not until December）回答的（A）為答案。（B）是對於why疑問句的回答方式，所以不是答案。

答案 (A)

**詞彙** potential client 潛在客戶

**2.** 英M 澳W

| | |
|---|---|
| 1 疑問詞＋助動詞 | Why did |
| 2 主詞 | Mr. Lawyer |
| 3 動詞（動作） | change his job |

Why did Mr. Lawyer change his job?
(A) We need to hire several new people.
(B) He found a more challenging position.

為什麼羅約先生換了他的工作？
（A）我們需要聘請一些新人。
（B）他找到一個更具挑戰性的職位。

**解說** 聽到了why did，就可以知道是詢問理由的why。兩個選項都是以句子的形式，所以是全部得聽完才能回答的考題。「找到了具有挑戰性的職位，所以換了工作」是有邏輯的組合，所以（B）為答案。（A）是故意用hire來誤導的選項。

答案 (B)

**詞彙** change 改變 job 職業 hire 雇用 challenging 具有挑戰性的

**3.** 美W 美M

| | |
|---|---|
| 1 疑問詞＋時間點 | When's |
| 2 主詞 | the next step of the study |
| 3 動詞（動作） | supposed to begin |

When's the next step of the study supposed to begin?
(A) I'll study it every day.
(B) It'll start within the next month.

這個研究的下一步預計什麼時候開始？
（A）我將每天學習。
（B）它將會在下月之內開始。

**解說** 聽到了when's，就可以知道要選包含未來時間的說法（within the next month）的（B）為答案。（A）是表達頻率的說法，所以是對於how often的回答方式，且也是故意用同音字study來誤導的選項。

答案 (B)

**詞彙** step 步驟 be supposed to 預計⋯ within 在⋯之中

**4.** 美M 英M

| | |
|---|---|
| 1 疑問詞＋助動詞 | Why has |
| 2 主詞 | the board |
| 3 動詞（動作） | reorganized our company |

Why has the board reorganized our company?
(A) To make us more efficient.
(B) In three hours.

董事會為什麼將我們公司改組的？
（A）為了使我們更加有效率。
（B）三小時之後。

**解說** 聽到Why has，就要知道是詢問理由的why，所以用「to＋動詞原型」回答的（A）為答案。（B）是未來時間點的說法，所以是對於when疑問句的回答方式。

答案 (A)

**詞彙** reorganize 重新組織 efficient 有效率的

**5.** 美W 澳W

| | |
|---|---|
| 1 疑問詞＋助動詞 | Why don't |
| 2 主詞 | we |
| 3 動詞（動作） | meet in the lobby |

Why don't we meet in the lobby?
(A) Because it's a good place.
(B) Sure, what time do you want to meet?

我們何不在大廳見面？
（A）因為它是一個好地方。
（B）當然，你想什麼時候見面呢？

**解說** 聽到why don't，就可以知道是建議的why，因此以表達肯定、許可回答方式的（B）為答案。（A）是對理由的why的回答方式。

答案 (B)

**詞彙** meet 見面 lobby 大廳 place 場所

## STEP 02 考題實戰練習

1. (B) 2. (C) 3. (C) 4. (C) 5. (B) 6. (B)
7. (B) 8. (C) 9. (A) 10. (C) 11. (C) 12. (B)

**1.** 美M 美W

When can I schedule an appointment with Dr. Yang?

(A) A ten minute walk from here.
(B) Any time after 4:00 p.m.
(C) Could you please?

我什麼時候能約楊博士？
（A）從這裡步行十分鐘。
（B）下午四點後的任何時間。
（C）可否麻煩您？

**解說** 聽到了when can，就可以知道以未來時間點說法（after 4:00 p.m.）回答的（B）為答案。（A）是對於where疑問句的回答方式。（C）是對於Could I的回答方式，也是故意誤導為和Could you混淆的選項。 答案 (B)

**詞彙** **schedule an appointment** 安排預約 **any time** 任何時候

**2.** 美W 英M

Why are you leaving so early?

(A) Do you know where he lives?
(B) Yes, I wake up early.
(C) I'm running late for the meeting.

你為何這麼早離開？
（A）你知道他住哪裡嗎？
（B）是的，我很早起床。
（C）我開會遲到了。

**解說** Why後面沒有don't，所以是詢問理由的疑問句，因此當作理由的（C）為答案。（A）的lives為leaving的類似發音，所以不是答案。（B）是對疑問詞疑問句用Yes來回答的，所以不是答案。 答案 (C)

**詞彙** **leave** 離開 **so early** 很早 **wake up** 起床 **late** 遲；晚

**3.** 美M 英W

Why didn't you come to the seminar?

(A) It's just down the hall.
(B) It went very well, thanks.
(C) I was too busy.

你為什麼沒來研討會？
（A）它就在走廊的盡頭。
（B）它進行得非常好，謝謝你。
（C）我太忙了。

**解說** Why後面聽到的不是don't而是didn't，所以是詢問理由的疑問句，因此作為沒有到研討會的理由的（C）為答案。（A）是對於where疑問句的回答方式。（B）是對於how的回答方式，且故意和come產生聯想而誤導的選項。 答案 (C)

**詞彙** **go very well** 進行得很好 **busy** 忙碌

**4.** 美M 美W

When did you finish the project?

(A) He finished it last week.
(B) You can't use the projector until three p.m.
(C) I'm still working on it.

你什麼時候完成這個計畫的？
（A）他上週完成了。
（B）你不能使用投影機，直到下午3點。
（C）我仍在處理當中。

**解說** 若是聽到了when did就立刻選包含過去時間點說法的（A）那就錯了。一樣包含時間點說法的（B）也不是答案。這兩個選項的主詞都不對。表達為「仍然處理當中」的（C）才是答案。 答案 (C)

**詞彙** **finish** 完成 **use** 使用 **work on** 處理

**5.** 澳W 英M

When does the department store open?

(A) Open the door, please.
(B) At 10 a.m., I think.
(C) Next to the payroll office.

百貨公司何時營業？
（A）請開門。
（B）我想是上午十點。
（C）在發薪辦公室旁邊。

**解說** 聽到了when does，就可以知道用未來時間點說法（at 10 a.m.）回答的（B）為答案。（A）是故意用同音字open來誤導的選項。（C）是對於where疑問句的回答方式，所以不是答案。 答案 (B)

**詞彙** **department store** 百貨公司 **payroll office** 發薪辦公室

**6.** 美M 美W

When's your business trip to Tokyo?

(A) Yes, it went pretty well.
(B) Next Friday.
(C) No, it's within walking distance.

你何時到東京出差？
（A）是的，它相當的好。
（B）下週五。
（C）不，它在步行距離之內。

**解說** 若聽到了when's，就可以知道以未來時間點說法（next Friday）回答的（B）為答案。因為是對於疑問詞疑問句用Yes來回答，所以（A）不是答案。（C）是對於疑問詞疑問句用No來回答，所以也不是答案。

答案 (B)

**詞彙** business trip 商務出差 go pretty well 進行得相當好 within walking distance 在步行距離

7. 英M 澳W
Why hasn't the new carpet arrived yet?
(A) By train, I think.
(B) I'll call the delivery company.
(C) I'll have it dry-cleaned.

為什麼新的地毯還沒到呢？
（A）我認為是搭火車。
（B）我會打電話給快遞公司。
（C）我會把它乾洗。

**解說** Why後面沒有聽到don't，所以是詢問理由的疑問句。（B）裡聽到間接迴避性的回答，所以是答案。（A）是對於詢問交通方式的how的回答方式，所以不是答案。（C）是故意用dry-cleaned來與carpet產生聯想而誤導的選項。 答案 (B)

**詞彙** arrive 抵達 delivery company 快遞公司 dry-cleaned 乾洗

8. 美M 美W
Why do you think everyone is so busy lately?
(A) Yes, all of them.
(B) Sorry, I can't be there on time.
(C) We got a lot of new orders.

你認為為什麼最近每個人都這麼忙？
（A）對，他們全部。
（B）抱歉，我無法準時到那兒。
（C）我們接到了很多新訂單。

**解說** Why後面沒有聽到don't，所以是詢問忙碌的原因的疑問句。因此（C）為答案。（A）是對於疑問詞疑問句用Yes來回答的，所以不是答案。（B）是對於建議的why的回答方式，所以不是答案。 答案 (C)

**詞彙** so busy 很忙 lately 最近；近期 on time 準時 a lot of 很多 order 訂單

9. 美W 英M
When is the next play going to start?
(A) Tonight, at 7:30.
(B) Yes, that's a good one.
(C) There are five players.

下一場舞台劇何時開始？
（A）今晚七點三十分。
（B）是的，這個不錯。
（C）有五名球員。

**解說** 聽到了when is，就可以知道用時間點說法（at 7:30）回答的（A）為答案。（B）是對於疑問詞疑問句用Yes來回答的，所以不是答案。（C）是故意用play的近似發音players來誤導的選項。 答案 (A)

**詞彙** play 演出；演劇 player 選手

10. 澳W 美W
Why was the itinerary changed?
(A) Sorry, I'm too busy.
(B) I'll make an appointment.
(C) Because Mr. Tanaka couldn't be here then.

行程為什麼改變的？
（A）很抱歉，我太忙了。
（B）我將會預約。
（C）因為田中先生那時不能在這裡。

**解說** Why後面沒有聽到don't，所以是詢問旅遊行程改變的理由的疑問句。因此（C）為答案。（A）是對於建議的why的回答方式，所以不是答案。（B）是故意用appointment（約定）來與itinerary（旅遊行程）產生聯想而誤導的選項。 答案 (C)

**詞彙** itinerary 旅程計畫 change 改變 too busy 太忙碌 make an appointment 預約 then 那時候

11. 英M 澳W
When will you return to your hometown?
(A) He'll be out of the town today.
(B) In the city.
(C) Within a week.

你什麼時候回到你的家鄉？
（A）他今天將出差。
（B）在城市。
（C）在一個星期內。

**解說** 若聽到了when will，就可以知道以時間點說法（within a week）回答的（C）為答案。（A）用了不對的主詞，所以不是答案。（B）是對於where疑問句的回答方式，所以不是答案。 答案 (C)

**詞彙** return 返回 hometown 故鄉 be out of the town 出差

12. 美W 美M
Why weren't you at the party this afternoon?
(A) Yes, I wrote part of it.
(B) I thought it was tomorrow.
(C) I'll bring it later tonight.

為什麼你今天下午不在宴會中？
（A）是的，我寫了一部分。
（B）我以為是明天。
（C）我今夜稍晚會帶去。

**解說** Why後面沒有聽到don't，所以是詢問「今天下午不在宴會場所的理由」的疑問句。因此（B）為答案。（A）是對於疑問詞疑問句用Yes來回答的，所以不是答案。（C）是故意用tonight來與afternoon產生聯想而誤導的選項。 答案 (B)

**詞彙** write 寫 part 部分 bring 帶來 later tonight 今夜稍晚

## Chapter 07 What、How 疑問句

### Quiz |

Q1. (1) What kind, buy (2) What time (3) What, doing (4) What, think

Q2. (1) ⓑ (2) ⓐ (3) ⓐ

Q3. (1) How long (2) How much (3) How do you like (4) How about

Q4. (1) ⓐ (2) ⓑ (3) ⓑ

### Q1

(1) What kind of ticket did you buy?
你買了哪一種票？

(2) What time did Mr. Rose leave the office?
羅斯先生什麼時候離開辦公室的？

(3) What are you doing after work?
下班後你將會做些什麼？

(4) What do you think of our advertising strategy?
你認為我們的廣告策略如何？

### Q2

(1) What are you ordering?
ⓐ No, thanks. I have one.
ⓑ **The chicken sandwich.**

你正在訂購什麼？
ⓐ 不，謝謝。我有一個。
ⓑ 雞肉三明治。

(2) What's the due date for this report?
ⓐ **Next Friday.**
ⓑ Only three.

報告的截止日期是什麼時候？
ⓐ 下星期五。
ⓑ 只有三個。

(3) What are you doing after work?
ⓐ **I'm going fishing.**
ⓑ She's not at home.

下班後你將會做些什麼？
ⓐ 我將會去釣魚。
ⓑ 她不在家。

### Q3

(1) How long did your interview last?
你的面試花了多久時間？

(2) How much did the lunch cost?
午餐花了多少錢？

(3) How do you like your coffee?
你要如何調配你的咖啡？

(4) How about shipping the orders this afternoon?
要不要今天下午將訂單出貨？

Q4

(1) How many rooms do you need to book?
ⓐ **Just one.**
ⓑ Around 3 o'clock.

您需要預訂多少房間呢？
ⓐ 只要一間。
ⓑ 大約是三點。

(2) How do you commute to work?
ⓐ No, not every day.
ⓑ **By train.**

你如何去上班？
ⓐ 不，不是每天。
ⓑ 乘火車。

(3) How would you like to play a game of tennis this afternoon?
ⓐ Unfortunately, I didn't.
ⓑ **Yes, that's a good idea.**

今天下午打網球賽如何？
ⓐ 真不幸，我沒有做。
ⓑ 是，那是個好主意。

## STEP 01 若沒答對會後悔的考題

1. (A) 2. (A) 3. (B) 4. (A) 5. (B)

**1.** 美M 美W

| | |
|---|---|
| 1 疑問詞 | What |
| 2 決定類別的單字 | drink |

What would you like to drink?
(A) A glass of water, please.
(B) I'd be delighted.

你想喝點什麼？
(A) 請給我一杯水。
(B) 我會很喜歡的。

**解說** What後面聽到及物動詞drink，所以這裡的what是詢問接受動作的對象。(A) 用接受drink的對象來回答，即為答案。(B) 是故意用與would you like發音相近的delighted來誤導的選項。 答案 (A)

**詞彙** **a glass of water** 一杯水 **delight** 高興、喜歡

**2.** 英M 澳W

| | |
|---|---|
| 1 疑問詞 | How |
| 2 決定類別的單字 | long |

How long will this light bulb last?
(A) At least five years.
(B) To make the room bright.

這個燈泡能一直用多久？
(A) 至少五年。
(B) 為了讓房間變明亮。

**解說** 聽到了how long，就可以知道用期間來回答的(A) 為答案。(B) 是故意用light的相似發音bright來誤導的選項。 答案 (A)

**詞彙** **light bulb** 燈泡 **last** 持續 **bright** 明亮

**3.** 美W 美M

| | |
|---|---|
| 1 疑問詞 | What |
| 2 決定類別的單字 | time |

What time is the meeting scheduled to start?
(A) He's just started working here.
(B) Not for an hour.

這個會議被訂在幾點開始？
(A) 他才剛到這兒開始工作。
(B) 在一小時後。

**解說** 聽到了what time，就可以知道是詢問時間的what，所以用時間說法 (not for an hour) 來回答的 (B) 為答案。(A) 的主詞不相合，所以不是答案。 答案 (B)

**詞彙** **be scheduled to** 預定⋯ **start** 開始

**4.** 美M 英M

| | |
|---|---|
| 1 疑問詞 | How |
| 2 決定類別的單字 | about |

How about meeting in the lobby?
(A) That would be nice.
(B) You should meet him.

在大廳見面如何？
(A) 那樣很好。

（B）你應該和他見面。

**解說** 這是建議的how。所以對於建議以肯定或允許說法來回答的（A）為答案。（B）是meeting的相似發音meet來故意誤導的選項，而且這裡的him也無法得知是誰。 答案 (A)

**詞彙** meet 見面 lobby 大廳

**5.** 美W 澳W

| | |
|---|---|
| 1 疑問詞 | What |
| 2 決定類別的單字 | think |

What do you think of our design proposal?
(A) I believe it's a good sign.
(B) I was very impressed.

你認為我們的設計方案如何？
（A）我相信它是個好徵兆。
（B）我印象很深刻。

**解說** 這是詢問意見的what。包含形容詞（impressed）的句子常常表達意見。（A）是故意用design的相似發音sign來誤導的選項。 答案 (B)

**詞彙** proposal 計畫方案 sign 徵兆 impressed 受深刻印象的

## STEP 02 考題實戰練習

| | | | | | |
|---|---|---|---|---|---|
| 1. (B) | 2. (A) | 3. (B) | 4. (B) | 5. (A) | 6. (B) |
| 7. (C) | 8. (B) | 9. (B) | 10. (B) | 11. (B) | 12. (A) |

**1.** 美M 美W
What flavor of soup would you like?
(A) Some soup and salad.
(B) What do you recommend?
(C) That's my favorite.

你想喝什麼口味的湯呢？
（A）一些湯和沙拉。
（B）你有什麼建議？
（C）這就是我喜歡的。

**解說** What後面聽到及物動詞like，所以這裡的what是詢問接受動作的對象。（B）是詢問「給我的建議」的「間接、迴避性回答方式」，即為答案。（A）是故意用一樣的單字（soup）來誤導的選項。（C）裡面無法知道that指的是什麼，所以不是答案。 答案 (B)

**詞彙** flavor 味道 soup 湯 recommend 建議 favorite 喜歡的（東西）

**2.** 美W 英M
What files do I need to bring on Tuesday?
(A) The ones on my desk.
(B) Yes, let's speak then.
(C) Because I haven't seen them.

我週二需要攜帶哪些檔案夾？
（A）我辦公桌上的。
（B）是的，我們到時說吧。
（C）因為我還沒有看見他們。

**解說** What後面聽到及物動詞bring，所以這裡的what是詢問接受動作的對象。因此，以bring的受詞來回答的（A）為答案。（B）是對於疑問詞疑問句用Yes來回答，所以不是答案。（C）是對於why疑問句的回答方式，而且無法知道這裡的them是指什麼。 答案 (A)

**詞彙** file 文件夾 bring 攜帶

**3.** 美M 澳W
How long have you worked at your company?
(A) About 4 kilometers from here.
(B) It will be three years next month.
(C) It doesn't work properly.

你有多久在貴公司工作？
（A）從這兒起約四公里。
（B）到下個月就三年了。
（C）它不能正常運作。

**解說** 聽到了how long，就可以知道以期間說法回答的（B）為答案。（A）是對於where的回答方式，且故意和long產生聯想而誤導的選項。（C）的work是worked的相似發音，但這裡的意思不是「工作」，而是「運作」。 答案 (B)

**詞彙** work 運作 properly 正常地

**4.** 美M 美W
How many people are attending the product demonstration?
(A) It tends to be.
(B) Everyone from the research division.
(C) For the next 10 to 12 months.

有多少人出席產品展示會？
（A）它傾向那樣。
（B）研究部門的每一個人。
（C）在未來十至十二個月當中。

**解說** 聽到了how many，所以用「全部」或「一部分」來回答的（B）為答案。（A）是故意用attend的相似發音tend來誤導的選項。（C）是對how long的回答方

式，所以不是答案。 答案 (B)

**詞彙** **attend** 出席 **demonstration** 示演會 **research division** 研究部門

**5.** 澳W 英M
What color are you painting the wall?
(A) Light brown, I think.
(B) Three weeks from now.
(C) The cooler's over there.

你用什麼顏色來塗牆壁？
（A）我打算用淺棕色。
（B）從現在起三個星期。
（C）冷卻器在那兒。

**解說** What color後面聽到及物動詞painting，所以這裡的what是詢問接受動作的對象。（A）用painting的受詞補語來回答，即為答案。（B）是對於when的回答方式。（C）是故意用color的類似發音cooler來誤導的選項。 答案 (A)

**詞彙** **paint** 塗 **wall** 牆壁 **light brown** 淺棕色 **cooler** 冷卻器；冷藏庫 **over there** 位在那裏

**6.** 美M 美W
How much are the admission to this museum?
(A) About an hour.
(B) Only 5 dollars.
(C) Bikes aren't allowed in this area.

這個博物館的入場費多少錢？
（A）大約一小時。
（B）只要五元。
（C）在這個地區不准帶腳踏車進來。

**解說** 聽到了how much和admission，就可以知道是詢問費用的how。因此以費用回答的（B）為答案。（A）是對於how long的回答方式。（C）是故意讓admission和allowed產生聯想的選項。 答案 (B)

**詞彙** **admission** 入場費 **museum** 博物館 **allow** 准許

**7.** 英M 澳W
What's the best way to reach your employer?
(A) I can't reach it.
(B) About ten kilograms.
(C) Try calling her mobile phone.

聯繫到你老闆最好的方式是什麼？
（A）我無法到達。
（B）約十公斤。
（C）試試致電她的手機。

**解說** 這是詢問方法（the best way）的what。（C）就是在論及方法，即為答案。（A）是故意用同音字（reach）來誤導的選項。（B）是故意讓way和ten kilograms產生聯想而誤導的選項。 答案 (C)

**詞彙** **way** 方法 **reach** 與…聯繫 **employer** 雇主 **about** 大約 **try** 嘗試 **mobile phone** 行動電話

**8.** 美M 美W
How did you learn about this job?
(A) I'm still learning how.
(B) I read about it in the newspaper.
(C) About a month ago.

你怎麼知道這個工作的？
（A）我現在仍然在學。
（B）我在報紙上讀到它的。
（C）大約一個月前。

**解說** 這是詢問方法的how。所以（B）為答案。（A）是故意用learn的相似發音learning來誤導的選項。（C）是對於when的回答方式，所以不是答案。 答案 (B)

**詞彙** **job** 職業 **newspaper** 報紙

**9.** 美W 英M
What time is the meeting scheduled to start?
(A) He's just started working here.
(B) Not for an hour.
(C) In the auditorium.

會議訂於什麼時候開始？
（A）他才剛到此開始工作。
（B）不會是一個小時之內。
（C）在演講廳。

**解說** 聽到了what time，就可以知道是詢問時間的what。因此，以時間說法（not for an hour.）來回答的（B）為答案。（A）是故意用start的相似發音started來誤導的選項，而且也無法知道He是指誰。（C）是對於where疑問句的回答方式，所以不是答案。 答案 (B)

**詞彙** **be scheduled to** 預訂 **start** 開始 **just** 剛才 **auditorium** 演講廳

**10.** 澳W 美W
What's Mr. Thomas doing during his leave of absence?
(A) No, I think he's in today.
(B) He's taking courses at the community center.
(C) He lives far away.

湯瑪士先生在他的休假期間要做什麼呢？
（A）不，我想他今天會在。
（B）他在社區活動中心參加課程。
（C）他住得很遠。

**解說** What後面聽到doing，所以是詢問行為的what。因此包含行為說法（將要參加課程）的（B）為答案。

（A）是對於疑問詞疑問句用Yes來回答的，所以不是答案。（C）是故意用leave的類似發音lives來誤導的選項。 答案 (B)

**詞彙** **during** 在…期間 **leave of absence** 休假 **be in** 有上班 **course** 課程 **community center** 社區活動中心 **far away** 相當遙遠

**11.** 英M 澳W

How do you like the new director?

(A) He's out of the office today.
(B) He's very demanding.
(C) No, that's not the right direction.

你的新主管怎麼樣呢？
（A）他今天不在辦公室。
（B）他的要求很高。
（C）不，這不是正確的方向。

**解說** 聽到了詢問意見的How do you like，所以表達意見的（B）為答案。若在考題裡只有聽到new director，就很容易選擇（A），但這是一種陷阱，而且（A）也不是表達意見的。（C）是故意用director的相似發音direction來誤導的選項。 答案 (B)

**詞彙** **director** 主管 **office** 辦公室 **demanding** 要求很高的 **direction** 方向

**12.** 美W 美M

How's the ice cream?

(A) It's quite good.
(B) I'm feeling better, thanks.
(C) Thanks for the favor.

這個冰淇淋如何？
（A）相當好。
（B）我感到好些了，謝謝。
（C）謝謝你的好意。

**解說** 對於詢問狀態的how is以包含形容詞的句子回答的（A）為答案。選項（B）的內容和冰淇淋無關，而是表達情緒的說法。（C）是故意用冰淇淋flaovor的相似發音favor來誤導的選項。 答案 (A)

**詞彙** **quite good** 相當好 **feel better** 感到較好一點 **favor** 善意；好意

# Chapter 08 建議、選擇疑問句

## Quiz

Q1. (1) Would you
(2) Could you
(3) Don't you want
(4) Let's

Q2. (1) ⓑ (2) ⓑ (3) ⓐ

Q3. (1) seven, eight
(2) talk now, you busy
(3) initial this, sign by full name
(4) Which

Q4. (1) ⓐ (2) ⓐ (3) ⓑ

## Q1

(1) Would you like to join us for the party?
你願意加入我們參加宴會嗎？

(2) Could you lend me your newspaper?
你能借我你的報紙嗎？

(3) Don't you want to see the baseball game tonight?
你今晚不想看棒球賽嗎？

(4) Let's try the new cafeteria.
我們試試看新的自助餐廳吧。

## Q2

(1) Could you give me a call at the office later?
ⓐ I've already put it on your desk.
ⓑ **Sure, I'll call you around five.**

你稍後能撥電話到辦公室找我嗎？
ⓐ 我已經放在你的桌上了。
ⓑ 當然，我大約在五點打電話給你。

(2) Do you need any help moving these boxes?
ⓐ He's moving to the city.
ⓑ **I'd appreciate that.**

你需要任何幫助來搬這些箱子嗎？
ⓐ 他正搬家到這個城市。
ⓑ 那樣我會很感激的。

(3) Let's go to the Italian restaurant on Main Street.
ⓐ **That sounds good.**
ⓑ The food wasn't ready.

我們去大街上的義大利餐廳吧。

ⓐ 那聽起來不錯。
ⓑ 食物還沒準備好。

## Q3

(1) Should we order seven dishes or eight?
我們應該點七道菜還是八道菜呢？

(2) Can we talk now or are you busy?
我們可以現在談嗎？還是你正在忙嗎？

(3) Should I just initial this or sign by full name?
我應該只簽姓氏還是簽全名？我應該只簽姓氏還是簽全名？

(4) Which parking area is for employees?
哪個停車場是給員工的？

## Q4

(1) Do you prefer a window or an aisle seat?
ⓐ **Either one is fine with me.**
ⓑ Sure, you can sit here.

你比較想要靠窗還是靠走道的座位？
ⓐ 對我來說哪個都好。
ⓑ 當然，你可以坐這兒。

(2) Would you rather fly or take a train to the meeting?
ⓐ **I'd prefer to take an airplane.**
ⓑ The training should be very useful.

你想要搭飛機還是搭火車去開會？
ⓐ 我想要搭飛機。
ⓑ 火車應該相當有用。

(3) Which restaurant should we eat dinner at?
ⓐ We can meet today.
ⓑ **Either one is fine.**

我們應該在哪家餐廳吃晚餐呢？
ⓐ 我們今天可以見面。
ⓑ 哪一家都很好。

## STEP 01 若沒答對會後悔的考題

1. (A) 2. (A) 3. (B) 4. (A) 5. (B)

### 1. 美M 美W

| | |
|---|---|
| 1 決定類別的線索 | Would you like me to |
| 2 動詞與其他 | make you some tea |

Would you like me to make you some tea?
(A) That's okay. I'll make some myself.
(B) She likes to see the dessert menu.

你要我幫您做點茶嗎？
（A）沒關係。我會自己弄的。
（B）她喜歡看甜點菜單。

**解說** 聽到了Would you like me to，就可以知道是建議。因此，否定或拒絕說法之後再附加說明的（A）為答案。（B）是故意用dessert menu來與tea產生聯想而誤導的選項，且也無法知道其主詞she指的是誰，所以不是答案。 答案 (A)

**詞彙** make 人 some tea 泡茶給某人 dessert 甜點

### 2. 英M 澳W

| | |
|---|---|
| 1 決定類別的線索 | in the cafeteria or my office |
| 2 動詞與其他 | prefer to meet |

Would you prefer to meet in the cafeteria or my office?
(A) Anywhere is fine.
(B) Yes, I agree with you.

你想在餐廳還是在我辦公室見面？
（A）任何地點都好。
（B）是的，我同意你。

**解說** 聽到了or就可以知道是選擇疑問句。因此包含表達「任何」的any的（A）為答案。（B）是對於選擇疑問句用Yes來回答，所以不是答案。 答案 (A)

**詞彙** prefer 較願意；較喜歡 cafeteria 自助餐廳 agree with 同意…

### 3. 美W 美M

| | |
|---|---|
| 1 決定類別的線索 | Please |
| 2 動詞與其他 | take a copy of the sales contract |

Please take a copy of the sales contract.
(A) Yes, I'm sure he did.
(B) I already have one, thanks.

請把一份銷售合約拿走。
（A）是的，我確定他做了。
（B）我已經有一份了，謝謝。

**解說** 聽到了Please就可以知道是建議。因此，省略了否定或拒絕說法而直接用附加說明來回答的（B）為答案。（A）裡無法知道he指的是誰、did指的是什麼行為，所以不是答案。 答案 (B)

**詞彙** **take a copy** 拿走一份 **sales contract** 銷售合約
**already** 已經

**4.** 美M 英M

| | |
|---|---|
| 1 決定類別的線索 | Monday or Tuesday |
| 2 動詞與其他 | reschedule the meeting |

Can you reschedule the meeting for Monday or Tuesday?
(A) How about Monday?
(B) No, they are behind schedule.

你能重新安排會議於星期一或是星期二嗎？
（A）星期一如何？
（B）不，他們的進度落後了。

**解說** 聽到了or就可以知道是選擇疑問句。（A）是拿選擇事項以反問句的方式回答，即是答案。（B）是對於選擇疑問句以No來回答，所以不是答案。 答案 (A)

**詞彙** **reschedule** 重新安排行程 **meeting** 會議
**be behind schedule** 落後於計畫的進度

**5.** 美W 澳W

| | |
|---|---|
| 1 決定類別的線索 | Do you mind |
| 2 動詞與其他 | waiting in the lobby |

Do you mind waiting in the lobby?
(A) To my mind, she's right.
(B) Absolutely not.

你介不介意在大廳等？
（A）照我的想法，她是對的。
（B）絕對不會。

**解說** 聽到了Do you mind就可以知道是建議。mind有「介意」的意思，所以（B）的「完全不」，也就是「允許」的意思，即為答案。（A）是故意用同義字mind來誤導的選項，且也無法知道she指的是誰。 答案 (B)

**詞彙** **mind** 介意 **lobby** 大廳 **to my mind** 照我的想法
**right** 正確；對 **absolutely not** 絕對不

## STEP 02 考題實戰練習

| | | | | | |
|---|---|---|---|---|---|
| 1. (B) | 2. (A) | 3. (B) | 4. (C) | 5. (B) | 6. (A) |
| 7. (B) | 8. (B) | 9. (B) | 10. (B) | 11. (C) | 12. (A) |

**1.** 美M 美W

Would you like to read the magazine when I finish?
(A) No, can you repair it?
(B) No thanks. I already bought a copy.
(C) Yes, I'd love to lead.

當我看完後，你想閱讀這本雜誌嗎？
（A）不，你可以修他嗎？
（B）不，謝謝。我已經買了一份。
（C）是的，我很喜歡當帶領的。

**解說** 聽到了建議的Would you，所以表達否定或拒絕的（B）為答案。（A）是無厘頭的回答。（C）是故意用read的類似發音lead來誤導的選項。 答案 (B)

**詞彙** **magazine** 雜誌 **finish** 完成 **repair** 修理
**a copy** 一份 **lead** 當領導

**2.** 美W 英M

Do you want some fruit or ice cream?
(A) Either one is okay.
(B) Sure. Help yourself.
(C) Yes, it was nice.

你想要一些水果或冰淇淋嗎？
（A）其中任一個都可以。
（B）當然，請隨意。
（C）是的，它是很好的。

**解說** 聽到了句子中間的or就可以知道是選擇疑問句。因此，表達「任何一個（either）」的（A）為答案。（B）是對於建議的回答方式，而不是答案。（C）是對於「單字or單字」的選擇疑問句用Yes來回答，所以不是答案。 答案 (A)

**詞彙** **help oneself** 隨意食用

**3.** 美M 澳W

Would you like to try this shirt on instead?
(A) It isn't that short.
(B) What size is it?
(C) Yes, we have.

你想換成這件襯衫試試看嗎？
（A）它不是那麼短。
（B）它的尺寸是多少？
（C）是的，我們有。

**解說** 聽到了Would you就可以知道是建議。（B）是反問形式的回答方式，總是能夠成為答案。（A）故意用了shirt的類似發音short來誤導的選項。（C）是不符合考題內容的回答。 答案 (B)

**詞彙** **try on** 試穿 **instead** 取代 **short** 短的 **size** 尺寸

**4.** 美M 美W

We need to check your passport or your driver's license for identification.

(A) Yes, I am.
(B) Leave your car here.
(C) Oh, I don't have either.

我們需要檢查您的護照或駕駛執照來確認身份。

（A）是，我是。
（B）把你的車留在這兒。
（C）噢，我任何一個都沒有。

**解說** 聽到了句子中間的or就可以知道是選擇疑問句。（C）用either來表達「任何一個」，即為答案。（A）是對於「單字or單字」的選擇疑問句用Yes來回答，所以不是答案。（B）是故意用car來與driver's license產生聯想而誤導的選項。 答案 (C)

**詞彙** **check** 檢查 **passport** 護照 **driver's license** 駕照 **identification** 身份檢查 **leave** 遺留；留下

**5.** 澳W 英M

Which is the fastest way to get to the bank, Islington Road or the highway?

(A) You can park your car in the garage.
(B) They're both about the same.
(C) To cash a check.

哪個是到銀行最快的方法呢？伊斯林頓路還是高速公路？
（A）你可以把車停在車庫。
（B）它們兩個都差不多。
（C）為了兌現一張支票

**解說** 聽到了Which與or就可以知道是選擇疑問句。（B）用both來表達「兩個都是」，即為答案。（A）是故意用car來與road和highway產生聯想來誤導的選項。（C）是故意用cash a check來與bank產生聯想來誤導的選項。 答案 (B)

**詞彙** **way to get to** 去某處的路 **park** 停車 **garage** 車庫 **cash a check** 兌現支票

**6.** 美M 美W

Do you need a lift to the convention?

(A) I'd appreciate that.
(B) I'm not sure I can lift this box alone.
(C) I enjoy their conversation too.

要不要載你到會議去？
（A）謝謝你。
（B）我不確定我能否獨自舉起這個箱子。
（C）我也喜歡他們的談話。

**解說** 聽到了建議的Do you need，所以表達肯定或允許的（A）為答案。（B）是故意用同音字lift來誤導的，則這裡的意思不是「載人」而是「舉起」，所以不是答案。（C）是故意用convention的相似發音conversation來誤導的選項。 答案 (A)

**詞彙** **lift** 搭載 **convention** 會議 **appreciate** 感謝 **alone** 獨自 **conversation** 對話 **too** 也

**7.** 英M 澳W

Could you come by my office before you leave?

(A) I don't know if the bill came this month.
(B) Sure. I'm on my way out now.
(C) No, she lives far away.

在你離開前，能到我辦公室來嗎？
（A）我不知道這個月帳單來了沒。
（B）當然，我正在下班當中。
（C）不，她住得很遠。

**解說** 聽到了建議的Could you，所以表達肯定或允許之後附加說明的（B）為答案。（A）是故意用come的類似發音came來誤導的選項。（C）也是故意用leave的類似發音lives來誤導的選項。 答案 (B)

**詞彙** **come by** 順路訪問 **leave** 離開 **bill** 帳單 **far away** 遠

**8.** 美M 美W

Which restaurant would you like to recommend?

(A) Dinner is at 7 p.m.
(B) How about the Korean one?
(C) Yes, it's quite good.

哪家餐廳是你想推薦的？
（A）晚餐在晚上7點。
（B）韓式餐廳如何？
（C）是的，它的相當不錯。

**解說** Which是表達選擇疑問句的單字，而此類型答案傾向於包含one。因此（B）為答案。（A）是故意用dinner來與restaurants產生聯想而誤導的選項。（C）是對於選擇疑問句用Yes來回答，所以不是答案。 答案 (B)

**詞彙** **recommend** 推薦 **dinner** 晚餐 **How about** 如何? **quite** 相當；很

**9.** 美W 英M

Have you contacted the travel agency or do you want me to call them?

(A) Is that your phone number?
(B) I don't have time. Do you?
(C) No, I haven't had much yet.

你和旅行社聯繫了沒？還是由我來打電話給他們？
（A）那是你的電話號碼嗎？
（B）我沒有時間。你有嗎？

（C）不，我目前沒有很多。

**解說** 聽到了句子中間有or就可以知道是選擇疑問句。在此，將B變形的（B）為答案。（A）是故意用phone number來與contacted產生聯想而誤導的選項。若只聽到Have you而立刻選（C）No, I haven't.的話就錯了。

答案 (B)

**詞彙** **contact** 聯絡 **travel agency** 旅行社 **phone number** 電話號碼

**10.** 澳W 美W

Don't you want to take a taxi?

(A) Thanks, I'll take some please.
(B) No, I'd like to walk.
(C) No, I talked to him this morning.

你不想搭計程車嗎？
（A）謝謝，我取用一些吧。
（B）不，我想走路。
（C）不，我今天上午和他說過。

**解說** 聽到了Don't you want，就可以知道是間接的建議。因此，表達否定或拒絕之後附加說明的（B）為答案。（A）是故意用同音字take來誤導的選項，在這裡的意思為「取用」。（C）是故意用相似發音talked來誤導的選項。

答案 (B)

**詞彙** **take a taxi** 搭計程車 **would like to** 想要…

**11.** 英M 英W

Can you stay a little longer or do you need to leave now?

(A) No, I don't need them.
(B) The sleeves are too long.
(C) I'll let you know in a second.

你能多待一下還是你現在就要離開呢？
（A）沒有，我不需要他們。
（B）袖子太長了。
（C）我很快會讓你知道。

**解說** 聽到了句子中間的or就可以知道是選擇疑問句。（C）是間接迴避性回答方式，即為答案。（A）是故意用同音字need來誤導的選項。（B）是故意用longer的相似發音long來誤導的選項。

答案 (C)

**詞彙** **stay** 停留；待著 **a little longer** 再久一點點 **sleeves** 袖子

**12.** 美W 美M

Let's stop by the construction site next week.

(A) I'll be out of town next week.
(B) That's the resident's apartment.
(C) To build a new convention hall.

下週到工地去一下吧。
（A）我下週將要出城。
（B）那是居民的公寓。
（C）為建立一個新的會議廳

**解說** 聽到了Let's就可以知道是建議。因此，表達否定或拒絕之後附加說明的（A）為答案。（B）是故意用apartment來與construction產生聯想來誤導的選項。（C）也是故意用build來與construction site產生聯想來誤導的選項。

答案 (A)

**詞彙** **stop by** 順路訪問 **construction site** 工地 **resident** 居民 **apartment** 公寓 **convention hall** 會議廳

Chapter 09 一般、否定、附加問句

## Quiz

Q1. (1) Are, happy (2) Did, arrive
(3) Do, have (4) Will, speak
Q2. (1) ⓐ (2) ⓑ (3) ⓐ
Q3. (1) like (2) been trained
(3) lived here (4) ordered
Q4. (1) ⓑ (2) ⓐ (3) ⓐ

### Q1

(1) Are you happy with your computer software?
你對你的新電腦軟體滿意嗎？

(2) Did the shipment arrive yesterday?
貨運昨天到了嗎？

(3) Do you have these shirts in other colors?
這些裙子你有其他顏色嗎？

(4) Will you speak at the sales meeting?
你將在銷售會議上演講嗎？

### Q2

(1) Did we renew that contract last month?
ⓐ **Yes, on 20th.**
ⓑ That's a great idea.

在上個月你更新過合約嗎？
ⓐ 是的，在二十號時。
ⓑ 那是個很棒的主意。

(2) Have you already had breakfast?
ⓐ This train does go fast.
ⓑ **No, I'm really hungry.**

你已經吃過早餐了嗎？
ⓐ 這台火車的確開得很快。
ⓑ 沒有，我真的很餓。

(3) Are there any extra tea cups?
ⓐ **In the cupboard, over the sink.**
ⓑ I made it this morning.

有任何多餘的茶杯嗎？
ⓐ 在水槽上方的櫥櫃裡。
ⓑ 我今天早上製做了。

### Q3

(1) Don't you like the book?
你不喜歡這本書嗎？

(2) Haven't you been trained to use that software?
你不是受過訓練使用那個軟體嗎？

(3) You've lived here for a while, haven't you?
你已經住在這兒一段時間了，沒有嗎？

(4) You ordered more stationary, didn't you?
你訂了更多的文具，不是嗎？

### Q4

(1) It's hot in the building, isn't it?
ⓐ Yes, it's pleasant weather.
ⓑ **I'll turn on the air conditioner.**

這棟大樓裡面很熱，不是嗎？
ⓐ 是的，這是個舒服的天氣。
ⓑ 我將打開冷氣。

(2) There's no restaurant around here, is there?
ⓐ **There used to be one.**
ⓑ I just bought some groceries.

這附近沒有餐廳，是嗎？
ⓐ 以前有一家。
ⓑ 我剛買了一些雜貨。

(3) Didn't Ms.Johnson buy printer papers last week?
ⓐ **She's getting them today.**
ⓑ Put them in his office.

上週強森沒有買印表機的紙嗎？
ⓐ 她今天會買的。
ⓑ 把那些放在他的辦公室。

## STEP 01 若沒答對會後悔的考題

1. (B) 2. (A) 3. (B) 4. (A) 5. (A)

**1.** 美M 美W

| | |
|---|---|
| 1 助動詞＋主詞＋動詞 | Are you going |
| 2 受詞與其他 | to the workshop next weekend |

Are you going to the workshop next weekend?
(A) About weekly training schedules.
(B) Yes, I'm looking forward to it.

你下週將會去工作坊嗎？
（A）有關於週訓練計畫。
（B）是的，我很期待。

**解說** 沒有出現疑問詞、否定詞、以及附加問句尾巴，所以是一般疑問句。若要回答「將要去」，用Yes，不

是的話用No。（B）說Yes之後以「很期待」來附加說明，即為答案。（A）是對於「這場工作方是有關什麼的？」的回答。 答案 (B)

**詞彙** **workshop** 工作坊 **training schedule** 訓練計畫 **look forward to** 名稱 對…期待

**2.** 英M 澳W

| | |
|---|---|
| 1 助動詞 + 主詞 + 動詞 | Didn't you organize |
| 2 受詞與其他 | the company banquet<br>last year |

Didn't you organize the company banquet last year?
(A) Yes, you attended, right?
(B) Which bank is closer?

你不是籌辦了公司去年的宴會嗎？
（A）是的，你參加了，對嗎？
（B）哪家銀行比較近？

**解說** 有否定詞在最前面出現了，所以是否定疑問句。將此否定詞拿掉了之後，如果要表達「籌辦了」，就是Yes，不是的話就是用No來回答。因此說Yes之後再附加說明的（A）為答案。（B）是故意用banquet的相似發音bank來誤導的選項。 答案 (A)

**詞彙** **organize** 籌畫舉辦 **banquet** 宴會 **attend** 參加

**3.** 美W 美M

| | |
|---|---|
| 1 助動詞 + 主詞 + 動詞 | Did you deliver |
| 2 受詞與其他 | the document in person |

Did you deliver the document in person?
(A) The personnel department.
(B) No, I sent it by fax.

你是親自遞送文件的嗎？
（A）是人事部門。
（B）不，我用傳真送過去的。

**解說** 沒有出現疑問詞、否定詞、以及附加問句尾巴，所以是一般疑問句。若要說「親自遞送的」就用Yes，不是的話用No來回答。（B）是說了No之後再說「用傳真送過去的」的，即為答案。（A）是用person的相似發音personnel來誤導的選項。 答案 (B)

**詞彙** **deliver** 投遞；配送 **document** 文件資料 **in person** 親自 **personnel department** 人事部 **by fax** 用傳真方式

**4.** 美M 英M

| | |
|---|---|
| 1 動詞 + 形容詞 | are delicius |
| 2 主詞與其他 | These sandwiches /<br>aren't they? |

These sandwiches are delicious, aren't they?
(A) Yes, I like this kind.
(B) No, I can't wait to have some.

這些三明治很美味，不是嗎？
（A）是的，我喜歡這一種。
（B）不，我等不及要吃一些。

**解說** 這是在最後部分有尾巴的附加問句。將此尾巴拿掉了之後，若要表達「好吃」，就用Yes，不是的話就用No來回答。因此，Yes後面附加說明的（A）為答案。（B）是說了No之後卻加上Yes的附加說明，所以不是答案。 答案 (A)

**詞彙** **delicious** 美味的 **kind** 種類 **can't wait to** 等不及

**5.** 美W 澳W

| | |
|---|---|
| 1 主詞 + 助動詞 + 動詞 | We haven't missed |
| 2 受詞與其他 | the train, have we? |

We haven't missed the train, have we?
(A) No, it's just arrived.
(B) She's been gone since yesterday.

我們還沒錯過這班火車，是嗎？
（A）不，它剛剛才到。
（B）她從昨天起不在的。

**解說** 這是在最後部分有尾巴的附加問句。將此尾巴和否定詞拿掉了之後，若要表達「錯過火車」就用Yes，若不是的話就用No來回答。因此，No後面附加說明的（A）為答案。（B）不是答案，因為無法知道she是在指誰。 答案 (A)

**詞彙** **miss** 錯過 **arrive** 抵達 **since** 自從…

## STEP 02 考題實戰練習

| | | | | | |
|---|---|---|---|---|---|
| 1. (B) | 2. (C) | 3. (B) | 4. (B) | 5. (B) | 6. (A) |
| 7. (A) | 8. (B) | 9. (B) | 10. (A) | 11. (A) | 12. (A) |

**1.** 美M 美W

Are you taking the clients out for lunch today?

(A) The chicken sandwich, please.
(B) Yes, would you like to join us?
(C) The food there is always delicious.

你今天要帶客戶出去吃午餐嗎？
（A）請給我雞肉三明治。
（B）是的，你想加入我們嗎？
（C）那兒的菜永遠很美味。

**解說** 沒有出現疑問詞、否定詞、以及附加問句尾巴，所以是一般疑問句。若要表達「帶出去」，就用Yes，不是的話就用No來回答。（B）是說了Yes之後將附加說明以反問形式來表達。（A）是故意用sandwich來與lunch產生聯想而誤導的選項。（C）不是答案，因為there指的是某地點。 答案 (B)

**詞彙** **take out** 帶出去 **always** 總是

**2.** 美W 英M
Aren't you going to call the doctor this afternoon?
(A) At our last meeting.
(B) I go about twice a month.
(C) I gave him a call this morning.

你今天下午不打電話給醫生嗎？
（A）在我們最後一次的會議。
（B）我大約每月去兩次。
（C）我今天上午打過電話給他了。

**解說** 有否定詞出現於最前面，所以是否定疑問句。將此否定詞拿掉了之後，若要表達「將要打電話」就用Yes，若要表達「不會打電話」就用No回答。因此，將No省略了之後，以「今天上午打過電話給他了」來附加說明的（C）為答案。（A）是對於未來時態用過去時態來回答，所以不是答案。（B）是故意用going的相似發音go來誤導的選項。 答案 (C)

**詞彙** **last** 上次的 **about** 大約 **twice a month** 一個月兩次

**3.** 美M 澳W
The concert starts at 9 o'clock, doesn't it?
(A) That's the music store.
(B) I think the time should be on the ticket.
(C) I found the ending better.

演唱會在9點鐘開始，不是嗎？
（A）那是間唱片店。
（B）我想入場票上應該有時間。
（C）我認為結局的部分好一些。

**解說** 這是在句子最後出現尾巴的，所以是附加問句。將此尾巴拿掉了之後，若要表達「在九點開始」就用Yes，若不是就用No來回答。因此將No省略了之後附加說明的（B）為答案。（A）是故意用music來與concert產生聯想來誤導的選項。（C）是故意用ending來與starts產生聯想來誤導的選項。 答案 (B)

**詞彙** **concert** 演唱會 **start** 開始 **music store** 唱片店 **ending** 結局；結束

**4.** 美M 美W
Our clothing sales have gone up this year, haven't they?
(A) No, he hasn't been there.
(B) Yes, I believe so.
(C) See you next month.

今年我們的服裝銷售增加了，不是嗎？
（A）沒有，他沒去過那裡。
（B）是的，我相信是這樣。
（C）下個月見。

**解說** 這是在句子最後出現尾巴的，所以是附加問句。將此尾巴拿掉了之後，若要表達「增加了」就用Yes，若不是就用No來回答。因此Yes後面附加說明的（B）為答案。（A）不是答案，因為無法知道主詞he指的是誰。（C）是故意用next month來與this year產生聯想而誤導的選項。 答案 (B)

**詞彙** **clothing** 衣服 **sales** 銷售量 **go up** 上升 **I believe so.** 我相信如此

**5.** 澳W 英M
Are there any tickets available for today's play?
(A) It's probably the most valuable skill.
(B) I'm afraid they're all sold out.
(C) You must present your ticket.

有今天舞台劇的任何門票嗎？
（A）它可能是最具價值的技術。
（B）恐怕已經都賣完了。
（C）你必須出示你的票。

**解說** 沒有出現疑問詞、否定詞、以及附加問句尾巴，所以是一般疑問句。若要表達「有門票」就用Yes，不是的話就用No來回答。（B）是將No省略之後以「都賣完了」來附加說明的答案。（A）是故意用valuable來與available產生混淆的選項。（C）是故意用相似發音ticket來產生混淆的選項。 答案 (B)

**詞彙** **available** 可用的 **play** 舞台劇 **probably** 可能；十之八九 **valuable** 具有價值的 **skill** 技術 **sold out** 賣完了 **present** 出示

**6.** 美M 美W
Did you make it to the new exhibit at the science museum?
(A) No, but I plan to next week.
(B) That's good news.
(C) Yes, to build a new museum.

你去過在科學博物館的新展覽會嗎?

(A) 不，但我打算下週去。
(B) 這真是個好消息。
(C) 是的，為了蓋新的博物館。

**解說** 沒有出現疑問詞、否定詞、以及附加問句尾巴，所以是一般疑問句。若要表達「能參加」就用Yes，不是的話就用No來回答。因此No之後附加說明的（A）為答案。（B）是故意用news來與new產生混淆的選項。（C）是故意用同音字new和museum來產生混淆的選項。 答案 (A)

**詞彙** **make it to** 到某處 **exhibit** 展示會 **museum** 博物館 **build** 建造

**7.** 英M 澳W
Didn't Ms. Johnson file the insurance paperwork last week?
(A) I'll ask her.
(B) The tiles arrived yesterday.
(C) The plastic ones look better.

強生女士上週沒有將保險文件歸檔嗎？
(A) 我將會問她。
(B) 昨天瓷磚到了。
(C) 塑膠的那個更好看。

**解說** 有否定詞出現於最前面，所以是否定疑問句。將此否定詞拿掉了之後，若要表達「將保險文件歸檔了」就用Yes，若不是就用No來回答。（A）是用成為答案機率很高的「間接迴避性回答」，即為答案。（B）是故意用file的相似發音tiles來產生混淆的選項。（C）是故意用plastic來與paper產生聯想來誤導的選項。 答案 (A)

**詞彙** **file** 整理歸檔 **insurance paperwork** 保險文件 **tile** 瓷磚 **arrive** 抵達 **plastic** 塑膠的

**8.** 美M 美W
Jacob will be able to reschedule the appointment, won't he?
(A) Yes, he's just been appointed.
(B) Yes, he will do it right away.
(C) Too many times.

雅各將能重新安排這個約會，不是嗎？
(A) 是的，他剛被任命。
(B) 是的，他會馬上做的。
(C) 太多次了。

**解說** 這是在句子最後出現尾巴的，所以是附加問句。將此尾巴拿掉了之後，若要表達「能重新安排約會」就用Yes，若不是就用No來回答。因此說Yes之後附加說明的（B）為答案。（A）是故意用appointment的相似發音appointed來產生混淆的選項。（C）是故意用times來與reschedule和appointment產生聯想來誤導的選項。 答案 (B)

**詞彙** **be able to** 動詞原型 能夠做某事 **reschedule an appointment** 重新安排約定 **appoint** 任命 **right away** 立刻

**9.** 美W 英M
The marketing associate wasn't very helpful, was he?
(A) No, in the accounting department.
(B) I didn't think he was either.
(C) Thanks for your help.

行銷合夥人不太能幫忙，是吧？
(A) 不，在會計部門。
(B) 我也不認為他很會幫忙。
(C) 謝謝你的幫忙。

**解說** 這是在句子最後出現尾巴的，所以是附加問句。將此尾巴拿掉了之後，若要表達「很有幫助」就用Yes，若不是就用No來回答。因此將No省略了之後附加說明的（B）為答案。選項（A）No之後的附加說明不妥當，而且故意用accounting department與marketing產生聯想來誤導。（C）是故意用help來與helpful產生混淆的選項。 答案 (B)

**詞彙** **associate** 同僚 **helpful** 有幫助的 **accounting department** 會計部門

**10.** 澳W 美W
Do you have any plans for this weekend?
(A) We're going hiking on Saturday.
(B) No, it was a guided tour.
(C) I put the plants by the window.

這個週末你有任何計劃嗎？
(A) 我們週六將要去健行。
(B) 不，這是導遊陪伴的旅遊。
(C) 我把植物放在窗邊。

**解說** 有否定詞出現於最前面，所以是否定疑問句。將此否定詞拿掉了之後，若要表達「預訂持續」就用Yes，若不是就用No來回答。因此說Yes之後附加說明的（A）為答案。選項（B）No後面的附加說明不妥當，而且故意用training的相似發音train來產生混淆。（C）是故意用yours來與hours產生混淆的選項。 答案 (A)

**詞彙** **plan** 計畫 **this weekend** 這個週末 **hiking** 登山 **guided** 導遊陪伴的 **put** 置放 **plant** 植物

**11.** 英M 澳W
Isn't that training session scheduled to last 2 hours?
(A) Yes, it will end on time.
(B) No, the train departs at 5:03.
(C) I believe it's yours.

培訓課不是預定持續兩個小時嗎？
（A）是的，它會準時結束。
（B）不，火車在五點零三分出發。
（C）我相信它是你的。

**解說** 有否定詞出現於最前面，所以是否定疑問句。將此否定詞拿掉了之後，若要表達「預訂持續」就用Yes，若不是就用No來回答。因此說Yes之後附加說明的（A）為答案。選項（B）No後面的附加說明不妥當，而且故意用training的相似發音train來產生混淆。（C）是故意用yours來與hours產生混淆的選項。

答案 (A)

**詞彙** training session 訓練課程 be scheduled to 動詞原型 預訂… last 持續 end 結束 on time 準時 depart 出發

12. 美W 美M

This plant was constructed about two years ago, wasn't it?

(A) Yes, I think that's right.
(B) Was the result satisfactory?
(C) It looks like a good plan.

這家工廠是大約兩年前建造的，不是嗎？
（A）是的，我認為那是對的。
（B）結果令人滿意嗎？
（C）它看起來像是個好計劃。

**解說** 這是在句子最後出現尾巴的，所以是附加問句。將此尾巴拿掉了之後，若要表達「建造的」就用Yes，若不是就用No來回答。因此說Yes之後附加說明的（A）為答案。（B）是故意用satisfactory來與factory、plant產生聯想來誤導的選項。（C）是故意用plant的相似發音plan來產生混淆的選項。

答案 (A)

**詞彙** plant 工廠 construct 建造 about 大約 result 結果 satisfactory 令人滿意的 plan 計畫

# Chapter 10 陳述句、間接疑問句

## Quiz

Q1. (1) I'd like to
(2) I thought
(3) There's
(4) I think, forgot

Q2. (1) ⓑ (2) ⓐ (3) ⓑ

Q3. (1) Can you tell me when
(2) Do you know why
(3) Have you decided which
(4) I don't remember who

Q4. (1) ⓐ (2) ⓐ (3) ⓐ

## Q1

(1) I'd like to make a reservation.
我想要預約。

(2) I thought you already left for Seoul.
我以為你已經往首爾去了

(3) There's a phone call for you.
這是一通找你的電話。

(4) I think I forgot my wallet.
我覺得我忘了我的皮夾。

## Q2

(1) I'd like to con rm my appointment time.
ⓐ Thanks, I'm glad you like it.
ⓑ **What is your name?**

我想確認我預約的時間。
ⓐ 謝謝，我很高興你喜歡它。
ⓑ 您的名字是什麼？

(2) I think Henry's a great designer.
ⓐ **I believe so.**
ⓑ I read the sign.

我認為亨利是個偉大的設計師。
我相信是這樣。
我看到告示了。

(3) I can't nd my notebook anywhere.
ⓐ I found it boring.
ⓑ **Have you checked the conference room?**

我到處都找不到我的筆記本。
ⓐ 我覺得很無聊。
ⓑ 你有確認過會議室嗎？

## Q3

(1) Can you tell me when you bought your car?
你能告訴我你什麼時候買了你的車呢？

(2) Do you know why the budget meeting was canceled?
你知道為什麼預算會議被取消嗎？

(3) Have you decided which computer to buy?
你決定要買哪台電腦了嗎？

(4) I don't remember who is supposed to water the plant.
我不記得是誰該給花草澆水。

## Q4

(1) Can you tell me when the report is due?
ⓐ **Next week, perhaps.**
ⓑ I can do it.

你能告訴我報告的截止日期嗎？
ⓐ 也許是下星期。
ⓑ 我能夠做。

(2) Do you know where I can buy a plane ticket?
ⓐ **You can purchase it on the Internet.**
ⓑ It does look plain.

你知道我在哪兒能買到機票嗎？
ⓐ 你可以上網訂購。
ⓑ 它的確看起來很平凡。

(3) I don't know how to use the copy machine.
ⓐ **Let me show you.**
ⓑ With sugar, please.

我不知道如何使用這台影印機。
ⓐ 讓我做給你看。
ⓑ 請加糖，謝謝。

## STEP 01 若沒答對會後悔的考題

1. (A) 2. (A) 3. (B) 4. (B) 5. (B)

**1.** 美M 美W

| | |
|---|---|
| 1 決定類別的單字 | I really like |
| 2 其他 | the magazine I'm reading |

I really like the magazine I'm reading.
(A) Which issue is it?
(B) No, you should follow me.

我真的很喜歡我正在讀的這本雜誌。
（A）是哪一期？
（B）不，你應該跟著我。

**解說** 有I really like而且也沒有尾巴，所以是表達意見的陳述句。因此以反問句來回答的（A）為答案。如果將考題裡面的reading聽成leading，就很容易選（B）當作答案，因為可能聯想到follow，但該選項就是陷阱。
答案 (A)

**詞彙** **magazine** 雜誌 **issue** 期數 **follow** 跟隨

**2.** 英M 澳W

| | |
|---|---|
| 1 決定類別的單字 | I've forgotten how |
| 2 其他 | to use this software |

I've forgotten how to use this software.
(A) Morris can help you figure it out.
(B) You may try a different size.

我忘了如何使用這個軟體。
（A）莫里斯可以幫助你瞭解。
（B）你可以試試看不同的尺寸。

**解說** 以I've forgotten開始，所以是陳述句，而句子裡面包含了how，所以也具有間接疑問句的色彩。選項（A）是對於how的回答方式，說別人會幫忙，此即為答案。如果將考題裡面software的ware聽成wear（穿衣服）的話，有可能選（B）為答案，因為可以聯想到「試穿別的大小」。
答案 (A)

**詞彙** **forget** 忘記 **figure out** 理解；瞭解 **try** 嘗試

**3.** 美W 美M

| | |
|---|---|
| 1 決定類別的單字 | I heard |
| 2 其他 | the show's been postponed |

I heard the show's been postponed.
(A) Thanks, I'll answer the phone.
(B) Really? When's the new date?

我聽說這個表演被延期了。
（A）謝謝，我將會接電話。
（B）真的嗎？新的日期是什麼時候？

**解說** 以主詞開頭而且也沒有尾巴，所以是陳述句。因此以反問句來回答的（B）為答案。（A）是故意用postponed的相似發音phone來誤導的選項。
答案 (B)

**詞彙** **postpone** 延期 **answer the phone** 接電話

**4.** 美M 英M

| | |
|---|---|
| 1 決定類別的單字 | Can you tell me how |
| 2 其他 | to fix the printer |

Can you tell me how to fix the printer?
(A) There are some papers in the staff room.
(B) I'm afraid I don't know.

你能告訴我如何修理這台印表機嗎？
（A）在職員室有一些紙。
（B）恐怕我不知道。

**解說** 得注意聽Can you tell me後面出現的how，然後找出對於how的回答。選項（B）是用「不知道」類型的間接迴避性回答，即為答案。（A）是故意用papers來與printer產生聯想來誤導的選項。 答案(B)

**詞彙** **fix** 修理 **papers** 紙 **staff room** 職員室

**5.** 美W 澳W

| | |
|---|---|
| 1 決定類別的單字 | I'll need |
| 2 其他 | some help moving these desks |

I'll need some help moving these desks.
(A) Yes, these days.
(B) I can give you a hand.

我需要一些幫忙來搬這些桌子。
（A）是的，是最近。
（B）我可以幫忙你。

**解說** 以主詞開頭而且也沒有尾巴，所以是陳述句。對於「需要幫忙」以答應幫忙的說法回答的（B）為答案。（A）是故意用和考題裡一樣的單字these來產生混淆的選項。 答案(B)

**詞彙** **move** 搬移 **these days** 最近 **give someone a hand** 幫助某人

## STEP 02 考題實戰練習

1. (B) 2. (B) 3. (A) 4. (A) 5. (A) 6. (A)
7. (B) 8. (B) 9. (A) 10. (B) 11. (A) 12. (A)

**1.** 美M 美W

I think the picture in the booklet is too light.
(A) I thought we needed two lights.
(B) Could it be darkened?
(C) Several color photos.

我認為這本小冊子的圖片太淡了。
（A）我以為我們需要兩個燈。
（B）它有可能被加深嗎？
（C）幾張彩色照片。

**解說** 出現I think而且沒有尾巴，所以是表達意見的陳述句。以反問句回答的（B）為答案。（A）是故意用同音字light來誤導的選項。（C）是故意用photos來與picture產生聯想的選項。 答案(B)

**詞彙** **booklet** 小冊子 **light** 淡；燈具 **darken** 加深顏色

**2.** 美W 英M

I thought Ms. Wagner was going to lead the workshop.
(A) I haven't read it yet.
(B) No, she's on vacation.
(C) It comes in today.

我以為華格納女士將會領導這個工作坊。
（A）我還沒有讀過。
（B）不，她在休假中。
（C）它在今天進來。

**解說** 出現I thought而且沒有尾巴，所以是表達意見的陳述句。先說No之後附加說明的（B）為答案。（A）是故意用lead的相似發音read來誤導的選項。（C）是故意用comes來與going產生聯想來誤導的選項。 答案(B)

**詞彙** **lead** 領導 **on vacation** 休假中 **come in** 進入

**3.** 美M 澳W

Have you heard when the construction of the new office will be finished?
(A) Yeah, by the end of December.
(B) We'll work on the instructions.
(C) About 5 years old.

你有聽說什麼時候新辦公室將會完工嗎？
（A）有啊，十二月底。
（B）我們將弄說明書。
（C）大約五歲左右。

**解說** 在Have you heard之後出現了when，所以是要對於when回答的間接疑問句。因此以時間說法回答的（A）為答案。（B）是故意用construction的相似發音instructions來誤導的選項。（C）是對於How old的回答方式。 答案(A)

**詞彙** **construction** 建設 **finish** 完成 **work** 工作 **instructions** 說明書 **about** 大約

**4.** 美M 美W
I'd like to make reservations for dinner tonight.
(A) Can I have your name?
(B) Two nights only.
(C) Let's have a rest for a while.

我想預訂今晚晚餐的座位。
（A）請告訴我您的大名。
（B）只有兩晚。
（C）我們休息一會兒吧。

**解說** 以I'd like to開始而且沒有尾巴，所以是陳述句。因此以反問句回答的（A）為答案。（B）是故意用tonight的相似發音two nights來產生混淆的選項。（C）是故意用reservations的相似發音rest來產生混淆的選項。
答案 (A)

**詞彙** **make a reservation** 預訂 **have a rest** 休息 **for a while** 一會兒

**5.** 澳W 英M
That construction work outside surely is noisy.
(A) Why don't you close the windows?
(B) The instructions are on the back.
(C) Inside the restaurant.

外面在施工真的很嘈雜。
（A）你為什麼不把窗關上？
（B）說明在背面。
（C）在餐廳內。

**解說** 以主詞開始而且沒有尾巴，所以是陳述句。聽到Noisy，因此可以知道是提出問題狀況的句子。因此提供解決方法的（A）為答案。（B）是故意用construction的相似發音instructions來產生混淆的選項。（C）是故意用inside來與outside產生聯想來誤導的選項。
答案 (A)

**詞彙** **construction work** 施工 **outside** 戶外 **noisy** 吵雜 **close** 關 **inside** 在…內

**6.** 美M 美W
Can you please tell me where to find Dr. Tang's office?
(A) He works in the next door building.
(B) We haven't been booked yet.
(C) She found it this morning.

你可以告訴我湯先生的辦公室在哪兒嗎？
（A）他在隔壁大樓工作。
（B）我們還沒有被預約。
（C）她今天上午發現的。

**解說** 出現Can you please tell me，所以接著得要聽到where的部分。這是要對於where做回答的間接疑問句。因此以場所說法回答的（A）為答案。（B）的主詞為we，但無法知道是在指誰。（C）也是無法知道she指的是誰，且故意用find的相似發音found來產生混淆的選項。
答案 (A)

**詞彙** **next door** 隔壁的 **book** 預約

**7.** 英M 澳W
I've hired two software engineers.
(A) It's hard to use.
(B) Are they going to start within this week?
(C) We projected higher sales.

我聘請了兩名軟體工程師。
（A）它很難用。
（B）他們將在這週內開始嗎？
（C）我們預估了更高的銷量。

**解說** 以主詞開始而且沒有尾巴，所以是陳述句。以反問句回答的（B）為答案。（A）是故意用hired的相似發音hard來產生混淆的選項。（C）也是故意用hired的相似發音higher來產生混淆的選項。
答案 (B)

**詞彙** **hire** 雇用 **hard** 困難 **use** 使用 **within** 在…之內 **project** 預估

**8.** 美M 美W
I can't get the computer to start.
(A) I went out this morning.
(B) Do you want me to try?
(C) He starts tomorrow.

我無法啟動電腦。
（A）我今天早上外出過。
（B）你要讓我試試看嗎？
（C）他從明天開始。

**解說** 聽到否定詞，所以是提出問題狀況的句子。以主詞開頭而且沒有尾巴，所以是陳述句。「can't get 名詞 to do」是一種提出問題狀況的說法。因此以包含解決方法的反問句回答的（B）就是答案。（A）是無厘頭的回答。（C）是故意用start的相似發音start來產生混淆的選項。
答案 (B)

**詞彙** **go out** 外出 **try** 嘗試

**9.** 美W 英M
Do you know who's responsible for this project?
(A) Yes, the marketing manager is.
(B) Yes, it's next Monday.
(C) About new products.

你知道誰負責這個計畫嗎？
（A）是的，是行銷經理。
（B）是的，在下週一。
（C）有關於新產品。

**解說** 聽到Do you know之後，還得要聽到who，然後對於who做回答的間接疑問句。說Yes之後以職稱來回答的（A）為答案。（B）是對於when的回答方式，所以不是答案。（C）是對於what的回答方式，而且故意用project的相似發音products來產生混淆的選項。答案 (A)

**詞彙** be responsible for 負責… marketing manager 行銷經理 product 產品

**10.** 澳W 美W

The microphones in the auditorium aren't working.

(A) Sometime this morning.
(B) I'll get the technician.
(C) The desk is next to the computer.

禮堂的麥克風壞掉了。
（A）今天上午某個時候。
（B）我會去找技師。
（C）那張桌子在電腦旁。

**解說** 以主詞開頭而且沒有尾巴，所以是陳述句。在句中有聽到否定詞，所以這是提出問題狀況的。因此以解決方法回答的（B）為答案。（A）是對於when的回答方式，所以不是答案。（C）是故意用desk和computer來與microphones產生聯想來誤導的選項。 答案 (B)

**詞彙** microphone 麥克風 auditorium 禮堂 work 運作 sometime 某個時候 get 找人

**11.** 英M 澳W

Our sales fell by ten percent last quarter.

(A) Decrease in demand is the main reason.
(B) Our new sales goals.
(C) I'm getting used to this weather.

我們上一季的銷售額下降了百分之十。
（A）需求下降是主要的原因。
（B）我們的新的銷售目標。
（C）我習慣於這種天氣。

**解說** 以主詞開頭而且沒有尾巴，所以是陳述句。因此做附加說明的（A）為答案。（B）是故意用同音字sales來產生混淆的選項。若將考題誤解為「溫度下降了」，有可能會錯選（C）的選項。 答案 (A)

**詞彙** fall 下降 last quarter 前一季 decrease 減少 demand 需要 main 主要 goal 目標 get used to 名詞 習慣於…

**12.** 美W 美M

Do you know why the company outing was cancelled?

(A) Probably because of the bad weather.
(B) Can we meet in two hours?
(C) I haven't heard of that company.

你知不知道為什麼公司郊遊被取消了？
（A）可能是因為天氣不好。
（B）我們能在兩小時內見面嗎？
（C）我沒聽說過那家公司。

**解說** 聽到Do you know之後，要注意聽why的部分，然後要對於why回答的間接疑問句。以「because of 名詞」回答的（A）為答案。若在考題裡只聽到了cancelled，那麼選項（B）的「見面吧」可能會產生聯想而選錯。（C）是故意用同音字company來產生混淆的選項。 答案 (A)

**詞彙** outing 郊遊 cancel 取消 probably 可能 because of 因為 bad weather 氣候不佳

## Chapter 11 概括性詢問的考題 I

### Quiz I

| | | | |
|---|---|---|---|
| 1. (A) | 2. (B) | 3. (A) | 4. (A) |
| 5. (A) | 6. (A) | 7. (A) | 8. (A) |

**Q1** 美M 美W

M : **Did you see** the new documentary with Larry Martin on television last night? It was so informative!

W : I wanted to see it, but I wasn't able to leave for the day until 9. I think Larry Martin is a great host.

男：昨晚你在電視上有看賴瑞馬汀主持的新記錄片嗎？它相當有教育性！

女：我想看，但是在九點前我不能下班。我認為賴瑞馬汀是很偉大的主持人。

這段談話主要是有關於什麼？

（A）一個電視節目

（B）一部新上映的電影

**解說** 聽到mainly about，就可以知道是「詢問主題的考題」。透過與Have you seen類似的Did you see，藉由其後面出現的「昨晚在電視上／新的紀錄片」，可以知道（A）為答案。 答案 (A)

**詞彙** **documentary** 記錄片 **informative** 有益的；有教育性的 **leave for the day** 下班 **host** 主持人

**Q2** 英M 澳W

M : Hi, Christina. We talked about going to a movie tonight. Do you still remember?

W : Oh no, **I forgot!** I'm sorry I can't make it to the movies tonight. My cousin is visiting me from New York, and I'm taking her out for dinner at a new restaurant near my house.

男：您好，克莉絲汀娜。我們討論過今晚要去看電影。你還記得嗎？

女：噢，我忘了！我很抱歉今晚我不能去看電影。我的表親從紐約來拜訪我，我要帶她出去到我家附近的一間新餐廳吃晚餐。

這個女人的問題狀況是什麼？

（A）她找不到可以坐的位子。

（B）她不能和這個男人去看電影。

**解說** 「有什麼問題／狀況？」類的考題就是在詢問主題。將I forgot後面聽到的「不能去看電影」做變化來表達的（B）為答案。 答案 (B)

**詞彙** **go to a movie** 去看電影 **can't make it to** 不能做… **take 人 out** 和某人出去

**Q3** 美W 英M

W : Hi. **I'm calling to** know what the number is for the city bank located in Middletown.

M : Do you have a particular address in mind? I see two branches in the computer listings.

女：您好。我打電話來是要知道在中區的城市銀行的電話是幾號。

男：您記得特定的地址嗎？我在電腦的列表裡看到有兩家分行。

這通電話的目的是什麼？

（A）為了得到一個電話號碼

（B）為了寄送一個包裹

**解說** 詢問通話目的的考題就是在詢問主題。將核心說法I'm calling to後面出現的「為了知道號碼」做變化來表達的（A）為答案。 答案 (A)

**詞彙** **located** 位於… **particular** 特定的 **have（名詞）in mind** 記得某事物 **computer listings** 電腦列表清單

**Q4** 澳W 英M

W : Dr. Min's office. How may I help you?

M : Hi, my name is Mike, one of Dr. Min's patients. **I'd like to** know the result of my physical examination. Can I speak to him for a minute?

女：閔醫師辦公室。我可以給您什麼幫助嗎？

男：您好，我的名字是麥可，我是閔醫師的病患之一。我想知道我的健康檢查結果。我能和他通一下電話嗎？

為什麼這個男人和這個女人聯繫？

（A）為了詢問有關檢查結果

（B）為了做預約

**解說** 「為什麼聯繫」類的考題也是在詢問主題的類型。將核心說法I'd like to後面出現的「為了知道健康檢查結果」做變化來表達的（A）為答案。 答案 (A)

**詞彙** **physical examination** 檢康檢查 **for a minute** 暫時；一下子 **exam result** 檢查結果 **make an appointment** 做預約

**Q5** 英M 英W

M : Good morning. Can you tell me where to go to open a savings account?

W : I can do that for you here. Do you have either a driver's license or a passport with you?

男：早安，你能告訴我要到哪裡可以開儲蓄帳戶嗎？

女：我可以在這兒幫你開。你有駕照或是護照其中之一嗎？

說話者很有可能在哪兒？

（A）在銀行

（B）在會計師事務所

**解說** 「開帳戶」類的說法是在「銀行」聽的到的。 答案 (A)

**詞彙** **open a savings account** 開儲蓄帳戶 **driver's license** 駕照 **passport** 駕照

### Q6 美W 美M

W : Here is my laptop. How long do you think it will take to fix the problem?

M : Please pick it up by five thirty. I think I'll need about an hour to cleanse the hard drive, check for viruses and upgrade the memory.

女：這是我的筆記型電腦。你認為修復這個問題會需要多久？
男：請在五點三十分時來拿。我想我需要大約一小時來清理硬碟、檢查有沒有病毒和升級記憶體。

說話者很有可能在哪兒？
（A）在電腦維修中心裡
（B）在汽車展覽會中

**解說** 聽到電腦有問題且詢問何時領取電腦，所以可以猜測是在「電腦維修中心」進行的對話。 答案 (A)

**詞彙** **laptop** 筆記型電腦 **take** 花時間 **pick up** 領取 **exhibition** 展覽會

### Q7 美W 英M

W : David, I heard there's going to be a product demonstration this afternoon for our computer models for next year.

M : Certainly. I'm going to attend it. Where is the meeting supposed to be held?

女：大衛，我聽說今天下午將有一場我們明年電腦模型的產品展示會。
男：確實。我將會去參加。會議應該會在哪裡舉辦呢？

說話者可能是為誰工作？
（A）一家電腦製造商
（B）一家廣告公司

**解說** work for（公司名稱）是指「某家公司的職員」。這個考題詢問說話者的公司是什麼，換句話說就是詢問說話者是誰的考題。以上的對話需將該女性的話全部都聽完才能瞭解內容。說出「參加我們電腦模型的產品展示會」的人，可以認為是在「電腦製造商」上班的。 答案 (A)

**詞彙** **product demonstration**產品展示會 **attend** 參加 **be supposed to** 應該 **hold** 舉行

### Q8 澳W 美M

W : Shawn, welcome to National Heavy Equipment. We're very happy you joined our sales team. Today, you'll start your training with Ms. Chen who will be your manager in the sales department.

M : Well, could you please let me know in detail what type of clients I'll be working with?

女：尚恩，歡迎來到國家重型設備。我們非常高興你加入我們的銷售團隊。今天，你和在銷售部門將當作你的上司的陳女士來開始你的訓練。
男：那麼，你能讓我詳細知道我將和哪一類型的客戶一起工作嗎？

這個男人很有可能是什麼人？
（A）一位銷售專員
（B）一個重要的客戶

**解說** 會聽到「很高興你加入了我們的銷售團隊」這句話的人，應該就是「銷售專員」吧。A representative不是指代表者，而是「職員／專員」的意思。 答案 (A)

**詞彙** **sales department** 銷售部門 **in detail** 詳細的 **work with...** 共事；一起工作

## STEP 01 若沒答對會後悔的考題

| | | | |
|---|---|---|---|
| 1 (A) | 2 (A) | 3 (B) | 4 (B) |
| 5 (A) | 6 (B) | 7 (B) | 8 (A) |
| 9 (A) | 10 (C) | 11 (C) | 12 (A) |
| 13 (B) | 14 (C) | | |

### 1. 英M 美W

| | |
|---|---|
| 1 找出核心語 | topic |
| 2 瞭解類型 | 詢問主題 |
| 3 看選項 | 停車規定或城市公園 |

M : Alicia, **have you heard** the parking rules on city streets are strictly enforced? I think you have to move your car off the street.

W : Really? I didn't know about that. I guess I'd better move my car before the meeting starts.

男：亞麗莎，你聽說過在市街的停車規定要嚴格執行嗎？我覺得你應該把你的車從街道移開。
女：真的嗎？我不知道有關那些。我想我最好在會議開始前把車移開。

這段談話主要是有關於什麼？
（A）新的停車規定
（B）一個城市公園

**解說** 透過核心語topic就可以知道是「詢問主題」的考題。藉由Have you heard後面出現的「停車規定要嚴格執行」，可以知道（A）為答案。 答案 (A)

**詞彙** **parking rules** 停車規定 **enforce** 實施 **move the car off** 把車移開 **had better** ~最好是

**2.** 澳W 英M

| | |
|---|---|
| 1 找出核心語 | problem |
| 2 瞭解類型 | 詢問主題 |
| 3 看選項 | 不能運作或寄錯東西 |

W : Hello, GW Telecom Technical Support. McDori speaking. What can I do for you?

M : Hi, **I have a problem** with this mobile phone that I bought yesterday. It shuts itself off whenever I try to make a call.

女：您好，GW電信科技支援中心。我是麥多莉。有什麼我能為您做的嗎？

男：您好，我昨天買的行動電話有點問題。每當我試著要打電話時，它會自動關機。

這個問題狀況可能是什麼？
(A) 電話不能正常運作。
(B) 送出了錯誤的樣本。

**解說** 「有什麼問題／狀況」也是在詢問主題的考題，在一段對話裡不會出現數個問題狀況。將「我有個問題」後面出現的「每當我試著要打電話時，它會自動關機」以概括性的敘述做變化來表達的（A）為答案。

答案 (A)

**詞彙** **mobile phone** 行動電話 **shut off**（指電器）關閉 **try to...** 嘗試做某事 **make a call** 打電話

**3.** 美W 美M

| | |
|---|---|
| 1 找出核心語 | discussing |
| 2 瞭解類型 | 詢問主題 |
| 3 看選項 | 銷售報告或午餐計劃 |

W : Hi, James. Several sales representatives are having lunch with our clients. Would you like to join us? We're going to the new Italian restaurant down the street.

M : I wish I could. But I have a budget meeting at 1 p.m.

女：您好，詹姆士。有好幾位銷售代表正在和我們的客戶吃午餐。你想要加入我們嗎？我們將會去在街底新開的義大利餐廳。

男：我希望我可以。但是我在下午一點鐘有預算會議。

說話者在討論什麼？
(A) 一個銷售報告
(B) 午餐計畫

**解說** 透過核心語discussing，就可以知道為「詢問主題的考題」。前面出現的疑問句就是詢問主題類型考題的答案線索。將「我們要吃飯，一起來吧」以概括性的敘述做變化來表達的（B）為答案。

答案 (B)

**詞彙** **sales representative** 銷售代表 **down the street** 在街底 **budget meeting** 預算會議

**4.** 澳W 英M

| | |
|---|---|
| 1 找出核心語 | call |
| 2 瞭解類型 | 詢問主題 |
| 3 看選項 | 寄送包裹或要求修理 |

W : Good afternoon, Campbell Property Management.

M : Hello, this is Andrew Peterson from TTS corporation. **I'm calling to** request that someone come over to do some repairs. We're having trouble with the lights in the front office. For some reason, they aren't working. Could you send someone over to fix them?

女：午安，坎貝爾物產管理。

男：您好，我是TTS公司的安德魯彼德森。我打電話是請求來一個人做點維修。我們前面辦公室裡的燈光正在有問題。因為某種原因，它們不能運作。你能派個人過來修理它們嗎？

為什麼這個男人打電話給這個女人？
(A) 他需要寄送一個包裹。
(B) 他的辦公室需要修理。

**解說** 「為什麼打電話」類型也是詢問主題的考題。將核心說法I'm calling to後面出現的「請求派一個人做點維修」做變化來表達的（B）為答案。

答案 (B)

**詞彙** **light** 燈具 **for some reason** 某個原因 **work** 運作 **send over...** 派送

**5.** 美W 美M

| | |
|---|---|
| 1 找出核心語 | where |
| 2 瞭解類型 | 詢問地點 |
| 3 看選項 | 郵局或禮品店 |

W : I want to send this gift to my friend in New York. Can you tell me how much it costs to send it there?

M : Well, for standard delivery, it costs 11 dollars per kilogram, but it will take about ten days to get there.

女：我想寄這個包裹給我在紐約的朋友。你能告訴我寄到那兒需要多少費用嗎？
男：那，一般郵寄每公斤費用是十一元，但是大約需要十天才能夠到達那邊。

說話者很有可能在哪兒？
（A）在郵局
（B）在一家禮品店

**解說** 透過「郵資多少錢」和「一般郵件」等說法，可以猜測是在「郵局」。 答案 (A)

**詞彙** cost 費用 standard delivery 一般配送 per... 每… about 大約 get 到達

**6.** 澳W 英M

| | |
|---|---|
| 1 找出核心語 | man |
| 2 瞭解類型 | 詢問說話者 |
| 3 看選項 | 電腦技師或營業員 |

W : Hi, I'm looking for a portable computer to use during my business trip. Can you help me?
M : Sure. Would you like a simple laptop or a laptop with more advanced features?

女：您好，我正在尋找一台在出差期間使用的攜帶型電腦。你能幫忙我嗎？
男：當然。你想要簡單的筆記型電腦還是有較多進階功能的筆記型電腦？

這個男人很有可能是什麼人？
（A）一個電腦技術員
（B）銷售員

**解說** 會聽到「尋找攜帶性電腦」這類話的人，可能就是「銷售員」。 答案 (B)

**詞彙** look for... 尋找 portable computer 攜帶用電腦 business trip 出差 feature 機能

**7.** 美W 美M

| | |
|---|---|
| 1 找出核心語 | woman work |
| 2 瞭解類型 | 詢問說話者 |
| 3 看選項 | 職業介紹所或機械公司 |

W : Welcome to Korea Heavy Machinery. After the morning orientation session, Ms. Yang, who will be your manager, will explain why our customers are proud to use our machinery.
M : Thank you.

女：歡迎來到韓國重機。在上午的訓練指導講習後，將成為你們經理的楊女士會說明為什麼我們的顧客很自豪使用我們的機械。
男：謝謝你。

這個女人很有可能是在哪裡工作呢？
（A）在一間職業介紹所
（B）在一家機械公司

**解說** 「說話者在哪裡工作」類的考題是詢問說話者的職業，所以有時候不一定與「對話的地點」有關。透過該女性話語當中的公司名稱與「使用我們的機械」，可以知道（B）為答案。 答案 (B)

**詞彙** orientation session（新生）訓練指導講習 be proud to... 自豪於…

**8.** 美M 澳W

| | |
|---|---|
| 1 找出核心語 | man |
| 2 瞭解類型 | 詢問說話者 |
| 3 看選項 | 辦公用品店或配送公司 |

M : GW's Office Mart, good afternoon. This is Martin. How may I help you?
W : Hi, this is Maria Hernandez with the Dublin office. I'm calling about the office supplies I ordered from your company last week.

男：這是GW辦公室市場，午安。我是馬汀。我可以如何幫助您嗎？
女：您好，我是杜賓辦公室的瑪莉亞荷南茲。我打電話來是有關於我上週從你們公司訂購的辦公室用品。

這個男人很有可能是在哪裡工作呢？
（A）在辦公用品店
（B）在配送公司

**解說** 透過該男性說的公司名稱與該女性說的「上週從你們公司訂購的辦公室用品」，可以知道該男性是在「辦公用品店」工作的。 答案 (A)

**詞彙** office supply 事務用品

問題9～10請參考以下對話。美W 英M

| | |
|---|---|
| 1 找出核心語 | calling, woman |
| 2 瞭解類型 | 詢問主題、說話者 |
| 3 看選項的詞彙 | 瑕疵品，丟失的東西，發 |
| | 店主，銷售人員，客服職 |
| 4 預測對話內容 | 店主，銷售人員，客服職 |

W : Hello, [10] M&D Pictures. Customer Service Department. This is Jane Fuller. How may I help you?
M : Hi, [9] I'm calling about a camera I bought

from your store two weeks ago but for some reason I haven't been able to get it to work properly.

W : Well, all our products have a one-year warranty, so your camera is still covered. The easiest thing would be for someone to take a look at it. I recommend you bring it to the service center.

女：您好，M&D相片公司顧客服務部。我是珍富勒。我可以如何幫助您嗎？

男：您好，我打電話來是有關於兩週前從你們店裡買的相機，因為某些原因我無法使它正確的運作。

女：好的，我們所有的產品都有一年的保固，因此您的相機仍在保固期。最簡單的方式是有人幫你看看。我建議您將它帶來服務中心。

**詞彙** for some reason 某原因 be able to 能做 properly 正確的 warranty 保固；保 covered 在保固有效期 take a look at 看一看

**9.**

這個男人為什麼打電話？

（A）討論一件有瑕疵的商品

（B）報告丟失的東西

（C）要求收據

**解說** 透過核心語calling，可以知道是詢問主題的考題。藉由在核心說法I'm calling about後面出現的「在你們商店買的相機、無法正常運作」，可以知道（A）為答案。 答案 (A)

**詞彙** defective merchandise 有缺點的製品 lost 弄丟；遺失 ask for 要求 receipt 收據

**10.**

這個女人很有可能是什麼人？

（A）店老闆

（B）手機銷售人員

（C）客戶服務職員

**解說** 接電話的女性話語裡有答案的線索。另外，聽到該男性說的「無法正常運作」這類的話的人應該是（C）。 答案 (C)

**詞彙** mobile phone 行動電話 salesperson 銷售員 representative 職員

問題11～12請參考以下對話。澳W 英M

| | |
|---|---|
| 1 找出核心語 | discussing, where |
| 2 瞭解類型 | 詢問主題、地點 |
| 3 看選項的詞彙 | 籌備活動，價格，地點 |
| | 音樂廳，樂器行，道路上 |
| 4 預測對話內容 | 在演奏廳準備表演。 |

W : Could you tell me [11]where the stage manager is? I want to ask him where to position some of these instruments on stage.

M : Well, I guess [12]he should be here 3 hours before the concert starts, but it seems like he's going to be a little late.

W : You have his mobile phone number, right? I'd better confirm the position over the phone.

女：你能告訴我舞台督導在哪裡嗎？我想問他把這些樂器要放在舞台哪裡？

男：嗯，我想在音樂會開始前三小時他應該會在這兒，但是看來他似乎將會有一點晚到。

女：你有他的行動電話號碼，對吧？我最好打電話來確認位置。

**詞彙** stage manager 舞台督導 where to position 位置在哪裡 instrument 樂器 seem like 似乎是… over the phone 透過電話

**11.**

說話者正在討論什麼？

（A）某些樂器的價格

（B）劇院的位置

（C）活動的準備工作

**解說** 透過核心語discussing，可以知道是詢問主題的考題。若Could you tell me等說法在對話前面部分出現，也能當作詢問主題的考題的答案線索。將後面出現的「問樂器要放在哪兒」以概括性的敘述做變化來表達的（C）為答案。 答案 (C)

**詞彙** price 價格 location 位置 theater 劇場 preparation 準備

**12.**

說話者很有可能在哪兒？

（A）在音樂廳

（B）在唱片店

（C）在路上

**解說** 透過「樂器要放哪兒」、「音樂會開始前在這兒」等線索，可以知道是在「音樂廳」。 答案 (A)

**詞彙** music shop 唱片店

問題13～14請參考以下對話。美M 美W

| | |
|---|---|
| 1 找出核心語 | where, man |
| 2 瞭解類型 | 詢問地點、說話者 |
| 3 看選項的詞彙 | 會議，詢問處，面試 |
| | 快遞人員，接待員，面試者 |
| 4 預測對話內容 | 求職者在服務台詢問面試地點。 |

M : Excuse me. [14]I'm here to interview with Mr. Dotson in the accounting department.

W : [13]Please sign in and here is your ID badge for visitors. The interview is going to be held on the 9th floor.

M : Certainly. [13]Can you tell me where the elevator is?

男：打擾一下。我是來這兒和會計部門的道森先生面試的。
女：請簽名，這是您的訪客證。面試將在九樓舉行。
男：沒問題。你能告訴我電梯在哪兒嗎？

**詞彙** **accounting department** 會計部門 **sign in** 簽名 **ID badge** 名牌

**13.**

這段談話很有可能是在哪兒發生的？
（A）在會議中
（B）在服務台
（C）在面試中

**解說** 「給訪客證的地方」、「有人告訴你電梯在哪兒的地方」應該是服務台。 答案 (B)

**詞彙** **reception desk** 服務台

**14**

這個男人很有可能是什麼人？
（A）快遞人員
（B）櫃檯人員
（C）求職面試者

**解說** 說出「我是來面試的」的人，應該是「求職者」。 答案 (C)

**詞彙** **delivery man** 快遞人員 **receptionist** 櫃檯人員 **job interviewee** 求職面試者 *cf.* interviewer（面試官）

## STEP 02 考題實戰練習

1. (B) 2. (D) 3. (B) 4. (B) 5. (D) 6. (B)
7. (C) 8. (D) 9. (D) 10. (C) 11. (C) 12. (A)

問題1～3請參考以下對話。美W 澳W

W1: Hi, Maria. It's Joanna. [1]Can you give me a ride to work this morning? My car broke down late last night, and it's being fixed in the repair shop.

W2: I'd be delighted to, but I have to go into work early to prepare for an important meeting. [2]Do you mind leaving 30 minutes earlier than usual?

W1: [2]Not at all! I will be ready to be picked up in 10 minutes.

W2: [3]You can make that 20. I need some time to get dressed before going out.

女1：您好，瑪麗亞，我是喬安娜。今天早上你能否載我一程去上班？昨天深夜我的車壞了，它在修車廠被維修。
女2：我很樂意，但我得很早去上班，為要準備一個重要會議。你介不介意比平常提早三十分鐘出門？
女1：不介意，我會加速在十分鐘內準備好。
女2：你可以有二十分鐘。外出前，我需要一些時間穿衣服。

**詞彙** **give someone a ride** 載某人一程 **repalr shop** 修理店 **30 minutes earlier than usual** 比平常早三十分鐘 **be ready to** 準備好做 **pick up** 整理 **make it**（時間）在某時間做… **get dressed** 穿衣服 **go out** 外出

**1.**

說話者主要在討論什麼？
（A）提早的會議
（B）到職場去的方式
（C）修理工人的問題
（D）一個新的工作時間表

**解說** 這是詢問主題的考題。在對話前段部分出現的疑問句可以當作答案線索。「載我一程去上班」已經決定其主題，所以將此變化後來表達的（B）即是答案。 答案 (B)

**詞彙** **way to get to** 去…的方向 **mechanic** 修理工人 **schedule** 日程表

**2.**

說話者同意做什麼事？
（A）順道去修理店。
（B）與客戶聯絡。
（C）共乘一台計程車。

（D）早一點到職場去。

**解說** 在此對話裡，由「介不介意…？」與「不介意」的問答過程當中，可以看出「同意」了什麼事情。將「比平常提早三十分鐘」以簡化的敘述來表達的（D）為答案。在此對話裡，由「介不介意…？」與「不介意」的問答過程當中，可以看出「同意」了什麼事情。將「比平常提早三十分鐘」以簡化的敘述來表達的（D）為答案。 答案 (D)

**詞彙** **stop by** 順道去… **contact** 聯絡 **share** 分享

**3.**

說話者在什麼時候可能見面？
（A）在十分鐘後
（B）在二十分鐘後
（C）在三十分鐘後
（D）在四十分鐘後

**解說** 這是詢問具體事項／具體時間點的考題。「十分鐘後」是陷阱，而「二十分鐘後」的（B）才是答案。 答案 (B)

**詞彙** **meet** 見面 **in**（時間名詞）在多久之後

問題4~6請參考以下對話 英M 美W

M: [4]Town Post Office, how may I help you?

W: Hi, [5]I'd like to know how much you charge for sending a package to Korea. And how long does it take for the package to get there?

M: Well, standard delivery for packages is 11 dollars per kilogram, and it could take up to 10 days to arrive. If you tell me how much it weighs, I can give you a price.

W: I'm not sure how heavy it is. [6]I'll weigh it then call you back. Thanks.

男：這是鄉鎮郵局，需要甚麼協助嗎？
女：您好，我想知道寄包裹到韓國要多少費用？還有要花多久時間可以寄達？
男：嗯，一般郵寄的包裹是每公斤十一元，而且可能需要十天會到。若你能告訴我它有多重，我可以告訴你費用。
女：我不太確定它的重量。我會秤一下然後回電給你。謝謝。

**詞彙** **charge for** 收費 **package** 包裹 **standard delivery** 一般寄送 **take up to 10 days** 要花十天 **weigh** 重量 **call back** 以電話回訊

**4.**

這個男人的工作很有可能是什麼？
（A）倉庫工人
（B）郵局職員
（C）旅行社職員
（D）電話公司接線員

**解說** 接電話時說「這是…郵局」，所以可以猜測為「郵局職員」。 答案 (B)

**詞彙** **warehouse** 倉庫 **worker** 工人 **clerk** 職員 **travel agent** 旅行社 **operator** 接線生

**5.**

這個女人為什麼打電話？
（A）詢問郵遞區號
（B）請教問路
（C）找一些有關旅遊的信息
（D）詢問價格

**解說** 聽到核心說法I'd like to。透過在後面出現的「多少費用」，可以知道是「詢問價格的狀況」。 答案 (D)

**詞彙** **ask for** 要求 **postal code** 郵遞區號 **driving direction** 道路指南 **tour** 旅遊 **inquire about** 詢問有關… **price** 價格

**6.**

這個女人接下來可能會做什麼？
（A）完成文書業務
（B）秤重一件包裹
（C）郵寄一些信件
（D）購買機票

**解說** 只要聽到在I'll後面的部分就可以回答。代名詞it是指包裹，所以（B）為答案。 答案 (B)

**詞彙** **complete** 完成 **paperwork** 文書業務 **mail** 郵寄 **purchase** 購買 **flight ticket** 飛機票

問題7~9請參考以下對話。美W 美M

W: Excuse me. Can you tell me where the dry cleaner is [7]here in the hotel? I spilt coffee on my shirt this morning, and [8]need to have it cleaned today.

M: Yes, there is one located on the second floor. However, I don't think they offer express service. You'd better go to the one across from the hotel. I'm sure they can do it within a few hours.

W: What a relief! I'll go there right away. [9]I need the shirt for a job interview tomorrow afternoon.

女：抱歉。請告訴我這家飯店的乾洗店在哪？今天早上我打翻咖啡在我的襯衫上，今日之內要清洗乾淨。
男：是，在二樓有。但我想他們不提供快速服務。您最好去飯店對面那家。我相信他們在幾個小時之內做得到。
女：真幸運！我要馬上去。我明天下午的求職面試需要這件襯衫。

**詞彙** **dry cleaner** 乾洗 **spill** 溢出 **express service** 快速服務 **across from** 在…對面 **right away** 立刻 **job interview** 求職面試

7.

說話者在哪兒？

(A) 在銀行
(B) 在購物中心
(C) 在飯店
(D) 在餐廳

**解說** 聽到線索「這家飯店」！若知道了對話的地點能聯想到相關核心語，就更容易回答考題。例如，銀行的核心語（open a bank account）、購物中心的核心語（looking for）、餐廳的核心語（order、menu）等。 答案 (C)

**詞彙** **shopping center** 購物中心 **restaurant** 餐廳

8.

這個女人想要做什麼？

(A) 下訂單
(B) 存款
(C) 更換她的房間
(D) 清潔一些衣服

**解說** 這是詢問要求事項的考題。該女性話裡的核心語為need to，將其後面的「清洗」做變化來表達的（D）為答案。 答案 (D)

**詞彙** **place an order** 下訂單 **make a deposit** 存款 **clean** 清洗 **clothes** 衣服

9.

面試是什麼時候？

(A) 今天上午
(B) 今天下午
(C) 明天早上
(D) 明天下午

**解說** interview和appointment的附近很常有答案的線索。在其後聽到的（D）為答案。 答案 (D)

**詞彙** **interview** 面試

問題10～12請參考以下對話。澳W 英M

W: [10]Thank you for calling Star Travel Service. How may I help you?

M: Hello, this is Antonio Chang from G&W Corporation. I'm planning to go on a business trip this weekend. I'd like to leave for New York tomorrow night and return on Sunday morning.

W: Let me check. [11]You can leave for 8 p.m. tomorrow, but all the economy class seats have been booked for Sunday morning. You may return Sunday afternoon or you'll have to seat in a business class that morning.

M: Well, [12]then book me on a business class. I have a meeting that afternoon. So, I have to come back before the meeting.

女：謝謝您來電星光旅遊服務，需要什麼服務嗎？
男：您好，我是G&W公司的安東尼奧張。我打算本週末去出差。我想明晚往紐約出發，並且在星期天早上返回。
女：請讓我確認一下。您可以在明天晚上八點離開，不過星期天早上所有經濟艙座位都已訂滿。您可以在週日下午返回，不然您要在上午搭商務艙返回。
男：嗯，那麼我訂商務艙，我那天下午有一個會議。所以我必須在會議之前回來。

**詞彙** **go on a business trip** 去出差 **leave for** 離開 **return** 返回 **book** 預約 **come back** 回來 **meeting** 會議

10.

這個女人很有可能是什麼人？

(A) 空服員
(B) 行李處理人員
(C) 旅行社職員
(D) 飛機乘客

**解說** 透過接到電話的女性的話語裡「謝謝您來電Star Travel Service」，可以知道（C）為答案。 答案 (C)

**詞彙** **flight attendant** 空中小姐 **luggage handler** 行李處理者 **travel agent** 旅行社 **airplane passenger** 飛機乘客

11.

這個問題狀況有可能是什麼？

(A) 有一些行李遺失了。
(B) 票的價格太高。
(C) 無法提供一些座位。
(D) 有一個航班延誤了。

**解說** 「問題／狀況是什麼？」類型是在詢問主題的，因為一個對話裡不會出現數個問題狀況。將中間部分出現的「沒有經濟艙，但有商務艙」以概括性的敘述做變化來表達的（C）為答案。 答案 (C)

**詞彙** **luggage** 行李 **missing** 錯過 **price** 價格 **available** 能夠 **be delayed** 延誤

12.

這個女人接下來很有可能會做什麼？

(A) 預訂一個航班
(B) 到登機口
(C) 舉辦一場會議
(D) 與她的上司聯絡

**解說** 將對話中男性說的「幫我訂商務艙」換成以該女性的角度來表達的（A）為答案。 答案 (A)

**詞彙** **make a reservation** 做預約 **departure gate** 登機口 **hold a meeting** 舉行會議 **contact** 聯絡 **supervisor** 長官

## Chapter 12 概括性詢問的考題 II

### Quiz I

| | | | |
|---|---|---|---|
| 1. (A) | 2. (B) | 3. (B) | 4. (A) |
| 5. (A) | 6. (B) | | |

**Q1** 美M 美W

M : You'll have to complete the application form and bring it to me. Would you like me to mail or fax the form to you?

W : Well, my fax machine is being fixed. **Could you** send it to me in the mail?

男：你必須完成這份申請表並且帶來給我。你希望我用郵寄還是傳真這份表格給你呢？
女：好的，我的傳真機正在修理中。你能用郵寄的給我嗎？

這個女人要求這個男人做什麼？
（A）郵寄一份資料
（B）派一位維修人員

**解說** 透過核心語ask，可以知道是詢問「要求事項」的考題。將核心說法Could you後面出現的「用郵寄的給我」以概括性的敘述做變化來表達的（A）為答案。

答案 (A)

**詞彙** **complete** 完成 **application form** 申請表 **bring** 帶來 **fix** 修理 **in the mail** 以電子郵件 **document** 文件 **repairperson** 修理工人

**Q2** 英M 澳W

M : Hello, my name is Henry Han from City Times. I'd like to talk to your sales manager, Sandra Oh.

W : I'm afraid she is no longer in our sales department. The new sales manager is John Celina. **Would you like me to** connect you with him?

男：您好，我是城市時報的亨利韓。我想和你們的銷售經理珊卓拉歐通話。
女：恐怕她已經不在我們的銷售部門了。新的銷售經理是約翰塞里納。你要我幫你轉接給他嗎？

這個女人提議做什麼？
（A）下材料訂單
（B）轉接這通電話

**解說** 出現核心語offer，可以知道是詢問「建議事項」的考題。透過與核心說法Could you類似的Would you like me，藉由其後面出現的「幫你轉接給他」，可以知道（B）為答案。

答案 (B)

**詞彙** **sales manager** 銷售經理 **be no longer** 不再是… **connect** 連接 **place an order for** 下訂某物 **transfer** （電話）轉接

**Q3** 英M 澳W

M : This copy machine broke down again! I'm worried because I need to make copies for my presentation tomorrow morning.

W : Don't worry. Why don't you keep preparing for your presentation? **I'll** call the technician about fixing this machine.

男：這台影印機又壞了！我很擔心，因為我明天早上的報告需要複本。
女：別擔心，你何不繼續準備你的報告？有關這台機器的修理，我會打電話給技師。

這個女人接下來很有可能會做什麼？
（A）修理這台機器
（B）打電話

**解說** 出現核心語do next，可以知道是詢問「下一個行程」的考題。透過在核心說法I'll後面出現的「打電話給技師」，可以知道（B）為答案。

答案 (B)

**詞彙** **copy machine** 影印機 **break down** 故障 **make a copy** 複印 **presentation** 發表 **prepare for** 準備… **technician** 技術員 **fix** 修理 **repair** 修理 **make a phone call** 打電話

**Q4** 美M 美W

M : I think we need to hire several part-time workers to help us move the office.

W : You're right. We can't do all of the preparation work ourselves. **Let me** search for a hiring agency to find us some people as soon as possible.

男：我想我們需要雇用幾位計時工作人員來幫忙我們搬遷辦公室。
女：你是對的。我們無法自己做全部的準備工作。讓我找招聘公司以儘可能快點幫我們找到人。

這個女人說她將會做什麼？
（A）尋找一間招聘公司
（B）申請一個臨時工作

**解說** 出現核心語she will do，可以知道是詢問「下一個行程」的考題。透過在核心說法Let me後面的「找招聘公司」，可以知道（A）為答案。

答案 (A)

**詞彙** **part-time worker** 計時工作人員 **move the office** 搬遷辦公室 **preparation work** 準備工作 **hiring agency** 招聘公司 **temporary** 臨時的

**Q5** 澳W 英M

W : Frank. How's it going with editing the new book? Will it be released to the bookstores as scheduled?

M : I don't think so. The author of the book wanted to make last-minute changes, so I **won't** be able to get the book out **until this March.**

女：法蘭克，新書的編輯進行的如何呢？它將會按照計畫在書店出刊嗎？

男：我不這麼認為。這本書的作者到最後突然要做修正，因此到三月前我將無法出版這本書。

根據這個男人的談話，在三月可能會發生什麼事？

（A）將會出一本新書。

（B）一位新的編輯將被雇用。

**解說** 透過未來時間點in March，可以知道是在詢問「下一個行程」的考題類型。「在三月之前無法出版」意思就是要三月以後才能出版。因此（A）為答案。

答案 (A)

**詞彙** **edit** 做編輯 **release** 出刊 **as scheduled** 依時間計畫表 **author** 作者 **make last-minute changes** 最終的修正 **not A until B** 在B時間前不會發生A

**Q6** 美W 美M

W: I'll be out of the town this week. Why don't I e-mail you a draft of the report first? You can take a look before I come back.

M: Definitely, **I'll** read it **this week.** Then we can set up a time to talk about it later.

女：我這週將要出差。我何不將報告的草稿用電子郵件先寄給你？你可以在我回來前先看看。

男：無論如何，我將會在這週先看它。然後我們晚一點可以約個時間來討論它。

這個男人說他這星期將會做什麼？

（A）去出差

（B）閱讀文件

**解說** this week是核心語，在對話內容與考題裡出現了相同的this week說法，因此在this week的前後會有答案的線索。因此把「將會看它」以概括性的敘述做變化來表達的（B）為答案。

答案 (B)

**詞彙** **out of the town** 出差 **a draft of the report** 報告的草稿 **take a look** 看 **definitely** 無論如何 **set up a time** 約時間 **talk about it later** 晚一點來討論它 **go on a business trip** 出差

## STEP 01 若沒答對會後悔的考題

| | | | |
|---|---|---|---|
| 1 (B) | 2 (B) | 3 (A) | 4 (A) |
| 5 (B) | 6 (A) | 7 (B) | 8 (B) |
| 9 (C) | 10 (A) | 11 (C) | 12 (C) |
| 13 (A) | 14 (C) | | |

**1.** 英M 美W

| | |
|---|---|
| 1 找出核心語 | woman ask |
| 2 瞭解類型 | 詢問要求事項 |
| 3 看選項 | 詢問要求事項 |

M: Hi. My name is Bill Brown. I'm calling about a printer that I ordered from you two weeks ago. It hasn't arrived yet.

W: Sure. I'd be happy to help you. **Can you** tell me your order number please?

男：我的名字是比爾布朗。我打電話來是有關於兩週前我和你們訂購的印表機。它到現在還沒有來。

女：當然。我很樂於幫助您。可否告訴我你的訂單編號嗎？

這個女人要求這個男人做什麼？

（A）給她正確的地址

（B）告訴她訂單編號

**解說** 出現核心語woman ask，可以知道是詢問「要求事項」的考題。透過在核心說法Can you後面出現的「告訴我你的訂單編號」，可以知道（B）為答案。

答案 (B)

**詞彙** **I'd be happy to** 我很樂於⋯ **order number** 訂單編號

**2.** 美W 美M

| | |
|---|---|
| 1 找出核心語 | request |
| 2 瞭解類型 | 詢問要求事項 |
| 3 看選項 | 別的預約時間，或去辦公室的方向 |

W : **Could you** tell me where Mr. Wilson's office is? I forgot to ask when I made the interview appointment.

M : He's on the 8th floor. Turn left after you get off the elevator and go all the way down the hallway. It's right next to the sales department. Good luck with the interview.

女：你能告訴我威爾森先生的辦公室在什麼地方嗎？我預約面試時忘記問了。
男：他在八樓。出電梯後左轉然後在走廊上一直走。它在銷售部門的右邊。祝您面試幸運。

這個女人請求什麼事？
(A) 別的預約時間
(B) 去辦公室的方向

**解說** 透過核心語request，可以知道是詢問「要求事項」的考題。透過在核心說法Could you後面出現的「告訴我威爾森先生的辦公室在什麼地方」，可以知道將此以概括性的敘述做變化來表達的（B）為答案。
答案 (B)

**詞彙** **interview appointment** 面試預約 **get off** 下車 **all the way down the hallway** 直接走到走廊 **next to** 在…旁 **sales department** 銷售部門 **Good luck.** 祝幸運 **directions to** 去…的方向

## 3. 英M 美W

| | |
|---|---|
| 1 找出核心語 | woman suggest |
| 2 瞭解類型 | 詢問建議事項 |
| 3 看選項 | 使用別的影印機，或打電話給技師 |

M : I want to make some copies before the budget meeting starts but all of the machines are being used. The only copier not being used is in the accounting department, but it's out of order.

W : In that case, **why don't you** try the photocopiers downstairs in the lobby? It should be available but you'll need to pay for the copies.

男：在預算會議前我想要影印一些東西，但是所有的機器都正被使用中。唯一沒有被使用的在會計部門，但是它壞了。
女：若是那樣，你何不試試在樓下大廳的影印機？它應該可以用，但是你將需要付費影印。

這個女人建議這個男人做什麼？
(A) 使用另一台影印機
(B) 打電話給技師

**解說** 透過核心語woman suggest，可以知道是詢問「建議事項」的考題。藉由在核心說法why don't you後面出現的「使用在樓下大廳的影印機」，可以知道將此以概括性的敘述做變化來表達的（A）為答案。 答案 (A)

**詞彙** **make a copy** 做複印 **accounting department** 會計部門 **out of order** 故障 **in that case** 那樣的話 **available** 可以使用 **pay for...** 為…付費 **technician** 技術員

## 4. 美M 澳W

| | |
|---|---|
| 1 找出核心語 | woman offer |
| 2 瞭解類型 | 詢問建議事項 |
| 3 看選項 | 拿名片或搬移書架 |

M : I need to confirm the position of the bookshelf first so that we can have the books placed correctly. But the library director hasn't come in yet. Do you know his mobile phone number?

W : Actually I have his business card in my car. **I'll** go and get it.

男：我需要先確認書架的位置，這樣我們才能把書置放正確。但是圖書館的管理人還沒有來。你知道他的行動電話號碼嗎？
女：事實上我車上有他的名片。我去拿。

這個女人提議做什麼？
(A) 拿名片
(B) 搬移書架

**解說** 透過核心語offer，可以知道是詢問「建議事項」的考題。透過在核心說法I'll後面出現的「去拿（名片）」，可以知道（A）為答案。 答案 (A)

**詞彙** **bookshelf** 書架 **library director** 圖書館管理人 **come in** 到達 **mobile phone number** 行動電話號碼 **business card** 名片

## 5. 英M 美W

| | |
|---|---|
| 1 找出核心語 | do next |
| 2 瞭解類型 | 詢問下一個行程 |
| 3 看選項 | 退費或帶來照片 |

M : Hi. I'm here to pick up some photos. My name is Jack Mayers. I had my photos taken on Monday. The person who helped me said they should be ready to be picked up today.

W : I have your information right here. You had passport photos taken. **I'll** go get them for you.

男：您好。我來拿一些照片。我的名字是傑克梅約。我在星期一拍了照片。幫忙我的人說它們應該在今天會被準備好可以領。
女：就在這邊我有您的資料。您照了護照相片。我去拿來給您。

這個女人接下來可能會做什麼？
(A) 發出退款
(B) 帶來一些照片

**解說** 透過核心語do next，可以知道是詢問「下一個行程」的考題。透過在核心說法I'll後面出現的「去拿（相片）來給您」，可以知道（B）為答案。 答案 (B)

**詞彙** pick up 領取 be ready to 動詞原型 準備好 passport photo 護照相片 get（某物）for you 拿某物給你 bring 帶來

**6.** 美W 美M

| | |
|---|---|
| 1 找出核心語 | do next |
| 2 瞭解類型 | 詢問下一個行程 |
| 3 看選項 | 完成表格或配送貨品 |

W : According to the company policy, all requests for office supplies must be made in writing. Probably the easiest thing to do would be to fill out a supplies request form placed at the human resources department's entrance.

M : Oh, I see. That certainly would be very easy. **I'll** do it right away. Thank you for your help.

女：依據公司的政策，所有的辦公用品申請書都必須用寫的。最簡單的方法可能是填寫放在人力資源部門入口處的辦公用品申請表格。

男：噢，我知道了。那當然非常容易。我將會馬上去做。謝謝你的幫忙。

這個男人接下來可能會做什麼？
（A）完成一份表格
（B）配送貨品

**解說** 透過核心語do next，可以知道是詢問「下一個行程」的考題。透過在核心說法I'll後面出現的「馬上去做（填寫申請表格）」，可以知道（A）為答案。 答案 (A)

**詞彙** according to 根據⋯ request 申請書 office supply 辦公用品 in writing 用書寫的 fill out 填寫 human resources department 人力資源部門 entrance 入口 right away 立刻 complete 完成 deliver 配送

**7.** 澳W 美M

| | |
|---|---|
| 1 找出核心語 | this afternoon |
| 2 瞭解類型 | 詢問下一個行程 |
| 3 看選項 | 報告或為會議準備 |

W : I heard you visited our office in New York to get some ideas about how we can expand our customers here in United States. Are you going to share your ideas at our marketing meeting tomorrow morning?

M : I will. **I'm going to** take some time **this afternoon** to get all my information organized.

女：我聽說關於我們在美國這兒如何擴大顧客群你想得到一些點子而拜訪了我們紐約的辦公室。你將會在明天上午的行銷會議上分享你的想法嗎？

男：我會的。今天下午我將會花一些時間整理我的資訊。

這個男人今天下午將會做什麼？
（A）報告
（B）為會議做準備

**解說** 這是詢問「下一個行程」的考題。在對話內容與考題裡出現了相同的this afternoon說法，因此在this afternoon的前後就有答案的線索。該女性同意「分享你的想法」這項建議，然後說「下午將會整理資訊」，這就是「準備會議」的意思。 答案 (B)

**詞彙** get some ideas 得到一些想法 share 分享 take some time 花一些時間 organized 整理 give a presentation 發表 prepare for 為⋯準備

**8.** 英M 美W

| | |
|---|---|
| 1 找出核心語 | Monday |
| 2 瞭解類型 | 詢問下一個行程 |
| 3 看選項 | 辦公室會關閉或介紹員工 |

M : I heard we're going to work with the new programmer soon. I guess she's in the middle of her training courses. Do you know when she starts in our office?

W : Yes, her first day will be **Monday**. She will be introduced to everyone at our team meeting on that day.

男：我聽說我們很快將要和新的程式設計師一起工作。我猜她還在她的訓練課程中。你知道她什麼時候來上班嗎？

女：是的，星期一將是她來的第一天。她將會在那天的會議裡被介紹給我們團隊的每一個人。

星期一將會發生什麼事？
（A）一間辦公室將被關閉。
（B）一位員工將被介紹。

**解說** Monday是核心語，在對話內容與考題裡出現了相同的Monday說法，因此在Monday前後就有答案的線索。將「她（新的程式設計師）將被介紹」以概括性的敘述做變化來表達的（B）為答案。 答案 (B)

**詞彙** in the middle of 在⋯當中 training course 訓練課程 first day 第一天 introduce 介紹 on that day 在那一天 be closed 被關閉

問題9～10請參考以下對話。美W 英M

| | |
|---|---|
| 1 找出核心語 | woman ask, do next |
| 2 瞭解類型 | 詢問要求事項、接下來的內容 |
| 3 看選項 | 確認配送，下訂單，修理 |
| | 電話，退還，尋找地址 |
| 4 預測對話內容 | 要求修理服務之後， |
| | 撥打電話確認細節。 |

W : Max, the sales department called and said something about a broken air conditioner. [9]Can you go and see if you can fix it? An important meeting with potential customers starts right after lunch and they want to make sure it works properly before the meeting.

M : Oh, I have a couple of urgent repairs first thing this morning. Can you check if someone can stay around until 12:00 p.m. or so? I should be able to look at it right before lunch time.

W : [10]I'll call and find out. I'll let you know in a while.

女：馬克司，有關壞掉的空調，銷售部門打電話來說了一些話。你能去看看你能否修理它嗎？有一場和潛在客戶的重要會議在午餐後馬上要開始，所以他們希望確認在會議前它能正常運作。

男：噢，今天早上我先有了兩個緊急的維修。你可以確認一下大約到中午十二點左右有人可以在附近嗎？我應該可以在午餐前去看看。

女：我會打電話找一下。我一會兒後會讓你知道的。

**詞彙** **sales department** 銷售部門 **broken** 故障 **fix** 修理 **potential customer** 潛在客戶 **properly** 正常的 **urgent** 修理 **repair** 在附近 **stay around** 在附近 **or so** 大約 **be able to** 可以 **look at** 看 **find out** 查找 **in a while** 一會兒後

## 9.

這個女人要求這個男人做什麼？
(A) 檢查配送
(B) 訂一些設備
(C) 做維修

**解說** 透過核心語woman ask，可以知道是詢問「要求事項」的考題。藉由在核心說法Can you後面出現的「去看看你能否修理它」，可以知道（C）為答案。

答案 (C)

**詞彙** **check on** 確認 **delivery** 配送 **order** 下訂單 **equipment** 設備

## 10.

這個女人接下來可能會做什麼？
(A) 打電話
(B) 退還一些商品
(C) 找一個地址

**解說** 透過核心語do next，可以知道是詢問「下一個行程」的考題。透過在核心說法I'll後面出現的「打電話找一下」，可以知道（A）為答案。

答案 (A)

**詞彙** **make a phone call** 打電話 **return** 返還 **merchandise** 製品 **address** 的指

問題11～12請參考以下對話。美W 美M

| | |
|---|---|
| 1 找出核心語 | woman ask, do next |
| 2 瞭解類型 | 詢問要求事項、接下來的內容 |
| 3 看選項 | 退款，餐點，換座位 |
| | 完成表格，取消預約，談話 |
| 4 預測對話內容 | 要求變更座位之後與家人確認 |

W : Hi, my sister and I just checked in. I found our seats are near the back of the plane in row 40. [11]Would it be possible to change them to exit row seats?

M : Let me see. You're flying to Detroit, right? Yes, I do have 2 seats available, but you'll have to pay extra 30 dollars for each seat.

W : Sounds reasonable, but [12]I should check with my sister before paying for them.

女：您好，我姊姊和我剛報到。我發現我們的座位靠近飛機後面的第四十排。有可能換到出口附近一排的座位嗎？

男：讓我看看。你們要飛行到底特律，對嗎？好的，我有兩個可用的位子，但是為每個座位您必須付額外三十元。

女：聽起來蠻合理的，但是付費前我必須和我姊姊確認。

**詞彙** **check in**（航空）報到 **Would it be possible...?** 某事有可能嗎？ **exit row seat** 出口附近一排的座位 **reasonable** 合理 **pay for** 為…付費

## 11.

這個女人要求什麼？
(A) 退款
(B) 一份餐點
(C) 換座位

**解說** 出現核心語ask，可以知道是詢問「要求事項」的考題。透過與核心說法Can you類似的Would it be possible，藉由其後面出現的「換到出口附近一排的座位」，可以知道將此以簡單型式變化來表達的（A）為答案。

答案 (C)

**詞彙** refund 返還 meal 餐食 seat change 換座位

### 12.

這個女人接下來會做什麼？
(A) 完成一份表格
(B) 取消預約
(C) 和她的姊姊談話

**解說** 出現核心語do next，可以知道是詢問「下一個行程」的考題。透過與核心說法I'll類似的I should，藉由其後面出現的「和我姊姊確認」，可以知道將此換句話說來表達的(C)為答案。 答案(C)

**詞彙** complete 完成 form 表格 cancel 取消 reservation 預約 talk to 和某人說話

問題13～14請參考以下對話。英M 澳W

| | |
|---|---|
| 1 找出核心語 | woman ask, do next |
| 2 瞭解類型 | 詢問要求事項、接下來的內容 |
| 3 看選項 | 保留，給收據，郵寄東西 |
| | 離開，閱讀，寫 |
| 4 預測對話內容 | 要求保管商品後，填寫名字。 |

M : Thank you for shopping at Shoes Heaven. What can I do for you?

W : I'd like to buy these shoes at a reduced price but I found the sale starts tomorrow. [13]Could you hold them for me? I'll be out of town all day tomorrow.

M : Sure, no problem. The sale goes through the weekend. So you can come anytime this weekend. [14]Just write your name here, and [14]I'll put the boots aside for you.

男：感謝您來到鞋子天堂購物。有什麼我能為您做的嗎？
女：我想要以降低的價格買這些鞋子，但是我發現明天才開始打折。你可以為我保留它們嗎？明天我將要出差一整天。
男：當然，沒有問題。打折活動會持續到週末。因此您可以在這個週末任何時間過來。將您的名字寫在這兒，我會為您把鞋子放在一旁。

**詞彙** at a reduced price 以降低的價格⋯ hold 保留 be out of town 出差 all day 整天 go 持續 put... aside 放在一旁

### 13.

這個女人要求這個男人做什麼？
(A) 把一些商品放在一旁
(B) 給這個女人一份收據
(C) 郵寄這個女人購買的東西給她

**解說** 出現核心語woman ask，可以知道是詢問「要求事項」的考題。透過在核心說法Could you後面出現的「為我保留它們」，與該男生說的「為您把鞋子放在一旁」，可以知道(A)為答案。 答案(A)

**詞彙** merchandise 商品 receipt 收據 mail 郵寄 purchase 購買

### 14.

這個女人接下來可能會做什麼？
(A) 離開這家店
(B) 看報紙
(C) 寫下來某件事

**解說** 透過核心語do next，可以知道是詢問「下一個行程」的考題。該男性說的最後一句會決定該女性的下一個動作。若該男生說「請寫下您的名字」，該女性接下來可能會進行(C)。 答案(C)

**詞彙** leave 離開 newspaper 報紙 write something down 寫一些東西

## STEP 02 考題實戰練習

1. (C) 2. (B) 3. (D) 4. (A) 5. (C) 6. (D)
7. (D) 8. (D) 9. (C) 10. (C) 11. (B) 12. (A)

問題1～3請參考以下對話。美M 美W

M : Good evening, Marie. [1]How's everything going with your bread factory? I was in the area and thought I'd come by to see how the new baking system is working.

W : Oh, [2]I find that the system you sold us is fantastic. It's a lot more convenient to have the bread dough shaped and baked automatically.

M : I am sure it is worth the money. It saves time and cuts back on flour use and it should increase your production. Does it seem that you produced more bread this month?

W : Hopefully. [3]We are expecting large orders next week, and I'm sure we can meet the deadline this time.

男：晚安，瑪麗。你的麵包工廠營運的如何？我在這個地區，我想是否能瞭解一下新烘烤系統運作的如何。
女：哦，我認為你賣給我們的系統太棒了。它非常方便於使生麵成型和自動烘烤。
男：我確信它值得花那筆錢，這樣可以節省時間和減少麵粉的使用，並增加您的產量。你覺得這個月生產了更多麵包嗎？

女：希望是。下週我們期待有大訂單，現在我敢確定我們能在截止日期前完成。

**詞彙** bread factory 麵包工廠 come by 來到 bread dough 生麵糰 shape 塑型 bake 烘培 automatically 自動的 worth 值得 cut back on 減少 meet the deadline 在截止日期時 this time 目前

**1.**

說話者很有可能在哪兒？

(A) 在施工現場
(B) 在一家花店
(C) 在一間工廠
(D) 在一家雜貨店

**解說** 將「你的麵包工廠營運的如何」與「我想是否能瞭解一下新烘烤系統運作的如何」連接起來推論的話，就可以知道是在「工廠」。 答案 (C)

**詞彙** construction 施工 grocery store 禮物店

**2.**

說話者正在談什麼？

(A) 降低包裹費用的方法
(B) 一些新設備的好處
(C) 一棟大樓的建設
(D) 訂購物品的過程

**解說** 透過核心語discussing，可以知道是詢問「主題」的考題。將「新的系統非常方便」與「節省時間和減少麵粉的使用，並增加產量」以概括性的敘述做變化來表達的 (B) 為答案。 答案 (B)

**詞彙** packaging 包裹 benefits 益處 equipment 設備 process 程序 order goods 訂貨物

**3.**

根據這段對話，下週將會發生什麼？

(A) 老舊的系統將會被檢查。
(B) 陳列箱將被換掉。
(C) 工人們將超時工作。
(D) 訂單將被處理。

**解說** next week是核心語，在對話內容與考題裡出現了相同的next week說法，因此在next week的前後會有答案的線索。將「我們期待有大訂單」以概括性的敘述做變化來表達的 (D) 為答案。若是主動句，常常會改成被動句來出現。 答案 (D)

**詞彙** inspect 檢查 display case 陳列箱 replace 替換 work overtime 超時工作 place an order 處理訂單

問題4～6請參考以下對話 英M 美W

M : Hello, [5]<u>I'd like two tickets for Thursday night's theater performance</u>.

W : [4]<u>I'm afraid all of the tickets are sold out</u> for that performance.

M : Oh then, what about next week? Do you have tickets for next Saturday's performance?

W : Yes, we do. There are tickets for 7 p.m. and 9 p.m. [6]<u>Which would you like?</u>

男：您好，我想要兩張週四晚上的戲劇演出門票。
女：那場演出所有的門票恐怕都賣完了。
男：哦，那麼下週的呢？有下週六演出的門票嗎？
女：是，有的。有晚上七點和晚上九點的。您想要哪一場？

**詞彙** performance 公演 sold out 賣完了

**4.**

這個女人很有可能是什麼？

(A) 一位銷售人員
(B) 一位運動選手
(C) 一位保全經理
(D) 一位博物館館長

**解說** 此為若能猜測到地點就很容易回答的考題。該男性想買票，而該女性回答票都賣完了，所以可以知道是售票處。將售票處賣票者以概括性的說法來表達的 (A) 為答案。 答案 (A)

**詞彙** salesperson 銷售人員 athlete 運動選手 security manager 保全經理 curator（博物館，圖書館）館長

**5.**

這個男人想要做什麼？

(A) 採購樂器
(B) 參觀博物館
(C) 參觀一場表演
(D) 做旅遊行程

**解說** 雖然是第二個考題，但此答案的線索在對話中比第一個考題出現的早。透過核心語man want，可以知道是詢問「要求事項」的考題。藉由在I'd like後面的「兩張門票」來推論，表達「參觀表演」的 (C) 為答案。 答案 (C)

**詞彙** purchase 購買 musical instrument 音樂設備 museum 博物館 travel itinerary 旅行日誌

**6.**

這個男人接下來可能會做什麼？

(A) 完成一份表格
(B) 和經理說話
(C) 聽音樂
(D) 買票

**解說** 由該女性的話語來決定該男性的下一個動作。「您想要哪一場？」是指「想要買哪一場的票？」，由此可推論該男性會「購買門票」。 答案 (D)

**詞彙** complete 完成 form 表格 manager 經理

問題7～9請參考以下對話。美M 澳W

M : Ms. Waldron? [7]Did you hear the decorations you ordered for the company awards banquet just arrived?

W : Yes, I did. [8]Could you pick up the supplies and deliver them to the main hall this Friday by 2:00? One truck should be enough. And [9]please don't forget to hand the receipt over to the accounting department when you're finished.

M : Certainly. [9]Don't you need a copy of it for your records?

W : Yes, I do. Please copy and give it to my assistant to file.

男：沃爾倫女士，你有聽到你幫公司頒獎典禮訂的裝飾品剛剛到達了嗎？

女：是的，我知道。你能取貨並在這週五兩點前把他們送到大廳？一台卡車應該就夠。當你完成時，請別忘了將收據給會計部門。

男：當然。你不需要一份影本做記錄嗎？

女：是的，我要。請複印並把它給我的助理歸檔。

**詞彙** **decoration** 裝飾品 **award banquet** 頒獎典禮 **pick up** 領取 **deliver A to B** 將A配送到B **hand... over to** 將…交給… **receipt** 收據 **accounting department** 會計部門 **be finished** 完成後 **file** 存檔；歸檔

## 7.

說話者正在討論什麼？

（A）退貨的規定

（B）預約時間表上的衝突

（C）會計軟體的問題

（D）即將來臨的活動的用品

**解說** 出現核心語discussing，可以知道是詢問「主題」的考題。透過在核心說法Did you hear後面出現的「你幫公司頒獎典禮訂的裝飾品」，可以知道將此以概括性的敘述做變化來表達的（D）為答案。 答案 (D)

**詞彙** **policy** 政策 **return** 返還 **goods** 貨物 **conflict** 衝突 **appointment schedule** 預約時間表 **upcoming** 即將到來的

## 8.

這個女人要求這個男人做什麼？

（A）參加典禮儀式

（B）準備工作坊

（C）領退款

（D）做配送

**解說** 透過核心語woman ask，可以知道是詢問「要求事項」的考題。透過在核心說法Could you後面出現的「取貨並送到大廳」，可以知道將此以概括性的敘述做變化來表達的（D）為答案。 答案 (D)

**詞彙** **ceremony** 儀式 **organize** 準備 **get a refund** 領退款 **make a delivery** 做配送

## 9.

這個男人詢問什麼？

（A）一個檔案夾

（B）一個旅遊行程

（C）一份收據

（D）一台影印機

**解說** 「詢問什麼」類型也是在詢問「要求事項」。「不需要一份（收據的）影本嗎？」就是詢問「收據」的說法。 答案 (C)

**詞彙** **file folder** 檔案夾 **itinerary** 日誌 **photocopier** 影印機

問題10～12請參考以下對話。英M 美W

M : [10]Have you heard the company just launched a new web site? I had a look at it, and found it wonderful.

W : Yes, I saw it this morning. At a glance, it looks a lot better than the old one. I think it should be very helpful for our business.

M : Of course, it will be much easier for customers to order our products online. And [11]a new web based e-mail system could keep employees updated even away from the office.

W : I didn't realize that. Well, that solves my problems. [12]I'm leaving for a conference on Monday and I was concerned about missing important e-mail.

男：你有聽說公司剛剛推出一個新的網站嗎？我看了一下，認為它太棒了。

女：是的，我今天早上看到了。略看一下，看起來比舊的好多了，我想它應該會對我們的業務非常有幫助。

男：當然，它將讓客戶更容易上網訂購我們的產品。而新的網路版電子郵件系統能讓員工們更新資料，即使員工離開辦公室。

女：我不太瞭解這個。不過，那解決了我的問題。我週一有個會議要去，而我正在擔心會錯過重要的電子郵件。

**詞彙** **launch** 開始 **at a glance** 看一眼 **online** 線上 **keep 人 updated** 讓某人可以更新… **away from** 離開某處 **realize** 實現 **solve** 解決 **leave** 離開某處 **conference** 瞭解 **be concerned about** 擔心有關於…

## 10.

這段談話的主題是什麼？

（A）一場即將來臨的會議

（B）修訂過的安全規定

（C）一個新網站
（D）網路購物

**解說** 透過核心語main topic，可以知道是詢問「主題」的考題。透過在核心說法Have you heard後面出現的「公司剛剛推出一個新的網站」，可以知道（C）為答案。 答案 (C)

**詞彙** **upcoming meeting** 即將來臨的會議 **revise** 修訂 **safety regulations** 安全規定

## 11.

根據這個男人的談話，這家公司的員工現在能做什麼？
（A）得到免費的配送
（B）離開辦公室可以確認電子郵件
（C）申請旅遊小冊子
（D）線上登錄活動

**解說** 這是詢問「具體事項的考題」。「員工能做」為核心語，而在對話中與此有關的，就是在中間出現的「能讓員工更新資料，即使員工離開辦公室」，即是指在辦公室以外的地方也能看電子郵件。 答案 (B)

**詞彙** **free delivery** 免費配送 **apply for** 申請… **sign up for** 登錄…

## 12.

這個女人說她星期一將會做什麼？
（A）離開去開會
（B）線上訂備品
（C）為預算得到許可
（D）升級網站

**解說** 這裡的Monday，在對話裡沒有經過paraphrasing，所以是核心語。因此Monday前後就有答案的線索。將「我週一有個會議要去」變化而表達的（A）為答案。 答案 (A)

**詞彙** **depart** 出發 **order** 下訂單 **supplies** 備品；材料 **approval** 同意 **budget** 預算

# Chapter 13 仔細詢問的考題

## Quiz I

1. (B) 2. (B) 3. (B) 4. (A)

### Q1 美M 美W

M : Hi, Christina. I just heard the assembly line was down at the Kings Bread factory. Will the shipment of the cakes for the Komparin Corporation be affected?

W : No, fortunately it won't. **I've got** an e-mail **this morning** saying that the order was sent yesterday.

男：克莉絲汀娜，您好。我剛聽說在金氏麵包工廠的裝配線停了。將要給康沛瑞公司的蛋糕的配送會受影響嗎？

女：不，很幸運不會。我今天上午收到一封電子郵件說那張訂單是昨天就被送出了。

這個女人今天早上收到了什麼？
（A）一份訂單
（B）一封電子郵件

**解說** 此為詢問及物動詞（receive）的受詞為何的簡短選項類的考題。在對話內容與考題裡常以相同的this morning說法出現，在此前後會出現答案；但Receive常被換句話說變成get。因此，在I've got之後、this morning之前聽到的an e-mail為答案的線索。（B）為答案。 答案 (B)

**詞彙** **assembly line** 裝配線 **factory** 工廠 **affect** 影響 **fortunately** 幸運 **get** 收到

### Q2 英M 澳W

M : Griffin, It's 4:10 p.m. now, and I think I heard you have to leave at 4 p.m. for an appointment today.

W : You're right. **I'm having my eyes examined** at 4:30 p.m., but I have to finalize this report.

男：格里芬。現在是下午四點十分，我想我有聽說你在今天下午四點鐘有約會要離開。

女：你說得對。我在下午四點三十分要檢查我的眼睛，但是我必須要做完這份報告。

這個女人的預約是什麼時候？
（A）在下午四點鐘
（B）在下午四點三十分

**解說** 透過核心語appointment，可以知道是詢問「時間點」的簡短選項類的考題。在與appointment有相關的I'm having my eyes examined前後聽的到時間點at 4:30

p.m.，所以（B）為答案。 答案 (B)

**詞彙** leave 離開 appointment 約會 examine 做檢查
finalize 使…完成

**Q3** 澳W 英M

W : Excuse me. Is there a grocery store around here? I'd like to buy some fresh fruit for dinner this evening.

M : There's one on Madison Street, just across the Central Bank. But **you'll have to hurry because** everything will be sold out quickly in the evening.

女：打擾一下。這附近有雜貨店嗎？為了今天晚餐，我想買點新鮮的水果。

男：在麥迪遜街上有一家，就在中央銀行的對面。但你必須快點，因為到了晚上什麼東西都將很快被搶購一空。

為什麼這個女人應該要快點？
（A）有某一個人正在等她。
（B）水果將快要缺貨了。

**解說** 這是詢問「理由」的「句子選項類的考題」，其核心語為hurry。將hurry後面表達理由的「什麼東西都將很快被搶購一空」做變化來表達的（B）為答案。 答案 (B)

**詞彙** grocery store 雜貨店 around here 附近
sold out 賣完 business 公司 out of stock 缺貨

**Q4** 美M 美W

M : Silvia, will the company pay the travel expenses this time?

W : They'll pay for the **registration fee**, but as for the airfare, I should cover it myself this time although the company paid for the plane tickets for the conference in January.

男：蘇維亞，這次公司將會支付出差費嗎？

女：他們將會支付註冊費，但是就機票費而言，這次我應該自己付的，雖然公司為一月份的會議支付過機票費。

有關於註冊費用的事這個女人說了什麼？
（A）它將由公司支付。
（B）到一月截止。

**解說** 出現say about，所以是詢問「意見」的「句子選項類的考題」。將registration fee前面的意見「他們（公司）將會支付」以被動語態句子作變化的（A）為答案。 答案 (A)

**詞彙** travel expense 出差費 pay for 為…付費
registration fee 註冊費 airfare 機票費
cover（費用上）負擔

## STEP 01 若沒答對會後悔的考題

| | | | |
|---|---|---|---|
| 1 (A) | 2 (B) | 3 (B) | 4 (A) |
| 5 (B) | 6 (B) | 7 (A) | 8 (B) |
| 9 (C) | 10 (A) | 11 (C) | 12 (A) |
| 13 (C) | 14 (C) | | |

**1.** 美W 英M

| | |
|---|---|
| 1 找出核心語 | presentation |
| 2 瞭解類型 | 詢問意見的考題 |
| 3 看選項 | 完成得很好，或送去給公司總裁 |

W : Tom! You gave an excellent **presentation** this morning! I wonder if you could give your input to Morris for his report.

M : Well, I wish. But I'm afraid I have to finish this feasibility analysis for the upcoming project by tomorrow.

女：湯姆！今天上午你的報告太棒了！我希望你能否對莫里斯的報告給些你的意見。

男：嗯，我希望。但是我恐怕為了即將到來的企劃案在明天之前要完成這份可行性分析。

有關於報告的事這個女人說了什麼？
（A）它相當好。
（B）它被送去給公司總裁。

**解說** 有say about，所以是詢問「意見」的「簡短選項類的考題」。透過在presentation附近的意見「報告太棒了」，可以知道（A）為答案。 答案 (A)

**詞彙** give a presentation 做報告 input 意見；協助
feasibility analysis 可行性分析 upcoming 即將到來的

**2.** 澳W 英M

| | |
|---|---|
| 1 找出核心語 | How, get, destination |
| 2 瞭解類型 | 詢問方法（交通方式）的考題 |
| 3 看選項 | 搭計程車或走路 |

W : I have a job interview at the GW Corporation in half an hour. I'm not sure if I have time to walk there or maybe I should take a taxi.

M : It's just a 5 minute walk. Go along this street and turn right then you **get to** the building. The company's really not that far.

女：我半小時之後在GW公司有場面試。我不確定我有沒有時間走到那兒，還是我也許應該搭計程車。

男：它只要走五分鐘。沿著這條街走然後右轉，那樣你就到那棟樓了。那家公司真的不太遠。

這個女人很有可能將如何到她的目的地？

（A）搭計程車

（B）走路

**解說** how後面聽到get與destination，就可以知道為詢問「交通方式」的「簡短選項類考題」。對於該女性的疑問「有沒有時間走到那兒，還是應該搭計程車」，該男性回答「只要走五分鐘」，所以（B）為答案。

答案 (B)

**詞彙** **job interview** 求職面試 **half an hour** 三十分鐘 **take a taxi** 搭計程車 **get to** 到達某處

**3.** 美M 美W

| | |
|---|---|
| 1 找出核心語 | leave work |
| 2 瞭解類型 | 詢問時間點的考題 |
| 3 看選項 | 晚上六點或晚上七點 |

M : Jessica, has the shipment of projectors arrived yet? We have to place them in the meeting room before we leave work.

W : Well, the shipping company said it should be here by 6 p.m. so I think we can finish all the preparation work by 7 p.m. Then we can **call it a day**.

男：傑西卡，投影機的貨運還沒有到嗎？我們得在下班前把它們置放在會議室呢。

女：嗯，貨運公司說它應該在下午六點半之前會到這兒，所以我想我們可以在晚上七點之前完成所有準備工作。然後我們就能下班。

說話者很有可能將在什麼時候下班？

（A）在晚上六點鐘

（B）在晚上七點鐘

**解說** 這是詢問「時間點」的「簡短選項類考題」。在Leave（或是意思相同call it a day）附近聽的到「我想我們可以在晚上七點之前完成所有準備工作」，所以可以知道（B）為答案。六點鐘是貨運來的時間，這是陷阱。

答案 (B)

**詞彙** **place** 置放 **leave work** 下班 **shipping company** 貨運公司 **preparation work** 準備工作 **call it a day** 下班

**4.** 英M 美W

| | |
|---|---|
| 1 找出核心語 | Mario Ortiz |
| 2 瞭解類型 | 詢問具體人物的考題 |
| 3 看選項 | 設計師或製造商 |

M : The sales figures on our mobile phone have been rising since last quarter. I think It's because the new GW phone incorporated **Mario Ortiz's** new design.

W : It's been a long time since we manufactured a phone that has had such a tremendous impact.

男：我們行動電話的銷售數據從上一季起上升當中。我認為這是由於新的GW電話結合了馬力歐奧蒂斯的新設計。

女：我們很久以來沒有生產過有這麼巨大影響的行動電話了。

馬力歐奧蒂斯是什麼人？

（A）一位設計師

（B）一位製造商

**解說** 這是詢問「具體人物」的「簡短選項類考題」。Mario Ortiz為核心語。在Mario Ortiz附近聽的到「結合了馬力歐奧蒂斯的新設計」，所以可以知道Mario Ortiz為設計師。

答案 (A)

**詞彙** **sales figures** 銷售數據 **mobile phone** 行動電話 **rise** 上升 **incorporate** 和…結合 **manufacture** 製造 **tremendous** 巨大的 **impact** 影響

**5.** 美M 澳W

| | |
|---|---|
| 1 找出核心語 | Saturday |
| 2 瞭解類型 | 詢問具體地點的考題 |
| 3 看選項 | 歌劇院或美術館 |

M : Mary, where are you planning on taking the overseas clients on **Saturday**? The art museum or the opera hall is convenient.

W : I'd like to take them to the art museum. They have an exhibit right now featuring work from several well-known contemporary artists.

男：瑪麗，你打算週六將帶海外客戶去哪裡？美術館或歌劇院都很方便。

女：我想帶他們去美術館。他們正在有一場展出一些知名當代藝術家的作品的展覽。

這個女人計畫星期六將要去什麼地方？

（A）去歌劇院

（B）去美術館

**解說** 這是詢問「具體地點」的「簡短選項類考題」。像Saturday這樣具體時間點為很好的線索，且其附近的句子也有答案的線索。對於「週六將帶海外客戶去哪裡？」，以「想帶他們去美術館」回答，所以（B）為答案。 答案 (B)

**詞彙** **take** 帶…去某處 **overseas client** 海外客戶 **art museum** 美術館 **right now** 正在 **A feature B** 以B為特色的A **well-known** 有名的 **contemporary artist** 當代藝術家

**6.** 美W 英M

| | |
|---|---|
| 1 找出核心語 | late |
| 2 瞭解類型 | 詢問理由的考題 |
| 3 看選項 | 弄錯時間表或航班耽誤 |

W : Excuse me. Do you know when the afternoon session for Newton Corporation begins? **I came late because** my flight was delayed.

M : No, I don't, but you can find a schedule of all the sessions at the information desk in the conference room.

女：抱歉，你知道牛頓公司下午的會議什麼時候開始嗎？因為我的班機被延誤，所以我遲到了。

男：不，我不知道，但你可以在會議室的諮詢台找到所有的會議日程。

為什麼這個女人遲到？

（A）她弄錯時間表了。

（B）她的航班耽誤了。

**解說** 這是詢問「理由」的「句子選項類考題」。在Late（或與late意思相同的句子）附近有線索。聽的到「我的班機被延誤」，所以（B）為答案。 答案 (B)

**詞彙** **session** 會議 **be delayed** 被延誤 **information desk** 諮詢台 **conference room** 會議室

**7.** 美M 美W

| | |
|---|---|
| 1 找出核心語 | must be completed |
| 2 瞭解類型 | 詢問行為對象的考題 |
| 3 看選項 | 培訓課程或辦公室整修 |

M : I heard the company has hired several new programmers to work on our new project. When will they start?

W : They're not actually working at our office yet. **They have to finish** their training session first. Their first day will be Monday.

男：我聽說我們公司為了處理新的企劃雇用了一些新程式設計人員。他們什麼時候將會開始？

女：他們還沒有實際在我們辦公室工作。他們要先完成他們的培訓課程。他們第一天上班將是在星期一。

根據這個女人的談話，什麼必須被完成？

（A）培訓課程

（B）辦公室整修

**解說** 這是詢問「行為的對象」的「簡短選項類考題」。核心語「必須被完成」變成「他們要先完成」，所以要被完成的就是培訓課程。（A）為答案。 答案 (A)

**詞彙** **programmer** 程式設計師 **work on** 在…工作 **finish** 完成 **training session** 培訓課程 **first day** 第一天

**8.** 美W 英M

| | |
|---|---|
| 1 找出核心語 | last week |
| 2 瞭解類型 | 詢問行為的考題 |
| 3 看選項 | 寄很大的包裹或訂購軟體 |

W : Hi, I ordered the computer software package from your company **last Monday**. And it hasn't arrived yet. Could you look up my order please?

M : Sure. What's the name on the order and when did you place it?

女：你好。上星期一我從你們公司訂了一套電腦軟體。它還沒有送到。你能查一下我的訂單嗎？

男：當然，訂單上的姓名是什麼，還有你什麼時候下的訂單？

這個女人說她上個星期做了什麼？

（A）寄了一大包包裹

（B）訂購了軟體

**解說** 這是詢問「行為」的「句子選項類考題」。核心語Last week在對話裡通常不會改變成其他說法，可以直接聽到。將在Last Monday附近的「訂了一套電腦軟體」簡化後來表達的（B）為答案。 答案 (B)

**詞彙** **order** 下訂單 **look up** 查閱 **place an order** 下訂單

問題9~10請參考以下對話。美W 美M

| | |
|---|---|
| 1 找出核心語 | woman surprised, wish to purchase |
| 2 瞭解類型 | 詢問理由、數量的考題 |
| 3 看選項 | 行程變化，沒有座位，沒有直航服務 |
| | 一，二，六 |
| 4 預測對話內容 | 訝異沒有直航班機，因此購買需轉機的機票 |

W : Excuse me, when's the next flight to Osaka?

M : Unfortunately there is no direct flight to Osaka. You need to stop over in Tokyo. Then there is a connecting flight to Osaka. The next flight to Tokyo departs at 6 p.m.

W : [9]No direct flight to Osaka? I'm surprised! I thought it would be a direct trip. Well, okay then, [10]please give me a single ticket to Tokyo.

女：打擾一下，下一個前往大阪的航班是什麼時候呢？
男：很不巧的，沒有直飛到大阪的航班。你需在東京停留。這樣的話有轉機航班到大阪。下一班到東京的班機在下午六點出發。
女：沒有直飛到大阪的班機？我真是驚訝！我以為這會是直飛的行程。嗯，好的，那麼請給我一張到東京的單程票。

**詞彙** **direct flight** 直飛航班 **stop over** 在中途停留 **connecting flight** 轉機航班 **single ticket** 單程票

### 9.

為什麼這個女人感到驚訝？
(A) 行程改變了。
(B) 沒有座位了。
(C) 沒有直航服務。

**解說** 這是詢問「理由」的「句子選項類考題」。將「我真是驚訝」附近的理由「以為這會是直飛的行程」做變化來表達的 (C) 為答案。 答案 (C)

**詞彙** **schedule change** 行程變更 **left** 留下 **direct service** 直航服務

### 10.

這個女人希望買多少張票？
(A) 一張
(B) 兩張
(C) 六張

**解說** 這是詢問「數量」的「簡短選項類考題」。核心語「希望買」（或與此相同意思的句子）附近出現「給我一張單程票」，所以 (A) 為答案。 答案 (A)

**詞彙** **purchase** 購買

問題11~12請參考以下對話。英M 澳W

| | |
|---|---|
| 1 找出核心語 | currently working on, man thank |
| 2 瞭解類型 | 詢問行為的對象、理由的考題 |
| 3 看選項 | 併購，發表，建設企劃 |
| | 推薦，延長期限，建議 |
| 4 預測對話內容 | 老闆正在進行建築個案當中，因為將他推薦給老闆而表達感謝。 |

M : Christina, the assignment you gave me is nearly complete. I'm in the process of taking a final look at it.

W : Oh, the top priority has changed. [11]The president just called. He is working on a construction project for a new client. [12]He needs someone with extensive knowledge about construction regulations, so I recommended you.

M : [12]Thanks. That sounds like a great opportunity for me.

男：克莉絲汀娜，你給我的任務已快完成了。我正在做最後瀏覽的過程。
女：噢，首要事項有變化了。總裁剛剛打過電話。他為一位新客戶正在進行一項建設企劃。他需要在建設法規上有廣泛知識的人，所以我推薦了你。
男：謝。對我來說，這聽來像是個相當好的機會。

**詞彙** **assignment** 任務 **nearly complete** 接近完成 **be in the process of** 在…的過程 **take a look at** 瀏覽 **top priority** 首要事項 **work on** 在…做事 **construction project** 建設企劃 **extensive knowledge** 廣泛的知識 **regulations** 法規 **recommend** 推薦 **opportunity** 機會

### 11.

這個總裁正在進行什麼事？
(A) 一項商業併購
(B) 一場會議的發表
(C) 一項建設企劃

**解說** 這是詢問「行為的對象」的「簡短選項類考題」。核心語「正在進行當中」附近出現「總裁剛剛打過電話、他正在進行一項建設企劃」，所以將此做變化來表達的 (C) 為答案。 答案 (C)

**詞彙** **currently** 現在 **merger** 併購 **presentation** 發表

## 12.

為什麼這個男人感謝這個女人？
(A) 因為向總裁推薦他
(B) 因為為他的報告延長期限
(C) 因為提供給他一些建議

**解說** 這是詢問「理由」的「句子選項類考題」。在核心語「感謝」附近出現「所以我推薦了你」，所以將此做變化來表達的（A）為答案。 答案 (A)

**詞彙** extend 延長 deadline 最後期限 offer 提供 advice 建議

問題13～14請參考以下對話。美M 美W

| | |
|---|---|
| 1 找出核心語 | waiting for, waiting |
| 2 瞭解類型 | 詢問具體人物、時間長短的考題 |
| 3 看選項 | 客戶，經理，修理工 |
| | 一小時，二小時，三小時 |
| 4 預測對話內容 | 等修理工等了三小時 |

M : Isn't the fax machine still working yet?

W : No, it isn't. [13, 14]We've been waiting for it to be fixed for three hours. But I called the maintenance department again and they can take a look at it sometime this afternoon.

M : This afternoon? I am expecting very important document to be faxed this morning. Is there another machine I can use?

男：傳真機仍然還不能用嗎？
女：不，它不能。我們一直在等它被修好等了三個小時。但是我已再次打電話給維修部，他們可以在今天下午某個時間來看看。
男：今天下午？我正在期盼的非常重要的文件今天早上要傳真過來。有另一台機器可以讓我使用嗎？

**詞彙** fax machine 傳真機 wait for 等待… maintenance department 維修部門 take a look at 看一下 important 重要 document 文件；資料

## 13.

這些工作者在等什麼人？
(A) 一位商業客戶
(B) 一位辦公室經裡
(C) 一位修理工

**解說** 這是詢問「具體人物」的「簡短選項類考題」。Waiting for為核心語，透過在該核心語附近出現的「等它被修好、打電話給維修部」等話語，可以猜測正在等「修理工」。 答案 (C)

**詞彙** business client 商業客戶 manager 經理 repairperson 修理工

## 14.

他們等了多長的時間？
(A) 一小時
(B) 兩小時
(C) 三小時

**解說** 這是詢問「時間長短」的「簡短選項類考題」。其核心語也是waiting，透過其後面出現的three hours，就可以知道答案。 答案 (C)

**詞彙** wait 等待

## STEP 02 考題實戰練習

1. (C) 2. (A) 3. (D) 4. (D) 5. (C) 6. (A)
7. (D) 8. (D) 9. (D) 10. (D) 11. (B) 12. (C)

問題1～3請參考以下對話 美W 英M

W : Good morning. Have you talked with Marsha about arranging for the sales meeting on Tuesday?

M : She just called. [1, 2]The quarterly sales report expected to arrive yesterday only came in this morning. She needs to analyze all the data so she asked if we could reschedule the meeting for Wednesday.

W : Well, [2]I'm leaving for a business trip on that day, but I can make myself available for an early morning meeting. Would you call her and reschedule the meeting?

M : Sure. [3]I'll reach her as soon as possible.

女：早安，你有和瑪莎談到關於在星期二安排銷售會議嗎？
男：她剛剛打電話來。預估昨天要到的季度銷售報告，在今天早上才來。她需要分析所有的數據，所以她要求我們是否能重新安排會議在星期三。
女：嗯，那天我要出差，但我能儘量參加晨間會議。你可以打電話聯繫她，並重新安排會議嗎？
男：當然，我會盡可能快點聯繫到她。

**詞彙** talk with 和…談話 arrange for 安排… quarterly sales report 季度銷售報告 come in 到達 analyze 分析 leave 離開 business trip 出差 reach 聯絡 as soon as possible 儘可能的快

## 1.

為什麼瑪莎要求將會議延後？
(A) 她正在等一位客戶。

(B) 她出差了。
(C) 某個訊息被延誤了。
(D) 沒有會議室可以提供。

**解說** 這是詢問「理由」的「句子選項類考題」。核心語「將會議延後」在對話中是以「是否能重新安排會議在星期三」來表達，且其前面出現「她需要分析所有的數據，所以她要求」，所以將此做變化來表達的（C）為答案。 答案 (C)

**詞彙** wait for 等待… client 客戶 be delayed 被延誤 available 能夠使用

**2.**

這個會議很有可能將在什麼時候被舉辦？
(A) 在星期三上午
(B) 在星期三下午
(C) 在星期四上午
(D) 在星期四下午

**解說** 這是詢問「時間點」的「簡短選項類考題」。該男性說「是否能重新安排會議在星期三」，接著該女性說「我能儘量參加晨間會議」，所以可以猜測「星期三上午」將開會。 答案 (A)

**詞彙** be held 被舉辦

**3.**

這個男人接下來很有可能會做什麼？
(A) 安排旅行時間表
(B) 準備銷售報告
(C) 尋找研究資料
(D) 想要和瑪莎聯絡

**解說** 這是「下一個行程」的考題。Do next為核心語，將核心說法I'll後面聽到的「聯繫到她」做變化來表達的（D）為答案。 答案 (D)

**詞彙** travel schedule 旅行時間表 prepare 準備 look for 尋找 research data 數據研究資料 try to 嘗試做… contact 聯絡

問題4～6請參考以下對話。澳W 美M

W : Becker, [4]how's the marketing manager search going? Did you find anyone who is a good fit?

M : No. The personnel department narrowed down the applications to two, but neither seems to be qualified. We're targeting young consumers in the clothing market. [5]We need someone who has extensive experience in the related field.

W : I have a friend who is really qualified for the job. He's been with a clothing company for decades. [6]Why don't you contact him to see if he's interested?

女：貝克，尋求行銷經理的事情進行得如何？你有找到任何不錯適合的人嗎？

男：沒有。人事部門縮小應徵者範圍到兩位，但似乎沒有一個具有資格。我們的目標是服裝市場的年輕消費者，我們需要一位在相關領域有豐富經驗的人。

女：我有一個朋友相當有資格來做這個工作。他在一家服裝公司幾十年了。你何不聯絡他，看看他有沒有興趣？

**詞彙** marketing manager 行銷經理 search 尋找 personnel department 人事部門 narrow down 縮小 application 申請 qualified 合格 target 目標 young consumer 年輕消費者 experience 經驗 related field 相關領域 decade 十年 contact 聯絡

**4.**

哪一個部門需要一位新的經理？
(A) 人事
(B) 客戶服務
(C) 會計
(D) 行銷

**解說** 這是詢問對象為什麼的「簡短選項類考題」。「需要一位新的經理」為核心語。透過「尋求行銷經理的事情進行得如何」，可以猜測新的經理就是行銷部門的經理。 答案 (D)

**詞彙** personnel 人事部門 customer service 客戶服務部門 accounting 會計部門 marketing 行銷部門

**5.**

這個男人提到什麼資格條件？
(A) 願意出差
(B) 強力的推薦
(C) 相關的經驗
(D) 大學學位

**解說** 這是詢問對象為什麼的「簡短選項類考題」。「資格條件」為核心語，在後面出現的「我們需要…的人」與核心語意思相同，因此將「一位在相關領域有豐富經驗」做變化來表達的（C）為答案。 答案 (C)

**詞彙** qualification 資格條件 mention 提及… willingness 願意 reference 推薦 relevant 關聯 university degree 大學學位

**6.**

這個女人建議了什麼？
(A) 聯絡可能的候選人
(B) 調到另一個分公司
(C) 在網路上登廣告
(D) 重新安排一些面試的時間

**解說** 透過woman recommend，可以知道是「詢問建議事項的考題」。由核心說法why don't you後面出現的

「聯絡他看看他有沒有興趣」，可以知道將此做變化來表達的（A）為答案。 答案 (A)

**詞彙** possible 可能性 candidate 候選人
transfer to 轉換到… place an advertisement 登廣告
reschedule 重新安排日程

問題7～9請參考以下對話。美W 英M

W : Hi, Mr. Writer. [7]I'm leaving my job here to move to New York. That's why I asked to meet with you.

M : Oh, we are sorry to lose you. [8]Your idea on our clothing design was very creative and garnered good feedback. Our market share has increased thanks to your effort.

W : Thank you. I've loved working with you. [8, 9]It's been a great honor to be a part of such a highly recognized clothing firm but the design school I dreamed of is in the New York area and I'd like to take this opportunity to expand my knowledge.

女：瑞特先生您好。我即將離開這兒的工作前往紐約。這是我要求和您見面的原因。

男：噢，我們很遺憾失去你。你的想法對我們的服裝設計來說很有創意，引起很好的回饋。我們的市場占有率已經增加，歸功於你的努力。

女：謝謝你，我很喜歡和您一起工作。能成為高名聲的服裝公司的一部份，這是很大的榮幸，但我夢想進入的設計學校在紐約，我想把握這個機會擴展我的學識。

**詞彙** leave a job 離職 move 移動 meet with 與…見面 lose 失去 creative 創意 garner 回饋 market share 市場佔有率 effort 努力 work with 與…一起工作 honor 光榮 highly recognized 高名聲 design school 設計學校 dream of 夢想… take an opportunity 把握機會 knowledge 知識

**7.**

為什麼這個女人想和這個男人談話？
（A）討論客戶滿意度
（B）要求調任
（C）要求一些建議
（D）提出她的辭呈

**解說** 這是詢問「理由」的「句子選項類考題」。「為什麼和這個男人談話」，在對話裡變成「要求和您見面的原因」，在其前後出現了「離開這兒的工作前往紐約」，所以將此做變化來表達的（D）為答案。

答案 (D)

**詞彙** talk to 和…談話 discuss 討論 customer satisfaction 顧客滿意度 transfer 轉換 ask for 要求 recommendation 辭呈 resignation 提交

**8.**

說話者很有可能在哪兒工作？
（A）在旅行社
（B）在廣告公司
（C）在設計學校
（D）在服裝公司

**解說** 透過「你的想法對我們的服裝設計來說很有創意，引起很好的回饋」、「能成為高名聲的服裝公司的一部份」，可以知道在「服裝公司」工作。 答案 (D)

**詞彙** travel agency 旅行社 advertising firm 廣告公司

**9.**

有關於紐約這個女人說了什麼？
（A）她的家族住在那兒。
（B）有很多觀光名勝。
（C）有很多服裝店。
（D）有她想去的學校。

**解說** 出現say about，所以是詢問「意見」的「簡短選項類考題」。透過在New York前後的線索「我夢想進入的學校在紐約」、「我想把握這個機會擴展我的學識」，可以知道答案為（D）。 答案 (D)

**詞彙** tourist attraction 觀光名勝

問題10～12請參考以下對話。澳W 美M

W : [10]Excuse me, when will our table be ready? It's been a half an hour since we arrived here.

M : Well, I wish I could seat you right away. But you reserved a table for only 4 people, but now you have 8 people in your group. We have tables that can accommodate only 4 people at the moment.

W : I'm sorry the others decided to join us just before leaving the office. [11]We have to get back to work for a meeting at 2 o'clock. And it's already 1 o'clock now, so we don't mind sitting in two different tables.

M : Oh, that won't be necessary. [12]The large group in the back room seems to be ready to leave soon. I'll go and check it out for you.

女：打擾一下，我們的桌次什麼時候可以準備好？我們已經到這兒半小時了。

男：嗯，我希望我能馬上給您座位。但為您保留的是四人桌，而現在您的團體有八位。我們當場能用的桌子只能容納四位。

女：我很抱歉，我們正要離開辦公室前其他人才決定加入。我們得回去工作開兩點鐘的會。現在已經快要一點鐘了，所以我們不介意分坐在兩張桌子。

男：噢，不需要那樣。在後面房間好像有一大群團體正準備要離開。我去為你們確認一下。

**詞彙** half an hour 半小時 right away 立刻 accommodate 使用 at the moment 當場；現下 get back to work 回去工作 mind 介意 necessary 需要 back room 後面房間 be ready to 被準備好 check it out 做確認

### 10.

這段對話很有可能在哪兒發生的？
(A) 在會計事務所
(B) 在傢俱店
(C) 在音樂廳
(D) 在餐廳

**解說** 透過「桌次什麼時候可以準備好」、「給您座位」等說法，可以猜測是在「餐廳」。 答案 (D)

**詞彙** take place 發生 accounting office 會計事務所 furniture 傢俱 concert hall 音樂廳 restaurant 餐廳

### 11.

這個女人在下午兩點打算做什麼？
(A) 配送一些傢俱
(B) 參加一場會議
(C) 打電話給一位客人
(D) 領取一些食物

**解說** 這是詢問「行為」的「句子選項類考題」。像2 p.m.這類的時間點，在對話內容和考題裡會出現一樣的說法。在2 o'clock附近敘述的「我們得回去工作開會」是「參加會議」的意思。 答案 (B)

**詞彙** deliver 做配送 attend 出席 customer 顧客 pick up 領取

### 12.

這個男人將要找什麼？
(A) 一張遺失的票
(B) 一份遺失的報告
(C) 一張能使用的桌子
(D) 一台空的計程車

**解說** 這是詢問動作的對象的「簡短選項類考題」。「找」在對話裡變成「確認」，而在此處是去確認別的團體是否即將離開，所以是找「可用的桌子」。 答案 (C)

**詞彙** look for 找… lost 遺失 missing 遺失 available 能夠使用的 empty 空的

# Chapter 14 與公司相關的對話

## Quiz

**1.** (B) **2.** (B) **3.** (A) **4.** (A)

### Q1 美W 英M

W : Hi, Peter. Have you booked your flight for the conference in **New York** yet? Do you prefer to take the 9 o'clock flight on Wednesday evening or the 11 o'clock flight on Thursday morning?

M : Wednesday's flight would be better. That way, we can take a short break before the conference begins Friday morning.

女：您好，彼得。您已經訂好到紐約開會的班機了嗎？您想要星期三晚上九點的航班還是星期四早上十一點的航班？

男：週三的航班比較好。這樣我們可以在週五上午開始的會議前暫時休息一下。

說話者為什麼要去紐約？
(A) 參觀名勝
(B) 參加會議

**解說** 看到考題裡的「去紐約」，可以預測以「業餘活動」或「通勤／交通／搜尋」為主體。透過該女性說的「到紐約開會」，可以知道答案為「參加會議」。 答案 (B)

**詞彙** book 預約 prefer 較願意… take a break 暫歇一下 attraction 觀光名勝 attend 參加

### Q2 澳W 美M

W : Hi, Richard. Are you ready for the presentation this afternoon?

M : Not quite. There is a **problem**. I've finished and saved the presentation files in my laptop. I tried to connect it with the projector but the projector is not working.

女：嗨，理查。今天下午的報告你準備好了嗎？

男：還沒有。有點狀況。我完成了之後把報告文件儲存在我的筆記型電腦裡面了。我試著把它連接到投影機，但是投影機無法運作。

這個男人提到什麼問題？
(A) 有些工作者很早離開了。
(B) 投影機故障了。

**解說** 看到考題裡的problem，可以預測以「故障／修理／維修」為主體。透過在problem後面出現的「投影機無法運作」，可以知道將此做變化來表達的（B）為答案。 答案 (B)

**詞彙** presentation 演講 not quite 尚未完成 laptop 筆記型電腦 connect 連接 work 運作 out of order 故

**Q3** 英M 美M

M1 : Thanks for meeting with me, Mr. Lee. As you can see in last year's expense report, we overspent last year. **I want to talk about** some ways to cut back on costs next year.

M2 : Well, to stay within the budget, I think we need to limit our expenses on office supplies.

男1：李先生，謝謝您和我見面。如您在去年的費用報告上所見，去年我們超支了。我想談談一些方法來削減明年的成本。

男2：嗯，為了保持在預算範圍內，我認為我們需要限制辦公用品上的支出。

這場會議的目的是什麼？
（A）如何減少花費
（B）如何擬訂預算

**解說** 藉由考題裡面的「會議的目的」與選項，可以預測其主題為「會議內容」。由「我想談談一些方法來削減明年的成本」能判斷（A）為答案。 答案 (A)

**詞彙** expense 費用 cut back on 削減… stay 保持 budget 預算 limit 限制 office supplies 辦公用品 reduce 減少 draw up 擬訂

**Q4** 美M 澳W

M : Have you heard that **Ms. Sato** has been promoted to vice president of sales?

W : Yes, and I heard she is hiring more salespeople to expand into the overseas market.

男：妳有聽說佐藤女士晉升為銷售副總了嗎？
女：是的，而且我聽說她正雇用更多銷售人員以拓展海外市場。

關於佐藤女士說到了什麼？
（A）她晉升了。
（B）她最近被雇用。

**解說** 藉由選項可以預測以「雇用／升遷／人事變動」為主體。Ms. Sato或she附近會出現答案，而在此就出現了「晉升」。 答案 (A)

**詞彙** promote 晉升；升遷 vice president 副總 hire 雇用 expand into 拓展；擴張 overseas market 海外市場

## STEP 01 若沒答對會後悔的考題

| | | | |
|---|---|---|---|
| 1 (A) | 2 (B) | 3 (A) | 4 (B) |
| 5 (A) | 6 (A) | 7 (B) | 8 (A) |
| 9 (B) | 10 (B) | 11 (C) | 12 (B) |
| 13 (C) | 14 (B) | | |

**1.** 美W 美M

| | |
|---|---|
| 1 找出核心語 | man want |
| 2 瞭解類型 | 訂票／開票或訂貨／配送 |
| 3 看選項 | 訂購來回票或旅行書 |

W : Thank you for calling Fantasia Travel Service. How may I help you?

M : Hello, this is Danny Kim from CS Corporation. I'm planning to go on a business trip this weekend. **I'd like to** take a flight leaving for New York tomorrow night and return on Sunday morning.

女：感謝您致電幻想曲旅遊服務中心。我能給您什麼幫助嗎？
男：你好，我是CS公司的丹尼金。我計畫這週末要出差。我想搭明天晚上去紐約的航班，並在週日上午回來。

這個男人想要做什麼？
（A）訂購來回票
（B）訂購一本旅行書

**解說** 透過選項可以預測以「訂票／開票」或「訂貨／配送」為主體。與旅行社職員通話的男性說「我想搭明天晚上去紐約的航班」，所以可以猜到他想訂購飛機票。 答案 (A)

**詞彙** business trip 出差 leave for 離開並去某地 return 返回 round trip ticket 來回票 order 下訂單

**2.** 英M 澳W

| | |
|---|---|
| 1 找出核心語 | man late to work |
| 2 瞭解類型 | 通勤／交通／搜尋 |
| 3 看選項 | 車禍或道路封閉 |

M : I can't believe that I spent 3 hours on the way to work today. I was caught in traffic on Highway 238.

W : Wow, what a long time! I heard that there was a car accident and the highway was temporarily blocked. You should have taken an alternate road to be here on time.

男：我不敢相信，我在路上花了三個小時才到公司。我今天堵車在238號高速公路上。

女：哇，這麼久！我聽說有車禍，道路暫時封鎖。你應該開替代道路就能準時了。

為什麼這個男人上班遲到？

（A）他遇到車禍。

（B）道路被封閉了。

**解說** 藉由選項可以猜測以「通勤／交通／搜尋」為主體。有事故所以道路封閉為原因。但在此並沒有暗示該男性發生車禍。 答案 (B)

**詞彙** **spend** 花費 **work** 上班 **accident** 事故 **temporarily** 暫時的 **blocked** 封鎖 **take an alternate road** 駕駛替代道路 **closed** 封閉

**3.** 美M 澳W

| | |
|---|---|
| 1 找出核心語 | their products |
| 2 瞭解類型 | 訂貨／配送 |
| 3 看選項 | 可在線上訂購或價錢合理 |

M : We're going to be so busy today. We got a batch of **orders** last night from our web site.

W : It's not that surprising. Since the holiday is coming, I expect many people will be ordering cakes and chocolates before or during the holiday.

男：我們今天將會很忙。昨晚從我們的網站收到了一批訂單。

女：這並不令人驚訝。因為假期即將來臨，我預計很多人會在節日前或這期間訂蛋糕和巧克力。

說話者對他們的產品做了什麼建議？

（A）可以在線上被訂購。

（B）價錢很合理。

**解說** 透過選項可以猜測以「訂貨／配送」為主體。「從我們的網站收到了一批訂單」即是指「可以在線上被訂購」。 答案 (A)

**詞彙** **batch** 一批；一次份量 **holiday** 節日 **product** 產品 **reasonably** 合理的 **priced** 價錢

**4.** 英M 美W

| | |
|---|---|
| 1 找出核心語 | problem |
| 2 瞭解類型 | 故障／修理／維修／改善 |
| 3 看選項 | 印得太深或雙面影印 |

M : Hi, **I'm having trouble** with my X2 photocopier. I can't make double-sided copies by using the special printing features. Can you help me with this?

W : Okay. Have you read the user manual? If not, please consult page 77 of the manual.

男：嗨，我的X2影印機有點問題。我不能使用特殊影印功能來做雙面複印。你能幫助我嗎？

女：好的。你讀過用戶手冊了嗎？如果沒有，請參考本手冊第七十七頁。

影印機有什麼問題？

（A）印得太深了。

（B）不能雙面影印。

**解說** 透過考題與選項可以猜測以「故障／修理／維修／改善」為主體。在此，problem變成trouble提供了線索，因此將其後面出現的「我不能做雙面複印」做簡單變化來表達的（B）為答案。 答案 (B)

**詞彙** **photocopier** 影印機 **make a copy** 影印 **double-sided** 雙面的 **by -ing** 在…的情形下 **feature** 功能 **user manual** 使用手冊 **consult** 參考 **copier** 影印機 **two sides** 雙面

**5.** 美M 美W

| | |
|---|---|
| 1 找出核心語 | meeting with the cu stomers |
| 2 瞭解類型 | 準備會議／安排時間 |
| 3 看選項 | 今天或明天 |

M : Ms. Leskey called me yesterday and said her flight back to Boston has been canceled due to the bad weather, and she couldn't get another flight.

W : But **the meeting with our customers** is at 5 p.m. today. We'd better push back the meeting until tomorrow if she doesn't get here on time.

男：雷思琪小姐昨天打電話給我，說由於天候不佳，她回波士頓的航班被取消了，而她無法接上其他航班。

女：但和我們客戶的會議在今天下午五點。如果她不能準時到這兒，我們最好延後會議到明天。

和顧客的會議是在什麼時候？

（A）今天

（B）明天

**解說** 透過考題可以猜測以「準備會議／安排時間」為主體。與顧客的會議是今天五點鐘，所以today為答案。必須注意不要被「延後會議到明天」誤導了。 答案 (A)

**詞彙** **cancel** 取消 **bad weather** 天候不佳 **push back** 延後 **on time** 準時

**6.** 英M 澳W

| | |
|---|---|
| 1 找出核心語 | topic of the seminar |
| 2 瞭解類型 | 會議內容 |
| 3 看選項 | 網路銀行或廣告趨勢 |

M : Hi, Christina. How was the **seminar** yesterday? It was about current trends in online banking, wasn't it?

W : Yes, and it was very good. Guwon, the instructor was well-organized and covered a lot in two hours.

男：嗨，克里斯汀娜。昨天研討會如何？它是有關於網路銀行目前的趨勢，是嗎？

女：是的，它非常好。講師高文很有條理並在兩小時內論及很多內容。

這場研討會的主題是什麼？

(A) 網路銀行

(B) 廣告趨勢

**解說** 透過考題可以猜測以「會議內容」為主體。這是該男性提及研討會的內容並向該女性確認的狀況。將seminar附近聽到的online banking做變化來表達的（A）為答案。 答案 (A)

**詞彙** **current** 現今的 **trend** 趨勢 **instructor** 講師 **well-organized** 很有系統 **cover** 涵蓋

**7.** 美M 美W

| | |
|---|---|
| 1 找出核心語 | going to Hong Kong office |
| 2 瞭解類型 | 僱用／升遷／人事變動 |
| 3 看選項 | 拜訪競爭對手的公司或管理 |

M : Did you hear that Ms. Adler is **moving to the Hong Kong office**? It was so unexpected because she has only been here for two months.

W : Yes, I heard. **She is going to** manage the sales team there.

男：你有聽說阿德勒女士將調到香港辦事處嗎？真是出乎意料，因為她在這裡只待了兩個月。

女：是的，我聽說她將要去管理那邊的銷售團隊。

為什麼阿德勒女士將要去香港辦公室？

(A) 拜訪競爭對手的公司

(B) 管理銷售團隊

**解說** 透過考題與選項可以猜測以「雇用／升遷／人事變動」為主體。對話裡「她將要去管理那邊的銷售團隊」，句中的there就是考題所指的Hong Kong office，句中的she就是考題所指的Ms. Adler。因此（B）就是答案。 答案 (B)

**詞彙** **manage** 管理 **visit** 拜訪 **rival company** 競爭對手的公司

**8.** 英M 美W

| | |
|---|---|
| 1 找出核心語 | man want to talk to Ms. Sato |
| 2 瞭解類型 | 薪水／費用 |
| 3 看選項 | 員工福利或加薪 |

M : Good morning, my name is James Keenan. I'm here to **meet with Ms. Sato to talk about** my employee benefits.

W : Ms. Sato is in the meeting right now. But, here is some information on health and other benefits to read while you are waiting.

男：早安，我的名字是詹姆斯基南。我來這兒和佐藤女士見面討論我的員工福利。

女：佐藤女士現在正是開會。不過這裡有一些關於健康和其他福利的資訊，在等待的時候可以看看。

為什麼這個男人想要和佐藤女士說話？

(A) 討論他的員工福利

(B) 討論加薪

**解說** 透過考題與選項可以猜測以「薪水／費用」為主體。透過出現於開頭部分自我介紹後面的話語，可以知道是要來談「員工福利」的。 答案 (A)

**詞彙** **benefit** 福利 **right now** 現在 **discuss** 討論 **pay raise** 加薪

問題9～10請參考以下對話 美M 澳W

| | |
|---|---|
| 1 找出核心語 | woman, man want |
| 2 瞭解類型 | 詢問說話者、行為的簡短選項類考題 |
| 3 看選項 | 旅行社職員，售票員，保全人員 |
| | 看電影，看表演，規劃旅行 |
| 4 預測對話內容 | 男人想買表演入場卷，和賣票的人對話 |

M : Hello, [9, 10]I'd like two tickets for Thursday night's theater performance.

W : [9]I'm afraid all of the tickets are sold out for that performance. Would you like me to check if there are some tickets for next week?

W : Yes, I'd appreciate that. Do you have tickets for next Saturday performance?

男：你好，我想要兩張週四晚上戲場表演的門票。
女：我恐怕那場表演所有的門票都已經賣完了。妳希望我幫妳看看下星期是否有票嗎？
男：是的，謝謝妳。有下週六表演的票嗎？

**詞彙** theater 劇場 performance 表演 sold out 賣完了 appreciate 感謝

## 9.

這個女人很有可能是什麼？
（A）旅行社職員
（B）售票員
（C）保全人員

**解說** 該男性說「想買門票」，而該女性說「都賣完了」，所以可以知道該女性為售票員。 答案 (B)

**詞彙** travel agent 旅行社 salesperson 銷售員 security guard 保全人員

## 10.

這個男人想要做什麼？
（A）看電影
（B）看表演
（C）做旅行規劃

**解說** 這是該男性想買表演門票的狀況，所以可以說是他想看表演。 答案 (B)

**詞彙** attend 參加 make arrangement 做規劃

問題11～12請參考以下對話。英M 澳W

| | |
|---|---|
| 1 找出核心語 | discussing, immediately |
| 2 瞭解類型 | 詢問主題、行為的簡短選項類考題 |
| 3 看選項 | 貨運費，損壞的部分，訂購物的配送，傳達訊息，配送商品，尋找遺失的商品 |
| 4 預測對話內容 | 配送上有問題，要求再次寄送 |

M : Hello, this is Nicholas Reed from AK Machine Parts. I'm returning your message regarding your concern about [11]getting your order within this week.

W : Yes, in fact most of our order came in yesterday, but one part is missing. Have you shipped all the parts we ordered?

M : Well, [12]the feed pump was temporarily out of stock yesterday. I'll send it immediately so you can get it no later than this weekend.

男：你好，我是AK機械零件公司的尼古拉斯瑞德。我是來回覆您的留言，您在意這週之內能否收到您的貨物。
女：是的，實際上我們貨物大多是在昨天收到的，但有一部不見。你有運送出我們訂購的所有的零件嗎？
男：嗯，供水幫浦昨天暫時缺貨。我會立即寄送它，所以您可以最晚在週末前收到。

**詞彙** return 回覆 in fact 事實上 part 部份 missing 遺失 ship 配送 feed pump 供水幫浦 temporarily 暫時的 out of stock 缺貨 immediately 立即 no later than 不晚於

## 11.

說話者在討論什麼？
（A）貨運費
（B）損壞的部分
（C）訂購物的配送

**解說** 透過考題與選項可以猜測以「訂貨／配送」為主體。但是這是只聽前段部分無法找到主題的難題，必須要聽到中間部分才行。由於是零件漏掉所以要求再配送的狀況，因此「訂購物的配送」為其主題。 答案 (C)

**詞彙** shipping charge 貨運費 damaged 損壞 delivery 配送 order 訂購

## 12.

這個男人說他將立刻要做什麼？
（A）傳達訊息
（B）運送一些商品
（C）找遺失的東西

**解說** immediately是常做為線索的副詞。Send it裡的send可以改成ship，it是指漏掉的零件，也就是merchandise，所以（B）為答案。 答案 (B)

**詞彙** deliver 配送 merchandise 產品 locate 找出某物 missing 遺失

問題13～14請參考以下對話。美W 美M

| | |
|---|---|
| 1 找出核心語 | applying for, interviewed |
| 2 瞭解類型 | 詢問動作的對象、數量的簡短選項類考題 |
| 3 看選項 | 人事經理，研究分析師，編輯助理<br>一位，兩位，三 |
| 4 預測對話內容 | 申請編輯助理職位的人總共有兩位 |

W : Hi, Jeff. [13]I'm here to see if you're having any luck finding me an assistant editor.

M : Well, we've got a lot of applications. [14]I've narrowed it down to two candidates, so I'd like to set up interviews with them. Do you have time to meet with them next Tuesday?

W : I'm afraid I'm not available at that time. But I'm free Thursday morning.

女：你好傑夫，我來這兒看看你有沒有運氣幫我找到一個編輯助理。
男：嗯，我們收到了很多申請書。我已經將範圍縮小到兩個候選人了，所以我想和他們安排面試。你下星期二有時間與他們會面嗎？
女：恐怕那個時候我不行。但我星期四上午有空。

**詞彙** **assistant editor** 編輯助理 **application** 申請者 **narrow down** 縮窄 **candidate** 候選人 **set up** 決定；選定 **available** 能夠用的

**13.**

應徵者申請的是什麼職位？
（A）人事經理
（B）研究分析師
（C）編輯助理

**解說** 透過考題與選項可以猜測以「雇用／升遷／人事變動」為主體。透過「幫我找到一個編輯助理」與「我們收到了很多申請書、想和他們安排面試」，可以知道應徵者是來申請編輯助理職位的。 答案 (C)

**詞彙** **position** 職位 **apply for** 申請… **personnel** 人事部 **research analyst** 研究分析師

**14.**

有多少申請者將被面試？
（A）一位
（B）兩位
（C）三位

**解說** 該男性說「已經將範圍縮小到兩個候選人了，所以我想和他們安排面試」，所以申請者為兩位。 答案 (B)

**詞彙** **applicant** 申請者 **interview** 面試

## STEP 02 考題實戰練習

1. (C) 2. (A) 3. (D) 4. (D) 5. (D) 6. (C)
7. (C) 8. (A) 9. (A) 10. (B) 11. (B) 12. (D)

問題1~3請參考以下對話。澳W 美M

W : David, [2]I got a phone call from King Corporation. They want me to fax them a written confirmation for their reservations this weekend. Did you process that?

M : Well, let me check. Yes, [1]I've given them all single rooms on the second floor for Friday and Saturday night and booked a conference room for Saturday afternoon. Is that right?

W : Actually, you missed one thing. They asked to reserve a banquet hall for dinner on Friday night too.

M : Oh, I forgot about that. [3]I'll book a banquet hall as well as prepare a written confirmation so you can fax it to them right away.

女：大衛，我接到從金氏企業來的電話。為了這週末的預訂他們要我傳真確認函。你有處理了嗎？
男：嗯，我確認一下。是的，我給了他們週五和週六晚上在二樓所有的單人房間，並在週六下午預訂了一間會議室。這樣對嗎？
女：事實上，你漏掉了一件事。他們也要求保留在週五晚上晚餐的宴會廳。
男：噢，我忘了那個。我會預訂好宴會廳以及準備書面確認，讓你可以立刻傳真給他們。

**詞彙** **get a phone call from** 接到…打來的電話 **written confirmation** 書面確認 **reservation** 預約 **process** 做處理 **book** 預約 **conference room** 會議室 **miss** 忘記 **banquet hall** 宴會廳 **as well** 同樣地做好 **prepare** 準備 **right away** 立刻

**1.**

說話者很有可能在哪兒？
（A）在餐廳
（B）在銀行
（C）在旅館
（D）在商店

**解說** 為別人「提供單人房，預約會議室與宴會場」的人在哪裡工作呢？可以知道是飯店。 答案 (C)

**詞彙** **restaurant** 餐廳 **store** 商店

**2.**

為什麼金氏公司打電話來？
（A）為了確認預約
（B）為了詢問到旅館的方向
（C）為了要求降價
（D）為了和活動舉辦者見面

**解說** 該女性說「為了這週末的預訂他們要我傳真確認函」，所以可以知道來電的目的是為了確認預約。 答案 (A)

**詞彙** **confirm** 確認 **booking** 預約 **ask about** 詢問有關於… **directions** 前往的方向 **price reduction** 降價 **event organizer** 活動舉辦者

**3.**

這個男人說他會做什麼？
（A）打電話給金氏公司

（B）檢查傳真機
（C）做出一份菜單
（D）準備一份文件

**解說** I'll是詢問「下一個行程」考題的核心說法，接在後面出現的是「準備書面確認」，所以將這部份以概括性的敘述做變化來表達的（D）為答案。 答案 (D)

**詞彙** check for 確認某事 create 設計製出

問題4～6請參考以下對話。美W 美M

W : Hi, my name is Sara Wilson and [4]I ordered some books from your store yesterday. However, I don't think I will be home next week to receive the delivery. [5]Can you have the package delivered to my office, instead?

M : I'm afraid we've already sent out your order, Ms. Wilson. If no one confirms the receipt of the delivery, [6]the package will be returned to us. Then, we will call you to set up a new delivery date.

W : Then should I pay for an extra fee to get it?

M : In fact, yes, you should. There will be an additional charge.

女：您好，我的名字是莎拉威爾遜，我昨天從您的商店訂購一些書籍。但是，我想我下週不會待在家收到投遞。你可以把包裹改送到我的辦公室嗎？
男：恐怕我們已經送出您的訂單了，莎拉威爾遜女士。如果沒有人確認簽收，包裹將被退還給我們。之後，我們會打電話給您安排新的寄送日期。
女：那我該付額外的費用嗎？
男：實際上來說，是的，您應該是。這將有一筆額外的收費。

**詞彙** order 下訂單 receive 收到 delivery 配送 package 包裹 confirm 確認 receipt 領取 pay for 付費 extra fee 額外費用 in fact 事實 additional charge 額外費用

**4.**
這個男人可能在哪裡工作？
（A）在郵局
（B）在快遞公司
（C）在修理廠
（D）在書店

**解說** 這是詢問該男性的職業的考題。透過該女性說的「從您的商店訂購一些書籍」，可以知道該男性在書店工作。 答案 (D)

**詞彙** post office 郵局 delivery company 快遞公司 repair shop 在修理廠 bookstore 在書店

**5.**
為什麼這個女人聯絡這個男人？
（A）為了登廣告
（B）為了付運費
（C）為了討論遺失的貨物
（D）為了變更配送地址

**解說** 對於電話上的對話，問「為什麼聯絡」的考題是詢問主題的。仔細看該考題與選項之後，大概可以知道「訂貨／配送」類的主題。Can you後面出現「把包裹改送到我的辦公室」，所以（D）為答案。 答案 (D)

**詞彙** place an advertisement 登廣告 shipping charge 運費 missing 遺失 change 變更

**6.**
當這個男人收到這個女人的包裹時，他將會做什麼？
（A）保留它待領
（B）提供免費配送
（C）安排新配送時間
（D）給她退費

**解說** 「收到這個女人的包裹時」，這句話以該男性角度來說就變成「包裹將被退還給我們，之後…」。將後面出現的「安排新的寄送日期 」做變化來表達的（C）為答案。 答案 (C)

**詞彙** pickup 領取 refund 退費

問題7～9請參考以下對話。英M 澳W

M : Rachel, [7, 8]can you help Jeff with the work on how to market our new line of ice cream? Jeff asked me to find someone to work with him.

W : Why not? We used to collaborate before, and the results were always successful.

M : Yes, that's why Jeff suggested working with you. He is well aware that you're experienced in marketing ice cream, so he needs your advice.

W : Okay, [8, 9]let me call him to see if he can begin the project today. I want to get it started as soon as possible.

男：瑞琪爾，有關於如何向市場推出我們新的冰淇淋，你能夠幫忙傑夫嗎？傑夫要我找人和他一起做。
女：有何不可？我們之前曾經合作，結果總是很成功。
男：對了，這就是為什麼傑夫提議與你一起工作。他很清楚你在行銷冰淇淋上有經驗，所以他需要你的意見。
女：沒問題，讓我給他電話看看他是否可以今天開始這個計畫。我想盡快開始。

**詞彙** Why not? 為何不 use to 曾經 collaborate 共事 successful 成功的 suggest 建議 be aware that 知道

be experienced in 有經驗於 advice 建議 as soon as possible 儘可能的快

**7.**

說話者很有可能在什麼部門工作？

(A) 顧客服務
(B) 技術支援
(C) 行銷
(D) 會計

**解說** 思考「如何向市場推出新的商品」的部門是哪裡？就是行銷部門嘛！ 答案 (C)

**詞彙** customer service 顧客服務 technical support 技術支援 marketing 行銷 accounting 會計

**8.**

這個男人說傑夫要求了什麼？

(A) 計畫上的協助
(B) 對行銷預算的許可
(C) 不同的工作時間安排
(D) 轉換到其他分公司

**解說** 考題裡的Jeff requested，在對話裡變成Jeff asked來出現。透過後面出現的「要我找人和他一起做」與「開始這個計畫」，可以知道是為了一項計劃來要求協助的。 答案 (A)

**詞彙** approval 同意 budget 預算 transfer 轉換 branch 分公司

**9.**

這個女人接下來將會做什麼？

(A) 與同事聯絡
(B) 與一些顧客見面
(C) 參加研討會
(D) 面試求職者

**解說** let me是詢問「下一個行程」考題的核心說法，接在後面出現的是「給他電話看看」，所以將這部份做變化來表達的（A）為答案。Contact是比call還要更概括性的說法。 答案 (A)

**詞彙** contact 聯絡 co-worker 同事 customer 顧客 attend 參加 job candidate 工作候選人

問題10～12請參考以下對話。 美M 美W

M : Hi, Susan. I was a little late for the meeting and [10]I missed some parts of the meeting. Could you tell me what the sales manager said about the Hong Kong office?

W : He said the [11]Hong Kong group's doing great. They've boosted their sales this quarter by focusing on teenage consumers in their advertisement.

M : Great! So the manager suggests that we target younger people so our branch may raise our sales too, right?

W : You're right. And [12]he said another meeting is scheduled for next week to discuss the details.

男：您好，蘇珊。我開會有點晚到，錯過了會議裡某些部分。你能告訴我關於香港辦公室銷售經理說了些什麼嗎？

女：他說，香港團隊做得非常好。他們在本季廣告中對準青少年消費者大力宣傳，快速提高了銷售量。

男：太棒了！所以經理建議我們將目標放在更年輕的人，而我們的分部也就更能提高我們的銷售，對嗎？

女：你說得對。他說下週要開另一次會議來討論細節。

**詞彙** late 遲；晚 miss 錯過 part 部份 manager 經理 boost 強力推銷 focus on 聚焦於⋯ advertisement 廣告 target 目標 branch 分公司 raise 上升 detail 細節事項

**10.**

這個男人要求這個女人做什麼？

(A) 去另一間辦公室的方式
(B) 會議內容的詳情
(C) 廣告商清單
(D) 支援銷售提案

**解說** 仔細觀察這三個考題，可以知道「會議內容」為主題，似乎是與「業績／策略」相關的內容呢！透過man ask，可以知道是詢問要求事項的考題，所以在對話裡其答案線索為Could you tell me附近的內容。這個狀況是錯過了會議並要求對方告訴他相關內容，所以（B）為答案。 答案 (B)

**詞彙** how to 做⋯的方法 list 清單 advertiser 廣告商 assistance 支援；協助 proposal 提案

**11.**

香港辦公室的員工做了什麼？

(A) 設計了新產品
(B) 增加了銷售量
(C) 分析了銷售報告
(D) 完成了他們的訓練

**解說** 專有名詞通常會以相同的型式在考題與對話錄音裡出現，是簡單又重要的核心語。因此，將Hong Kong office改說Hong Kong group的部分附近會出現答案。Boost與increase是意思相近的單字。 答案 (B)

**詞彙** increase 增加 analyze 分析 finish 完成

**12.**

根據這個男人所言，下週將會發生什麼？

(A) 一位經理將退休。
(B) 一位客戶將抵達。
(C) 一間公司將被併購。
(D) 一場會議將被舉辦。

**解說** 這是詢問「下一個行程」的考題，且next week為核心語。該女性說「要開另一次會議來討論細節」，所以（D）為答案。 答案 (D)

**詞彙** occur 發生 retire 退休 customer 顧客 acquire 獲取 hold 舉行

## Chapter 15 與業餘活動、特定場所相關的考題

### Quiz I

1. (A) 2. (A) 3. (B) 4. (A)

**Q1** 美W 美M

W : Have you heard about the GWF Restaurant on Main Street?

M : Yes. **I saw** a really positive review **in the newspaper**. It said that the newly hired chef apparently specializes in international dishes.

女：你聽說了關於在大街上的GWF餐廳的事嗎？
男：是的。我在報上看到了很正面的評論。它說新聘用的主廚顯然專長於國際化的料理。

根據這段對話，這個男人在報紙上看到了什麼？
（A）一則評論家的評語
（B）一個職缺

**解說** 若先知道在報紙上常常出現的，是針對電影／表演／餐廳的評論，就可以猜測到對話主題為「電影／表演／外食／興趣」。因此將核心語saw與in the newspaper之間的positive review以概括性的敘述做變化來表達的（A）為答案。 答案 (A)

**詞彙** positive 正面的 review 評論 newspaper 報紙 apparently 看起來 specialize in 專長於… international 國際化的 dish 料理 critic 批評 job opening 職缺

**Q2** 澳W 英M

W : Hi, Jim, it's Mary. Do you **have any plans for the long weekend**?

M : Yes. I am excited to go to Dubai. I heard about some good restaurants near my hotel and also a wonderful museum in the city.

女：吉姆你好，我是瑪麗。這個長週末你有任何計畫嗎？
男：是的。我很興奮要去杜拜。我聽說在我住的旅館附近有一些不錯的餐廳，而且在市區也有很棒的博物館。

這個男人這週末將要做什麼？
（A）參觀一座城市
（B）舉辦派對

**解說** 透過考題裡的do this weekend，可以預測以「度假計劃」為主題。核心語weekend後面出現的「很興奮要去杜拜」，可以知道他要去參觀一座城市。 答案 (A)

**詞彙** plan 計畫 weekend 週末 museum 博物館 visit 參觀 hold 舉辦

Q3 澳W 英M

W : **This photocopier** is one of the most popular models we have in the store. **It comes with** complimentary copy papers and ink cartridges.

M : That's a good offer, but isn't it too difficult to install it by myself?

女：這台影印機是在我們店裡最受歡迎的款式之一。它附有免費的影印紙和墨水匣。
男：這是個很好的銷售活動，但是由我自己來安裝它不會太困難嗎？

什麼東西被包含於這台影印機的購買？
（A）免費安裝
（B）免費備品

**解說** 看考題與選項可以預測到對話的地點為「商店」。「和影印機一起提供…」的說法是以it comes with來表達的，而後面出現的免費的影印紙和墨水匣可以換成「免費備品」來表達。 答案 (B)

**詞彙** **photocopier** 影印機 **popular** 受歡迎 **come with** 與…一起的 **complimentary** 免費的 **offer** 提供 **by oneself** 藉由某人自己 **include** 包括 **installation** 安裝 **supply**（事務）用品

Q4 美W 美M

W : Dr. Min's office. How may I help you?

M : My name is John Clark. **I'd like to** make a dental appointment. I'd like to see a doctor as soon as possible. It seems I developed a cavity in one of my lower back teeth.

女：閩醫生辦公室。我能如何幫助您？
男：我的名字是約翰克拉克。我想要做牙科預約。我想要儘可能快點就診。在我的後下方牙齒好像有了蛀牙。

為什麼這個男人打電話到閩醫生辦公室？
（A）為了安排預約
（B）為了推銷產品

**解說** 透過考題與選項可以知道接電話的人工作的地方是「醫院」。為什麼打電話到醫院呢？聽對話之前已經可以預測到答案了，在核心說法I'd like to後面出現的「牙科預約」簡化成「預約」。 答案 (A)

**詞彙** **make an appointment** 做預約 **see a doctor** 就診 **as soon as possible** 儘可能的快點 **develop a cavity** 有了蛀牙 **lower back teeth** 後下方牙齒

## STEP 01 若沒答對會後悔的考題

| | | | |
|---|---|---|---|
| 1 (B) | 2 (A) | 3 (B) | 4 (A) |
| 5 (A) | 6 (B) | 7 (B) | 8 (A) |
| 9 (A) | 10 (A) | 11 (C) | 12 (A) |
| 13 (C) | 14 (C) | | |

1. 美M 澳W

| | |
|---|---|
| 1 找出核心語 | going to Tokyo |
| 2 瞭解類型 | 通勤／交通／搜尋或度假計劃 |
| 3 看選項 | 進行調查或拜訪同事 |

M : I heard you'll be taking off next week. Where are you **going**?

W : **To Tokyo**. I'm visiting a former colleague I got to be very close with when I worked there. I've been itching to meet her but I'm worried because the bank has been so busy lately. We're understaffed.

男：我聽說你下週將要休假。你要去哪裡？
女：去東京。我要去拜訪以前我在那裡工作時非常要好的同事。我很渴望與她見面但是我很擔心，因為銀行最近相當忙。我們的人員不足。

為什麼這個女人要去東京？
（A）為了進行調查
（B）為了拜訪以前的同事

**解說** 核心語going to Tokyo附近有答案。在選項中，將「拜訪以前的同事」的colleague改成了co-worker來表達。 答案 (B)

**詞彙** **take off** 休息 **former** 以前的 **colleague** 同事 **itching to** 對…渴望 **understaffed** 人員不足 **conduct a survey** 執行；進行 經營管理 **co-worker** 同事

2. 英M 美W

| | |
|---|---|
| 1 找出核心語 | not yet gone to the event |
| 2 瞭解類型 | 電影／表演／外食／興趣 |
| 3 看選項 | 沒空或不喜歡 |

M : **Have you been to the Magic Art exhibition yet?** It's amazing to see so many three-dimensional paintings and drawings.

W : **I wish. But** I've been too busy working since I got promoted to manager. How long will the exhibit be in town?

男：你去過神奇美術展了嗎？看到那麼多立體的繪畫和素描真令人感到驚奇。
女：我希望可以。但是自從我晉升成為經理工作一直很忙。這個展覽將會在市區多久呢？

為什麼這個女人還沒有去過這個活動？
（A）她沒有太多空閒時間。
（B）她不喜歡這項活動。

**解說** event是具體活動的概括性單字。在此將「工作一直很忙」改成了「沒有太多空閒時間」來表達。
答案 (A)

**詞彙** **exhibit** 展覽 **three-dimensional** 三度空間；立體的 **get promoted** 晉升 **event** 活動 **free time** 空閒時間

**3.** 美W 美M

| | |
|---|---|
| 1 找出核心語 | shopping for |
| 2 瞭解類型 | 商店 |
| 3 看選項 | 妹妹或兒子 |

W : Hi, I'm looking for a sweater. I hope to get it for my son's birthday next week. I think he'd like one of these sweaters but are any of these available in blue?
M : Unfortunately we don't have any blue sweaters in stock, but we can order one from our warehouse. They usually deliver in less than three days.

女：你好，我正在找一件毛衣。為了我兒子下個禮拜的生日我希望拿到它。我想他會喜歡這些毛衣的其中之一，但是這其中任何一件有藍色的嗎？
男：很不巧的我們庫存裡沒有任何藍色的毛衣，但是我們可以從我們的倉庫訂一件。他們通常會在三天之內配送。

這個女人買東西給誰？
（A）她的姊妹
（B）她的兒子

**解說** 透過核心語shopping for，可以知道這是在「商店」裡，店員與客人之間發生的對話。looking for為商店相關的核心語，藉由在其後面出現的「為了我兒子下個禮拜的生日我希望拿到它」，可以知道（B）為答案。
答案 (B)

**詞彙** **look for** 尋找 **sweater** 毛衣 **available** 能夠 **unfortunately** 不幸的；不巧 **warehouse** 倉庫 **deliver** 配送

**4.** 美W 英M

| | |
|---|---|
| 1 找出核心語 | Where |
| 2 瞭解類型 | 詢問對話地點的考題 |
| 3 看選項 | 錄影帶出租店或汽車出租店 |

W : Good morning. I want to return this videotape that I borrowed last week. Is it overdue?
M : Let me check. Oh, this was due last Friday. You have to pay a $1 late charge per day.

女：早安。我要還上週借的錄影帶。它逾期了嗎？
男：讓我確認一下。噢，上週五是到期日。你要付每日一元的逾期費。

這段談話很有可能是在哪兒發生的？
（A）錄影帶出租店
（B）汽車出租店

**解說** 這是詢問對話地點的考題。需要看著選項反向預測答案。若（A）為答案，可能會出現borrowed、return等的單字。若（B）為答案，可能會出現book或check out等的說法。對話裡出現的是歸還videotape的狀況，所以（A）為答案。
答案 (A)

**詞彙** **return** 歸還 **borrow** 借出 **overdue** 逾期 **due** 期限 **pay** 付費 **late charge** 逾期費 **per** 每… **take place** 發生 **video rental store** 錄影帶出租店

**5.** 英M 澳W

| | |
|---|---|
| 1 找出核心語 | Where |
| 2 瞭解類型 | 詢問對話地點的考題 |
| 3 看選項 | 藥局或餐廳 |

M : Hello, I'd like to get this prescription refilled please. My name is Mark Johnson and I have used this pharmacy before.
W : All right. As we're busy, it will take a little while. Why don't you come back in an hour to pick it up?

男：你好，我想要補充這個處方藥。我的名字是馬克強森，我之前利用過這間藥局。
女：好的。因為我們很忙，這將需要一段時間。你何不在一個小時後回來領取它呢？

說話者在哪裡？
（A）在藥局
（B）在餐廳

**解說** 這是詢問對話地點的考題。需要看著選項反向預測答案。若（A）為答案，可能會出現prescription等的單字。若（B）為答案，可能會出現order或menu等的單字。在此對話裡除了出現prescription，也聽得到「之前利用過這間藥局」，所以（A）為答案。 答案 (A)

**詞彙** **get prescription refilled** 以處方箋再次領藥 **pharmacy** 藥局 **come back** 回來 **pick up** 領取

**6.** 美M 美W

| | |
|---|---|
| 1 找出核心語 | call the bank |
| 2 瞭解類型 | 銀行 |
| 3 看選項 | 詢問營業時間或開戶資訊 |

M : Hello, **I'm calling to** know how long it usually takes to open a new bank account.

W : Well, usually it takes about half an hour except in the morning when our bank gets crowded. If you want to save some time, download the application form from our web site and fill it out before your visit.

男：你好，我打電話來是想知道開一個新帳戶需要多久時間？

女：嗯，除了早上我們銀行人很多的時候之外，平常大約要花半小時。如果你要省一點時間，在你來之前先從我們網站上下載申請表之後填寫它。

為什麼這個男人打電話給銀行？

（A）為了詢問營業時間

（B）為了得到開戶資訊

**解說** 透過考題可以知道該接電話的人在銀行工作。將核心語I'm calling to後面的「想知道開一個新帳戶需要多久時間」以概括性的敘述做變化來表達的（B）為答案。 答案 (B)

**詞彙** **open a bank account** 開銀行帳戶 **about** 大約 **crowded** 擁擠 **save** 存款 **download** 下載 **application form** 申請表 **fill out** 填寫 **inquire about** 詢問有關… **opening hours** 營業時間

**7.** 澳W 英M

| | |
|---|---|
| 1 找出核心語 | mechanic not able to help the woman |
| 2 瞭解類型 | 修理站 |
| 3 看選項 | 無法拿到零件或太忙 |

W : Hi. I'd like to drop off my car for repairs. I got into an accident last night.

M : Well, **our mechanic** is really busy today. But if you want to leave your car here tonight, we will call you to give you an estimate in the morning.

女：您好，我要把我的車留下來修理。我昨晚遇上了事故。

男：我們的修理師今天真的很忙，但如果你想今晚把你的車留在這兒，在早上我們會給你打電話來估價。

為什麼修理師今天無法幫忙這個女人？

（A）他無法拿到零件。

（B）他今天太忙。

**解說** 透過考題可以知道對話的地點為「修理站」。因此將「修理師真的很忙、早上會給你打電話」做變化來表達的（B）為答案。 答案 (B)

**詞彙** **drop off my car for repairs** 為了修車而把車留置 **accident** 事故；意外 **mechanic** 修理師 **leave** 留下 **give an estimate** 估計 **be able to** 能夠… **parts** 零件

**8.** 美W 英M

| | |
|---|---|
| 1 找出核心語 | fee |
| 2 瞭解類型 | 停車場或博物館 |
| 3 看選項 | 五元或二元 |

W : Excuse, me. I parked my car here in the parking area all this morning. But I found I am a little short of cash. Can I pay by credit card?

M : Yes, you can. Let me see how much you should pay. Well, you came here at 9:30 and now it's 11:30. **You owe** 5 dollars for 2 hours.

女：抱歉，我今天整個上午將車停在這個停車場。但是發現我現金有點不夠。我可以用信用卡支付嗎？

男：是的，可以。讓我看看你應該付多少。嗯，你在九點三十分到這兒，現在是十一點三十分。兩小時你要付五元。

費用是多少錢？

（A）五元

（B）兩元

**解說** 透過考題可以知道對話地點為「停車場」或「博物館」。在對話裡，將fee改成了「你要付」來表達，所以後面出現的五元為答案。 答案 (A)

**詞彙** **park** 停車 **parking area** 停車場 **all morning** 整個上午 **pay** 付費 **by credit card** 用信用卡… **owe** 尚未付的款項 **fee** 費用

問題9～10請參考以下對話。美W 英W

| | |
|---|---|
| 1 找出核心語 | discussing, see on the web site |
| 2 瞭解類型 | 詢問主題或行為對象的簡短選項類考題 |
| 3 看選項 | 購物中心，公寓，天氣 |
| | 購物中心，公寓，天氣 |
| 4 預測對話內容 | 透過廣告得知新購物中心的相關消息。 |

W1 : What a rainy day outside! [9]I was hoping that I'd go to the outdoor shops downtown today but not in this weather.

W2 : [9]Do you want to go to the Mega Mall with me instead? It's just opened.

W1 : That sounds good to me. I've wanted to shop there since [10]I saw the ad on the web site.

女：外面真是個大雨天了！我本來希望今天去市區的戶外商店，但不是在這樣的天氣。

男：你想改成和我一起去巨霸商場嗎？它是剛開業的。

女：這聽起來不錯。自從我在網站上看到了廣告，我一直想去那兒購物。

**詞彙** **a rainy day** 下雨天 **outdoor shop** 戶外運動用品店 **instead** 替換 **ad** 廣告

## 9.

這些女人主要在討論什麼？

（A）購物中心

（B）一間公寓

（C）天氣

**解說** 在對話裡，對於建議的說法「去商場」表達了同意，所以可以知道（A）為答案。 答案 (A)

**詞彙** **discuss** 討論 **shopping complex** 購買的東西 **apartment** 公寓 **weather** 天氣

## 10.

說話者在網站上看到了什麼？

（A）一則廣告

（B）一則評論家的評論

（C）天氣資訊

**解說** see on the web site為核心語，此對話裡在saw（由see變化而來）與on the web site之間會出現答案。Ad是advertisement的縮寫。 答案 (A)

**詞彙** **advertisement** 廣告 **critic** 批評 **review** 評論

問題11～12請參考以下對話。英M 美W

| | |
|---|---|
| 1 找出核心語 | Where, concern |
| 2 瞭解類型 | 詢問地點、主題的考題（問題狀況或令人擔心的事情也是一種主題） |
| 3 看選項 | 服裝店，街角，乾洗店 |
| | 需要快速服務，需要去電影院的方向，遺失票 |
| 4 預測對話內容 | 詢問有關快速服務的洗衣店。 |

M : Hi, [11, 12]I'd like to have this business suit cleaned for a banquet I am attending tonight. Can you do it right away?

W : [12]I'm afraid that I can't do it today. We are too busy to process your order at this time.

M : Okay. [11, 12]Are there any other dry cleaners that might be able to take care of my order?

男：您好，為了我今晚參加的宴會，我想要清洗這套西裝。你能馬上做嗎？

女：恐怕我今天沒辦法做。我們今天太忙而不能在這個時候處理您的要求。

男：好的。有任何其他的乾洗店可以處理我的要求嗎？

**詞彙** **business suit** 西裝 **cleaned** 清洗 **banquet** 宴會 **attend** 參加；出席 **right away** 立刻 **process** 處理 **dry cleaner** 乾洗 **take care of** 做處理

## 11.

說話者在哪兒？

（A）在服裝店

（B）在街角

（C）在乾洗店

**解說** 這是詢問對話地點的考題。透過「我想要清洗這套西裝」，可以知道是在乾洗店。 答案 (C)

**詞彙** **clothing store** 服裝店 **dry cleaner's** 乾洗店

## 12.

這個男人在擔心什麼？

（A）他需要快速完成的服務。

（B）他需要去電影院的方向。

（C）他遺失了音樂會的票。

**解說** 此狀況為乾洗店職員說「今天太忙而不能在這個時候處理」，所以該男性再找別的店，因此（A）為答案。 答案 (A)

**詞彙** **concern** 擔心 **finish** 完成 **quickly** 快速的 **directions** 方向 **theater** 電影院 **lose** 遺失

問題13～14請參考以下對話。美M 澳W

| | |
|---|---|
| 1 找出核心語 | Where, in Sydney |
| 2 瞭解類型 | 詢問地點、理由的句子選項類考題 |
| 3 看選項 | 戲院，辦公室，博物館 |
| | 參加會議，買房子，度假 |
| 4 預測對話內容 | 在博物館的男人說他正在雪梨度假。 |

M : Excuse, me. [13]Can you tell me where the science exhibit is being held?

W : It's on the second floor up to the main stairways to your left. [13]Have you ever been to our museum?

M : No. [14]This is the first time visiting to Sydney. I'm spending my vacation here at my uncle's house. He moved here several months ago.

男：抱歉，你能告訴我科學展覽在哪裡舉辦嗎？
女：在二樓，到你左邊的主樓梯間的空間。你有來過我們的博物館嗎？
男：沒有。這是我第一次來雪梨參觀。我在這兒我叔叔的家渡假。他在幾個月前搬到這裡的。

**詞彙** exhibit 展覽 hold 舉辦 stairway 樓梯 museum 博物館 move 搬移 several 數個

**13.**

說話者很有可能在哪兒？
(A) 在戲院
(B) 在辦公室
(C) 在博物館

**解說** 透過「科學展覽在哪裡舉辦」與「我們的博物館」，可以知道博物館為對話地點。 答案 (C)

**詞彙** theater 電影院

**14.**

為什麼這個男人在雪梨？
(A) 他正在參加會議。
(B) 他正在買房子。
(C) 他在渡假。

**解說** 地名或人名本身成為很好的核心語。對話裡出現Sydney，所以其附近有答案。該男性說在度假，(C) 即為答案。 答案 (C)

**詞彙** attend 參加；出席 conference 會議 buy 買 vacation 休假

## STEP 02 考題實戰練習

1. (A) 2. (B) 3. (A) 4. (A) 5. (B) 6. (D)
7. (B) 8. (C) 9. (A) 10. (B) 11. (A) 12. (C)

問題1～3請參考以下對話。英M 美W

M : I haven't been able to go out since [1]I moved into my new apartment. Finally, I'm done unpacking. So I can look around the city.

W : Well, [2]I recommend you go to the outdoor music concert this weekend.

M : I heard about that concert from a radio ad. The city holds it every year, right?

W : Yeah, unless you hate large crowds, you will have fun. There will be several music stages installed and [3]the local restaurants will be giving out samples of their food. I'm sure you'll be excited.

男：自從搬到新公寓後我一直無法出門。終於我都拆箱完畢了。因此我可以好好看看這個城市。
女：那麼，我建議你這週末去戶外音樂會。
男：我從電台廣告裡知道這個音樂會。城裡每年都舉辦。對嗎？
女：對啊，你會覺得很好玩的，除非你討厭一大堆人群。那邊會安裝幾個演出舞台還有當地的餐廳將會給免費試吃。我相信你會很興奮的。

**詞彙** go out 外出 finally 終於 unpack 拆封 look around 四處看看 recommend 建議 outdoor 戶外 ad 廣告 hold 舉行 install 設置 give out 分發

**1.**

這個男人最近做了什麼？
(A) 搬到一間新公寓
(B) 管理一間餐廳
(C) 申請一個職位
(D) 休假

**解說** 透過在前面部分出現的「自從搬到新公寓後我一直無法出門、終於可以好好看看這個城市」。可以知道「最近搬來的」。 答案 (A)

**詞彙** recently 最近 manage 管理 apply for 申請 open position 職缺 take time off work 休假

**2.**

這個女人建議了什麼？
(A) 在戶外市場購物
(B) 去一場音樂表演
(C) 聽廣播
(D) 與導遊商量

**解說** 核心語suggest在對話中是以recommend表達，在對話裡recommend附近會出現答案。 答案 (B)

**詞彙** performance 表演 consult 諮詢；商談 travel guide 旅行導覽

**3.**

當地的餐廳將會提供什麼？

（A）提供免費試吃
（B）持續營業到很晚
（C）舉辦烹飪課
（D）發行禮券

**解說** 對話裡的核心語為the local restaurants，將核心語附近的「給免費試吃」在選項裡中改以「提供免費試吃」來表達。 答案 (A)

**詞彙** provide 提供 offer 提供 complimentary 免費的 organize 舉辦 class 教室

問題4~6請參考以下對話。澳W 美M

W : Thank you for calling Ellen Jay Bookstore. What can I do for you?

M : Hello, I'd like to buy a newly released book, *Back To Nature*, reviewed in today's newspaper. But 4 I don't remember how to get to your store. Is it on 14th street or 16th street? I'm going to stop by your store on my way home.

W : Neither. We're located on 17th Street, and you need to walk three blocks down. However, 5 we're closing in five minutes. 6 You'll have to come tomorrow, instead. We're open at 9 a.m.

女：感謝您來電艾倫傑書店。我能為您做些什麼嗎？
男：您好，我想購買在今天的報上受評論的新上市的書「回歸自然」。但我不記得怎麼去你的店。是在第十四街還是十六街？我要在我回家的途中順便到你的商店。
女：都不是。我們位於第十七街附近，你需要往下走三個街區。但是我們在五分鐘內將打烊。您得明天再來，我們在上午九點營業。

**詞彙** bookstore 書店 newly released book 新上市的書 newspaper 報紙 stop by 順便去 on one's way 在…的途中 locate 位在 close 打烊 instead 做為替代

**4.**

為什麼這個男人要打電話？

（A）為了得到去書店的方向
（B）為了詢問營業時間
（C）為了要求配送
（D）為了取消一項訂購

**解說** 詢問來電的目的的考題是要詢問「主題」的。在核心說法I'd like to後面接著but，在but之後的內容即為答案。 答案 (A)

**詞彙** directions 方向 inquire about 詢問有關於… store's hours 營業時間 ask for 要求 delivery 配送

**5.**

有關於這家店這個女人說了什麼？

（A）它遷移到新地區。
（B）它快打烊了。
（C）某些項目缺貨。
（D）有個職缺。

**解說** 這是詢問意見的句子選項類考題，答案在於對話的後面部分。將「在五分鐘內將打烊」做變化來表達成「快打烊了」的（B）為答案。 答案 (B)

**詞彙** be about to 能夠… be short of …短缺 job vacancy 職缺

**6.**

這個女人要求這個男人做什麼？

（A）參考地圖
（B）稍晚再回撥電話
（C）完成某件工作
（D）明天到店裡來

**解說** 這是詢問要求事項的考題。將核心說法you'll have to後面出現的「明天再來」做變化來表達的（D）為答案。 答案 (D)

**詞彙** consult 參考 map 地圖 call back 回撥電話 later 稍晚一點 complete 參觀 visit 拜訪

問題7~9請參考以下對話。美W 英M

W : Thank you for calling Dr. Johnson's office. How may I help you?

M : Hello, my name is David Wilson, one of Dr. Johnson's patients. 8 I'm calling about the medicine he prescribed. I want to change it to another one.

W : I'm afraid 7 Dr. Johnson is away from the office to attend a medical conference. Since it doesn't seem to be an emergency, 9 let me put you through to Dr. Lee's office. She's been taking his job during his absence.

女：謝謝您來電強生醫生辦公室。我能給您什麼幫助嗎？
男：您好，我的名字是大衛威爾遜，是強生醫生的病人之一，我打電話來是有關他開給我的藥。我想改換成另一種。
女：很可惜強生醫生離開辦公室去參加一場醫學會議了。既然這事似乎不緊急，我把你電話接到李醫生的辦公室。在他不在時她一直代他的工作。

**詞彙** patient 病人 medicine 藥 prescribe 處方 away from 離開…的 conference 會議 emergency 緊急狀況 take 承擔 absence 不在

**7.**

強生醫生在哪裡？
（A）和病人在一起
（B）在一場會議
（C）在別的辦公室
（D）在渡假

**解說** 這不是詢問對話的地點，而是詢問特定人物所在地點的考題。Dr. Johnson的附近出現「離開辦公室去參加一場醫學會議」，所以（B）為答案。 答案 (B)

**詞彙** on vacation 休假中

**8.**

為什麼這個男人打電話到強生醫生的辦公室？
（A）為了說有關報告的事
（B）為了做預約
（C）為了討論處方
（D）為了有關帳單詢問

**解說** 透過該男性說的核心語calling about後面出現的「關他開給我的藥」與「我想改換成另一種」等的線索，可以知道（C）為答案。 答案 (C)

**詞彙** talk about 討論 presentation 演講 schedule an appointment 預約時間 ask about 詢問有關於… bill 帳單

**9.**

這個女人接下來很有可能會做什麼？
（A）轉接電話
（B）聯絡強生醫生
（C）做預約
（D）取消訂單

**解說** 這是詢問下一個行程的考題。將核心語let me後面出現的put you through改成類似說法的（A）為答案。 答案 (A)

**詞彙** transfer 轉換 contact 聯絡 make an appointment 做預約 cancel 取消

問題10～12請參考以下對話。澳W 美M

W : Hi, [10, 11]I saw a painting by John Harrison in the contemporary art wing, and I'm here to buy a print of it.

M : Sure, we have quite a few reproductions of past paintings here in the gift shop. Can you describe it in detail?

W : Okay, well, the painting's mostly green and it has a lot of grass in it. I think the painting was called 'Rural Scenery'.

M : Yes, I know that one. There are reproductions available in several different sizes. [12]Please find them on the second floor up to the main stairway.

女：您好，我在當代藝術的側廳看到了一幅約翰哈里森的畫，我來這兒買它的複製品。

男：當然，我們這裡的禮品店有很多以前畫作的複製品。你能描述的詳細些嗎？

女：好，那幅畫大多是綠色，而且裡面有許多草。我想那幅畫被稱為「田園風光」。

男：是的，我知道那個。它有幾種不同尺寸的複製品。請到二樓的樓梯間旁找它們。

**詞彙** painting 繪畫 contemporary 當代的 wing 側廳 quite 相當的 reproduction 製品 gift shop 禮物店 describe 說明 in detail 詳細的 grass 草 available in 可以於… stairway 樓梯

**10.**

說話者在哪兒？
（A）在塗裝用品店
（B）在博物館的禮品店
（C）在鄉間地區
（D）在售票處

**解說** 透過「看到了一幅畫」、「買印刷品」、「這兒禮品店」等的線索可以知道（B）為答案。 答案 (B)

**詞彙** paint supply shop 顏料用品店 museum 博物館 box office 售票處

**11.**

說話者們在討論什麼？
（A）一幅畫的複製品
（B）房子改裝
（C）雕刻品展覽
（D）鄉間旅行

**解說** 對話內容為「我來這兒買它的印刷品、在哪兒找得到」，所以「一幅畫的複製品」為其主題。 答案 (A)

**詞彙** remodeling 改裝；修改 sculpture 雕刻品 countryside 鄉村地區

**12.**

這個女人接下來很有可能會做什麼？
（A）登船
（B）買票
（C）到二樓去
（D）與有名的藝術家見面

**解說** 這是詢問該女性下一個行程的考題，在該男性的建議裡會出現答案線索。可以預測到，該女性聽到「請到二樓的樓梯間旁找它們」後，就會到二樓去。 答案 (C)

**詞彙** board 搭乘 famous 有名的 artist 藝術家

## Chapter 16 電話錄音

### Quiz |

1. (B)　2. (A)　3. (A)　4. (A)

**Q1** 美W

This is Emily Wang from Dr. Edgar's office. **I would like to speak with you about** your appointment at 4 p.m. tomorrow. As this is your first visit, please arrive 10 minutes earlier to fill out some forms.

我是埃德加醫生辦公室的艾蜜莉王。我想告訴您有關您明天下午四點的預約。由於這是您第一次來，請您提早十分鐘到填寫一些表格。

這通留言的目的是什麼？
（A）為了邀請一位演講者
（B）為了確認預約

**解說** 在考題裡看到message的同時，就可以知道該錄音為「電話錄音」類型。由考題的purpose也能知道這是詢問主題的，答案線索在錄音的前段／中間部分。錄音裡聽的到詢問主題類考題的核心語I'd like to speak with you，在此之後就有線索。將「我想告訴您有關您明天下午四點的預約」改成「為了確認預約」來表達的（B）為答案。　答案 (B)

**詞彙** appointment 預約　fill out 填寫　form 填寫
confirm 確認

**Q2** 美M

Hi, this is Mark Peterson from Central Bank. I was very impressed with your resume, and I would like to meet you for an interview. **Please bring** a picture ID on the interview date.

你好。我是中央銀行的馬克彼得森。我對你履歷的印象很深刻，因此為了面試我想跟你見面。在面試當日請你攜帶有照片的身份證件。

面試者被要求要帶什麼？
（A）有照片的身份證件
（B）文件影本

**解說** 在「電話錄音」類的錄音裡，詢問要求事項的考題其答案線索在錄音的後段部分。該錄音裡出現要求／建議的暗示please並接著出現bring，所以在此之後就有答案線索。將picture ID做變化來表達的（A）為答案。　答案 (A)

**詞彙** impressed 印象深刻的　resume 履歷表　bring 帶來
picture ID 有照片的　photo identification 身份證件　copy
有照片的身份證件　document 影印本

**Q3** 美W

**You have reached** Alabama Power Company. Residents in the downtown area are currently experiencing a power outage. If you want to talk to a customer service representative, please stay on the line.

您所聯絡的是阿拉巴馬電力公司。市中心區的居民目前是停電的。若您想和客服專員說話，請等待別掛斷。

這位打電話者想要聯絡什麼人？
（A）電力公司
（B）網路服務供應商

**解說** 考題裡的trying to reach告訴你該錄音為「電話錄音」類型，且看到選項就可以知道是「機構的自動語音系統錄音」。這是詢問說話者的考題，答案線索在you have reached附近。Power company是指電力公司，所以使用相似詞的（A）為答案。　答案 (A)

**詞彙** power company 電力公司　resident 居民
downtown area 市中心區　currently 目前
power outage 停電　representative 專員
stay on the line 在線上等待　electric company 電力公司
provider 供應商

**Q4** 澳W

If you want to make a reservation, **press '1' now.** If you want to leave a message please wait for the beep and then begin speaking.

若您想預約，請按「1」。若您想留言，等到聽見嗶聲再開始說話。

為什麼打電話者會按「1」？
（A）為了預約
（B）為了留言

**解說** 看考題就可以知道該錄音為「機構的自動語音系統錄音」。Press 1為核心語，所以press 1 now附近就有答案線索。出現了與錄音裡相同說法make a resevation的（A）為答案。　答案 (A)

**詞彙** make a reservation 預約　press 按　leave a message 留言　wait for 等…　beep 嗶聲

### STEP 01 若沒答對會後悔的考題

| | | | |
|---|---|---|---|
| 1 (A) | 2 (A) | 3 (B) | 4 (B) |
| 5 (A) | 6 (A) | 7 (B) | 8 (A) |
| 9 (C) | 10 (C) | 11 (A) | 12 (B) |
| 13 (B) | 14 (B) | | |

**1.** 英M

| | |
|---|---|
| 1 找出核心語 | purpose of the message |
| 2 類型與答案的位置 | 類型與答案的位置 |
| 3 看選項 | 重新安排時間或參加運動俱樂部 |

Hello, Annie. This is Brian from Bodies Athletic Club. **I'm calling to** inform you that we have to reschedule this weekend's soccer game for next Saturday.

安妮您好。我是身體運動俱樂部的布萊恩。我打電話是要通知您，我們需要把這週末的足球比賽重新安排到下週六了。

這通留言的目的是什麼？
（A）為了重新安排一場比賽
（B）為了參加運動俱樂部

**解說** 透過考題裡的message與選項，就可以知道該錄音為「個人電話留言」類型。這是詢問主題的考題，答案線索出現於錄音的前段／中間部分。將核心語I'm calling to後面出現的「要通知您，我們需要把這週末的足球比賽重新安排」做變化來表達的（A）為答案。

答案 (A)

**詞彙** **inform** 通知 **reschedule** 重新安排（時間） **this weekend** 這個週末 **join** 加入

**2.** 美W

| | |
|---|---|
| 1 找出核心語 | caller reached |
| 2 類型與答案的位置 | 主題／前面、中間部分 |
| 3 看選項 | 重新安排時間或參加運動俱樂部 |

**You've reached** the Tokyo branch of International Bank. We are not open today. Our business hours are 9 a.m. to 4 p.m., except on weekends and national holidays.

安妮您好。我是身體運動俱樂部的布萊恩。我打電話是要通知您，我們需要把這週末的足球比賽重新安排到下週六了。

這通留言的目的是什麼？
（A）為了重新安排一場比賽
（B）為了參加運動俱樂部

**解說** 透過考題裡的message與選項，就可以知道該錄音為「個人電話留言」類型。這是詢問主題的考題，答案線索出現於錄音的前段／中間部分。將核心語I'm calling to後面出現的「要通知您，我們需要把這週末的足球比賽重新安排」做變化來表達的（A）為答案。

答案 (A)

**詞彙** **business hours** 通知 **except** 重新安排（時間） **national holiday** 這個週末 **embassy** 加入

**3.** 美M

| | |
|---|---|
| 1 找出核心語 | speaker work |
| 2 類型與答案的位置 | 說話者／前面部分 |
| 3 看選項 | 會計部門或行銷部門 |

Hi, Mary, **this is Jason** from the marketing department. I would like to know if you want to join us for our accounting director, Mr. Johnson's retirement party tonight.

瑪莉你好。我是行銷部門的傑森。我想知道你要不要跟我們一起參加我們會計部門經理強生先生的退休晚會。

說話者工作於什麼部門？
（A）會計部門
（B）行銷部門

**解說** 詢問說話者為誰的考題，答案線索都是在錄音的前段部分。From是出現公司或部門名稱時的線索。

答案 (B)

**詞彙** **marketing department** 行銷部門 **accounting director** 會計部門經理 **retirement party** 退休派對

**4.** 澳W

| | |
|---|---|
| 1 找出核心語 | intended for |
| 2 類型與答案的位置 | 聽話者／前面部分 |
| 3 看選項 | 旅館員工或旅館顧客 |

**Thank you for calling** the Oceanview Hotel. **If you are calling to** make a reservation, please press '1'. For further assistance, please press 'zero' to be connected to an operator.

感謝您致電海洋風景飯店。若您打電話要預約，請按「1」。若需要別的服務，請按「0」來聯絡總機人員。

這通留言是為誰的？
（A）旅館的員工們
（B）旅館的顧客們

**解說** 透過考題裡的message與選項，就可以知道該錄音為「機構的自動語音系統錄音」類型。透過intended for，可以知道這是詢問聽眾為誰的考題，答案在錄音的前段部分。連接到的地方是旅館，訂房的人就是「旅館的顧客」。

答案 (B)

**詞彙** make a reservation 預約 press 按 assistance 幫助；服務 operator 總機人員 employee 職員 customer 顧客

**5.** 英M

| | |
|---|---|
| 1 找出核心語 | problem |
| 2 類型與答案的位置 | 論及問題／中間部分 |
| 3 看選項 | 庫存不足或支付完成 |

Hi, Ms. Kim, this is Mark from Central Bookstore. I am calling regarding the book you ordered. **Unfortunately**, it's sold out. I can place a special order if you don't mind waiting a few days for delivery.

金先生您好，我是中央書店的馬克。我打電話過來是有關於您所訂購的書。很不幸的，它都售完了。若您不介意再等幾天配送，我可以下特別訂單。

這個問題是什麼？
（A）有個東西不能提供了。
（B）帳單已經付了。

**解說** 詢問電話錄音裡是什麼問題狀況的考題，答案線索出現於錄音的中間部分。表示問題狀況的核心語為unfortunately，其後面的「都售完了」就是這裡的問題狀況。Available是有庫存的狀況，但這裡有not，所以是沒有庫存的意思。 答案 (A)

**詞彙** regarding 有關於… order 訂購 unfortunately 很不幸的 sold out 售完 place an order 下訂單 don't mind -ing 不介意 wait 等待 delivery 配送 available 可用的 payment 支付

**6.** 美M

| | |
|---|---|
| 1 找出核心語 | why closed |
| 2 類型與答案的位置 | 具體內容／前面部分 |
| 3 看選項 | 整修或國定假日 |

Hello. This is an automated message from Verto's Law Firm. We're sorry but we are closed all through this week **because** our office is being remodeled. Please call back next week.

你好。這是維多法律事務所的自動留言。很抱歉我們這週之內都不上班，因為我們的辦公室正在整修當中。請下週再次來電。

為什麼最近辦公室不上班？
（A）由於整修
（B）由於國定假日

**解說** 透過考題裡的「為什麼不上班」，就可以知道該錄音為「機構的自動語音系統錄音」類型。將核心語because後面出現的「辦公室整修」做變化來表達的（A）為答案。 答案 (A)

**詞彙** automated message 自動留言 law firm 法律事務所 all through this week 持續於這週內 remodel 整修 call back 再次來電 due to 由於… renovation 整修

**7.** 英M

| | |
|---|---|
| 1 找出核心語 | suggest |
| 2 類型與答案的位置 | 要求事項／後面部分 |
| 3 看選項 | 回撥電話或訪問門市 |

Hello, Ms. William, this is Brian from Anna Home Design. I wanted to tell you that the living room chairs you ordered aren't available in brown, but the gray fabric is available. I think you will like them in the gray fabric, too, but **need you to** stop by the store to confirm. Thank you.

威廉小姐您好。我是安娜住宅設計的布萊恩。我想跟您說，您訂購的客廳椅子沒有咖啡色的，但是有的灰色布料。我覺得您也會喜歡那些灰色的布料，不過需要您順路到門市確認。謝謝。

打電話者建議接聽電話的人做什麼？
（A）回撥電話
（B）到門市來

**解說** 透過考題裡的caller，可以知道是「電話錄音」類型，由suggest得知這是詢問要求／建議事項的考題。答案出現於後段部分，將核心語need you to後面出現的「順路到」做變化來表達的（B）為答案。 答案 (B)

**詞彙** order 訂購 be available in 顏色 有…顏色的 fabric 布料 stop by 順路拜訪 confirm 確認 return the phone call 回撥電話 visit 訪

**8.** 美W

| | |
|---|---|
| 1 找出核心語 | ask |
| 2 類型與答案的位置 | 要求事項／後面部分 |
| 3 看選項 | 在線上等候或按1 |

Thank you for calling Anywhere Tour Agency. All our lines are busy due to high volume of calls. **Please** hold the line, and our next available agent will answer your call shortly.

謝謝您撥電話到環遊旅行社。由於大量的來電，我們所有的專線都被佔用當中。請等待別掛斷，我們下一個有空的人員會立即接聽您的電話。

說話者要求打電話者做什麼？
（A）在線上等候

（B）按「1」

**解說** 對撥電話的人提出要求的錄音是「機構的自動語音系統錄音」。答案在錄音的後段部分，核心語please後面出現的「等待別掛斷」，用相同意思來表達的（A）為答案。 答案 (A)

**詞彙** lines are busy 專線被佔用當中 volume of calls 通話量 hold the line 在線上等候 available 有空的 answer the call 接電話 shortly 立即 stay on the line 在線上等候

問題9～10，請參考以下訊息。澳W

| | |
|---|---|
| 1 找出核心語 | business / closed |
| 2 類型與答案的位置 | 類型與答案的位置 說話者／前面部分 |
| | 具體內容／中間部分 |
| 3 看選項 | 餐廳，電影院，辦公用品店 |
| | 星期一，星期五，星期日 |
| 4 預測對話內容 | 聯絡到了辦公用品店，但週末休息 |

[9]Thank you for calling Fine Office Supplies, your place for the lowest prices on office supplies. Sorry, but we are currently closed. [10]Our hours of operation are from 10 a.m. to 6 p.m. on weekdays. If you would like to browse our stock and shop online, please visit our web site. Thank you.

謝謝您致電精品辦公用品店，最低價辦公用品的總匯。很抱歉我們現在不營業。我們營業時間為平日上午十點至下午六點。若您想瀏覽我們的貨物以及線上購物，請至我們的網站。謝謝。

**詞彙** the lowest prices 最低價 office supply 辦公用品 closed 不營業的 hours of operation 營業時間 on weekdays 在平日 browse 瀏覽 shop online 線上購物 visit 訪問

**9.**

這是什麼型態的公司？
（A）餐廳
（B）電影院
（C）辦公用品店

**解說** 透過考題裡的business（營業場所）與「不營業」，就可以知道這是「機構的自動語音系統錄音」，因此考題是在詢問說話者為何，答案會在錄音的前段部分。核心語Thank you for calling後面出現的名稱與「最低價辦公用品的總匯」都是答案的線索。 答案 (C)

**詞彙** movie theater 電影院

**10.**

這家店什麼時候不營業？
（A）星期一
（B）星期五
（C）星期日

**解說** 在「機構的自動語音系統錄音」裡，營業時間公告是在中間部分出現。聽到「營業時間為平日」，所以可以猜測到週末是打烊的。 答案 (C)

**詞彙** store 商店

問題11～12，請參考以下訊息。英M

| | |
|---|---|
| 1 找出核心語 | man calling / ask |
| 2 類型與答案的位置 | 主題／前面、中間部 |
| | 要求事項／後面部分 |
| 3 看選項 | 傳遞訊息，重新安排會議 |
| | 得到同事的電話號碼 |
| | 到行銷部門，打電話，搭上早班班機 |
| 4 預測對話內容 | 為了通知而撥電話，並要求回電 |

Good morning, Ms. Baker. This is Dan Henry calling from the marketing department. [11]Mr. Shawn asked me to let you know that he will be a little late for the 1:30 meeting with you. He's going to be back a little later from New York. [12]Please call directly on his cell phone at 217-555-4738. Thank you very much.

貝克爾小姐早安。我是行銷部門的丹亨利。尚恩先生要我通知您，和您約在一點半的會議他會晚一點到。他稍晚會從紐約回來。請直接撥電話到他的行動電話217-555-4738。謝謝。

**詞彙** marketing department 行銷部門 meeting 會議 a little later 稍晚 directly 直接 cell phone 行動電話

**11.**

為什麼這個男人打電話來？
（A）為了傳遞一項訊息
（B）為了重新安排會議
（C）為了得到同事的電話號碼

**解說** 這是「個人電話留言」類錄音，且該考題為詢問主題的，所以答案在前段／中間部分。答案線索是接在自我介紹後面就出現。「通知」也可以說成是「傳遞一項訊息」。（B）是陷阱，因為這是Mr. Shawn的來電目的，並非錄音裡撥電話者的目的。 答案 (A)

**詞彙** deliver 配送 reschedule 重新安排時間 co-worker 同事 phone number 電話號碼

**12.**

這個男人要求接聽電話的人做什麼？
(A) 來到行銷部門
(B) 打電話
(C) 搭上很早的班機

**解說** 這是詢問「個人電話留言」裡的要求事項的考題，答案線索在錄音的後段部分。將核心語please後面出現的「直接撥電話到他的行動電話」做簡化來表達的（B）為答案。 答案 (B)

**詞彙** make a phone call 撥電話 catch 搭乘 early flight 早班飛機

問題13～14，請參考以下訊息。美W

| | |
|---|---|
| 1 找出核心語 | complaint / ask |
| 2 類型與答案的位置 | 論及問題／中間部分 |
| | 要求事項／後面部分 |
| 3 看選項 | 貨物受損，貨物還沒送到，送錯東西 |
| | 退還總金額，打電話，立刻配送貨物 |
| 4 預測對話內容 | 訂購的商品尚未到達，而要求回電 |

Hello there. [13]I'm calling about a problem with my order. My name is Gina Rotelli and my order number is SBB-934. [13]I was promised delivery within two weeks of the date I placed the order, but it still hasn't come in. [14]Please check on this and give me a call today. My number is 555-0703. Thank you.

你好。我打電話過來是有關於我的訂單的問題。我的名字是吉娜羅泰里，我的訂單編號是SBB-934。我得到的保證是我下訂單之後兩週內配送，但它還沒有來。請確認這點，並在今天給我電話。我的號碼是555-0703。謝謝。

**詞彙** problem 問題 order 訂單 delivery 配送 place an order 下訂單 come in 進來 check 確認

**13.**

這個打電話的人在抱怨什麼？
(A) 送來的貨物受損了。
(B) 貨物還沒送到。
(C) 送錯東西了。

**解說** 透過考題裡的caller可以知道這是「個人電話留言」類錄音。Complaint是「論及問題」類的核心語，相關答案線索在錄音中間部分出現。將「還沒有來」做變化來表達的（B）為答案。 答案 (B)

**詞彙** complaint 抱怨 arrive 到達 damaged 受損的 wrong item 不對的商品 deliver 配送

**14.**

打電話的人要求這家公司做什麼？
(A) 退還總金額
(B) 打電話
(C) 立刻配送貨物

**解說** 這是詢問要求事項的考題。將核心語please後面出現的「請確認、給我電話」做簡化來表達的（B）為答案。 答案 (B)

**詞彙** refund 退款 amount 金額 right away 立刻

## STEP 02 考題實戰練習

| | | | | | |
|---|---|---|---|---|---|
| 1. (C) | 2. (A) | 3. (A) | 4. (C) | 5. (A) | 6. (C) |
| 7. (B) | 8. (B) | 9. (D) | 10. (D) | 11. (C) | 12. (A) |

問題1～3，請參考以下訊息。美M

Hi, Erica. [1]This is Madison Morton calling from Westwood Furniture store, and I'm a sales manager. I'm calling about the dress hanger you ordered from us last week. [2]Unfortunately, the second type model you selected is not in stock. We can place a special order for it but I don't think we can get it in less than two months. However, we have the third type model available now. So [3]I'd like to know whether you want to order the third type model or would rather wait for the second type model. I will leave for the day around six, so please call me back as soon as you get this message. Thank you.

您好，艾瑞卡。這是西木傢俱店麥迪森摩頓的留言，我是銷售經理。我是有關上週您和我們訂購的衣架來電的。很不巧的，您選的第二款沒有庫存。我們可以下特別訂單，但我不認為我們能在兩個月之內拿到。然而，我們目前有第三款可提供。所以我想知道您是否要訂購第三款，或寧願等第二款。我今天六點左右會離開，所以當您聽到這個留言，請儘快回電給我。謝謝！

**詞彙** furniture 傢俱 sales manager 銷售部門負責人 dress hanger 衣架 unfortunately 不幸的 type 類型 select 挑選 in stock 有庫存的 place an order 下訂單 get 得到 available 可用的 wait for 等待 leave for the day 下班 as soon as …之後立刻 get the message 收到留言

**1.**

打電話者是什麼人？
(A) 一位會計
(B) 一位服裝製造商
(C) 一位行銷經理
(D) 一位時尚設計師

**解說** 透過考題裡的caller與problem，可以知道這是「個人電話留言」類錄音。該考題是詢問說話者為誰的，所以其答案線索在錄音的前段部分。在前段的自我介紹的話語裡可以直接聽到「行銷經理」。 答案 (C)

**詞彙** accountant 會計師 clothing maker 衣服製造業者

**2.**

這個問題是什麼？

（A）有個東西沒有了。

（B）有些文件遺失了。

（C）有些產品被損壞了。

（D）配送延誤了。

**解說** 問題狀況通常出現於電話錄音的中間部分。透過核心語unfortunately，可以知道將「沒有庫存」做變化來表達的（A）為答案。 答案 (A)

**詞彙** item 商品 document 文件 missing 遺失的 product 產品 damaged 受損的 delivery 配送 late 晚；延誤

**3.**

這個打電話者想由艾瑞卡這兒知道什麼？

（A）她想要的款式。

（B）她回到辦公室的時間。

（C）特別訂購項目的費用。

（D）預計收貨的時間。

**解說** 在電話錄音裡，要求事項出現於後段部分。將核心語I'd like to know後面出現的「是否要訂購第三款，或寧願等第二款」以概括性的敘述做變化來表達的（A）為答案。 答案 (A)

**詞彙** return 回來 cost 費用 specially 特別 expected 預估的 arrival time 到達時間

**問題4～6，請參考以下訊息。** 美W

[4] Thank you for calling the offices of Family Security Systems, the company that takes care of all your insurance needs. We are sorry we're not here to take your call right now because of the national holiday. We are open from 9 a.m. to 5 p.m. Monday through Friday, and closed on weekends and holidays. [5] If this is an emergency, please press 1. An agent is available to assist you immediately 24 hours a day. [6] To register a change in your mailing address using our automated system, press 2. You may also change your address and check your policy on our company's web site at www.fss.com. We hope you enjoy the holiday.

感謝您致電家庭安全系統辦公室，我們處理您所有的保險需求。我們很抱歉，目前因國定假日，我們不上班無法接聽您的電話。我們週一至週五早上九點到下午五點營業，週末和假日休息。若您有緊急情況，請按一。有代理人員可二十四小時立即協助您。若需要用我們的自動系統登記變更您的通訊地址，請按二。您也可以變更您的地址和確認您的保單於我們公司的網頁www.fss.com。祝您佳節愉快。

**詞彙** take care of 照顧；處理 insurance 保險 national holiday 國慶假日 emergency 緊急狀況 press 按 available 可用的；有空的 assist 幫助 immediately 立刻 24 hours a day 一天二十四小時 register 登記 automated system 自動系統 policy 條款

**4.**

家庭安全系統是什麼型態的公司？

（A）警察局

（B）旅行社

（C）保險公司

（D）鎖製造商

**解說** 透過第二個考題裡的「要按幾號鍵」，可以知道是「機構的自動語音系統錄音」類。第一個考題是詢問說話者為誰，答案線索在錄音的前段部分。透過在核心語thank you for calling後面出現的「我們處理您所有的保險需求」，可以猜測為「保險公司」。 答案 (C)

**詞彙** police station 警察局 travel agency 旅行社

**5.**

緊急狀況應該要按幾號鍵？

(A) 1

(B) 2

(C) 5

(D) 9

**解說** 這是詢問各個號碼所提供的資訊是什麼的考題。錄音內容裡，在urgent problem的相關詞emergency附近有答案。 答案 (A)

**詞彙** urgent 緊迫的

**6.**

為什麼某些人會看網站？

（A）為了收到樣品

（B）為了找到最近的服務點

（C）為了登錄地址變更

（D）為了預約洽談

**解說** 在網頁上通常會出現附加資訊。與此有關的答案線索大部分出現於錄音的後段部分，也就在web site附近。將「變更您的地址和確認您的保單」做簡化來表達的（C）為答案。 答案 (C)

**詞彙** receive 收到 nearby 附近的 location 地點 reserve 預約 consultation 洽談

**問題7～9，請參考以下訊息。** 英M

Hello, this message is for Mr. Jefferson. My

name is John Franklin. [7]I'm calling regarding the electronics engineering position posted in today's newspaper. I'm sure that I am an excellent candidate for the position. [8]I have over 5 years of experience working for an electronics company. I designed circuit layouts for a variety of electronics products. Also, I was the leader of my team for the last 2 years. I will be visiting near your downtown office next week so I was wondering if I could show you my previous work at that time. [9]I will send you a copy of my resume this afternoon. I hope to hear from you soon. Thanks and have a good day.

您好，這是給傑佛森先生的留言。我的名字是約翰富蘭克林。我打電話是因注意到今天報紙上刊登的電子工程師職位。我肯定我會是這個職位出色的候選人。我在一家電子公司工作已經有超過五年的經驗。我為多種電子產品設計電路佈局。而在過去兩年我也是團隊的領導者。下週我會在你們市中心辦公室的附近，所以我在想，那時是否能給你們看我以前設計的電路佈局。今天下午我會寄出我的簡歷給您。希望能很快得到您的回覆。謝謝，祝您有美好的一天。

**詞彙** **regarding** 有關於… **electronics engineering position** 電子工程師職位 **posted** 公佈的 **newspaper** 報紙 **candidate** 申請者 **design** 設計 **circuit layout** 電路佈局 **a variety of** 多種的 **wonder** 想知道 **at that time** 那時候 **copy** 影印本 **resume** 履歷表

**7.**

這通留言的目的是什麼？
(A) 為了訂一項電子產品
(B) 為了申請一個職缺
(C) 為了追蹤一項申請進度
(D) 為了得到一家公司的資訊

**解說** 透過考題裡的message與she will do，可以知道是「個人電話留言」。該考題是詢問主題的，答案線索在錄音的前段／中間部分。透過在核心語I'm calling regarding後面出現的「因注意到今天報紙上刊登的電子工程師職位」，可以猜測到（B）為答案。（C）是有關已提交申請書之後的狀況，所以不是答案。 答案 (B)

**詞彙** **electronics product** 電子產品 **apply for** 申請 **job opening** 職缺 **follow up on** 追蹤 **application** 申請；申請書 **get information** 得到資訊

**8.**

這位打電話者有關於她自己說了什麼？
(A) 她在報社工作。
(B) 她有相關的經驗。
(C) 她聽說了很多關於這家公司的事。
(D) 她最近搬到這個地區。

**解說** 個人電話留言的中間部分，通常出現與主題相關具體內容，所以該考題的答案就在這兒。將「有超過五年的經驗」做變化來表達「有相關的經驗」的（B）為答案。 答案 (B)

**詞彙** **relevant** 相關的 **recently** 最近 **move to** 搬到… **area** 地區

**9.**

這個女人說她將要做什麼？
(A) 順道拜訪這間辦公室
(B) 給對方看合約
(C) 下週回電
(D) 提交履歷

**解說** 這是詢問下一個行程的考題。該類考題的答案線索通常在錄音後段部分，並且有核心語I will出現。將「寄出我的簡歷」做變化來表達的（D）為答案。 答案 (D)

**詞彙** **stop by** 順道拜訪 **contract** 合約 **call back** 回撥電話 **submit** 提交

**問題10～12，請參考以下訊息。** 澳W

[10]You've reached Countway Computers. We value your call. All of our lines are busy now. If you want to inquire about our computer products, hang up and dial 222-3456. If you would like to speak to a customer service representative, please stay on the line and your call will be answered in turn. [11]Right now there is a wait of approximately five minutes. Otherwise, please leave a brief voice mail message with your name and telephone number by pressing 2. [12]Your call will be returned by our next available customer service representative. Thank you.

您已連接至康威電腦。我們重視您的來電。目前所有線路均忙線中。如果你想詢問我們的電腦產品，請掛斷電話並撥打222-3456。如果您希望與服務人員通話，請在線上等候，您的電話將被依序應答。目前大約要五分鐘等候。或是您可以按二，留下您的姓名和電話號碼的語音訊息。我們下一位服務人員將回撥給您。謝謝您。

**詞彙** **reach** 聯絡到 **value** 珍惜 **line** 電話專線 **busy** 忙線中 **hang up** 掛斷電話 **dial** 撥打電話 **representative** 專員 **stay on the line** 在線上等候 **answer** 回應 **in turn** 輪流 **voice mail message** 語音信箱留言 **press** 按

**10.**

這個打電話者聯繫的可能是什麼型態的公司？
(A) 網路服務供應商
(B) 電影院
(C) 汽車修理廠
(D) 電腦公司

**解說** 透過考題裡的caller reached，可以知道該錄音是

「機構的自動語音系統錄音」類。這是詢問說話者為誰的考題，答案線索在錄音的前段部分。透過其公司名稱，可以猜測到是「電腦公司」。「我們的電腦產品」也是答案的線索。 答案 (D)

**詞彙** **provider** 供應商 **movie theater** 電影院 **auto repair shop** 汽車修理廠

### 11.

這個打電話者需要等多久？
（A）一分鐘
（B）兩分鐘
（C）五分鐘
（D）十分鐘

**解說** 這是詢問具體事項的考題，答案出現於錄音的中間部分。追踪數字也是找答案的好方法。出現「五分鐘等候」，所以（C）為答案。 答案 (C)

**詞彙** **wait** 等候

### 12.

為什麼接聽電話的人會按「2」？
（A）為了要有電話回覆
（B）為了訂票
（C）為了詢問產品
（D）為了瞭解付費的方式

**解說** 這是詢問各個號碼所提供的資訊是什麼的考題。Press 2附近會出現答案。按2號的話，可以留姓名與電話號碼，同時下一位能夠接電話的服務員會回覆，所以（A）為答案。 答案 (A)

**詞彙** **reserve** 預約 **payment option** 支付方法

# Chapter 17 正式公告 I

## Quiz I

1. (A) 2. (A) 3. (A) 4. (A)

### Q1 美W

Thank you for coming to today's meeting. I have a quick announcement before we start our meeting. The repainting of the underground parking garage will begin tomorrow and it's going to last three days. So, please park in the outdoor parking area.

謝謝你們來到今天的會議。在我們開始會議之前，我有個簡短的公告事項。地下停車場重新塗裝工程將明天開始，而且會持續三天。因此，請在戶外停車區停車。

這則談話主要的目的是什麼？
（A）公告維修工作
（B）招募工作志願者

**解說** 這是詢問公告主題的考題。「地下停車場重新塗裝工程」是屬於維修工程。 答案 (A)

**詞彙** **announcement** 公告 **repaint** 重新塗裝 **underground** 底下的 **parking area** 停車區 **maintenance** 維修

### Q2 英M

I've asked you all here for a short meeting to discuss our quarterly sales report. Sales went down by 10 percent. **I'd like** all of you to think of the reasons for the decline and come up with new strategies for increasing sales.

我召集你們開簡短的會議，是為了討論我們的季度銷售量報告。銷售掉了百分之十。我希望你們全部都思考其減少的原因，而且為了增加銷售量想出新的策略。

說話者要求聽眾做什麼？
（A）對於改善計劃做腦力激盪
（B）策劃季度銷售資料

**解說** 會議上的公告裡，要求事項會出現於錄音後段部分。將核心說法I'd like後面出現的「思考其減少的原因，而且為了增加銷售量想出新的策略」做變化來表達的「對於改善計劃做腦力激盪」為答案。 答案 (A)

**詞彙** **quarterly sales report** 季度銷售量報告 **go down** 掉下 **reason** 原因 **decline** 減少 **come up with** 想起（新的想法） **strategy** 策略 **brainstorm** 腦力激盪 **improvement** 改善 **draw up** 策劃

### Q3 美W

Ladies and gentleman, I'm sorry to announce that tonight's baseball game will be pushed back by one hour due to heavy rain conditions.

各位女士，各位先生。很抱歉要公告今晚的棒球比賽，由於豪雨的狀況將延後一個小時。

這則公告很有可能是在哪裡發出的？
（A）在戶外運動場
（B）在商店裡

**解說** 會聽到廣播延期棒球比賽的地方，應該就是棒球場吧。 答案 (A)

**詞彙** **announce** 公告 **baseball game** 棒球比賽 **push back** 延後 **heavy rain** 豪雨 **condition** 狀況 **stadium** 戶外（露天）運動場

### Q4 澳W

Attention, shoppers. The store will be closing in ten minutes. **Please** proceed to the checkout counter immediately to complete your purchase. Thank you for your cooperation.

各位顧客請注意。本店即將在十分鐘之內打烊。請立刻到收銀台來完成您的採購。謝謝您的合作。

說話者建議顧客做什麼？
（A）到結帳處
（B）和經理做確認

**解說** 考題裡有suggest，就是在詢問要求事項的。將核心語please後面出現的「到收銀台來」當中的proceed改成go來表達的（A）為答案。 答案 (A)

**詞彙** **shopper** 顧客 **proceed** 到 **checkout counter** 收銀台 **immediately** 立刻 **complete** 完成 **cooperation** 合作 **customer** 客人 **check with** 和…確認

## STEP 01 若沒答對會後悔的考題

| | | | |
|---|---|---|---|
| 1 (A) | 2 (B) | 3 (A) | 4 (B) |
| 5 (B) | 6 (A) | 7 (A) | 8 (B) |
| 9 (B) | 10 (C) | 11 (A) | 12 (C) |
| 13 (B) | 14 (C) | | |

### 1. 英M

| | |
|---|---|
| 1 找出核心語 | speaker work for |
| 2 瞭解類型 | 說話者／前面部分 |
| 3 看選項 | 連鎖咖啡店或人力中介公司 |

First on our staff meeting agenda today, I'd like to tell you about the results of our customer survey. As you may know, we conducted a nationwide survey among our customers at all of our 100 coffee shop locations.

今天員工會議的第一個議題，我想告訴你們我們的顧客調查結果。如同你們可能知道的，我們在我們全部一百個咖啡店地點，對我們的客人執行了全國性的調查。

說話者在什麼型態的公司工作？
（A）連鎖咖啡店
（B）人力仲介公司

**解說** 這是詢問說話者為誰的考題。在公告裡，說話者與聽話者相關的答案線索會在前段部分出現。聽到「我們全部一百個咖啡店地點」，可以知道說話者是在連鎖咖啡店工作。 答案 (A)

**詞彙** **agenda** 議題 **result** 結果 **survey** 調查 **conduct** 執行 **nationwide** 全國性的 **location** 地點

### 2. 美W

| | |
|---|---|
| 1 找出核心語 | purpose of the talk |
| 2 瞭解類型 | 主題／前面部分 |
| 3 看選項 | 討論增加資金的計畫，或介紹新同事成員 |

Good afternoon. I'm glad you could all make it to this meeting. **I'm very pleased to** introduce our new accountant at the GW Theater, James Donovan. Mr. Donovan brings a great deal of money management experience to the job.

午安。我很高興你們全部都能來到這場會議。我非常高興介紹我們在GW戲院的新的會計師詹姆是唐納文。唐納文先生把相當多的資金管理經驗帶到這份工作上。

這則談話主要的目的是什麼？
（A）為了討論增加資金的計畫
（B）為了介紹新同事成員

**解說** 若錄音的前段部分出現introduce，很有可能是屬於「會議上公告」的「人物介紹」類型。將「新的會計師」做變化來表達成「新同事成員」的（B）為答案。 答案 (B)

**詞彙** make it 能夠前來 introduce 介紹 accountant 會計師 theater 戲院 bring 帶來 a great deal of 相當多的 management 管理 raise 籌（款）

**3.** 美M

| | |
|---|---|
| 1 找出核心語 | ask |
| 2 瞭解類型 | 要求事項／後面部分 |
| 3 看選項 | 送出某項要求給人事部門，或立即報告問題狀況 |

Before we start today's meeting, I'd like to tell you about the new company policy. From now on, **you must** submit your vacation requests not to your immediate supervisor but to the personnel department. Thank you for your cooperation.

在我們開始今天會議之前，我想告訴你們新的公司政策。從今以後，你們的休假申請單不是給你們的直屬上司，而是得要提交給人事部門。謝謝你們的合作。

說話者要求聽眾做什麼？
(A) 送出某項要求給人事部門
(B) 立即報告問題狀況

**解說** 將詢問要求事項的考題的核心說法you must後面的「提交休假申請單」做變化來表達的（A）為答案。 答案 (A)

**詞彙** policy 政策 from now on 從此以後 submit 提交 vacation request 休假申請單 immediate supervisor 直屬上司 personnel department 人事部門 cooperation 合作 report 合作 problem 問題 immediately 立即

**4.** 澳W

| | |
|---|---|
| 1 找出核心語 | asked to check for |
| 2 瞭解類型 | 要求事項／後面部分 |
| 3 看選項 | 工作時間表或每日的公告 |

I just want to give a quick reminder to all workers on the assembly line. As soon as you get here in the morning, **check** the display board next to the factory manager's office for daily notices.

我想給在裝配線上所有的員工一項簡短的提醒。當早上你們一到這裡，就要確認工廠經理辦公室旁邊公佈欄上的當日公告。

聽眾被要求要確認什麼？
(A) 工作時間表
(B) 每日的公告

**解說** 核心語check後面出現「工廠經理辦公室旁邊公佈欄上的當日公告」，所以可以知道所要求事項是要確認「每日的公告」。 答案 (B)

**詞彙** quick 簡短的 reminder 提醒 assembly line 裝配線 as soon as 一…就 get 到達 display board 公佈欄 factory 工廠 daily 當日的

**5.** 英M

| | |
|---|---|
| 1 找出核心語 | topic of the meeting |
| 2 瞭解類型 | 主題／前面部分 |
| 3 看選項 | 搭乘計程車或辦公室花費 |

Thank you for taking time to come to this meeting. Let me get straight to the point. As you all know, many of you have been making unauthorized charges to the office expense account for things such as lunches and taxi rides that are not related to your jobs.

謝謝你們撥冗來到這場會議。讓我直接切入重點。如同你們都知道的，你們當中很多人將未經許可的費用記在辦公室消費帳戶上，例如和你們的工作無關的午餐和計程車費用等。

會議的主題是什麼？
(A) 搭乘計程車
(B) 辦公室花費

**解說** 透過考題可以知道該錄音為「會議上的公告」。這是「未經許可的費用不可以記在辦公室消費帳戶上」的內容，所以（B）為答案。 答案 (B)

**詞彙** take time 撥冗 unauthorized 未經許可的 charge 費用 expense 消費 account 帳號 taxi ride 計程車 related 有關聯的 job 工作

**6.** 美M

| | |
|---|---|
| 1 找出核心語 | Where |
| 2 瞭解類型 | 公告地點／前面部分 |
| 3 看選項 | 飛機或火車 |

Attention passengers. This is your captain speaking. I hope you're enjoying the flight. It's a beautiful day out there. However, the radar indicates that we will be experiencing some turbulence soon, so please fasten your seat belt and stay in your seats.

各位乘客請注意。我是機長。我希望您正在享受飛行當中。外面的天氣很好。但雷達顯示我們將快經歷氣流，所以請繫安全帶，而且留在您的座位上。

這則公告是在哪裡發出的？
（A）在飛機上
（B）在火車上

**解說** 能聽到「我是機長」的地方，就是在飛機上了。 答案 (A)

**詞彙** **captain** 機長 **radar** 雷達 **turbulence** 氣流；亂流 **fasten** 繫緊 **stay** 留

**7.** 英M

| | |
|---|---|
| 1 找出核心語 | event taking place |
| 2 瞭解類型 | 主題／前面部分 |
| 3 看選項 | 表演或歡迎會 |

Hello, everyone! **Welcome to** Palmer Theater. I know you're all looking forward to an exciting evening. Before this evening's performance begins, I have a couple of reminders.

大家好！歡迎來到帕瑪戲院。我知道你們都很期待一個很令人興奮的晚上。在今晚的表演開始之前，我有兩個提醒事項。

什麼活動將被舉辦？
（A）一場表演
（B）一場歡迎會

**解說** 透過「歡迎來到戲院」與「表演開始」，可以知道即將要發生的事情就是「表演」。 答案 (A)

**詞彙** **theater** 戲院 **performance** 表演 **a couple of** 兩個的 **reminder** 提醒事項 **take place** 發生 **play** 表演 **reception** 歡迎會

**8.** 美W

| | |
|---|---|
| 1 找出核心語 | asked |
| 2 瞭解類型 | 要求事項／後面部分 |
| 3 看選項 | 測試警鈴或做日常的工作 |

Attention, employees. The fire alarm system is being tested this morning. You may hear the alarm go off several times through the morning. When you hear the alarm, **please** remain calm and continue with your usual routine. Thank you for your patience.

各位同仁請注意。今天早上火災警報系統將被測試。在整個早上您會聽到警報響起多次。在您聽到警報時，請保持平靜並持續做您日常的工作。感謝您的耐心。

員工被要求去做什麼？
（A）測試警鈴
（B）做他們日常的工作

**解說** please為詢問要求事項考題的核心語，透過在其後面出現的「保持平靜並持續做您日常的工作」，可以知道（B）為答案。 答案 (B)

**詞彙** **alarm** 警報 **go off** 響起 **through** 在整個… **remain calm** 保持平靜 **continue** 持續 **routine** 日常工作 **patience** 耐心

**問題9～10，請參考以下訊息。** 澳W

| | |
|---|---|
| 1 找出核心語 | report say, happen next |
| 2 類型與答案的位置 | 具體事項／中間部分 |
| | 下一個行程／前面部分 |
| 3 看選項 | 廣告成功，顧客滿意，銷售下降 |
| | 舉辦發表會，發出回應卡，討論調查結果。 |
| 4 預測對話內容 | 意見調查表示顧客滿意，所以另外討論。 |

Good afternoon. I'm glad so many of you could make it to this meeting. I'd like to share the results of our recent customer survey. As you know, we conducted a survey to find ways to boost our sales. Overall, [9]customers show satisfaction with our product designs and our competitive prices. In front of you, you'll find the complete results of the survey. [10]Let's discuss them now point by point.

午安。我很高興你們這麼多人能來到這場會議。我想分享我們最近的顧客意見調查結果。如您所知，我們為了大幅增加銷售量執行了調查。大致上，顧客對我們產品的設計和具有競爭力的價格表達了滿意。在你們面前，你們會看到完整的調查結果。現在我們針對每一項討論吧。

**詞彙** **make it** 達到 **share** 分享 **result** 結果 **survey** 意見調查 **conduct** 執行 **boost** 大幅增加 **customer** 顧客 **satisfaction** 滿意 **competitive** 具有競爭力的 **complete** 完整的 **discuss** 討論 **point by point** 針對每一項

**9.**

這份調查報告說了什麼？
（A）廣告成功了。
（B）顧客很滿意。
（C）銷售下降了。

**解說** 透過「執行了調查、顧客對我們產品表達了滿意」，可以知道「顧客很滿意」。 答案 (B)

**詞彙** **report** 報告書 **advertisement** 廣告 **successful** 成功的 **satisfied** 滿意的 **decline** 下降

**10.**

根據這則談話，接下來將會發生什麼？

(A) 這個團體將舉辦發表會。
(B) 將發出回應卡。
(C) 這個調查結果將被討論。

**解說** let's為詢問「下一個行程」的考題的核心說法，其後面出現的「針對每一項討論吧」，即是指對於意見調查結果進行討論。 答案 (C)

**詞彙** **happen** 發生 **make a presentation** 發表 **give out** 分發 **survey result** 調查結果

問題11～12，請參考以下訊息。 英M

| | | |
|---|---|---|
| 1 找出核心語 | announcement for, asked | |
| 2 類型與答案的位置 | 說話者／前面部分 | |
| | 要求事項／後面部分 | |
| 3 看選項 | 員工們，購物者，觀光客 | |
| | 填表格，和保全經理談話， | |
| | 確認有沒有遺失的東西 | |
| 4 預測對話內容 | 向員工公告：請確認是否遺失什麼東西 | |

[11]Attention all staff. This is Alex Kim, the security manager at Walters Corporation. A set of house keys was found in the cafeteria this morning at approximately 10:30 a.m. [12]Please check your wallets, pockets, and purses to make sure you haven't misplaced your keys. If you think the keys are yours, please come to the main office and ask for Mr. Chang to identify them. Thank you.

各位同仁請注意。我是沃特企業的保全經理艾力克司金。今天早上大概十點半的時候，在自助餐廳發現了一套房子的鑰匙。請看看你們的皮夾、口袋和手提包來確認你們是否將鑰匙放錯地方。如果你覺得這些鑰匙是你的，請來到總辦公室並找張先生來認領。謝謝。

**詞彙** **cafeteria** 自助餐廳 **approximately** 大概 **wallet** 皮夾 **pocket** 手提包 **purse** 放 **misplace** 錯地方

## 11.

這則公告是要給誰的？
(A) 員工們
(B) 購物者
(C) 觀光客

**解說** 這是詢問公告的對象，就是詢問聽眾為誰的考題，答案在錄音的前段部分，而且通常在attention後面出現。此題又出現了將staff改成employees來表達的方式。 答案 (A)

**詞彙** **employee** 員工 **shopper** 顧客 **visitor** 訪客

## 12.

聽眾被要求做什麼？
(A) 填表格
(B) 和保全經理談話
(C) 確認有沒有遺失的東西

**解說** please為詢問要求事項的考題的核心語，其後面出現的「請確認你們是否將鑰匙放錯地方」，指的就是「確認有沒有遺失的東西」的意思。 答案 (C)

**詞彙** **fill out** 填寫 **form** 表格 **security manager** 保全經理 **missing** 遺失的 **item** 東西

問題13～14，請參考以下訊息。 美M

| | | |
|---|---|---|
| 1 找出核心語 | Where, park until the garage is completed | |
| 2 類型與答案的位置 | 地點／前面部分 | |
| | 要求事項／後面部分 | |
| 3 看選項 | 停車場，辦公室，購物中心 | |
| | 在街上，沿著轉角 | |
| 4 預測對話內容 | 在購物中心停車場 | |
| | 在辦公室停車相關的公告 | |

[13]This is the facility manager with an important announcement for all company employees. Since our company is building a new parking garage that will replace the old parking lot we've been using, [14]all employees should park their cars across the street during construction. We've made special arrangements with the shopping center to use one of their lots. We apologize for the inconvenience, but it'll be worth it.

我是設備管理者。對於全公司員工我有項很重要的公告。由於我們公司正在建設新的停車塔以取代我們一直以來用的舊停車場，在施工當中所有的員工們得將車子停在對面。我們和那邊的購物中心做了特約來使用他們的停車場。造成不便很抱歉，但這是值得的。.

**詞彙** **facility** 設備 **important** 重要的 **announcement** 公告事項 **build** 建設 **parking garage** 停車塔 **replace** 代替 **parking lot** 停車場 **park** 停車 **construction** 施工 **arrangement** 約定 **apologize** 道歉 **inconvenience** 不便 **worth** 值得

## 13.

這則公告很有可能是在哪裡發出的？
(A) 在停車場
(B) 在辦公室
(C) 在購物中心

**解說** 「由於正在建設新的停車塔，所以將車子停在別的地方」這不能視為在停車場廣播的公告，應該是在辦公室對職員做的公告。 答案 (B)

**詞彙** office 辦公室 shopping mall 購物中心

**14.**

聽眾直到車庫完工前，應該在哪兒停車？
(A) 在街上
(B) 沿著轉角
(C) 在購物中心停車場

**解說** 先說「員工們得將車子停在對面」，接著說「和那邊的購物中心做了特約來使用他們的停車場」，所以就是「在購物中心的停車場停車」的意思。在此必須注意，是在對面停車而不是在街上停車的。 答案 (C)

**詞彙** completed 完成的 corner 角落

## STEP 02 考題實戰練習

1. (B) 2. (B) 3. (D) 4. (A) 5. (C) 6. (B)
7. (C) 8. (A) 9. (C) 10. (B) 11. (A) 12. (B)

**問題1～3，請參考以下訊息。** 美W

Good afternoon, passengers for Star Train 157 to Budu station. [1]We are sorry to inform you of the change in our departure time. Unfortunately, a disabled train was ahead of us and it caused a serious delay. Several maintenance crews are working on it now, and it should be moved off the tracks in 10 minutes. [2]The train is now scheduled to depart at 5:45 p.m. The boarding process will begin shortly. [3]Please stay adjacent to the gate.

午安，搭乘一五七星際列車到巴度站的乘客們。我們抱歉通知您出發時間變更，一台故障的列車停在前方，因而造成嚴重的延誤。維修工班現在正處理中，列車應該在十分鐘內會離開軌道。火車目前定於下午五時四十五分離開。不久將開始登車。請待在閘口附近。

**詞彙** passenger 乘客 inform 通知 change 變更
departure time 出發時間 unfortunately 很不幸的
disabled 拋錨的 cause 造成 serious 嚴重的 delay 延誤
maintenance crew 維修團隊 track 鐵路
be scheduled to 動詞原形 預定… depart 出發
boarding process 登記程序 shortly 不久；立刻 stay 留
adjacent to 接近…的 gate 出入口

**1.**

為什麼出發時間要重新安排？
(A) 設備的一小部份壞了。
(B) 有一台故障的火車。
(C) 有些鐵軌還沒有被修理。
(D) 鐵道封閉了。

**解說** 透過考題與選項就知道該錄音為火車站裡的公告。聽到「一台故障的列車停在前方」，所以 (B) 為答案。 答案 (B)

**詞彙** departure 出發 reschedule 重新安排時間
equipment 裝備 broken 故障的 malfunctioning 不正常運作的 repair 修理 railway 鐵道 closed 關閉的

**2.**

火車離開的時間是什麼時候？
(A) 在下午四點三十分
(B) 在下午五點四十五分
(C) 在下午六點十五分
(D) 在下午八點三十分

**解說** 在錄音裡就可以聽到「火車目前定於下午五時四十五分離開」。 答案 (B)

**3.**

乘客們被要求做什麼事？
(A) 依團體編號上車
(B) 看指南手冊
(C) 確認他們的座位分配
(D) 待在出發閘口附近

**解說** please為詢問要求事項的考題的核心語，在其後面出現的「待在閘口附近」以同義詞來表達的 (D) 就是答案。 答案 (D)

**詞彙** board 搭乘 according to 依照… look at 看…
guidebook 旅行指南 assignment 安排 departure gate 出發閘口

**問題4～6，請參考以下訊息。** 英M

As you all know, our network equipment sales have gone up. We expect that sales will continue to increase, so we're planning to start a new branch in Busan in early August. [5]I've been appointed to head the sales department in Busan, [4]so I will be leaving my position as sales manager in July. Several new employees will be hired to deal with the increased business. [6] All of you are invited to consider the possibility of transferring to Busan. Please give us some feedback within the next few weeks if you're interested in making this move.

如同大家所知道的，我們在首都地區的網絡設備銷售量上升了。我們期待銷售量將繼續增加，所以我們計劃在八月初開始在釜山有新的分公司。我被安排帶領釜山銷售部門，所以我在七月離開銷售經理的職位。將有幾位新員工被雇用來處理增加的業務，當然，同樣的機會也會給予公司內經驗豐富的銷售代表們。邀請大家考慮轉換到釜山的可能性。若您有興趣此一變動，請在未來幾週之內給我們回應。

**詞彙** equipment 裝備 go up 增加 branch 分部 appoint 任命 head 領導 sales department 銷售部門 leave 離開… position 職位 hire 僱用 deal with 處理 invite 邀請 consider 考慮 possibility 可能性 feedback 反饋 interested 有興趣的 move 移動

### 4.

說話者是什麼人？
(A) 一位銷售經理
(B) 一位維修工人
(C) 一位軟體設計師
(D) 一位維修技師

**解說** 聽到「離開銷售經理的職位」就知道說話者為銷售經理。 答案 (A)

**詞彙** maintenance work 維修工人 designer 設計師 repair technician 維修技師

### 5.

在七月將會發生什麼事？
(A) 一家公司將結束運作。
(B) 一棟新大樓的整修將會開始。
(C) 說話者將調動到新城市。
(D) 一場發表將在會議中被舉辦。

**解說** 特定時間點是很重要的核心語，所以錄音裡July附近就有答案。將「被安排帶領釜山銷售部門，所以我在七月離開銷售經理的職位」以概括性的敘述做變化來表達的（C）為答案。 答案 (C)

**詞彙** operation 營運 renovation 整修 transfer 調動 make a presentation 做發表

### 6.

說話者要求聽眾考慮什麼事？
(A) 遵守計畫的最後期限
(B) 調到不同的辦公室
(C) 招募更多員工
(D) 變更一棟大樓的設計

**解說** 「be invited to 動詞原型」是「被鄭重要求做…」的意思，屬於詢問要求事項的考題的核心說法。在另一個核心語consider後面出現了「轉換到釜山的可能性」，將此做變化來表達的（B）就是答案。 答案 (B)

**詞彙** meet 處理；面對 deadline 截止期限 recruit 招募 modify 變更；修正

**問題7~9，請參考以下訊息。** 澳W

Good morning, everyone. [7] I would like to start the meeting by extending a warm welcome to Danny Kim, our new marketing analyst. Danny worked for Chungsol Motors, where he has been analyzing data on consumer trends in China over the past five years. As you all know, [8] we've signed the deal with several large dealers in Korea and Japan to sell a line of our vehicles. We value Danny's experience and [9] are sure that it will help us determine which of our newest lines of cars are likely to appeal to consumer taste in those two countries.

大家早。我以熱烈的歡迎新的營銷分析師丹尼金來開始這個會議。丹尼曾任職於青松汽車，在過去五年做中國的消費趨勢數據分析的工作。大家都知道，我們簽下韓國和日本的幾家大的經銷商銷售我們的車輛。我們重視丹尼的經驗，並相信這將幫助我們確定哪種我們新系列車子，在這兩個國家能吸引消費者的口味。

**詞彙** analyst 分析師 analyze 分析 customer 顧客 trend 趨勢 sign 簽名 deal 交易 dealer 經銷商 sell 銷售 value 重視 determine 決定 be likely to 可能會… appeal to 被…吸引

### 7.

這則談話主要的目的是什麼？
(A) 為了檢討工作成果
(B) 為了分配一項新計畫
(C) 為了介紹一名新員工
(D) 為了在新工作上給予指示

**解說** 詢問公告主題的考題，答案線索總是在錄音的前段部分。在此出現「熱烈的歡迎新的營銷分析師」，所以「介紹一名新員工」為目的。 答案 (C)

**詞彙** review 檢討 performance 成果；業績 assign 分配 introduce 介紹 instructions 指示 task 工作；任務

### 8.

說話者的公司銷售的是什麼型態的產品？
(A) 汽車
(B) 廚房用品
(C) 行動電話
(D) 行銷服務

**解說** 出現了兩次「我們的車輛」，所以將此以同義詞來表達的（A）為答案。 答案 (A)

**詞彙** automobile 汽車 kitchen appliance 廚房用品 mobile phone 行動電話

### 9.

這家公司要金先生做什麼事？
(A) 管理海外分公司
(B) 訓練新員工
(C) 協助瞭解顧客的偏好
(D) 簽署銷售合約

**解說** 「幫助我們確定哪種新系列車子能吸引消費者的口味」是指這位被介紹者要做的事。換句話說，就是該公司要這個人做這項工作。 答案 (C)

**詞彙** manage 管理 overseas 海外的 branch 分公司

train 訓練 understand 瞭解 preference 偏愛
contract 合約

問題10～12，請參考以下訊息。美M

[10]Attention shoppers. Our store will be closing in twenty minutes. Please make your final selections and proceed to the checkout lane. Don't forget to stop by the produce department for today's specials. There are fresh vegetables and a variety of fruit on sale, but only for a few more minutes. The customer service counter is now closed. [11]Please direct all questions to the manager on duty. [12]Shoppers purchasing fifteen or fewer items can use express checkout lanes. Just follow the red signs to the express lanes at the front of the store. Thank you for shopping with us, and we look forward to seeing you again.

顧客們請注意。我們的商店將在二十分鐘內打烊。請完成您的選購並前往結帳通道。別忘了於農產品部看看今天的特價品。有新鮮的蔬菜和多種水果在拍賣，但只限最後這幾分鐘。目前客戶服務櫃檯已關閉。所有的問題請直接向值班經理洽詢。購買十五個或更少項目可以使用快速結帳通道。只需依照店前方的紅色標誌前往快速結帳通道。感謝您來店購物，我們期待再次見到您。

**詞彙** shopper 顧客 final selection 最後的選擇 proceed to 往…移動 checkout line 收銀台 stop by 順便訪問 produce department 農產品專區 special 特價品 a variety of 多種的 on sale 有折扣的 customer service counter 客服櫃檯 closed 關閉的 direct questions to 向…詢問 manager 負責人 on duty 執行任務當中的 fewer 少於… item 商品 look forward to -ing 期待…

**10.**

這則公告主要的目的是什麼？
(A) 為了通知新的安全程序
(B) 為了公告商店要打烊
(C) 為了介紹付費的方式
(D) 為了廣告肉品的價格

**解說** 詢問公告主題的考題，答案線索會在錄音的前段部分出現。聽到「將在二十分鐘內打烊」，所以（B）為答案。 答案 (B)

**詞彙** announcement 公告 inform 通知 safety procedure 安全措施程序 closing 關閉 introduce 介紹 payment 支付 advertise 廣告 price 價格

**11.**

有疑問的顧客被指示到哪裡？
(A) 找經理
(B) 到結帳處
(C) 到詢問處
(D) 到客戶服務台

**解說** 這是詢問具體事項的考題。在錄音的中間部分會聽到「請直接向值班經理洽詢」，所以答案為（A）。 答案 (A)

**詞彙** question 疑問 be directed to 被指向於… information center 詢問處

**12.**

誰可以使用快速結帳處？
(A) 買蔬菜的人
(B) 買少於十五樣東西的人
(C) 等候超過二十分鐘的人
(D) 簽署意見調查表的人

**解說** 特定的名詞也能成為核心語。在Express checkout lane附近會聽到「購買十五個或更少項目的購物者」，這就是答案。 答案 (B)

**詞彙** buy 買 wait 等待 sign 簽名 survey form 意見調查表

## Chapter 18 正式公告 II

### Quiz I

1. (A)　2. (A)　3. (A)　4. (A)

### Q1 美W

**Welcome** everyone, and congratulations on starting a new career here at Mary Kacy Cosmetics. My name is Rebeca Mori, and I'm the sales manager. Let me start off by saying how happy we are to have you as part of the Mary Kacy Cosmetics sales team.

歡迎大家。恭喜你們在瑪莉凱西化妝品公司開始新的職業生涯。我的名字叫瑞貝卡莫莉。我是銷售部門的經理。請讓我開始來表達對於你們加入瑪莉凱西化妝品公司的銷售團隊我們有多高興。

聽眾很有可能是在哪兒？
(A) 在員工迎新會
(B) 在頒獎宴會

**解說** 透過考題與選項可以知道該錄音為活動相關公告。錄音內容裡，在welcome後面通常出現活動名稱。這是恭喜聽眾開始新的職業生涯，所以是在員工歡迎會上的話語。. 答案 (A)

**詞彙** **career** 職業生涯 **start off** 開始 **be happy to 動詞原型** 很高興… **as part of** 以…的一部分 **employee orientation** 員工歡迎會 **award banquet** 頒獎宴會

### Q2 英M

Make sure to make an appointment to get your I.D. photo taken before noon. We will have a short lunch break at 12:30, and then **in the afternoon**, each of you will meet the managers you'll be working with.

請你們確實記得預約並拍你們身份證的照片。我們在十二點半將會有簡短的午餐休息時間，然後在下午的時候你們每個人將要與和你們一起工作的經理見面。

聽眾將會在下午做什麼？
(A) 與經理見面
(B) 為了身份證拍照

**解說** 時間點為很好的核心語。錄音的後段部分出現in the afternoon，接著聽得到「和經理見面」。 答案 (A)

**詞彙** **make an appointment** 預約 **I.D. photo** 身份證照片 **lunch break** 午餐休息時間 **work with** 和…一起工作

### Q3 英M

Good morning, class. My name is Tran, and I will be your biology professor this semester. I've been teaching at York College for over 15 years, and before that I was a student here, just like the rest of you. I'm going to begin tonight by talking about the scientific method.

全班同學，早安。我的名字叫泉恩。我將成為你們這個學期的生物課教授。我在約克大學教書教了十五年以上。之前，我和你們其他人一樣也是這裡的學生。今天晚上我想就討論科學的方法來開始。

這個演講的聽眾很有可能是什麼人？
(A) 學生們
(B) 教師們

**解說** class也有「上課的學生們」的意思，且說話者說自己是教授，所以其聽眾應該是學生。 答案 (A)

**詞彙** **class** 全班同學 **biology professor** 生物課教授 **semester** 學期 **rest** 其餘的 **by -ing** 以… **scientific method** 科學的方法

### Q4 美M

Hello. **My name is Steven Reynolds** and I'm very happy to speak today on Money Talk. I'd like to thank GW Radio for inviting me today. I've been a financial consultant for over twenty years, and I'm here to share several money management tips with today's listeners.

你好。我的名字叫史提芬雷諾。我非常高興今天在「金錢開講」中演講。我想感謝GW廣播電台今天邀請我來。在過去二十年以上我一直當財經顧問。我在這兒要和今天的聽眾一起分享一些金錢管理上的資訊。

史提芬雷諾是什麼人？
(A) 一位財經顧問
(B) 一位廣播主持人

**解說** 錄音裡，人名的附近有答案。這是在節目上說的話語，可以知道他是來賓。在錄音的中間部分論及自己為財經顧問。 答案 (A)

**詞彙** **invite** 邀請 **financial consultant** 財經顧問 **tip** 資訊

### STEP 01 若沒答對會後悔的考題

| | | | |
|---|---|---|---|
| 1 (A) | 2 (B) | 3 (B) | 4 (A) |
| 5 (B) | 6 (B) | 7 (A) | 8 (A) |
| 9 (A) | 10 (B) | 11 (C) | 12 (A) |
| 13 (A) | 14 (B) | | |

**1.** 英M

| | |
|---|---|
| 1 找出核心語 | asked |
| 2 類型與答案的位置 | 要求事項／後面部分 |
| 3 看選項 | 看行程表或在會議廳做登記 |

Welcome everyone. I hope you're enjoying the refreshments that we provided free of charge. I'm Jonathan Lee, the organizer for this year's Professional Cooking conference. First, **let's** take a look at the conference schedule.

歡迎大家。我希望你們正享受著我們免費提供的茶點。我是今年度專業烹飪會議的籌辦人強納生李。首先，我們看會議行程吧。

聽眾被要求做什麼？
(A) 看行程表
(B) 在會議廳做登記

**解說** 這是詢問要求事項的考題。將核心說法let's後面出現的「看會議行程吧」以同義詞做變化來表達的（A）為答案。 答案 (A)

**詞彙** **refreshment** 茶點 **free of charge** 免費的 **organizer** 籌辦人 **take a look at** 看 **schedule** 行程 **conference hall** 行程

**2.** 美W

| | |
|---|---|
| 1 找出核心語 | changed |
| 2 類型與答案的位置 | 具體事項／中間部分 |
| 3 看選項 | 演講者或研習會的時程 |

Attention everyone. **I'd like to announce a slight change** to today's conference schedule. Because of a problem with the presenter's flight arrangement, the 11 a.m. workshop on management techniques will be postponed to 4 p.m., but will be held in the same conference room.

請大家注意。我想公佈今天會議行程上小小的變更事項。因為演講者的飛機時間的問題，上午十一點的管理技巧研習會將延後到下午四點，但是會在同樣的會議室舉辦。

什麼被改變了？
(A) 演講者
(B) 研習會的時程

**解說** 「活動前公告」裡常出現的就是活動行程上的變動。錄音裡change後面出現「會議行程」，接著可以聽到「講習會將延後」，所以（B）為答案。 答案 (B)

**詞彙** **slight** 小小的 **change** 變更事項 **presenter** 演講者 **management technique** 管理技巧 **postpone** 延後 **hold** 舉辦 **conference room** 會議室

**3.** 美M

| | |
|---|---|
| 1 找出核心語 | in the afternoon |
| 2 類型與答案的位置 | 下一個行程／後面部分 |
| 3 看選項 | 與部門經理們會面或熟悉顧客的問題 |

You will start today's session by greeting all the department managers from sales, advertising, accounting, and so on. **In the afternoon**, you will familiarize yourselves with customer service issues and learn about inventory management.

你們將和銷售、廣告、會計等所有部門的經理打招呼來開始今天的議程。在下午的時候，你們將認識客服議題，然後學習庫存管理。

聽眾在下午將會做什麼？
(A) 與部門經理們會面
(B) 熟悉顧客的問題

**解說** 時間點為很好的核心語。將錄音裡出現的In the afternoon後面的「認識客服議題」做變化來表達的（B）為答案。 答案 (B)

**詞彙** **greet** 和…打招呼 **department** 部門 **and so on** 等等 **familiarize oneself with** 熟悉… **issue** 議題 **inventory management** 庫存管理

**4.** 英M

| | |
|---|---|
| 1 找出核心語 | speaker |
| 2 類型與答案的位置 | 說話者／前面部分 |
| 3 看選項 | 公司總裁或軟體工程師 |

Good evening, ladies and gentlemen. I'm Michael Chang. Welcome to our annual banquet. **As** CEO and founder of this company, I'm pleased to present this year's award for best product developer to Jong Min Kim.

各位先生、女士們早安。我是麥可張。歡迎來到我們的年度宴會。以這家公司的總裁與創辦人的身份，我很高興將今年的最佳產品開發者獎頒給金鐘民。

說話者是什麼人？
(A) 一位公司總裁
(B) 一位軟體工程師

**解說** 詢問說話者為誰的考題，其答案線索在錄音裡以

as來出現。As是身份的介系詞，所以將CEO做變化來表達的（A）為答案。 答案 (A)

**詞彙** **CEO** 總裁 **founder** 創辦人 **award** 獎賞 **developer** 開發者

**5.** 澳W

| 1 找出核心語 | after the lecture |
|---|---|
| 2 類型與答案的位置 | 要求事項／後續行程／後面部分 |
| 3 看選項 | 報名將來的演講或參加招待會 |

Our guest speaker today is Dr. Emma Lubiano, who will be speaking to us about new advances in the IT industry and how they affect software companies like ours. **Following the lecture**, there will be a reception. Please join us in the reception where Dr. Lubiano will be answering questions.

我們今天的客座演講者為愛瑪露比安諾博士。她將告訴我們電子產業裡的新進展，以及它們如何影響像我們一樣的軟體公司。演講之後會有歡迎會。請你們參加歡迎會，在此露比安諾博士會答覆問題。

說話者邀請聽眾在演講後做什麼？
（A）報名將來的演講
（B）參加招待會

**解說** after the lecture的近似說法following the lecture為錄音裡的核心語，所以將其後面出現的「請你們參加歡迎會」做簡化來表達的（B）為答案。 答案 (B)

**詞彙** **guest speaker** 客座演講者 **advance** 進展 **industry** 產業 **affect** 影響 **following** …之後 **lecture** 演講 **reception** 歡迎會 **join** 參加 **answer questions** 答覆問題

**6.** 美M

| 1 找出核心語 | want to be when he was young |
|---|---|
| 2 類型與答案的位置 | 具體事項／中間部分 |
| 3 看選項 | 教師或科學家 |

I'd like to start off by answering your questions about how I started my career as a scientist. I dreamed of being a scientist **from the time I was very young**. It felt so interesting to read books about science and many famous scientists, so I hardly ever spent time with my friends.

有關我如何開始我的科學家職業生涯，我想開始回答你們的問題。自從我很小的時候我夢想成為科學家。對於看有關科學和很多著名科學家相關的書感到很有趣，所以我幾乎沒有花時間在我朋友們身上。

演講者在年輕的時候想成為什麼？
（A）一位教師
（B）一位科學家

**解說** 考題裡的he就是「演說／演講」類錄音裡的speaker，也就是錄音內容的I。將「自從我很小的時候我夢想成為科學家」改成「想成為科學家」來表達的（A）為答案。 答案 (B)

**詞彙** **start off** 開始 **dream** 夢想 **hardly** 幾乎不… **spend time** 花時間

**7.** 英M

| 1 找出核心語 | purpose of the speech |
|---|---|
| 2 類型與答案的位置 | 主題／前面部分 |
| 3 看選項 | 對頒獎表示感謝或解釋公司的規定 |

I'm very pleased to be honored for my research into the use of the audio video materials to improve language education. **I'd like to** thank all of my fellow workers for this award. Without their commitment, I couldn't have received this award.

我很高興我對視聽材料使用於語言教育的發展上的研究得到了榮譽。為了這個獎賞我想感謝我所有的同仁們。若沒有他們的投入，我不可能得到這個獎賞。

這個演講的目地是什麼？
（A）對頒獎表示感謝
（B）解釋公司的規定

**解說** 這是詢問演講目的的考題，所以在錄音前段部分的內容有答案。將thank改成appreciation來表達的（A）為答案。 答案 (A)

**詞彙** **honor** 榮譽 **research** 研究 **material** 材料 **language** 語言 **education** 教育 **fellow** 同仁 **award** 獎賞 **commitment** 投入 **receive** 得到

**8.** 美M

| 1 找出核心語 | giving out |
|---|---|
| 2 類型與答案的位置 | 具體事項／中間、後面部分 |
| 3 看選項 | 發表記錄或軟體 |

Good morning, I'm Berry Moor, a senior manager from the head office in Seoul. I'm really happy to get a chance to visit the Bangkok office and demonstrate the new database management program. Before I tell you more about this new program, I'd like to **hand out** these presentation notes.

早安，我是首爾總部的首席經理貝瑞摩爾。我很高興有機會訪問曼谷辦公室並示範新的資料庫管理軟體。在我告訴你們更多有關這個新的軟體之前，我想分發這些發表資料。

說話者發給參加的人什麼東西？
(A) 發表記錄
(B) 軟體

**解說** 錄音裡出現give out的同義詞hand out，在其附近會有答案。「發表記錄」為記載發表內容的文件。 答案 (A)

**詞彙** **senior** 首席的 **head office** 總部 **chance to** 動詞原型 做…的機會 **demonstrate** 示範 **hand out** 分發 **give out** 分給

問題9～10，請參考以下訊息。澳W

| | |
|---|---|
| 1 找出核心語 | Where, Sofia Russo do |
| 2 類型與答案的位置 | 地點／前面部分 |
| | 具體事項／中間部分 |
| 3 看選項 | 宴會廳，在會議室，在書店 |
| | 在醫院工作，出版書籍，開發醫療藥物 |
| 4 預測對話內容 | 在宴會介紹演講者的經歷 |

[9]Good evening and welcome to the Connor Company's Annual Employee Appreciation Dinner. I would like to extend special thanks to the Grace Hotel for providing us with this wonderful banquet hall. And now it's time to introduce our guest speaker for this evening. [10]Please welcome Dr. Sofia Russo, author of the best-selling book *The Future of Medicine*, who will tell us about her experiences writing this book.

晚安。歡迎來到康納公司的年度員工感恩晚餐。我想表達特別感謝葛莉思飯店提供給我們這麼棒的宴會廳。那麼現在是介紹今晚的客座演講者的時間。請歡迎暢銷書「醫學的未來」的作者蘇菲亞羅素博士來告訴我們她寫這本書的時候的經驗。

**詞彙** **extend** 表達（歡迎、同情等） **provide A with B** 提供B給A **banquet hall** 宴會廳 **guest speaker** 客座講師 **author** 作者 **experience** 經驗

### 9.

說話者在哪兒？
(A) 在宴會廳
(B) 在會議室
(C) 在書店

**解說** 在錄音的前段分出現「晚餐」，所以（A）或（B）為可能的答案。透過「感謝提供給我們這麼棒的宴會廳」，可以知道演講的地點為宴會廳。 答案 (A)

**詞彙** **conference room** 會議室 **bookstore** 會議室

### 10.

蘇菲亞羅素做過什麼？
(A) 她曾在醫院工作。
(B) 她曾出版書籍。
(C) 她曾開發醫療藥物。

**解說** 錄音內容裡出現的人名附近會有答案。受邀而來的講師很多時候是作者。將「作者」改成「出版書籍」來表達的（B）為答案。 答案 (B)

**詞彙** **hospital** 醫院 **publish** 出版 **develop** 開發 **medical** 醫學的

問題11～12，請參考以下訊息。英M

| | |
|---|---|
| 1 找出核心語 | speaker work, his previous work experience |
| 2 類型與答案的位置 | 說話者／前面部分 |
| | 具體事項／中間部分 |
| 3 看選項 | 電腦程式編寫，會計，新聞業 |
| | 有助於學習如何執行多種工作， |
| | 沒有包含新的工作，到國外出差 |
| 4 預測對話內容 | 說話者在面試當中說明自己足夠的經歷 |

First of all, I'm very happy for the opportunity to tell you more about my qualifications for this position. [11]I have been a reporter with the Korea Times for the last 5 years. [12]During those 5 years, I've learned patience, the ability to multi-task and the importance of hard work. Now I can manage a variety of tasks and these have become my professional strengths. I think these are probably the most valuable skills for any journalist.

首先，我很高興有機會告訴你們對於這個職位我的資格條件。在過去五年當中，我在韓國時報當了記者。在此五年的時間裡，我學會了耐心、同時處理多項工作的能力、以及勤勞的重要性。現在我能處理多種的任務，而且這些成為我的專業上的優勢。我認為對任何一位新聞工作者而言，這些可能是最具有價值的技術。

**詞彙** **opportunity** 機會 **qualification** 資格條件 **position** 職位 **patience** 耐心 **ability** 能力 **multi-task** 同時處理多項工作 **importance** 重要性 **hard work** 勤勞 **manage** 管理 **a variety of** 多種的 **task**

任務 **professional** 專業上的 **strength** 優勢 **probably** 可能是 **valuable** 具有價值的 **journalist** 新聞工作者

## 11.

說話者在什麼領域工作？
(A) 電腦程式編寫
(B) 會計
(C) 新聞業

**解說** 「在過去五年當中當了記者」是「在新聞業工作的」的意思。 答案 (C)

**詞彙** **programming** 編寫電腦程式 **accounting** 會計 **journalism** 新聞業

## 12.

關於他之前的工作經驗，說話者說了什麼？
(A) 有助於他學習如何執行多種工作。
(B) 它沒有包含新的工作。
(C) 他常到國外出差。

**解說** 「在五年當中學會的東西」就是指「工作經驗」，而且也說了「現在我能處理多種的任務」，所以可以瞭解成「工作經驗有助於執行多種工作」。 答案 (A)

**詞彙** **previous** 以前的 **various** 多種的 **cover** 包含

**問題13～14，請參考以下訊息。** 美M

| | |
|---|---|
| 1 找出核心語 | purpose of the talk, happen after the speech |
| 2 類型與答案的位置 | 主題／前面部分<br>後續行程／後面部分 |
| 3 看選項 | 介紹客座演講者，公告旅館的開幕，說明旅遊的行程，簡短的中場休息，問答時間，播放短片 |
| 4 預測對話內容 | 介紹演講者之後有提問時間 |

[13]Welcome to the Business Management lecture series. Our speaker this evening is Mr. John Thompson, an accountant with over twenty years' experience, and he also coordinates the annual Small Business Conference at City College. The title of his talk tonight is "What Every Small Business Administrator Needs to Know About Taxes." [14]After his speech, Mr. Thompson will answer questions in the Great Hall, and coffee and snacks will be served.

歡迎來到企業管理講座。我們今晚的演講者為約翰湯普生先生。他是具有超過二十年以上經驗的會計師，而且也籌辦城市大學的小型企業年度研討會。今晚他的演講題目為「每一個小型企業管理者都需知的稅務」。演講之後，在「宏偉廳」湯普生先生將會回答問題，而且也提供茶點。

**詞彙** **lecture** 講座 **accountant** 會計師 **experience** 經驗 **coordinate** 籌辦 **speech** 演講 **answer questions** 回答問題

## 13.

這段談話的目的是什麼？
(A) 為了介紹客座演講者
(B) 為了公告一間旅館的開幕
(C) 為了說明旅遊的行程

**解說** 「演講者為某某」即為介紹演講者的狀況。 答案 (A)

**詞彙** **guest speaker** 客座演講者 **explain** 說明 **travel itinerary** 旅遊行程

## 14.

在演講之後很有可能將會發生什麼事？
(A) 將有一個簡短的中場休息。
(B) 將會接著進行問答時間。
(C) 將播放短片。

**解說** 考題裡的after the speech為核心語。將錄音裡的「將會回答問題」改成了「將會接著進行問答時間」。 答案 (B)

**詞彙** **intermission** 休息時間 **a question and answer session** 問答時間 **follow** 接續著 **video footage** 短片

## STEP 02 考題實戰練習

1. (A) 2. (C) 3. (C) 4. (C) 5. (B) 6. (B)
7. (A) 8. (B) 9. (A) 10. (A) 11. (B) 12. (A)

**問題1～3，請參考以下訊息。** 美W

[1]Welcome everyone to this year's global Conference on Community Health. We're pleased to have more than 200 professionals who work in various fields of community health programs throughout the world give presentations. Our presenters will be sharing their experiences, survey results, and ideas for providing medical treatment to citizens of the world. Before I present our keynote speaker, [2]I have an important announcement about the small group sessions on the program. Because of limited space, you need to register for the sessions in advance. Your

tickets should be in your welcome kit for each session you sign up for. If not, [3]check our web site to confirm that you are really registered.

歡迎大家來到今年的社區衛生服務全球會議。我們很高興能有超過兩百名工作於世界各地社區衛生計畫多樣領域的專業人員來演講。我們的發表者將分享他們為世界公民提供醫療的經驗、調查結果和想法。在介紹今天的主講人之前，有關於程序當中的小團體會議，我有一項重要的公告。因空間有限，這個會議您需要預先登記。每一場您登記的會議門票應該在您邀請卡上。如果沒有，請於我們的網站確認您是否已真正註冊。

**詞彙** be pleased to 很高興… professional 專家 various 多種的 field 領域 throughout 遍布於… presentation 發表 presenter 發表者 keynote speaker 主要演講者 important 重要的 announcement 公告事項 limited 有限的 register for 登錄 in advance 提前 sign up for 報名

**1.**

這場會議的主題是什麼？

（A）社區衛生

（B）報告方式

（C）軟體設計

（D）醫療工具

**解說** 透過這三個考題與選項可以知道該錄音為「活動前公告」類型。錄音前段部分出現介系詞on，接著聽得到「社區衛生」，所以很容易找到答案。 答案(A)

**詞彙** methods 方法 tool 道具

**2.**

有關於小團體會議，說話者說了什麼？

（A）它們將在不同的地點被舉辦。

（B）它們不包含在程序中。

（C）它們需要預先登記。

（D）它們是產品演示的一部份。

**解說** 這是詢問具體事項的考題，所以答案會在錄音內容的中間部分。將「需要預先登記」以相似說法表達的（C）為答案。 答案(C)

**詞彙** location 地點 include 包含 prior registration 事前登錄 a part of …的一部分

**3.**

根據說話者所言，聽眾能在會議網站上找到什麼？

（A）調查報告

（B）一項評估

（C）登記確認

（D）程序單

**解說** 錄音內容裡的web site附近有答案。若是與web site資訊相關內容，大部分在後段部分出現答案線索。尤其第三個考題的答案線索通常是在錄音的後段部分。將「確認是否已真正註冊」做變化來表達的（C）為答案。 答案(C)

**詞彙** report 報告書 estimate 評估資料 registration 登錄 confirmation 確認資料 list 目錄

問題4～6，請參考以下訊息。 英M

Welcome to our annual conference. Before we get started with this morning's program, [4]I'd like to make an important announcement regarding the schedule. Our first group speaker will begin her presentation thirty minutes later than originally scheduled. She will now speak at nine-fifteen, instead of at eight forty-five, in our main meeting room. At twelve o'clock, [5]lunch will be served in the Red River Room instead of the Blue Mountain Room, which will be used for dinner. [6]This evening, as listed in your pre-printed schedules, don't forget to attend our keynote speaker's presentation. Thank you.

歡迎來到我們的年度會議。在我們開始今天上午的程序前，有關時間表我想做個重要的公告。我們第一組的演講者將比原本預定的時間晚三十分鐘開始她的演講。現在她將於九點十五分而不是八點四十五分，在大會議室演講。十二點鐘時，將在紅河室午餐而不是將用於晚餐的藍山室。今晚，如同印好的時間表所列，別忘了參加我們主講人的演講。感謝您。

**詞彙** start with 以…開始 important 重要的 announcement 公告事項 schedule 行程 presentation 發表 originally scheduled 原來預定的 instead of 而不是… meeting room 會議室 serve 提供 pre-printed 已印好的 attend 參加 keynote speaker 主要演講者

**4.**

為什麼發出這則公告？

（A）為了表揚一位員工

（B）為了介紹一些新菜色

（C）為了公告時間表變更

（D）為了慶祝公司的成功

**解說** 透過第二題的「提供午餐」，可以猜測到該錄音為「活動前公告」類。這是詢問主題的考題，所以答案在錄音的前段部分。將「有關時間表我想做個重要的公告」以相似說法來表達的（C）為答案。 答案(C)

**詞彙** honor 表揚 introduce 介紹 dish 菜 celebrate 祝賀 success 成功

**5.**

將會在哪裡提供午餐？

（A）在主會議室

（B）在紅河室

（C）在藍山室

(D) 在自助餐廳

**解說** 錄音裡的lunch附近會出現答案。(C)是陷阱，因為(C)是晚餐場地。 答案 (B)

**詞彙** cafeteria 自助餐廳

**6**

說話者建議聽眾在晚上做什麼？

(A) 與好友吃晚餐
(B) 參加一場報告
(C) 領取問卷
(D) 拿到已簽名的書

**解說** 時間點為很重要的核心語。錄音裡的this evening附近會出現答案。將錄音後段聽到的「參加我們主講人的演講」做簡化來表達的(B)為答案。 答案 (B)

**詞彙** close friend 要好的朋友 pick up 領取 questionnaire 問卷

**問題7~9，請參考以下訊息。** 澳W

Welcome everyone to today's lecture series. [7]Our featured speaker today is Mr. John Park, once the chairman of the Stock Analyst Association. [7, 8]He is also an award-winning author of Secrets of a *Millionaire*. Mr. Park will read excerpts from his book and answer questions from the audience. Following that, he will be available to sign copies of his book. [9]You can purchase the book at the back of the auditorium for twenty-five dollars. To get more information on his other books, you may refer to the brochures available there. Now, let's give a warm welcome to Mr. John Park.

歡迎大家來到今天的系列講座。我們今天的特別演講者，是曾為股票分析協會主席的約翰帕爾可先生。他也是百萬富翁先生的秘密的獲獎作者。帕爾可先生將讀出他書中的摘要和回答聽眾的問題。之後，他將會為他的書簽名。您可於觀眾席後面以二十五美元購買這本書。若想知道有關於他其他書籍的更多資訊，您可以參考這邊提供的小冊子。現在，請給予約翰帕爾可先生熱烈的歡迎。

**詞彙** lecture 講座 featured speaker 特別演講者 chairman 主席 analyst 分析師 award-winning 獲獎的 author 作家 excerpt 摘錄 audience 聽眾 following …之後 available 可用的 sign 簽名 purchase 購買 auditorium 演講廳 refer to 參考… brochure 小冊

**7**

帕爾可先生是什麼人？

(A) 一位作家
(B) 一位會議舉辦人
(C) 一位書店老闆
(D) 一位旅館接待員

**解說** 透過第二題的「帕爾可先生將會談些什麼」可以知道該錄音為「活動前公告」。那麼Mr. Park很有可能是應邀前來的演講者。所以錄音裡的Mr. Park附近會出現答案，因此用he來指稱之後，接著就告訴聽眾他是「作家」。 答案 (A)

**詞彙** organizer 舉辦人 bookstore owner 書店主人 receptionist 接待人員

**8**

帕爾可先生將會談些什麼？

(A) 他的經驗
(B) 他的書
(C) 他的健康
(D) 他做為一位分析師的角色

**解說** 錄音裡出現「讀出他書中的摘要和回答聽眾的問題」，可以猜測到他將會討論他的書。 答案 (B)

**詞彙** experience 經驗 role 角色

**9**

聽眾可以在演講廳的後面做什麼？

(A) 買書
(B) 看一些標誌
(C) 小歇一下
(D) 登記之後的演講

**解說** 特定地點也是很重要的核心語。將「可在觀眾席後面購買這本書」做變化來表達的(A)為答案。 答案 (A)

**詞彙** buy 買 read 看；閱讀 sign 標誌 coffee break 休息時間 register for 登錄

**問題10~12，請參考以下訊息。** 美M

Good afternoon, everyone. Thanks for taking time to attend this training session out of your busy schedule. I'm Mario Rossi, software engineer from the head office in New York. As you all know, [11]our team recently developed a new software system to keep track of our warehouse inventory. The new system will enable us to keep our warehouse well-stocked and organized. [10]As inventory manager, you have to become familiar with using this software, so I'd like to make sure all of you know how the new system works. [12]First, I'd like to play a short video footage that shows you the general features of this new system. Please direct your attention to the screen.

各位午安，感謝大家在百忙之中抽空參加本次培訓會議。我是紐約總部的軟件工程師馬力歐羅西。如你們所知，我們小組最近開發出掌握我們倉庫庫存的新軟體系統。新系統將能使我們的倉庫能充份儲存和系統化。作為庫存經理，您必須會熟悉使用這個軟體，所以我想確認你們全體都知道這個新系統如何運作。首先，我想先放一段錄影短片讓大家看這個新系統的一般功能。請將您的注意力朝向螢幕。

**詞彙** take time 撥冗 attend 出席 training session 訓練課 head office 總公司 recently 最近 develop 開發 enable 使得可能 inventory 庫存 manager 經理 familiar with 熟悉…的 work 運作 general 一般的 feature 功能

**10**

聽眾很有可能是什麼人？
(A) 公司的經理們
(B) 農民協會的會員們
(C) 在電腦店的顧客們
(D) 在餐廳的員工們

**解說** 若是詢問聽眾為誰的考題，大部分在錄音的前段部分出現答案，但這是比較難的錄音，必需要聽到中間部分才能找的到答案。身份的介系詞as後面出現「作為庫存經理」，以此做簡化來表達的 (A) 為答案。

答案 (A)

**詞彙** audience 聽眾 association 協會 customer 顧客 store 商店

**11**

最近開發出了什麼？
(A) 潛在的客戶們
(B) 一套軟體系統
(C) 辦公室用品
(D) 一項醫療設備

**解說** 在錄音中間出現developed。將「新軟體系統」以簡化來表達的 (B) 為答案。 答案 (B)

**詞彙** potential customer 潛在的顧客 office supplies 辦公用品 device 裝置

**12**

說話者接下來將會做什麼？
(A) 做視聽發表
(B) 引導參觀設備
(C) 介紹公司的總監
(D) 採購一套軟體系統

**解說** 這是詢問下一個行程的考題。將「放一段錄影短片」改成「做視聽發表」來表達的 (A) 為答案。

答案 (A)

**詞彙** show 顯示 audiovisual 視聽的 tour 參觀 facility 設備 director 主管 purchase 購買

# Chapter 19 廣播

## Quiz |

1. (A) 2. (A) 3. (A) 4. (B)

**Q1** 美W

**This is** Angela Booth with your 30-second afternoon weather report. Though it's been a relatively dry week for this time of year, we can expect showers tonight. There's an 80 percent chance of precipitation tomorrow morning.

我是三十秒氣象報導的安琪拉布斯。儘管相較於每年的這個時間，目前算是較乾燥的一週，但我們預測今晚有陣雨。明天早上則有百分之八十的降雨機率。

說話者很有可能是什麼人？
(A) 一位廣播播報員
(B) 一位旅館經理

**解說** 在錄音內容的前段部分就可以決定是廣播節目種類的「天氣預報」類型，說話者就是廣播播報員。

答案 (A)

**詞彙** weather report 氣象報導 relatively 相對的 dry 乾燥的 shower 陣雨 precipitation 降雨

**Q2** 英M

If you are coming into the city from the east side now, try to avoid Clover Street. **We recommend** you take highway 15 where traffic is running smoothly. Stay tuned. I'll be back in 10 minutes with another traffic update.

如果您現在要從東側進入本市，請盡量避開幸運草街。我們建議您行駛目前交通順暢的十五號高速公路。請繼續收聽。我將在十分鐘之後回來報導另一項路況更新。

說話者建議聽眾做什麼？
(A) 行駛備用道路
(B) 開慢一點

**解說** 若為「路況報導／天氣預報」，在錄音後段部分會提供有用的資訊。在此篇錄音裡，用suggest的同義詞recommend來提供了答案線索。「不要走Clover Street，而改走十五號高速公路」是「行駛備用道路」的意思。

答案 (A)

**詞彙** east side 東邊 try to 試著；盡量 avoid 避開 recommend 建議 highway 高速公路 smoothly 流暢地 stay tuned 繼續收聽 traffic update 路況報導

Q3 美W

Good evening. **This is Sandra Johnson** and with your Business World Now. Hana Computer Group's chairman, Michael Rogers, announced today that the company's new laptop 'the Sensation' will go on sale next Friday.

晚安。這是現今商業界新聞，我是珊卓拉強生。漢納電腦集團的董事長麥可羅傑斯今天公佈，該公司的新筆記型電腦「轟動」在下週五將開始銷售。

珊卓拉強生很有可能是什麼人？
（A）一位新聞播報員
（B）一位企業總裁

**解說** 在錄音裡提到的名字附近有答案。出現了新聞節目的名稱，所以說話者為主持新聞節目的人。 答案 (A)

**詞彙** **chairman** 董事長 **announce** 公佈 **laptop** 筆記型電腦 **go on sale** 開始銷售

Q4 英M

The construction of the new highway will begin on May 1st and is estimated to cost two million dollars. **The project will take** approximately four months. However, citizens are skeptical that the current traffic congestion will be alleviated.

新高速公路的建設將在五月一日開始，且預計花費兩百萬元。該計劃大約將需要四個月。然而，市民對於現在的交通堵塞將變緩和感到懷疑。

這個計畫將會進行多久？
（A）兩個月
（B）四個月

**解說** 這是詢問具體內容的考題。只要有聽到錄音內容裡出現的project... take後面的數字「四」就可以了。 答案 (B)

**詞彙** **construction** 建設 **estimate** 預計 **approximately** 大概 **citizen** 市民 **skeptical** 懷疑的 **current** 現在的 **traffic congestion** 交通堵塞**alleviate** 緩和

## STEP 01 若沒答對會後悔的考題

| | | | |
|---|---|---|---|
| 1 (A) | 2 (B) | 3 (B) | 4 (A) |
| 5 (B) | 6 (A) | 7 (A) | 8 (B) |
| 9 (B) | 10 (B) | 11 (C) | 12 (B) |
| 13 (C) | 14 (C) | | |

1. 美M

| | |
|---|---|
| 1 找出核心語 | reason of the delay |
| 2 類型與答案的位置 | 具體內容／中間部分 |
| 3 看選項 | 車禍或馬路維修 |

Thanks for listening to 102.7, your local station for news, traffic and weather. I'm Chris Lee with a traffic report. **We have heavy traffic** this morning because of a car accident on Route One near the airport. Avoid Route One if possible.

感謝您收聽102.7新聞、交通資訊和氣象的在地電台。我是路況報導的克里斯李。由於在一號路線上機場附近的車禍，今天早上交通堵塞。如果可以的話請避開一號路線。

延遲的原因是什麼？
（A）一起車禍
（B）馬路維修

**解說** 透過考題與選項可以預測該錄音內容為「路況報導」。這是詢問問題狀況原因的考題，所以在錄音裡because of後面出現的「車禍」為答案。 答案 (A)

**詞彙** **traffic report** 路況報導 **because of** 因為 **accident** 事故 **if possible** 如果可以的話 **delay** 延誤 **repair** 維修

2. 美W

| | |
|---|---|
| 1 找出核心語 | asked |
| 2 類型與答案的位置 | 要求事項／後面部分 |
| 3 看選項 | 調高收音機的聲量或繼續收聽廣播 |

This is a special weather report. Please be aware that the entire region is under a flood watch. We are currently experiencing heavy rains, which we expect to continue for the next twenty-four hours. **Everyone** living within a mile of the Han River **should** stay tuned for evacuation orders.

這是特別氣象報導。請注意，全區域正在發布洪水特報。我們正有豪雨，而且預計它會持續二十四小時。居住於漢江一英哩以內的所有的人，請務必不要轉台並注意疏散令。

聽眾被要求做什麼？
（A）調高收音機的聲量
（B）繼續收聽廣播

**解說** stay tuned是「將電台維持固定」，也就是「不要轉台持續收聽」的意思，所以（B）為答案。 答案 (B)

**詞彙** **weather report** 氣象報導 **be aware that** 注意到⋯ **entire region** 全區域 **flood watch** 洪水特報 **heavy rain** 豪雨 **stay tuned** 不要換台 **evacuation order** 疏散令

**3.** 英M

| | |
|---|---|
| 1 找出核心語 | report mainly concern |
| 2 類型與答案的位置 | 主題／前面部分 |
| 3 看選項 | 天氣或交通 |

You will be happy to know this is the last day for the renovation of Clover Street and it will be open to the public again tomorrow morning. So from tomorrow, it will be wise to take Clover Street instead of Main Street, where traffic is always heavy. I'll be back for another traffic update in 15 minutes.

你們將很樂於知道今天是幸運草街維修工程的最後一天，而且它將於明天早上重新對大眾開放。因此從明天起，請明智地行駛幸運草街來代替總是堵塞的幹線道路。我在十五分鐘之後將帶著另一項路況更新回來。

這則報導主要在關切什麼？
(A) 天氣
(B) 交通

**解說** 是否為「廣播節目」的類型，大部分能在錄音的前段部分決定。但此篇錄音在前段部分先提供路況，用以暗示出類別，在後段部分再說出「將帶著另一項路況更新」來確定其節目類型。 答案 (B)

**詞彙** **renovation** 維修 **public** 大眾 **again** 重新 **instead of** 而不是… **traffic update** 路況報導

**4.** 澳W

| | |
|---|---|
| 1 找出核心語 | needed in the morning |
| 2 類型與答案的位置 | 具體內容／後面部分 |
| 3 看選項 | 厚外套或雨傘 |

Cold weather will continue, but that is usual for this time of the year. You may want to take a heavy coat when you go out **in the morning**. That's the morning weather report on SY Radio. Now back to our regular classical music program.

冷天氣將會持續，但這是每年此時很平常的事。早上外出時，您應該要帶著很厚的外套。這是SY廣播電台的晨間氣象報導。現在回到我們固定的古典音樂節目。

根據說話者所言，在早上將會需要什麼？
(A) 一件厚外套
(B) 一把雨傘

**解說** 時間點為很好的答案線索。透過該考題與選項可以預測該錄音為「天氣預報」。在該錄音裡的時間說法in the morning附近可以聽到heavy coat。 答案 (A)

**詞彙** **usual** 平常的 **heavy coat** 厚外套 **go out** 外出 **weather report** 氣象報導 **regular** 固定的

**5.** 美M

| | |
|---|---|
| 1 找出核心語 | recommend |
| 2 類型與答案的位置 | 要求事項／後面部分 |
| 3 看選項 | 小心開車或帶雨傘 |

Good morning, it's time for the GW Radio morning weather report. We'll have heavy rain throughout the morning. After the rain stops, temperature will drop sharply in the afternoon. So **we recommend** taking an umbrella and keeping yourself warm when you go out.

早安。現在是GW廣播電台的晨間氣象報導時間。我們在上午將持續有豪雨。雨停了之後，下午時氣溫將會劇降。因此我們建議您外出時要帶著雨傘並且保暖。

說話者建議聽眾在今天下午做什麼？
(A) 小心開車
(B) 帶雨傘

**解說** 這是與「天氣預報」有關，詢問有用資訊的考題。在錄音裡recommend後面就出現答案。 答案 (B)

**詞彙** **heavy rain** 豪雨 **throughout** 在…一直 **temperature** 氣溫 **drop** 下降 **sharply** 劇烈地 **recommend** 建議 **warm** 溫暖 **go out** 外出

**6.** 澳W

| | |
|---|---|
| 1 找出核心語 | Mr. Chen |
| 2 類型與答案的位置 | 具體人物／前面或中間部分 |
| 3 看選項 | 公司總裁或廣播業者 |

Good morning and welcome to the Morning 4 on national radio. I am your host, Maria Rega. We're happy to have **Mr. James Chen**, the president of James Enterprises, in our studio as our special guest today. Mr. Chen will talk about how his childhood experiences helped him develop his career.

早安。歡迎收聽公共電台的晨間四節目。我是主持人瑪莉亞瑞佳。我們很高興邀請詹姆士企業的董事長詹姆士陳先生來到我們的播音室作為特別來賓。陳先生將談談他兒童時代的經驗如何幫助他發展出他的事業。

陳先生是什麼人？
(A) 一位公司總裁
(B) 一位廣播業者

**解說** 這是「受訪節目」類的錄音內容，會在人名附近出現答案，很有可能是詢問有關來賓或主持人的內容。該錄音的前段部分，人名附近出現了「詹姆士企業的董事長」，而這就是答案。 答案 (A)

**詞彙** **host** 主持人 **president** 董事長 **guest** 來賓 **childhood experience** 童年時代的經驗 **career** 職業 **broadcaster** 廣播員

**7.** 美W

| | |
|---|---|
| 1 找出核心語 | report mainly about |
| 2 類型與答案的位置 | 主題／前面部分 |
| 3 看選項 | 商業收購或建設計劃 |

And now for this evening's business news. Nanjing Industries formally announced that their acquisition of GW Package will proceed as planned. The profits of Nanjing Industries this quarter increased sharply nearly 12 percent over the second quarter, which convinced the company to proceed with the acquisition.

現在是今晚的商務新聞。南京工業正式公佈他們對GW包裝公司的收購案將依照計劃進行。南京工業這一季的利潤比起第二季劇增了將近百分之十二，這使該公司有信心將收購案進行下去。

這則報導主要是有關於什麼？
(A) 一項商業收購
(B) 一個建設計畫

**解說** 這是詢問廣播節目類型的考題，看選項就可以知道為「一般報導」類。在錄音前段部分的announced後面出現答案。 答案 (A)

**詞彙** **formally** 正式地 **acquisition** 收購 **profits** 利潤 **quarter** 季 **sharply** 急劇地 **nearly** 幾乎 **over** 比起… **convince** 使相信 **proceed with** 進行…

**8.** 美M

| | |
|---|---|
| 1 找出核心語 | at noon |
| 2 類型與答案的位置 | 後續行程／後面部分 |
| 3 看選項 | 廣告或聽眾來電 |

Good morning Vancouver. This morning, we invited a famous critic, Arthur George to our studio. He will be discussing changes in the film industry over the last century. Then **at noon**, Mr. George has agreed to take calls from our audience.

早安，溫哥華。今天早上我們邀請了著名評論家亞瑟喬治到我們的播音室。他將要討論上一個世紀裡電影產業的變化。接下來在中午的時候，喬治先生同意接聽我們聽眾的電話。

在下午將會發生什麼？
(A) 插播商業廣告。
(B) 聽眾們將會打電話到廣播電台。

**解說** 時間點為很好的答案線索。將錄音後段部分的「同意接聽聽眾的電話」改成了「聽眾們將會打電話到廣播電台」來表達。 答案 (B)

**詞彙** **invite** 邀請 **critic** 評論家 **discuss** 討論 **take a call** 接電話 **audience** 聽眾

問題9～10，請參考以下訊息。 澳W

| | |
|---|---|
| 1 找出核心語 | Who, tomorrow |
| 2 類型與答案的位置 | 說話者／前面部分 |
| | 具體內容／中間部分 |
| 3 看選項 | 飛機駕駛，氣象播報員，旅行社職員 |
| | 雨天，晴天，陰天 |
| 4 預測對話內容 | 氣象預報員說明天是晴天 |

[9] Welcome to the five o'clock weather report. I know you're all tired of this long day of rain, but the good news is that the skies will finally clear up tonight. [10] By tomorrow morning there shouldn't be a cloud in the sky, and it'll be warm and sunny all day. For all you people who've been waiting to make a trip to the beach, tomorrow should be the perfect day for it.

歡迎收聽五點整氣象報導。我知道你們對這次漫長的下雨天都感到厭倦，但有個好消息是今晚天空將會變晴朗。到明天早上天空上應該不會有雲彩，而且一整天都會溫暖又有陽光。對於一直等待到海邊旅行的所有的人來說，明天應該是最完美的一天。

**詞彙** **finally** 終於 **clear up** 變晴朗 **warm** 溫暖 **sunny** 有陽光的 **all day** 一整天 **make a trip** 旅行 **beach** 海邊

**9.**

正在說話人的很有可能是誰？
(A) 一位飛機駕駛
(B) 一位氣象播報員
(C) 一位旅行社職員

**解說** 錄音前段部分以出現「氣象報導」，可以判斷出類型，所以該位說話者為氣象播報員。 答案 (B)

**詞彙** **pilot** 飛機駕駛 **weather forecaster** 氣象播報員 **travel agent** 旅行社職員

## 10.

明天將可能什麼樣的天氣？
(A) 雨天
(B) 晴天
(C) 陰天

**解說** 在錄音裡出現tomorrow相關的具體說法tomorrow morning，又說了「不會有雲彩、有陽光」，所以sunny為答案。 答案 (B)

**詞彙** **rainy** 下雨的 **cloudy** 陰天的

**問題11～12，請參考以下訊息。** 英M

| | |
|---|---|
| 1 找出核心語 | subject of the report, new product arrive |
| 2 類型與答案的位置 | 主題／前面部分<br>具體內容／後面部分 |
| 3 看選項 | 商業合併，行銷活動，新電腦的上市今天，兩週之內，三週之內 |
| 4 預測對話內容 | 新電腦將在兩週之內上市的新聞 |

Computer Magazine reported today that the [11]California Computer Company has announced that it will launch a new computer. The spokesman of the company said the new computer will be smaller and faster than other computers currently on the market. [12]The new computer will be available in stores within the next two weeks. To learn more about these innovative systems, visit Computer Magazine's web site.

電腦月刊今天報導，加州電腦公司公佈將推出新款電腦。該公司的代言人說該新款電腦和現今市場上其他電腦相比更小又更快。該款新電腦在接下來的兩個星期之內在商店可以購買。若想知道更多有關這些創新的系統，請至電腦月刊網站。

**詞彙** **report** 報導 **launch** 推出開賣 **currently** 現今 **on the market** 在市場上 **available** 可購買的 **within** 在…之內 **innovative** 創新的

## 11.

這則報導的主題是什麼？
(A) 一項商業合併
(B) 一項行銷活動
(C) 新電腦的上市

**解說** 這是「一般報導」類型的錄音內容，在錄音前段部分的announced附近有答案。將「推出新款電腦」以相似說法來表達的（C）為答案。 答案 (C)

**詞彙** **subject** 主題 **merger** 合併 **release** 上市

## 12.

新產品將於什麼時候到達商店？
(A) 今天
(B) 在兩週之內
(C) 在三週之內

**解說** 「新產品」是指「新的電腦」，所以如果注意聽「在商店可以購買」後面出現的時間點，就可以知道「兩週之內」為答案。 答案 (B)

**問題13～14，請參考以下訊息。** 美M

| | |
|---|---|
| 1 找出核心語 | recommend, next traffic report |
| 2 類型與答案的位置 | 要求事項／後面部分<br>後續行程／後面部分 |
| 3 看選項 | 搭乘大眾運輸，慢速開車，行駛替代道路<br>五分鐘，十分鐘，十五分鐘 |
| 4 預測對話內容 | 請走別的道路、下一次路況報導在十五分鐘之後 |

This is Ken Harrison from Radio 5's traffic desk. A traffic accident downtown is causing major delays on several main roads. Drivers are asked to avoid North State Street. [13]So, if you must drive downtown, we recommend using Constitution Avenue instead. Even on Constitution Avenue, however, you may experience some delays. [14]Our next traffic report will be in 15 minutes, so keep listening.

我是廣播五交通部門的肯哈里遜。市中心的一場車禍正造成一些幹線道路上嚴重的延誤。請駕駛人避開北州街。若是你得開到市中心，我們建議改行駛憲法路。但即使在憲法路上您可能也會遇到一些延誤狀況。我們下一次的交通播報將於十五分鐘之後，所以請繼續收聽。

**詞彙** **accident** 事故 **downtown** 市中心的 **cause**（原因）（結果）因某原因造成某種結果 **delay** 延遲 **road** 道路 **avoid** 避開 **recommend** 建議 **instead** 作為代替 **traffic report** 路況報導 **keep -ing** 繼續…

## 13.

說話者建議了什麼？
(A) 搭乘大眾運輸系統
(B) 開車比平常開慢一點
(C) 行駛替代道路

**解說** 透過考題與選項可以知道該錄音為「路況報導」類型。這是詢問「路況報導」的有用資訊的考題。核心語recommend後面出現了「改行駛憲法路」，而將此改

以「行駛替代道路」來表達的（C）為答案。 答案 (C)

**詞彙** **recommend** 建議 **public transportation** 公共交通 **than usual** 比起平時 **alternate rout** 替代道路

**14.**

下一次的交通報導是在什麼時候？
(A) 在五分鐘之後
(B) 在十分鐘之後
(C) 在十五分鐘之後

**解說** 這是「廣播節目」類型，在錄音後段部分就能找到答案的簡單考題。在此直接就可以聽到數字十五。
答案 (C)

## STEP 02 考題實戰練習

| | | | | | |
|---|---|---|---|---|---|
| 1. (A) | 2. (C) | 3. (D) | 4. (D) | 5. (A) | 6. (B) |
| 7. (A) | 8. (A) | 9. (D) | 10. (D) | 11. (B) | 12. (D) |

**問題1～3，請參考以下訊息。** 英M

[1,3]This is Jeffrey Jones in the GWC Traffic Helicopter. It's now quarter to five. Traffic is running smoothly on most streets into and out of the city. [2]However, Route 4's northbound lane is blocked because of major accident. Cars are backed up for more than three kilometers. It will take a few hours to clear the road, so we recommend taking the South Central by-pass into the city. Other than that, there are no major incidents to report, and it looks like most of you will have a smooth commute home. I'll be back for another traffic update in 15 minutes. [1, 3]This is Jeffrey Jones in the GWC Traffic Helicopter wishing you safe travel!

這是在GWC交通直升機上的傑弗瑞瓊斯。現在在還差十五分鐘就到五點。進城和出城大部分的街道交通運行流暢。不過，四號路線的北向車道因為一個重大事故而被封閉。車輛受阻超過三公里。這將要花幾小時來疏通道路，因此我們建議由市區南邊繞路進城。除此之外，沒有重大的事件報告，看來你們大部分都能順暢下班回家。我會在十五分鐘後回來做路況更新。這是在GWC交通直升機上的傑弗瑞瓊斯，祝您行車安全。

**詞彙** **smoothly** 流暢地 **block** 封鎖 **accident** 事故 **clear** 建議 **recommend** 建議 **by-pass** 旁道 **traffic update** 路況報導

**1.**

這則公告是給誰的？
(A) 駕駛人
(B) 飛機駕駛
(C) 新聞報導者
(D) 警官

**解說** 透過考題與選項可以預測該錄音為「路況報導」類型。在錄音前段與後段出現答案線索traffic，同時整體內容是在說明交通狀況，因此是給駕駛人聽的廣播節目。
答案 (A)

**詞彙** **driver** 駕駛人 **pilot** 飛機駕駛 **police officer** 警官

**2.**

四號路線有了什麼問題？
(A) 有施工。
(B) 有直升機墜毀。
(C) 有意外事故。
(D) 有太多的旅行者。

**解說** 具體的地名為很好的答案線索。「四號路線」附近出現「事故」，所以（C）為答案。 答案 (C)

**詞彙** **problem** 問題 **construction** 施工；建築工程 **crash** 墜毀

**3.**

說話者在什麼地點？
(A) 在新聞播音室
(B) 在車上
(C) 在地面上
(D) 在直升機上

**解說** 在錄音前段與後段出現了兩次「在直升機上」，所以（D）為答案。（A）是陷阱。 答案 (D)

**詞彙** **studio** 播音室 **on the ground** 在地上

**問題4～6，請參考以下訊息。** 澳W

The following is a public service announcement, brought you by Radio ABC. [4]Because of the drought, government officials are asking all city residents to conserve water. [5]Residents are asked not to fill their swimming pools or water their gardens until further notice. Right now, the government is asking residents to do this on a voluntary basis, although if the situation becomes severe, it is possible that fines will be imposed. For more information, [6]find energy conservation tips at our web site at www.energytips.or.uk.

以下由ABC電台為您帶來一則公共服務公告。由於乾旱，政府官員要求各城市的居民節省用水。直到進一步通知前，居民被要求不在游泳池注水或花園澆水。此刻，政府要求居民基於自願來做這些，但如果情況變嚴重，有可能會加以罰款。有關訊息，請在我們網站www.enrgytips.or.uk.搜尋節能小建議。

**詞彙** **public service announcement** 對大眾的公告事項 **because of** 由於… **drought** 旱災 **government official**

政府官員 resident 居民 conserve 節省 fill 灌注 swimming pool 游泳池 water 澆水 until further notice 到後續通知之前 right now 正在 on a voluntary basis 自願地 situation 狀況 severe 嚴重的 possible 有可能的 fine 罰款 impose 徵收；課取

**4.**

這則談話是要指示什麼人？
（A）廣播電台員工
（B）公務員
（C）政府官員
（D）居民

**解說** 透過考題與選項可以預測該錄音為「一般報導」類型。錄音裡重複出現「要求居民」這類的話，所以可以知道居民為聽眾。 答案 (D)

**詞彙** radio station 廣播電台 public servant 公務員

**5.**

聽眾被要求避免些什麼？
（A）給植物澆水
（B）在游泳池游泳
（C）散步
（D）丟垃圾

**解說** 「要求不要在花園澆水」也可以說是「避免給植物澆水」，所以（A）為答案。 答案 (A)

**詞彙** avoid 避免 plant 植物 throw 扔 garbage 垃圾

**6.**

在說話者提到的網站上可以發現什麼？
（A）目前氣象資訊的地圖
（B）節約能源的方式的列表
（C）政府官員的地址
（D）園藝工具的價格表

**解說** 網站名稱附近出現「節能小建議」，將此內容做變化來表達的（B）為答案。 答案 (B)

**詞彙** mention 論及 (a) list of …的目錄 way to 動詞原型 …的方法 address 地址 tool 工具

問題7～9，請參考以下訊息。美W

And now for this afternoon's lead news story. Residents of Melton city are still without power. [7]The heavy rains and strong winds swept through the county last night and tore down power lines. As a result, 150,000 residents are without electricity until this afternoon. Work crews have been working hard to restore power, [8]but the winds, which remain strong, are making their work difficult. The Power Company expects that the western part of the city will be able to turn on their lights this evening, but [9]the rest of the city will be lucky to have electricity by tomorrow morning.

現在是今天下午頭條新聞。梅爾頓市的居民依然沒有電力。昨晚大雨和強風席捲該城同時拆毀了電力線。導致十五萬居民到今天下午無電使用。施工班盡全力恢復供電，但因風勢仍強而使他們的工作困難。電力公司預計今天傍晚該城西部將能夠開燈，但城市其餘地區若到明天早上供電就算是幸運的。

**詞彙** resident 居民 heavy rain 豪雨 sweep through 橫掃；席捲 tear down 拆毀 power line 輸電線 as a result 其結果 restore 復原 be able to 能… turn on the light 開燈

**7.**

為什麼該城市的居民失去了電力？
（A）有大風暴。
（B）有太多居民住在該城市。
（C）機組工作人員正在安裝新系統。
（D）電力公司員工罷工。

**解說** 這是詢問具體內容的考題。透過考題與選項可以知道該錄音為「一般報導」類型。錄音裡，在without electricity的前面有問題狀況的原因。將「大雨和強風」改以「風暴」來表達的（A）為答案。 答案 (A)

**詞彙** lose 失去 electric power 電力 big storm 大規模暴風雨 install 安裝 on strike 罷工當中

**8.**

是什麼使得工作人員的工作變困難？
（A）強風
（B）低溫
（C）有霧的狀況
（D）豪雨

**解說** difficult為核心語，在錄音裡的difficult附近會出現答案。 答案 (A)

**詞彙** low 低 temperature 氣溫 foggy 有霧氣的 condition 狀態

**9.**

什麼時候整座城市將會有電力？
（A）今天下午
（B）今天傍晚
（C）今晚
（D）明天早上

**解說** 「今天傍晚該城西部將能夠開燈、城市其餘地區在明天早上供電」，就是指整座城市在「明天早上」才有電的意思。 答案 (D)

**詞彙** entire 全部的

問題10～12，請參考以下訊息。美M

Good evening this is Joe Butler, host of the Butler

Live. [10]Today I will be interviewing Mary Stein, one of the country's leading communication specialists. [11]She will talk about useful tips from her new book, *10 Steps to Effective Communication* which has been on the best seller's list of most major newspapers for more than 6 weeks. At the end of the interview, Ms. Stein has agreed to take calls from our audience. [12]If you have any questions for Ms. Stein, give us a call at 555-4343 and we will try to get you on the show.

晚安，我是巴特勒實況秀的主持人喬巴特勒。今天我將訪問國家領導級的溝通專家之一瑪麗斯坦。她將談到在大部分主流報紙中名列最佳銷售超過六週的她的新書「有效溝通的十個步驟」裡的有用的建議。在訪談的最後，瑪麗斯坦女士同意接聽由我們聽眾打來的電話。若您想問瑪麗斯坦女士任何問題，請致電555-4343我們會盡力在節目中接通。

**詞彙** **host** 主持人 **leading** 領導的 **communication** 溝通 **specialist** 專家 **useful** 有用的 **tip** 資訊 **major** 主要的 **audience** 聽眾

**10.**

瑪麗斯坦是誰？
(A) 一間書店的老闆
(B) 一位雜誌編輯
(C) 一位廣播主持人
(D) 一位通信專家

**解說** 透過考題與選項可以知道該錄音為「廣播節目」，而且是「受訪節目」類型，因此在人名附近會有答案。答案中的expert是將錄音裡的specialist做變化來表達的。 答案 (D)

**詞彙** **owner** 主人 **editor** 編輯人員 **host** 主持人 **expert** 專家

**11.**

為什麼斯坦女士上這個節目？
(A) 為了談一項獎賞
(B) 為了談論她的書
(C) 為了訪談一位來賓
(D) 為了介紹一個新節目

**解說** 將錄音中間部分出現的「將談到她的新書裡的有用的建議」做簡化來表達的（B）為答案。 答案 (B)

**詞彙** **award** 獎賞 **guest** 來賓 **introduce** 介紹

**12.**

說話者邀請聽眾們做什麼？
(A) 訂閱雜誌
(B) 申請免費產品
(C) 登錄一項服務
(D) 撥電話進來提問

**解說** 「受訪節目」的後面部分常出現接受聽眾來電詢問的狀況。將「若您想問問題，請致電」做簡化來表達的（D）為答案。 答案 (D)

**詞彙** **invite** 邀請 **subscribe** 訂閱 **magazine** 雜誌 **apply for** 申請 **register for** 登錄 **call in** 撥電話進來

Chapter 20 購買、參觀、觀光

Quiz |

1. (A) 2. (A) 3. (A) 4. (A)

**Q1** 英M

Is your company looking for skilled computer technicians? Do you want to hire technicians who have been trained with state-of-the-art equipment? Look no further. You can find highly trained and skilled graduates at the Computer Technology Institute.

貴公司正在尋找熟練的電腦技師嗎？您想雇用以最先進的設備來訓練的技師嗎？不用再殷殷期盼了。在電腦技術學院您能找到有完善訓練與技術好的畢業生。

什麼型態的公司正在被廣告？
（A）一家訓練機構
（B）一家電腦店

**解說** 這是詢問在廣告哪項產品的考題。錄音裡的疑問句後面有答案線索。培養「有完善訓練與技術好的畢業生」的地方就是教育訓練機構。 答案 (A)

**詞彙** look for 尋找 skilled 熟練的 technician 技師 hire 僱用 train 訓練 state-of-the-art 最先進的 equipment 設備 highly 相當高的 graduate 畢業生 institute 學院

**Q2** 澳W

Are you satisfied with your health insurance? Does it cover all your needs? Don't spend your life worrying as your insurance rates get higher and higher. Our insurance plan covers all your medical expenses at reasonable prices. **Call 555-1942** to obtain a free consultation.

您對您的健康保險滿意嗎？它涵蓋了您所有的需求嗎？別將您的人生浪費在擔心變得越來越貴的保險費率上。我們合理的價格的保險商品涵蓋了您所有的醫療費用。請撥555-1942來得到免費諮詢。

根據這則廣告，為什麼聽眾會撥這個電話號碼？
（A）為了得到諮詢
（B）為了看醫生

**解說** 這是「廣告」類型的錄音。將「得到免費諮詢」簡化成「得到諮詢」來表達的（A）為答案。 答案 (A)

**詞彙** satisfy 滿足 health insurance 健康保險 cover 提供保障 need 需求 rate 費率 insurance plan 保險商品 expense 費用 at reasonable prices 以合理的價錢 obtain 得到 free consultation 免費諮詢

**Q3** 英M

**Welcome to** the Garnet Company. My name is Ditman. I am a sales manager in charge of this factory tour. I'll be leading you around the production plant today and help you understand how we make our product durable and reliable.

歡迎到佳網公司。我的名字叫迪特門。我是負責這間工廠導覽的銷售經理。我將帶領你們到生產工廠，並幫助你們瞭解我們如何製造耐用又可靠的產品。

這則公告是在哪裡發出的？
（A）在一間工廠
（B）在一場銷售會議上

**解說** 詢問地點的考題，答案線索大部分在錄音的前段部分。尤其是「參觀／觀光」類的錄音，在welcome後面會出現線索。說話者「負責這間工廠導覽」，所以該錄音是在「工廠」做的公告。 答案 (A)

**詞彙** sales manager 銷售經理 in charge of 負責…的 factory 工廠 tour 參觀 lead 帶領 plant 工廠 durable 耐用的 reliable 可靠的

**Q4** 美M

Please remember that eating and drinking are not allowed in the exhibit areas. Instead, you can go to a very good restaurant on the second floor of the museum. **Now let's** look at the large piece of pottery standing in the center of the room.

請記住在展示區不可以飲食。但是你們可以去博物館二樓的一間很棒的餐廳。現在我們來看立在這間房間中央很大的陶瓷。

街下來很有可能會發生什麼事？
（A）一場導覽將開始。
（B）一部電影將播放。

**解說** 這是詢問「參觀／觀光」後續行程的考題。先出現禁止事項的公告，之後聽到「開始」的核心語Now let's look at，所以可以知道接下來就是開始參觀。 答案 (A)

**詞彙** remember 記住 allow 允許 exhibit 展示會 instead 不過；反而 museum 博物館 pottery 陶瓷

## STEP 01 若沒答對會後悔的考題

| | | | |
|---|---|---|---|
| 1 (A) | 2 (B) | 3 (A) | 4 (A) |
| 5 (B) | 6 (A) | 7 (A) | 8 (B) |
| 9 (C) | 10 (A) | 11 (B) | 12 (B) |
| 13 (A) | 14 (C) | | |

**1.** 美M

| | |
|---|---|
| 1 找出核心語 | advertised |
| 2 類型與答案的位置 | 主題／前面部分 |
| 3 看選項 | 雜誌或電視節目 |

Do you get your sports news from television? Are you getting tired of all the commercial interruptions on TV? You don't have to be annoyed by commercials any more. Our magazine gives you all the latest sports news commercial-free.

你從電視上得知運動新聞嗎？你對於被電視廣告打斷感到厭倦嗎？你再也不用被廣告煩擾了。我們的雜誌給你所有最新的運動新聞而且沒有廣告。

什麼東西正在被廣告？
（A）一本雜誌
（B）一個電視節目

**解說** 這是詢問在廣告哪項產品的考題。在錄音裡疑問句後面出現「我們的雜誌給你新聞而且沒有廣告」，所以（A）為答案。 答案 (A)

**詞彙** **tired** 感到厭倦的 **commercial interruption** 因廣告而來的中斷 **annoyed** 被煩擾 **any more** 不再 **magazine** 雜誌 **latest** 最新的 **commercial-free** 沒有廣告

**2.** 美W

| | |
|---|---|
| 1 找出核心語 | true about the restaurant |
| 2 類型與答案的位置 | 特點／中間部分 |
| 3 看選項 | 提供免費點心或專門做海鮮料理 |

Want to try the traditional Japanese food with a modern style? Then stop by Fuji House, which is full of wonderful aromas and tastes. We specialize in seafood and our sushi is the best you can't find anywhere else. All the dishes are moderately priced. Visit us today!

你想嘗試具有新風味的傳統日本料理嗎？那麼請順到來充滿美妙香氣和味道的富士之家吧。我們專門做海鮮，而且我們的壽司是你在任何地方都找不到的頂級品。所有的餐飲都有合理的價錢。今天就來到我們這裡吧！

有關於這個餐廳，何者為對？
（A）它提供免費點心。
（B）海鮮料理是它的專業。

**解說** 該錄音為餐廳的廣告。這個考題是在詢問特色為何。出現「我們專門做海鮮」，所以（B）為答案。 答案 (B)

**詞彙** **traditional** 傳統的 **stop by** 順便來 **full of** …充滿的 **aroma** 香氣 **taste** 味道 **specialize in** 專門做… **seafood** 海鮮 **anywhere else** 別的地方 **dish** 餐 **moderately** 合理地 **priced** 有定價的 **visit** 訪問

**3.** 澳W

| | |
|---|---|
| 1 找出核心語 | speaker |
| 2 類型與答案的位置 | 說話者／前面部分 |
| 3 看選項 | 導遊或保全人員 |

Good morning, and welcome to the ruins of Machu Picchu. My name is Lisa and I'll be your guide this morning. We'll start our walk at the main gate of the city, where you'll see the Temple of the Sun, and finish at the main plaza, which you can see behind me.

早安。歡迎到馬丘比丘遺址。我的名字叫莉莎，是你們今天早上的導遊。我們將由該城市的大門開始，在此你們會看到太陽神殿，然後在你們所看到我身後的大廣場結束。

說話者是誰？
（A）一位導遊
（B）一位保全人員

**解說** 錄音裡聽到「Welcome to + 地點名稱」就能知道為「參觀／觀光」類型。該錄音裡接著出現「我是你們今天早上的導遊」，所以（A）為答案。 答案 (A)

**詞彙** **ruins** 遺址 **main gate** 大門 **temple** 神殿 **finish** 結束 **main plaza** 大廣場

**4.** 英M

| | |
|---|---|
| 1 找出核心語 | stay at the Wilson House |
| 2 類型與答案的位置 | 具體內容（參觀行程）／前面或中間部分 |
| 3 看選項 | 半小時或一小時 |

Good afternoon. I hope you're all feeling well-rested and energetic after that delicious lunch. For our next stop, we'll visit **the Bob Wilson House**. Mr. Wilson was our city's first mayor. We'll spend 30 minutes **there**.

午安。我希望你們在好吃的午餐之後都感到充分休息且有活力。我們的下一站將參觀鮑伯威爾森之家。威爾森先生是我們城市的第一任市長。我們在那兒會花三十分鐘的時間。

他們將會在威爾森之家停留多久？
(A) 半小時
(B) 一小時

**解說** 這是詢問參觀行程的考題。在錄音中專有名詞用there來替代，並且在其後接著說出「三十分鐘」。

答案 (A)

**詞彙** **well-rested** 休息得好的 **energetic** 有活力的 **delicious** 好吃的 **stop** 停靠站 **mayor** 市長 **spend** 花（時間）

**5.** 美M

| | |
|---|---|
| 1 找出核心語 | offering discounts |
| 2 類型與答案的位置 | 主題／前面部分 |
| 3 看選項 | 為了慶祝它的週年或為了結束營業 |

Conner Bookstore is going out of business. Come in today for the most amazing bargains you've ever seen. All books are 80 percent off the ticketed price. So hurry on down to Conner Bookstore before we are gone forever.

彎角書店即將歇業。請今天就來得到你所見過的最令人驚喜的優惠。所有的書以標價打二折。所以在我們永遠消失之前請趕快到彎角書店吧。

為什麼這家店提供折扣？
(A) 為了慶祝它的週年。
(B) 為了結束營業。

**解說** 「廣告」類型錄音當中，打折活動經常出現。活動的背景、理由出現在錄音前段部分。將「歇業」以相似說法來表達的（B）為答案。

答案 (B)

**詞彙** **go out of business** 歇業 **amazing** 令人驚訝的 **bargain** 特價品 **ticketed price** 定價 **gone** 消失的 **celebrate** 慶祝 **anniversary** 紀念日 **close** 關門

**6.** 澳W

| | |
|---|---|
| 1 找出核心語 | use the service |
| 2 類型與答案的位置 | 具體內容（購買方法）／後面部分 |
| 3 看選項 | 打電話或看網站 |

Do you want to make your house look like a new house? If so, GW's Painting and Decorating is the answer. We specialize in both interior and exterior painting. We've been painting homes in this city for 13 years. Don't wait. Call us today.

你想讓你的家看起來像新家一樣嗎？若是如此，GW油漆與裝飾公司就是答案。我們專門做室內和室外油漆。我們在此城市塗裝住宅十三年了。請別等待，今天就打電話給我們。

人們如何能使用這項服務？
(A) 藉由打電話過去
(B) 藉由拜訪網站

**解說** 這是「廣告」類錄音，購買方法的線索出現在後段的部分。最常出現以撥打電話為方法的內容，而此處果然也在最後句子裡出現了。使用call的同義詞give a call的（A）為答案。

答案 (A)

**詞彙** **look like** 看起來像⋯ **answer** 答案 **specialize in** 專門做⋯ **wait** 等待 **call** 撥打電話

**7.** 美W

| | |
|---|---|
| 1 找出核心語 | receive if they call now |
| 2 類型與答案的位置 | 具體內容（優惠）／後面部分 |
| 3 看選項 | 免費配送或免費安裝 |

And if you order today, you'll also **receive** free shipping. But remember! This offer is good only until the end of this week. Don't wait any longer! Call 216-555-3411 now to place your order.

若於本日訂購，您將會得到免費配送的服務。但請記住！這項優惠只在這週有效。別再等待了！現在撥打216-555-3411來下訂單吧。

若顧客現在就打電話，他們將會得到什麼？
(A) 免費的配送
(B) 免費的安裝

**解說** 這是詢問「廣告」的優惠內容為何的考題。「現在打電話」在錄音裡是以「本日訂購」與「現在撥打」來表達。在錄音前段就可以聽到「免費配送」。

答案 (A)

**詞彙** **order** 訂購 **receive** 得到 **free shipping** 免費配送 **remember** 記住 **offer** 優惠 **good** 有效的 **place an order** 下訂單

**8.** 美M

| | |
|---|---|
| 1 找出核心語 | asked |
| 2 類型與答案的位置 | 要求事項／後面部分 |
| 3 看選項 | 安靜或帶走垃圾 |

We value our environment, so please don't throw your garbage on the trail. Since there are no garbage cans while climbing up the mountain, **you need to** carry your garbage with you until we return. Now, let's begin our hike.

我們非常重視我們的環境，所以請不要丟垃圾在小徑上。由於在登山途中沒有垃圾桶，您需要帶著您的垃圾直到我們返回。現在，讓我們開始步行吧。

觀光客被要求做什麼？
(A) 安靜的待著
(B) 帶走他們的垃圾

**解說** 這是「參觀」類錄音當中，談論「注意事項」的。考題裡的asked，在錄音裡是以you need to表達，因此接在後面聽到的「帶著您的垃圾」就是答案。 答案(B)

**詞彙** **value** 重視 **throw** 丟 **garbage** 垃圾 **trail** 小道 **climb up** 登 **carry** 帶 **return** 回來 **begin** 開始 **hike** 步行

問題9～10，請參考以下訊息。澳W

| | |
|---|---|
| 1 找出核心語 | being offered, the sale start |
| 2 類型與答案的位置 | 具體內容（優惠）／中間或後面部分 |
| | 具體內容（期間）／後面部分 |
| 3 看選項 | 免費禮物包裝，免費配送，免費安裝 |
| | 星期一，星期五，星期天 |
| 4 預測對話內容 | 免費安裝的優惠在星期一開始 |

Looking for a new appliance with affordable prices? As of tomorrow, Sweet Home Appliances is having our annual sale with fantastic bargains for every appliance. We have a variety of products such as stoves, dishwashers, drying machines and more. And during this time only, [9]we are offering free installation services for all appliances. [10]The sales start at 8 a.m., Monday and continue until 7 p.m. Sunday night. Don't miss this fantastic deal.

正在找經濟實惠的新家電嗎？從明天起，甜蜜家庭家電行舉辦年度行銷活動，每一件家電都有難以至信的特價。我們有多種產品，例如爐子、洗碗機、乾燥機等等。而且只有在此期間，我們將對所有的家電提供免費安裝服務。銷售活動在星期一上午八點開始持續到星期天晚上七點。別錯過這個超級好的交易。

**詞彙** **look for** 尋找 **appliance** 家電 **affordable price** 負擔得起的價錢 **as of** 自從… **annual** 年度的 **fantastic** 難以至信的 **bargain** 特價品 **a variety of** 多種的 **product** 產品 **stove** 爐子 **dishwasher** 洗碗機 **drying machine** 乾燥機 **offer** 提供 **installation** 安裝 **start** 開始 **miss** 錯過 **deal** 交易

**9.**

什麼服務將被提供給顧客們？
(A) 免費的禮物包裝
(B) 免費的配送
(C) 不收費的安裝

**解說** 若選項裡出現free，其錄音內容很有可能是「廣告」類。考題裡的being offered，在錄音裡是變成are offering，在其後面聽到的內容就是答案。錄音裡的free，在選項裡變成以without charge來表達。 答案(C)

**詞彙** **customer** 顧客 **complimentary** 贈送的 **gift wrapping** 禮物包裝 **delivery** 配送 **installation** 安裝 **without charge** 免費

**10.**

銷售活動什麼時候開始？
(A) 在星期一
(B) 在星期五
(C) 在星期日

**解說** 這是詢問優惠期間的考題。大部分在錄音內容後段部分出現答案線索。透過「星期一八點開始」可以知道（A）為答案。 答案(A)

問題11～12，請參考以下訊息。英M

| | |
|---|---|
| 1 找出核心語 | come to see, asked to return |
| 2 類型與答案的位置 | 地點／前面部分 |
| | 要求事項／後面部分 |
| 3 看選項 | 美術館，歷史遺址，汽車工廠 |
| | 機場，巴士，禮品店 |
| 4 預測對話內容 | 參觀古蹟的民眾在公車上集合。 |

Hello everybody, [11]I'd like to welcome you to the most historic and beautiful site in Namwon City. The building before us was first built nearly 500 years ago, and it was once destroyed, but recently restored to its original 16th century condition. Since the ground here is very slippery from the rain, please watch your step while walking around the site. We'll spend one hour here, so [12]be sure to return to the bus on time since we'll be leaving promptly at 2 o'clock.

大家好。歡迎你們到南園市裡最具有歷史價值又美麗的地點。我們前面的這棟建築物是將近五百年前初次建造的，並且曾過一次被破壞，但最近修復為原本十六世紀的狀態。由於下雨，這裡的地面相當滑溜，於此走動的時候請注意步行。我們將在這兒待一個小時，所以請你們記得準時回到公車上，因為我們將在兩點立刻出發。

**詞彙** historic 具有歷史價值的 building 建築物 build 建造 nearly 幾乎 destroy 破壞 recently 最近 restore 修復 original 原來的 condition 狀態 ground 地面 slippery 滑溜的 watch one's step 注意步行 site 地點 return 回來 on time 準時 leave 出發 promptly 立刻

**11.**

觀眾要看看什麼？

（A）一間美術館

（B）一個歷史遺址

（C）一間汽車工廠

**解說** 透過考題與選項可以預測到該錄音為「參觀／觀光」類型。該考題是詢問訪問地點為何的，答案線索在錄音裡welcome後面出現。將「具有歷史價值又美麗的地點」簡化成「具有歷史價值的地點」即「歷史遺址」的（B）為答案。 答案 (B)

**詞彙** art museum 美術館 historic site 歷史遺址 automobile factory 汽車工廠

**12.**

人們被要求返回到哪裡？

（A）到機場

（B）到巴士

（C）到禮品店

**解說** 透過考題裡的asked可以知道這是詢問要求事項的。錄音裡，在be sure to後面就是答案線索。其要求為回到公車上。 答案 (B)

**詞彙** airport 機場 gift shop 禮品店

問題13～14，請參考以下訊息。 美W

| | |
|---|---|
| 1 找出核心語 | convenient, find the product |
| 2 類型與答案的位置 | 具體內容（優點）／中間部分 |
| | 具體內容（購買方法）／後面部分 |
| 3 看選項 | 容易攜帶，能被折疊，非常輕 |
| | 百貨公司，美髮店，超市 |
| 4 預測對話內容 | 商品很容易搬運、在超市有貨 |

Do you like healthy beverages? Not only healthy but also tasty? Well, Lion Beverage has something for you. Try "Naturalia", which is full of only natural ingredients without any type of preservatives. In addition, [13]it's packaged in a small, convenient box, so you can conveniently carry it to work or to school. If you are health conscious, "Naturalia" is the best choice for you. [14]Find it now at your local supermarket.

你喜歡健康飲料嗎？不僅要健康而且也要美味嗎？那麼，獅子飲料公司為你有了某樣東西。嚐嚐「自然飲」，它只有充足的天然成分不含任何防腐劑。此外，它是小巧又方便的盒裝，所以能便於攜帶到職場或學校。如果你在意健康，「自然飲」對你來說就是最好的選擇。現在就在你們當地的超市尋找它吧。

**詞彙** healthy 健康的 beverage 飲料 full of …充滿的 ingredient 成分 preservative 防腐劑 in addition 另外 package 包裝 convenient 方便的 carry 攜帶 conscious 在意的 supermarket 超市

**13.**

關於這個產品，有什麼是很便利的？

（A）它很容易攜帶。

（B）它能被折疊。

（C）它非常的輕。

**解說** 透過考題與選項可以知道該錄音為「廣告」類型。該考題是詢問優點的。在錄音的中間部分出現convenient，可以聽到用被動語態表達的「容易攜帶」。 答案 (A)

**詞彙** easily 容易地 fold 折疊 lightweight 輕的

**14.**

聽眾可以在哪裡找到這個產品？

（A）在百貨公司

（B）在美髮店

（C）在超市

**解說** 這是詢問「廣告」敘述的購買方法為何的考題。該錄音最後的句子出現了find，在此後面就能聽到答案。 答案 (C)

**詞彙** department store 百貨公司 hair salon 美髮店

## STEP 02 考題實戰練習

| | | | | | |
|---|---|---|---|---|---|
| 1. (A) | 2. (D) | 3. (A) | 4. (D) | 5. (D) | 6. (D) |
| 7. (A) | 8. (B) | 9. (A) | 10. (A) | 11. (C) | 12. (C) |

問題1～3，請參考以下訊息。 澳W

Have you ever been late for an important meeting due to bad weather or heavy traffic? Looking for a comfortable way to get to your destination on time? [1]Then check out Koreana Railways. Koreana Railways has trains to every major business destination throughout the country, and to better meet customers' business needs, [2]we've just started providing wireless Internet service on board, so you can get on the Internet while moving to your destination. In addition, [3]we are offering special discounts for new customers. This offer will be good until the end of the month. For more information, visit our web site at www.koreanrailway.com. We look forward to seeing you soon at Koreana Railways.

你曾因惡劣的天氣或繁忙的交通而在重要會議中遲到嗎？在尋找一種舒適的方式讓您準時到達目的地嗎？那麼看看可麗安納鐵路吧。可麗安納鐵路有到全國各地每一個主要商業區的列車，同時為了更適合於客戶的需求，我們開始於車上提供無線上網服務，因此您能在移動到目的地的時候上網。此外，我們也提供特別折扣給新客戶。這項優惠將持續到本月底。有關更多訊息，請至我們的網站www.koreanrailway.com。我們期待很快與您在可麗安納鐵路相見。

**詞彙** late 晚到 important 重要的 bad weather 壞天氣 heavy traffic 交通堵塞 comfortable 舒服的 way to 動詞原型 …的方法 destination 目的地 on time 準時 throughout the country 全國到處 meet needs 滿足需求 provide 滿足需求 wireless Internet 無線網路 in addition 另外 offer 提供 discount 折扣 good 有效的 look forward to -ing 期待…

**1.**

什麼型態的公司正在被廣告？

(A) 一列火車
(B) 一項網路服務
(C) 一間搬家公司
(D) 一家飯店

**解說** 這是詢問廣告商品為何的考題，錄音前段部分的疑問句之後會出現答案。藉由錄音裡聽到的公司名稱能得到線索，而透過「有列車」也可以知道有關火車的廣告。 答案 (A)

**詞彙** advertise 打廣告 moving company 搬家公司

**2.**

這家公司最近做了什麼改變？

(A) 它招募了新人員。
(B) 它擴大進入了新市場。
(C) 它更新了網站。
(D) 它增加了服務。

**解說** 錄音中間出現的we've just started是指「最近做了某事」的意思。將其後出現的「開始於車上提供無線上網服務」做簡化來表達的 (D) 為答案。 答案 (D)

**詞彙** change 變更 recently 最近 hire 招募 add 招募

**3.**

根據說話者所言，這個月誰將會得到折扣？

(A) 第一次來的顧客
(B) 老顧客
(C) 本地居民
(D) 競賽優勝者

**解說** discount為核心語。錄音裡，在discount附近出現了new，將此改成first來表達的 (A) 為答案。 答案 (A)

**詞彙** receive 得到 first-time 第一次的 patron 老顧客 contest 競賽 winner 優勝者

**問題4~6，請參考以下訊息。** 美W

Good morning, everyone. Welcome to the City Museum of Art tour. My name is Maria Sinbaldi and I'll be your tour guide. Please line up over here, and have your ticket ready. [4]If you don't have a ticket, get one now. They cost just seven dollars. Don't worry, we'll wait for you. Now then, today we'll look at modern paintings and sculpture in the second floor galleries and [5]works by local artists, including paintings and prints, on the third floor. But [6]we'll begin in the main gallery right here on the ground floor, looking at portraits. Is everybody ready? All right, let's go.

大家早安。歡迎來到市立藝術博物館之旅。我的名字是瑪麗亞辛巴迪，我是您今天的導遊。請在此排隊並準備好您的門票。如果您沒有門票，請現在去買。門票只要七元。請別擔心，我們會等待您。那麼，今天我們將要看看在二樓畫廊裡的現代繪畫和雕塑，包含三樓由本地藝術家製作的繪畫和版畫。但我們將由現在位於的一樓主畫廊開始，先看看這些人像畫。大家都準備好了嗎？好，出發吧。

**詞彙** line up 排隊 tour 參觀 over here 往這邊 ready 準備好的 cost 需要付（價錢） wait for 等待 look at 看 modern 現代的 painting 繪畫 sculpture 雕像 work 作品 artist 藝術家 including 包括… print 版畫 ground floor 第一層樓 portrait 肖像

**4.**

這個導覽票價是多少錢？

(A) 兩元
(B) 三元
(C) 五元
(D) 七元

**解說** 這是詢問具體內容的簡短選項類考題。錄音裡，介紹地點與說話者之後，可以聽到數字七元，很容易找到答案。 答案 (D)

**5.**

本地藝術家的作品在哪兒？

(A) 在一樓
(B) 在一樓
(C) 在二樓
(D) 在三樓

**解說** 這是詢問具體內容的簡短選項類考題。Local artists為核心語，只要能聽到錄音內容裡，接在核心語後面的「三樓」就行。 答案 (D)

**6.**

這個導覽的參加者將會先去看什麼？
（A）現代繪畫
（B）雕塑
（C）版畫
（D）肖像

**解說** 在「參觀／觀光」類型錄音的後段部分會出現後續行程，而此考題就是詢問下一個行程的。錄音內容中有「先看看這些人像畫」，所以（D）為答案。

答案 (D)

**詞彙** **participant** 參加者

**問題7～9，請參考以下訊息。** 英M

Hello everyone, welcome to Big Mountain National Park. My name is George, and I'll be your guide for the day. I have a few reminders before we begin our tour. This morning, [7]we will have a 90 minute drive to the Big Waterfalls. On the way, we'll see a lot of animals. [7, 8]We will stop a few times along the way, so that you can take photos if you want. However, please don't attempt to feed the animals. Also, it's so warm today, [9]it is recommended to drink water frequently. After spending an hour at the Big Waterfalls, we will have lunch for one hour at the Jinsan Restaurant [7]where our bus will be standing by for us to move onto the next stop.

您好，大家好，歡迎來到巨山國家公園。我的名字是喬治，我將是你今天的導遊。在我們開始行程之前我有幾項提醒。今天上午，我們將開90分鐘車程去大瀑布。在路上，我們將看到很多動物。沿路上我們會停車幾次，因此如果您願意您可以拍照。不過，請不要企圖餵食動物。另外，今天如此溫暖，我們建議您經常補充水費。在大瀑布待一小時之後，我們將在津森餐廳用餐一小時，我們的巴士將在那兒等候我們移動到下一站。

**詞彙** **reminder** 公告事項 **on the way** 在路上 **stop** 停留 **take photos** 拍照 **attempt** 嘗試；試圖 **feed** 餵 **warm** 溫暖的 **recommend** 建議 **frequently** 頻繁地 **stand by** 等候；待命

**7.**

這則公告很有可能會在哪裡被聽到？
（A）在公車上
（B）在船上
（C）在火車上
（D）在飛機上

**解說** 「參觀／觀光」類錄音裡，地點相關線索總是在前段部分出現。但此考題的選項為交通工具，所以答案線索可能不在錄音前段部分。該錄音內容裡有「九十分鐘車程」、「停車」、「巴士等候」等說法，所以（A）為答案。

答案 (A)

**詞彙** **announcement** 公告事項

**8.**

他們今天早上為什麼會有數次的停車？
（A）為了購買一些食物
（B）為了照相
（C）為了休息
（D）為了搭載其他團體

**解說** 錄音中間部分能聽到「如果您願意您可以拍照」，此為停車的理由。在這一句裡的pictures與photos是同義詞。

答案 (B)

**詞彙** **purchase** 購買 **take pictures** 拍照 **take a rest** 休息 **pick up** 搭載

**9.**

說話者鼓勵人們做什麼事？
（A）喝水
（B）餵食動物
（C）輕聲說話
（D）帶走他們的垃圾

**解說** 「參觀／觀光」類型的後面部分會出現注意／勸導／許可事項。該考題裡的核心語encourage，在錄音裡以recommended來表達，其後面就有答案線索。

答案 (A)

**詞彙** **encourage** 鼓勵 **quietly** 安靜地 **carry** 帶

**問題10～12，請參考以下訊息。** 美M

[10]Hi, I'm Richard Steeves, director of the award-winning film, *The Exodus*. To celebrate Busan's international film festival, we're offering free admission or discounts to previews scheduled during the next two weeks. [11]We've been sponsored by Busan City Council to offer a special package to audience members. For the low price of two dollars, you can take a guided city tour and enjoy refreshments before or after the film. The festival venue is conveniently located near public transportation stops. [12]Sign up for the special package online at www.busanfestival.com. Availability is limited, so don't wait!

您好，我是獲獎影片出埃及記的導演李察史提夫。為了慶祝釜山國際電影節，我們提供免費入場或折扣在預定於未來兩星期的試映會。我們被釜山市議會贊助提供觀眾一個特別配套方案。用兩塊錢的低價，能得到一趟市區導覽和在看片之前或之後享受茶點。電影節舉辦的地點接近大眾運輸站。請上網www.busanfestival.com登記這個特別的配套方案。名額有限，所以請不要等待！

**詞彙** **director** 導演 **award-winning** 得獎的 **celebrate** 慶祝 **offer** 提供 **free admission** 免費入場 **discount** 折

扣 **preview** 試映會 **sponsor** 贊助 **guided tour** 有導遊的旅行 **refreshment** 茶點 **venue** 活動場地 **conveniently located** 位置方便的 **public transportation** 公共交通 **sign up for** 登錄 **online** 在線上 **availability** 可得性 **limited** 有限

**10.**

說話者很有可能是誰？

（A）一位電影導演

（B）一位導遊

（C）一位餐廳經理

（D）一位市長

**解說** 在錄音前段部分出現I'm與說話者的身份。於此題中直接說「導演」。 答案 (A)

**詞彙** **tour guide** 導遊 **manager** 經理 **mayor** 市長

**11.**

這個特別配套方案中包含了什麼？

（A）博物館的票

（B）在紀念品店的折扣

（C）市區觀光

（D）導覽手冊

**解說** 在錄音當中直接能聽到有關special package的說明，也就是「用兩塊錢能享受旅遊與茶點」。 答案 (C)

**詞彙** **include** 包含 **museum** 博物館 **gift shop** 紀念品店 **guidebook** 手冊

**12.**

為什麼聽眾應該到網站看？

（A）為了得到停車指示

（B）為了看目前表演的清單

（C）為了登錄一項配套活動

（D）為了更多瞭解城市的景點

**解說** 錄音內容裡，在網址的附近可以聽到register for的同義詞sign up for。在其後面出現的special package改成了event package來表達。因此（C）為答案。 答案 (C)

**詞彙** **visit** 訪問 **parking** 停車 **tip** 資訊 **a list of...** 的目錄 **register for** 登錄 **attraction** 旅遊景點

# 模擬試題答案與解析

| 001 (C) | 002 (D) | 003 (C) | 004 (D) | 005 (D) | 006 (C) | 007 (D) | 008 (B) | 009 (C) | 010 (C) |
|---|---|---|---|---|---|---|---|---|---|
| 011 (A) | 012 (B) | 013 (B) | 014 (A) | 015 (A) | 016 (C) | 017 (A) | 018 (B) | 019 (A) | 020 (B) |
| 021 (B) | 022 (C) | 023 (A) | 024 (B) | 025 (B) | 026 (C) | 027 (A) | 028 (B) | 029 (B) | 030 (B) |
| 031 (A) | 032 (A) | 033 (A) | 034 (B) | 035 (A) | 036 (A) | 037 (A) | 038 (B) | 039 (B) | 040 (B) |
| 041 (B) | 042 (A) | 043 (B) | 044 (D) | 045 (D) | 046 (A) | 047 (A) | 048 (B) | 049 (D) | 050 (A) |
| 051 (B) | 052 (B) | 053 (D) | 054 (B) | 055 (D) | 056 (D) | 057 (C) | 058 (C) | 059 (D) | 060 (B) |
| 061 (B) | 062 (B) | 063 (D) | 064 (A) | 065 (B) | 066 (A) | 067 (C) | 068 (D) | 069 (B) | 070 (B) |
| 071 (C) | 072 (A) | 073 (D) | 074 (D) | 075 (D) | 076 (D) | 077 (D) | 078 (A) | 079 (B) | 080 (A) |
| 081 (D) | 082 (A) | 083 (A) | 084 (C) | 085 (D) | 086 (C) | 087 (A) | 088 (A) | 089 (C) | 090 (B) |
| 091 (C) | 092 (B) | 093 (C) | 094 (B) | 095 (C) | 096 (C) | 097 (A) | 098 (C) | 099 (A) | 100 (B) |

# 模擬試題答案與解析

## Part 1

**1.** 美W

(A) A boy is riding a bicycle.
(B) A boy is purchasing a tire.
(C) A boy is working on a bicycle.
(D) A boy is sweeping the floor.

(A) 一個男孩正在騎自行車。
(B) 一個男孩正在購買輪胎。
(C) 一個男孩正在修理自行車。
(D) 一個男孩正在掃地。

**解說** 照片裡的少年正在修理腳踏車，所以(C)為答案。(A)是用聽到bicycle來做誤導。(B)必須要照片裡出現錢才會成為有可能的選項。(D)不是答案，因為少年是在修理腳踏車而不是在掃地。 答案 (C)

**詞彙** **ride a bicycle** 騎自行車 **purchase** 購買 **tire** 輪胎 **work on** 處理；修理 **sweep** 掃 **floor** 地板

**2.** 美M

(A) She's drinking from a water fountain.
(B) She's removing her necklace.
(C) She's reaching for a cup.
(D) She's wearing her glasses.

(A) 她正在從飲水台喝水。
(B) 她正在解開她的項鍊。
(C) 她正在伸手拿杯子。
(D) 她戴著眼鏡。

**解說** 一位女性戴著眼鏡，所以(D)為答案。(A)論及了照片裡沒有的名詞water fountain，所以不是答案。(B)不是答案，因為該女性不是正在解開項鍊，而是戴著項鍊的狀態。(C) 不是答案，因為該女性不是正在伸手拿杯子。 答案 (D)

**詞彙** **drink from** 從…喝水 **water fountain** 飲水台 **remove** 去掉 **necklace** 項鍊 **reach for** 向…伸手 **wear** 穿戴

**3.** 英M

(A) A man is assembling a bookcase.
(B) A man is bending to pick up the newspaper.
(C) The women are sitting next to each other.
(D) Some benches have been disassembled.

(A) 一個男人正在組裝書櫃。
(B) 一個男人正在彎腰拿起報紙。
(C) 女人們正並排坐著。
(D) 一些長椅被拆解了。

**解說** 有兩位女性並排坐著，所以(C)為答案。(A)是用與book相近的發音bookcase來誤導的選項。(B)論及了照片裡沒有的名詞newspaper，所以不是答案。(D)是故意用周遭背景的單字benches來誤導的選項。 答案 (C)

**詞彙** **assemble** 組裝 **bookcase** 書櫃 **bend** 彎腰 **pick up** 拾取 **newspaper** 報紙 **each other** 互相 **disassemble** 拆解

**4.** 澳W

(A) Some sofas are being arranged around the table.
(B) Some chairs are being cleaned.
(C) Some file folders are being stacked.
(D) Some furniture is being moved.

(A) 一些沙發被圍著桌子擺設。
(B) 一些椅子正在被清潔。
(C) 一些文件夾正在被堆放。
(D) 一些家具正在被搬移。

**解說** 有兩個男性在搬沙發上樓，因此以概括性說法來表達的(D)為答案。(A)出現了照片裡沒有的名詞table，所以不是答案。(B)也出現了照片裡沒有的名詞chair，所以不是答案。(C)也不是答案，因為出現了照片裡沒有的名詞file folders。 答案 (D)

**詞彙** **arrange** 擺設 **clean** 清掃乾淨 **stack** 堆放 **furniture** 家具 **move** 搬移

**5.** 美M

(A) A doorframe is being measured.
(B) A fence runs along the edge of the road.
(C) A worker is holding a ladder.
(D) Some workers are building a roof.

(A) 門框正在被測量。
(B) 圍欄沿著道路的邊緣。
(C) 一個工人正抓著梯子。
(D) 一些工人正在建設屋頂。

**解說** 有兩個男人在建築物上該屋頂，所以(D)為答案。(A)出現了照片裡沒有的名詞doorframe，所以不是答案。(B)也出現了照片裡沒有的名詞fence，所以不是答案。(C)是故意用周遭背景的單字ladder來誤導的選項。 答案 (D)

**詞彙** **doorframe** 門框 **measure** 測量 **fence** 圍欄 **worker** 工人 **hold** 抓著 **ladder** 梯子 **roof** 屋頂

**6.** 美W

(A) Some trees line both sides of the street.
(B) Some people are riding on a boat.
(C) Some cars are crossing a bridge.
(D) Some pedestrians are crossing a bridge.

(A) 一些樹木排列在街道的兩側。

(B) 一些人正在搭船。
(C) 一些車輛正在通過橋樑。
(D) 一些行人正在通過橋樑。

**解說** 有一些車子正在過橋，所以(C)為答案。(A)不是答案，因為樹木是在道路的單側。選項(B)和(D)不是答案，因為在照片中沒有人出現。 答案 (C)

**詞彙** **line** 排成一列 **both sides of the street** 街道的兩側 **ride** 搭乘 **cross a bridge** 通過橋樑 **pedestrian** 行人

**7.** 英M
(A) Some people are waiting in line to buy a lunch.
(B) Some people are collecting some bottles.
(C) Some people are setting up equipment for a meeting.
(D) Some people have gathered around a table.

(A) 一些人正在排隊等候買午餐。
(B) 一些人正在收集一些瓶子。
(C) 一些人正在為會議安置設備。
(D) 一些人正圍著桌子聚集。

**解說** 照片裡的人們繞著桌子坐著，所以(D)為答案。(A)不是答案，因為人們不是在排隊等買午餐。(B)出現了照片裡沒有的bottles，所以不是答案。(C)出現了照片裡沒有的equipment，所以也不是答案。 答案 (D)

**詞彙** **wait in line** 排隊等候 **buy** 買 **collect** 收集 **bottle** 瓶子 **set up** 安置 **equipment** 設備 **meeting** 會議 **gather** 聚集

**8.** 澳W
(A) A plaque is hanging on the wall.
(B) A television has been placed next to the lamp.
(C) Dishes are being cleared from the table.
(D) Cushions are piled on a sofa.

(A) 一塊牌匾掛在牆上。
(B) 一台電視被放在檯燈旁邊。
(C) 餐盤被從餐桌上清除。
(D) 墊子被堆在沙發上。

**解說** 電視被放在檯燈旁邊的位置，所以(B)為答案。(A)出現了照片裡沒有的plaque，所以不是答案。選項(C)因為照片裡沒有人卻聽到being，所以不是答案。另外照片中也沒有dishes出現。(D)也是出現照片中沒有的cushions和sofa，所以不是答案。 答案 (B)

**詞彙** **plaque** 牌匾 **hang** 掛 **dish** 餐盤 **clear** 清除 **cushion** 墊子 **pile** 堆置

**9.** 美W
(A) Some cars are waiting at the railroad crossing.
(B) Passengers are exiting a train.
(C) A train is traveling on the tracks.
(D) A man is checking his time schedule.

(A) 一些車輛正在平交道口等著。
(B) 乘客正在離開列車。
(C) 一列火車行駛在軌道上。
(D) 一個男人正在確認他的時間表。

**解說** 火車在鐵道上移動，所以(C)為答案。(A)出現照片中沒有的railroad crossing，所以不是答案。(B)和(D)因為照片中沒有人出現，所以不是答案。 答案 (C)

**詞彙** **railroad crossing** 平交道口 **passenger** 乘客 **exit** 離開 **travel** 行駛 **track** 軌道 **time schedule** 時間表

**10.** 美W
(A) A spiral staircase winds around the building.
(B) A woman is going down a flight of stairs.
(C) A handrail runs up the middle of the steps.
(D) A light is being installed on the window frame.

(A) 螺旋式的樓梯圍繞著這棟建築。
(B) 一個女人正走下一段樓梯。
(C) 有扶手在階梯的中間。
(D) 燈正被安裝在窗框上。

**解說** 扶手在樓梯的中段，所以(C)為答案。選項(A)因為照片裡沒有螺旋形的樓梯，所以不是答案。選項(B)因為照片中沒有人物出現，不能用A woman，所以不是答案。選項(D)是因為照片裡沒有人卻聽到being，所以不是答案。 答案 (C)

**詞彙** **spiral staircase** 螺旋式的樓梯 **wind** 圍繞 **a flight of stairs** 一段樓梯 **handrail** 扶手 **light** 燈 **install** 安裝 **window frame** 窗框

## Part 2

**11.** 美M 英M
Have you read the new software manual?
(A) Not yet. Where is it?
(B) He's in charge of the annual banquet.
(C) Here's your newspaper.

你看過新的軟體手冊嗎？
(A) 還沒有，它在哪裡？
(B) 他在負責年度晚宴。
(C) 這是您的報紙。

**解說** 這是一般疑問句的考題。對於詢問是否「看過」，以否定與補充說明方式來回答的(A)為答案。(B)是故意用manual的類似發音annual來誤導的選項。(C)是故意用new的類似發音newspaper來誤導的選項。 答案 (A)

**詞彙** **manual** 手冊；說明書 **in charge of** 負責…的 **banquet** 宴會 **newspaper** 報紙

12. 美W 澳W

How do you commute to work every day?
(A) No later than 7:00.
(B) I walk there.
(C) Yes, in the afternoon.

你每天如何上下班？
(A) 不晚於七點。
(B) 我走路到那裡。
(C) 是的，在下午。

**解說** 這是詢問通勤方式的how。(B)「用走路去」指的就是通勤的方式，就是答案。(A)是對於when的回答方式，所以不是答案。(C)是對於疑問詞疑問句用Yes／No來回答，所以不是答案。 答案 (B)

**詞彙** **commute to work** 通勤 **no later than** 不晚於… **walk** 走路

13. 英M 美W

Can you tell me your camera serial number?
(A) Contact me at 555-6556.
(B) Where is it?
(C) Yes, very serious.

你能告訴我你相機的序號嗎？
(A) 撥555-6556與我聯絡。
(B) 它在哪裡？
(C) 是的，非常嚴重。

**解說** 這是建議疑問句的考題。(B)是反問形式的回答方式，總是能成為答案。(A)是故意用電話號碼來與number產生聯想做誤導的選項。(C)故意用了serial的類似發音serious來誤導的選項。 答案 (B)

**詞彙** **serial number** 序號 **contact** 聯絡 **serious** 嚴重的

14. 美M 美W

Did you go to the department meeting yesterday?
(A) It was cancelled.
(B) Okay, let's talk later.
(C) It will be informative.

你昨天去了部門會議嗎？
(A) 它被取消了。
(B) 好吧，我們晚點再說吧。
(C) 那將是很有教育性的。

**解說** 這是一般疑問句的考題，選項(A)在回答是否「去了部門會議」時省略了No，直接說「被取消了」，此即為答案。(B)是對於建議疑問句的回答方式。而若只有考慮meeting就很容易會聯想到選項(C)的內容，但這與該考題無關，在時態上也不一致。 答案 (A)

**詞彙** **department** 部門 **meeting** 會議 **cancel** 取消 **later** 稍後 **informative** 有教育性的

15. 美M 美W

Where is the product manual?
(A) In the drawer.
(B) Once a month.
(C) Mr. Jackson is the owner.

產品說明書在哪裡？
(A) 在抽屜裡。
(B) 每個月一次。
(C)傑克遜先生是主人。

**解說** 對where疑問句以地點說法來回答的(A)為答案。(B)是對於How often的回答方式，(C)是對於Who的回答方式，所以都不是答案。 答案 (A)

**詞彙** **product manual** 產品說明書 **drawer** 抽屜 **owner** 主人

16. 美M 澳W

When will you guys finish the pamphlet?
(A) On your desk, I believe.
(B) I haven't met with them before.
(C) Later today.

你們什麼時候完成這本小冊子？
(A) 我相信是在你辦公桌上。
(B) 我之前沒有與他們見面。
(C) 今天稍晚。

**解說** 這是詢問未來時間的when疑問句考題，所以用時間點說法來回答的(C)為答案。(A)是對於where的回答方式，(B)的them在考題中不能夠知道是指誰，所以不是答案。 答案 (C)

**詞彙** **you guys** 大家；諸位 **finish** 完成 **pamphlet** 小手冊 **meet with** 與…會面 **later today** 今天稍晚

17. 美W 英M

The copy machine is making strange noises again.
(A) We have to get a new one.
(B) No, the 100 to 300 dollars price range.
(C) I spilt coffee on it by mistake.

影印機又發出奇怪的聲音。
(A) 我們得買一台新的。
(B) 不，是一百到三百元的價格範圍。
(C) 我不小心把咖啡灑在上面了。

**解說** 該考題是論及問題狀況的陳述句，所以對此提出解決方法的(A)為答案。(B)是故意用strange的相似發音range來誤導的選項。(C) 是故意用copy的相似發音coffee來誤導的選項。 答案 (A)

**詞彙** copy machine 影印機 make a strange noise 發出怪聲音 price range 價格範圍 spill 潑灑 by mistake 潑灑

**18.** 美M 美W

What are you doing this afternoon?
(A) Yes, I have to.
(B) I'm going shopping.
(C) Fine, thanks.

今天下午你將要做什麼？
(A) 是的，我得做。
(B) 我將去購物。
(C) 很好，謝謝您。

**解說** 這是詢問行為的what疑問句。回答中包含了行為的(B)為答案。(A)不是答案，因為對疑問詞疑問句不能用Yes／No來回答。(C)是對於How的回答方式。 答案 (B)

**詞彙** have to 得… go shopping 去購物 fine 去購物

**19.** 美W 美M

Didn't you think the speech was interesting?
(A) No, it was long and boring.
(B) No, there's no interest fee.
(C) Sure, let's have some coffee.

你不覺得演講很有趣嗎？
(A) 不，它漫長又無聊。
(B) 不，它沒有利息。
(C) 當然，我們來一點咖啡吧。

**解說** 該考題是否定疑問句。對「有趣」以No來回答，之後再附加說明的(A)為答案。(B)是故意用interesting的相似發音interest來誤導的選項。(C)是對建議的說法回答的方法。 答案 (A)

**詞彙** speech 演講 interesting 有趣的 boring 無聊 interest fee 利息

**20.** 英M 美W

Where did you leave the new catalog?
(A) Sorry, we're going to produce them next year.
(B) In the top drawer of this cabinet.
(C) Of course not.

你把新的型錄放在哪了？
(A) 對不起，我們明年才要生產它們。
(B) 在這個櫃子最上面的抽屜裡。
(C) 當然不是。

**解說** 對where疑問句用地點說法來回答的(B)為答案。(A)沒有包含地點說法，所以不是答案。(C)是對Do you mind...?疑問句的回答方式。 答案 (B)

**詞彙** leave 留置 catalog 型錄 produce 生產 drawer 抽屜

**21.** 美W 美M

You like Italian cooking, don't you?
(A) She hasn't ordered the soup.
(B) Yes, very much.
(C) Beside the grill.

你喜歡義大利料理，不是嗎？
(A) 她沒有點這道湯。
(B) 是的，非常喜歡。
(C) 在烤架的旁邊。

**解說** 該考題是附加問句。先將否定詞或尾巴去掉了之後對此表達肯定，再附加說明的(B)為答案。(A)和(C)是故意用與cooking產生聯想的soup、grill來誤導的選項。 答案 (B)

**詞彙** cooking 料理 order 點(菜) beside …的旁邊 grill 烤架

**22.** 澳W 英M

Who's going to lock up the office tonight?
(A) I bought it at the office supply store.
(B) For three night only.
(C) I'm working late, so I will.

今晚誰要鎖辦公室？
(A) 我在辦公用品店買到它的。
(B) 只有三個晚上。
(C) 我將工作到很晚。所以我會。

**解說** 對who疑問句的回答方式中，包含有「我」的(C)為答案。(A)是故意用同音詞office來產生混淆的選項。(B)是對how long疑問句的回答方式。 答案 (C)

**詞彙** lock up 將…鎖上 office supply store 辦公用品店 work late 工作到很晚

**23.** 美M 美W

I'd like to change my appointment time.
(A) I can help you with that.
(B) Which apartment do you like?
(C) Sorry, I have no change.

我想變更我的預約時間。
(A) 我可以幫你。
(B) 你喜歡哪一間公寓？
(C) 抱歉，我沒有零錢。

**解說** 該考題是以I'd like to開始的陳述句，因此以「我幫助你」回答的(A)為答案。(B)是故意用appointment的相似發音來誤導的選項。(C)是將考題裡change的原來意思「變更」故意改成「零錢」來誤導的選項。

答案 (A)

**詞彙** **change** 變更 **appointment time** 預約時間 **apartment** 公寓

**24.** 美M 英M

Can I expect your reply today or tomorrow?
(A) By regular mail.
(B) This afternoon, if possible.
(C) Yes, I can.

我今天可以得到你的回覆，還是明天？
(A) 通過普通郵件。
(B) 如果可能的話，是今天下午。
(C) 是的，我可以。

**解說** 該考題是選擇疑問句。(B)的this afternoon是today的變化說法。(A)是對how的回答方式。而選項(C)其主詞不對。

答案 (B)

**詞彙** **reply** 回覆 **regular mail** 普通郵件 **if possible** 如果可能的話

**25.** 美W 美M

Which is the key to the supply closet?
(A) We don't need supplies.
(B) The one with the yellow tag.
(C) No, it isn't very close.

哪一隻是供應品倉庫的鑰匙？
(A) 我們不需要用品。
(B) 有一個黃色標籤的那個。
(C) 不，它不會很近。

**解說** which疑問句也是一種選擇疑問句。用代名詞one來回答的(B)為答案。(A)是故意用supply的相近發音supplies來誤導的選項。(C)是故意用closet的相近發音close來誤導的選項。

答案 (B)

**詞彙** **supply closet** 供應品倉庫 **tag** 標籤 **close** 近

**26.** 美M 美W

Why is the book's publication being delayed?
(A) Lay it on the table.
(B) No, the deadline is firm.
(C) We need to get final approval from our CEO.

這本書的出版為什麼被延後？
(A) 把它放在桌子上。
(B) 不，截止期限是固定的。
(C) 我們需要得到來自我們總裁的最終批准。

**解說** 對why疑問句以理由來回答的(C)為答案。(A)是對where的回答方式。(B)是對疑問詞疑問句用Yes／No回答的，所以不是答案。

答案 (C)

**詞彙** **publication** 出版 **delay** 延後 **lay** 放置 **deadline** 截止期限 **firm** 固定不變的 **final approval** 最終的批准

**27.** 美M 英M

When do you expect the budget plan to be approved?
(A) By the end of this week.
(B) Yes, things should improve.
(C) Looks like we need money.

你預期預算案什麼時候被批准？
(A) 在本週末之前。
(B) 是的，工作應該改進。
(C) 看來我們需要經費。

**解說** 該考題是詢問未來時間的when疑問句，所以以未來時間點回答的(A)為答案。(B)是對疑問詞疑問句用了Yes／No回答，所以不是答案。(C)是故意用money來與budget產生混淆的選項。

答案 (A)

**詞彙** **expect** 預期 **budget plan** 預算案 **approve** 批准 **by the end of this week** 在這一週末之前 **improve** 改進 **look like** 看起來…

**28.** 美M 澳W

How do you turn off the copy machine?
(A) I'll return it soon.
(B) Press the red button.
(C) The copier is over there.

怎麼關影印機？
(A) 我將很快就返還它。
(B) 按紅色的鈕。
(C) 影印機就在那兒。

**解說** 該考題是方法的how疑問句，因此有表達方法的(B)為答案。(A)是故意用turn的相近發音return來產生混淆的選項。(C)是對where的回答方式。

答案 (B)

**詞彙** **turn off** 關掉 **copy machine** 影印機 **return** 返回 **press** 按 **copier** 影印影印 **over there** 在那兒

**29.** 美M 美W

Could you please turn the radio up?
(A) It's Sandy's turn to go.
(B) No problem. I'll turn it up.
(C) Down the hall and to the right.

你可否將收音機聲量開大一點？
(A) 現在輪到珊蒂去了。
(B) 沒問題，我會開大一點。
(C) 到大廳底之後右轉。

**解說** 該考題是建議的疑問句。因此以肯定／允許回答之後再附加說明的(B)為答案。(A)是故意用同音詞turn來產生混淆的選項。在選項(C)中，若將考題裡的turn解釋為「轉彎」，是可以列入考慮的選項，但不是答案。 答案 (B)

**詞彙** **turn up** 提高聲量

**30.** 美W 美M

Don't we need to order more office supplies?
(A) It's hard to open.
(B) No, let's do it later.
(C) Yes, I was surprised.

我們不需要訂購更多的辦公用品嗎？
(A) 它很難打開。
(B) 不，晚一點做吧。
(C) 是的，我很驚訝。

**解說** 該考題是間接建議的疑問句。以否定／拒絕回答之後，再附加說明的(B)為答案。(A)是完全無關的選項。(C)是故意用supplies的類似發音surprised來產生混淆的選項。 答案 (B)

**詞彙** **order** 訂購 **office supplies** 辦公用品 **hard** 困難 **open** 打開 **later** 稍晚一點 **surprised** 驚訝

**31.** 美W 英M

The printer's run out of ink.
(A) You can get some in the top drawer of this cabinet.
(B) Yes, I'm having trouble running this program.
(C) No, I think she headed out for lunch.

印表機的墨水用完了。
(A) 你可以在這個櫃子最上面的抽屜裡拿到一些。
(B) 是的，我在運用這個程序時遇到困難。
(C) 不，我想她出去吃午餐了。

**解說** 該考題是論及問題狀況的陳述句。因此提供解決方法的(A)為答案。(B)是論及另一個問題來產生混淆的選項。(C)是故意用同音詞out來產生混淆的選項，而且也不知道she指的是誰。 答案 (A)

**詞彙** **out of ink** 沒有墨水的 **drawer** 抽屜 **have trouble -ing** 於…遇到困難 **head out** 出去

**32.** 澳W 美W

How was your trip to London?
(A) I had a great time.
(B) A few weeks.
(C) On the plane.

你去倫敦的旅行如何？
(A) 我有了很棒的時光。
(B) 幾個星期。
(C) 在飛機上。

**解說** 該考題是詢問狀態的how疑問句。以包含形容詞的句子回答的(A)為答案。(B)是對how long的回答方式。(C)是對where的回答方式。 答案 (A)

**詞彙** **trip** 旅行

**33.** 美W 美M

Who's going to review the sales projections?
(A) I heard the marketing director will do it.
(B) It's a nice view.
(C) No, I don't know that salesperson.

誰將會審閱銷售預測？
(A) 我聽說是行銷總監將會做。
(B) 很不錯的景觀。
(C) 不，我不認識那個營業員。

**解說** 對who疑問句以「職稱」來回答的(A)為答案。(B)是故意用review的相近發音view來產生混淆的選項。(C)是對疑問詞疑問句用了Yes／No來回答，所以不是答案。 答案 (A)

**詞彙** **review** 審閱 **sales projections** 銷售預測 **marketing director** 行銷總監 **view** 景觀 **salesperson** 營業員

**34.** 英M 美W

It's a bit chilly today.
(A) It looks like a pot.
(B) Maybe you should get your sweater.
(C) I'll talk to you later today.

今天有點冷。
(A) 它看起來像一個鍋子。
(B) 也許你應該穿你的毛衣。
(C) 今天晚點我將會和你談話。

**解說** 對「冷」的狀況提出解決方法的(B)為答案。(A)是完全無關的內容。(C)是故意用同音詞today來產生混淆的選項。 答案 (B)

**詞彙** **a bit** 有一點 **chilly** 冷的 **look like** 看起來像… **pot** 鍋子 **later** 稍晚一點

**35.** 美M 美W

We need to register for the workshop.
(A) Thanks for reminding me.
(B) I took a walk earlier today.
(C) In a store downtown.

我們需要為研習會做登錄。
(A) 謝謝你提醒我。
(B) 我今天早一點的時候散步的。

(C) 在市中心的店。

**解說** 該考題是一種提出建議的陳述句。對提供的資訊表達謝意的(A)為答案。(B)是故意用register的類似發音earlier來產生混淆的選項。(C)是故意用store來與workshop產生混淆的選項。 答案 (A)

**詞彙** **register for** 為…做登錄 **remind** 提醒 **take a walk** 散步 **store** 商店 **downtown** 市中心

**36.** 澳W 英M

Why are you cleaning your shirt?
(A) I noticed a spot.
(B) Since yesterday.
(C) I'll take this to the dry cleaner's.

你為什麼清洗著你的襯衫？
(A) 我看到了一個污漬。
(B) 從昨天起。
(C) 我將會把它拿去乾洗店。

**解說** 該考題是理由的why疑問句。以理由來回答的(A)為答案。(B)是對how long的回答方式。選項(C)若沒有聽到考題裡的疑問詞，很容易將cleaning與dry cleaner's之間產生連結而誤選，但不是答案。 答案 (A)

**詞彙** **clean** 清洗 **notice** 看到；發現 **spot** 污點
**since** 自從…起 **take**（事物）**to**（場所）把某物帶到某處
**dry cleaner's** 乾洗店

**37.** 美W 美M

I'm looking for a set of headphones to use with my CD player.
(A) What brand do you have in mind?
(B) The player will be here in a week.
(C) Yes, I'm looking forward to it.

我在尋找一組耳機來和我的CD播放機使用。
(A) 你在考慮什麼品牌？
(B) 播放器將在一星期內到這兒。
(C) 是的，我很期待。

**解說** 若考題為陳述句，則以反問句當作答案的機率為百分之三十三。(B)是故意用同音詞player來產生混淆的選項。(C)是故意用looking for的相近發音looking forward來誤導的選項。 答案 (A)

**詞彙** **look for** 尋找 **have in mind** 在心裡考量 **look forward to** 對於…期待

**38.** 美M 美W

Who's working extended hours tonight?
(A) I don't think it's ours.
(B) Shouldn't the project manager do that?
(C) Here's his extension.

今天晚上誰將會加班？
(A) 我不認為它是我們的。
(B) 不是企劃經理應該做嗎？
(C) 這是他的分機號碼。

**解說** 對who疑問句用包含「職稱」的反問句回答的(B)為答案。(A)是故意用hours的相近發音ours來產生混淆的選項。(C)是故意用extended的類似發音extension來產生混淆的選項。 答案 (B)

**詞彙** **work extended hours** 加班 **extension** 分機號碼

**39.** 澳W 英M

You didn't finish processing those payments yet, did you?
(A) For our current list of prices.
(B) No, not quite.
(C) Yes, you may not.

你還沒有完成這些付費程序，對嗎？
(A) 針對我們目前的價格清單。
(B) 沒有，還沒有。
(C) 是的，你不可以。

**解說** 將否定詞去掉之後，句子以否定說法回答，再附加說明的(B)為答案。(A)是故意用payments來與prices產生聯想來做誤導的選項。(C)是用錯了主詞，若以you來詢問，應該以I來回答。 答案 (B)

**詞彙** **finish** 完成 **process** 處理 **payment** 付費 **list** 清單
**price** 價格 **not quite** 尚未

**40.** 美M 美W

Don't you think we should take a short break?
(A) He can fix it.
(B) Okay, in 10 minutes.
(C) It was a lovely vacation.

你不覺得我們需要暫時休息一下嗎？
(A) 他可以修好它。
(B) 好的，十分鐘之後。
(C) 這真是個美好的假期。

**解說** 該考題是間接建議的疑問句。因此以肯定／允許回答，之後再附加說明的(B)為答案。在選項(A)中，若將考題裡的break解釋成「故障」而不是「休息」，會成為有可能選擇的選項。(C)是對how疑問句的回答方式。 答案 (B)

**詞彙** **take a short break** 暫時休息一下 **fix** 修理
**lovely** 美好的 **vacation** 休假

## Part 3

**問題41～43，請參考以下對話。** 美M 英M

M1 : Well, [41]I've almost finished all of the work for the roof except I have to drive nails into these last pieces of woods. After that we can start painting. Have you prepared all of the supplies we need for the painting?

M2 : Yes, [42]except the brushes. I couldn't find them in the truck. I must have left them at the store this morning. I'll call the store to see if the brushes are still there.

M1 : Sounds like a good plan. [43]I think we can still have the roof completed by this afternoon. I mean, it won't take longer than two hours for us to finish the painting.

男1：嗯，除了在最後這塊木頭上得把釘子敲進去，我幾乎完成屋頂所有的工作了。之後我們就可以開始塗油漆了。你把我們塗油漆時需要的所有用品準備好了嗎？

男2：是的，除了刷子。我在卡車上找不到它們。我一定是今天早上把他們留在店裡了。我會打電話給店裡看看刷子是否還在那兒。

男1：聽起來是個好計劃。我想我們仍然可以在今天下午完成屋頂工作。我的意思是，我們要是完成塗油漆不會需要兩小時以上。

**詞彙** **finish** 完成 **work** 工作 **roof** 屋頂 **except** 除了 **drive** 敲 **wood** 木頭 **prepare** 準備 **brush** 刷子 **leave** 留置 **still** 仍然 **completed** 被完成的

### 41

說話者正在做什麼？

(A) 正在訂辦公室用品

(B) 正在屋頂工作

(C) 正在儲存建材

(D) 修理卡車

**解說** 該考題是詢問主題的，因此答案大部分在錄音的前段部分。出現「我幾乎完成屋頂所有的工作了」與大致的作業行程，所以可以瞭解成「正在屋頂工作」。

答案 (B)

**詞彙** **order** 下訂單 **office supply** 辦公室用品 **store** 儲存 **building material** 建材 **fix** 修理

### 42

說話者遺忘了什麼？

(A) 刷子

(B) 汽車零件

(C) 一些畫作

(D) 工作時間表

**解說** 考題中的lost，在錄音裡是變化為「找不到」來表達，並作為線索。在其前面出現的brushes為答案。

答案 (A)

**詞彙** **automobile part** 汽車零件 **painting** 圖畫

### 43

這個工作很有可能在什麼時候被完成？

(A) 今天上午

(B) 今天下午

(C) 明天上午

(D) 明天傍晚

**解說** 這是若有錄音的後段部分聽到時間點，就能回答的考題。在錄音裡，以finished的同義字completed來出現答案線索，其後面的「今天下午」為答案。 答案 (B)

**問題44～46，請參考以下對話。** 美W 美M

W : Good afternoon. [44]I'd like to make a reservation for dinner tonight at 7. I'd like a table that accommodates a large group.

M : Let me check. [45]I'm afraid we don't have any large tables at 7. However, 6 o'clock should be okay. Will that time work for you?

W : As a matter of fact, that works too because we will go there directly from work. [46]My name is Susan, and do you need anything else to reserve our table?

M : That's enough. So I'll put you down for a large table at 6 o'clock tonight.

女：午安。我想預約今天晚上七點的晚餐。我想要可以容納大團體的桌子。

男：讓我確認一下。在七點時我們恐怕沒有任何大的桌子。但是六點的時候應該可以。那個時間對您方便嗎？

女：事實上那也可以，因為我們會直接從公司去那裡。我的名字是蘇珊，你還需要其他任何資訊來預訂我們的桌位嗎？

男：那就夠了。那麼我將安排你們在今晚六點的大桌子。

**詞彙** **make a reservation** 做預約 **accommodate** 能容納 **as a matter of fact** 事實上 **directly from** 直接從⋯ **reserve** 預約 **enough** 足夠的

### 44

這則談話的主題是什麼？

(A) 一個工作職缺

(B) 一項產品的價錢

(C) 一個團體發表會

(D) 一項餐廳的預約

**解說** 這是詢問主題的考題。在錄音前段部分出現「預約晚餐」，所以「餐廳預約」為主題。 答案 (D)

**詞彙** **main** 主要的 **topic** 主題 **conversation** 談話 **job opening** 工作職缺 **product** 工作職缺 **presentation** 發表會 **reservation** 預約

## 45

這個男人建議什麼？

(A) 稍晚回電給他

(B) 和經理談話

(C) 寄一些推薦函

(D) 在不同的時間過來

**解說** 出現「七點不行，但六點可以」，所以將此以概括說法來做表達的(D)為答案。 答案 (D)

**詞彙** **recommend** 建議 **later** 晚一點 **send** 寄 **reference** 推薦函 **different** 不同的

## 46

這個女人提供了什麼訊息？

(A) 她的名字

(B) 她的訂單號碼

(C) 她的住宅地址

(D) 她的電話號碼

**解說** 在該女生的最後一句話裡出現她的名字，所以(A)為答案。 答案 (A)

**詞彙** **provide** 提供 **order number** 訂單編號 **home address** 住宅地址

**問題47～49，請參考以下對話。** 澳W 美M

W : [47]Thank you for calling Anywhere Travel Service. How may I help you?

M : Hello, this is Daniel Kim from TTS corporation. I'm planning to go on a business trip this weekend. [48]I'd like to leave for New York tomorrow night and return on Sunday morning.

W : Let me check. You can leave for 8 p.m. tomorrow, but all of the seats in economy class have been booked for Sunday morning. [49]You can return Sunday afternoon or you'll have to seat in business class that morning.

M : Well, [49]then book me on business class. I have a meeting that afternoon. So I have to come back before the meeting.

女：謝謝您來電任你旅遊服務，需要什麼服務嗎？

男：哈囉，我是TTS公司的丹尼爾金。我打算本週末去出差。我想明晚往紐約出發，並且在星期天早上返回。

女：請讓我確認一下。您可以在明天晚上八點離開，不過星期天早上所有經濟艙座位都已訂滿。您可以在週日下午返回，不然您要在上午搭商務艙返回。

男：嗯，那麼我訂商務艙，我那天下午有一個會議。所以我必須在會議之前回來。

**詞彙** **go on a business trip** 去出差 **leave for** 往…離開 **return** 返回 **book** 預約 **come back** 回來

## 47

這個女人很有可能是什麼人？

(A) 旅行社職員

(B) 行李搬運工

(C) 空服人員

(D) 飛機乘客

**解說** 透過公司名稱可以猜測該女生的職業。錄音裡出現了旅行社的名字，所以可以知道該女生為旅行社職員。 答案 (A)

**詞彙** **travel agent** 旅行社職員 **baggage handler** 行李搬運工 **flight attendant** 空服人員 **passenger** 乘客

## 48

這個男人想要做什麼？

(A) 變更他的座位號碼

(B) 預定來回票

(C) 尋找出發閘口

(D) 確認他的行李

**解說** 在錄音裡可以聽到出發與回來的日期，所以這是訂票的狀況。 答案 (B)

**詞彙** **reserve** 預約 **round trip ticket** 來回票 **departure gate** 來回票 **luggage** 行李

## 49

這個男人可能將於什麼時後返回？

(A) 在星期五傍晚

(B) 在星期六上午

(C) 在星期六下午

(D) 在星期日上午

**解說** 該女生提出「星期天下午或星期天上午」的選擇事項，而該男生選擇了「星期天上午」。因此(D)為答案。 答案 (D)

**問題50～52，請參考以下對話。** 英M 美W

M : Hi, [50]I saw some car photos posted on your web site. Are they all available for sale?

W : Most of them are for sale except some of them have already been sold. If you could tell what type of cars you are interested in I can check the inventory for you.

M : [51]I'd like a car that is fuel-efficient and reliable since I drive to a lot of places. I don't need a luxury car.

W : That narrows it down a little bit. [52]I'll check the computer for cars that have what you're looking for.

男：您好，我在您的網站上看到張貼了一些汽車的照片。它們全部都是可供出售的嗎？

女：他們大部分都可供出售，除了其中一些已經售出的。如果你能告訴我什麼類型的車你感興趣，我可以幫你查查庫存。

男：由於我要開車去很多地方，我想要省油又可靠的車。我不需要豪華的車子。

女：這樣範圍縮小了一點。我會在電腦上確認有沒有你要找的汽車。

**詞彙** **post** 刊登；張貼 **available** 可供的 **except** 除了 **fuel-efficient** 省油的 **reliable** 可靠的 **drive to** 開去(某處) **a lot of** 很多 **place** 地點 **luxury car** 豪華的汽車

## 50

這個男人想要做什麼？

(A) 買一輛汽車

(B) 換不同的工作

(C) 租公寓

(D) 為一台車拍照

**解說** 該考題是詢問主題的，答案線索在錄音前段部分的疑問句裡出現。該男生說「看到了一些汽車的照片、都是可供出售的嗎」，所以可以知道他想「買汽車」。

答案 (A)

**詞彙** **buy** 買 **automobile** 汽車 **different** 不同的 **rent** 租 **apartment** 公寓 **photograph** 拍照

## 51

這個男人說了什麼有關於他的偏好？

(A) 他想要一台昂貴的車子。

(B) 可靠性很重要。

(C) 他喜歡一家薪水更高的公司。

(D) 他通常使用大眾交通工具。

**解說** 「我要開車去很多地方，我想要省油又可靠的車」，可以簡單瞭解為「可靠性很重要」。 答案 (B)

**詞彙** **expensive** 貴的 **usually** 通常 **public transportation** 大眾交通工具

## 52

這個女人接下來可能會做什麼？

(A) 簽一份合約

(B) 在電腦上做確認

(C) 給折扣

(D) 安裝一些設備

**解說** 這是詢問下一個行程的考題。在錄音的後段部分該女生的話語裡，出現核心語I'll，接著可以聽到「在電腦上確認」。

答案 (B)

**詞彙** **sign** 簽名 **contract** 合約 **check** 確認 **discount** 折扣 **install** 安裝 **equipment** 設備

**問題53～55，請參考以下對話。** 美W 美M

W : Hi, Peter. This is Jenny. The printer in our marketing department isn't working. This is the third time it broke down. [53]I thought you placed an order for a new one. Is that right?

M : Yes. I ordered the new printer last week and the company said [54]it will be delivered tomorrow afternoon.

W : If that's the case, it doesn't pay to try to get the old printer up and running. [55]I'm going to use the printer in the accounting department until tomorrow. Thanks.

女：你好彼得，我是珍妮。我們行銷部門的印表機不能運作了。這是它第三次故障的。我想你已訂了一台新的了，對嗎？

男：是的，我上週訂了新的印表機，該公司說明天下午將會送到。

女：若是那樣，就不用花時間試著讓舊印表機運作。到明天之前，我要用會計部門的印表機。謝謝你。

**詞彙** **marketing department** 行銷部門 **work** 運作 **break down** 故障 **place an order** 下訂單 **order** 訂購 **deliver** 配送 **if that is the case** 若是那樣 **up and running** 正常運轉的 **accounting department** 會計部門

## 53

為什麼這個女人打電話來？

(A) 為了取消會議

(B) 為了安排約會

(C) 為了要求服務

(D) 為了詢問有關一份訂單

**解說** 這是詢問主題的考題。在錄音前段部分的疑問句裡會出現答案線索。「印表機不能運作了、已訂了一台新的了，對嗎？」，所以(D)為答案。 答案 (D)

**詞彙** **cancel** 取消 **meeting** 會議 **appointment** 約定 **inquire about** 詢問有關於⋯

## 54

在明天下午將會發生什麼？

(A) 一位新會計師將被雇用。

(B) 一項產品將被配送。

(C) 一份合約將被簽署。

(D) 一個預約將被取消。

**解說** 時間點為很好的答案線索。錄音裡的Tomorrow afternoon附近出現「送達」。(B)的product是指printer。 答案 (B)

**詞彙** accountant 會計師 hire 雇用 contract 合約 sign 簽名 reservation 預約

## 55

根據珍妮所言，員工們能在會計部門做什麼？

(A) 取得薪水資訊

(B) 使用新影印機

(C) 領取辦公室用品

(D) 列印一些文件資料

**解說** accounting department為核心語。將「用印表機」改成「列印文件」來表達的(D)為答案。 答案 (D)

**詞彙** access 取得 copier 影印機 pick up 領取 office supply 辦公室用品 document 文件資料

**問題56～58，請參考以下對話。** 英M 澳W

M : Wow, you haven't even started packing up. [56, 57]You forgot that the movers are going to be here in the office at 7:30 tomorrow morning, didn't you?

W : Oh! No! I was thinking they won't be here until tomorrow noon. I think I have no choice but to stay up late tonight.

M : Well, since I'm almost done with my packing, I'd be happy to come by to help you if you want. But it's almost lunch time. Would you like to join us for lunch?

W : Certainly. [58]Let me just tidy up the desk and the bookshelves before leaving so I can start packing up right after lunch.

男：哇，你竟然還沒有開始打包。你忘了明天早上七點半搬家公司就會到這間辦公室了，不是嗎？

女：哦！不會吧！我以為他們明天中午前不會到。我想除了今天晚上留晚一點，我已經別無選擇。

男：嗯，因為我幾乎已經完成打包我的，如果你要，我很樂意過來幫忙你。但是已經接近午餐時間了。你想加入我們吃午餐嗎？

女：當然。在離開之前讓我整理一下書桌和書架，這樣午餐後我就可以開始打包。

**詞彙** pack up 打包 forget 忘記 office 辦公室 have no choice but to 除了…之外別無選擇 packing 打包 come by 順便過來 tidy up the desk 整理書桌 bookshelf 書架

## 56

這段談話可能在哪兒發生的？

(A) 在路上

(B) 在一家書店

(C) 在一間傢俱店

(D) 在一間辦公室

**解說** 在錄音前面部分出現「這間辦公室」，所以知道對話的地點為「辦公室」。 答案 (D)

**詞彙** take place 發生 road 道路 bookstore 書店

## 57

搬家公司應該在什麼時候會來？

(A) 今天上午

(B) 今天下午

(C) 明天上午

(D) 明天下午

**解說** 考題裡的supposed to come為核心語，而錄音裡的going to be here為答案線索。在此附近出現未來時間點tomorrow morning。 答案 (C)

**詞彙** be supposed to 應該…

## 58

這個女人接下來會做什麼？

(A) 準備用餐的餐桌

(B) 打包一些書本

(C) 清掃一些傢俱

(D) 寄出包裹

**解說** 這是詢問下一個行程的考題。錄音裡該女生說的let me為核心說法，將其後面出現的「整理書桌和書架」改成「清掃」來表達的(C)為答案。 答案 (C)

**詞彙** set the table 準備餐桌 meal 餐食 pack 打包 clean up 打包 furniture 傢俱 parcel 包裹

**問題59～61，請參考以下對話。** 美M 美W

M : Hi, [59]I'm here to talk to someone about hosting a company dinner in your restaurant. My boss said that the food and the service are excellent here.

W : I'm just a restaurant server, and [60]the manager in charge of hosting events isn't here at the moment. You'll need to contact her. Here is her business card.

M : Thanks. I'll get in touch with her as soon as I can. By the way, when is she available?

W : [61]She'll be in tomorrow. How about calling her in the morning? I'm sure you can set up a meeting with her within a few days.

男：你好，我來這兒是要和某人洽談在你們餐廳主辦一場公司的晚宴。我的老闆說這裡的食品和服務都很優質。

女：我只是個餐廳的服務生，負責舉辦活動的經理此刻不在。你將會需要與她聯繫。這是她的名片。

男：謝謝。我會儘快與她聯繫。順便問一下，她什麼時間可以呢？

女：她明天會在。早上打電話給她怎麼樣呢？我相信在幾天之內你可以安排與她會面。

**詞彙** host 舉辦 in charge of 負責…的 at the moment 此刻；現在 contact 聯絡 business card 名片 get in touch with 與…連繫 as soon as 儘快 by the way 順便提一下 available 可用的 set up a meeting 約定見面

## 59

這個男人為什麼去餐廳的？

(A) 為了要應徵一個職位

(B) 為了要和同事一起晚餐

(C) 為了配送一件貨物

(D) 為了安排一場活動

**解說** 這是詢問理由的考題。將錄音前面部分出現的「來洽談主辦一場公司的晚宴」做簡化來表達的(D)為答案。 答案 (D)

**詞彙** apply for 應徵… position 位置 colleague 同事 deliver 配送 order 訂單；貨物

## 60

有什麼樣的問題？

(A) 所有的房間都被預訂了。

(B) 經理不在。

(C) 餐廳因假日而不營業。

(D) 一位客人對於服務抱怨。

**解說** 詢問問題狀況為何的考題，答案大部分會包含否定詞或論及問題的說法。將錄音裡出現的「經理此刻不在」以相近意思的not available表達的(B)為答案。 答案 (B)

**詞彙** problem 問題 fully 完全的 book 預約 closed 不營業的 due to 由於… holiday 假日 complain 抱怨

## 61

這個女人建議了什麼？

(A) 去不同的餐廳

(B) 隔天打電話來

(C) 參考網站資訊

(D) 和朋友一起回來

**解說** 這是詢問建議事項為何的考題。錄音裡，接在how about後面的「早上打電話」改成「隔天打電話」來表達的(B)為答案。 答案 (B)

**詞彙** recommend 建議 consult 參考 come back 回來

**問題62～64，請參考以下對話。** 美W 英M

W : Alex, can you join me in the meeting with our clients from GW electronics tomorrow morning? [62]They tell me your magazine ad layout is very impressive and they would like to apply your ideas to their online advertisements and store displays.

M : Tomorrow morning? Well, I thought the meeting wasn't for 2 days. [63]I'm not sure I can finalize the entire ad proposal on time.

W : Oh, that's fine. [64]What we need is to generate some concepts for them to report to their managers.

女：艾力克斯，你能加入我明天早上和GW電子來的客戶開的會議嗎？他們告訴我，你的雜誌廣告的版面設計讓人印象非常深刻，他們想在線上廣告和店內展示中應用你的構想。

男：明天早上嗎？嗯，我以為要兩天後才會開會。我不確定我能否準時完成整個廣告企劃案。

女：哦，那好。我們需要的是為他們想出一些概念以讓他們向他們的經理報告。

**詞彙** client 顧客 magazine 雜誌 ad(=advertisement) 廣告 layout 版面設計 impressive 印象深刻的 apply 應用 display 展示 finalize 完成 entire 整個的 proposal 企劃案 on time 準時 generate 引發；產生出 report 報告 manager 經理

## 62

說話者很有可能是在什麼型態的公司工作？

(A) 會計公司

(B) 廣告公司

(C) 建設公司

(D) 電子公司

**解說** 這是詢問說話者的職業為何的考題。說話者為了與廣告相關的案子所以與客戶見面，因此說話者可能在「廣告公司」工作。 答案 (B)

**詞彙** accounting firm 會計公司 advertising agency 廣告公司 construction firm 建設公司 electronics company 電子公司

## 63

為什麼這個男人擔心明天的會議？

(A) 沒有會議室可以用。

(B) 出席率會很低。

(C) 由於家庭因素，他無法參加。

(D) 他將沒有足夠的時間做準備。

**解說** 錄音中間部分出現的I'm not sure為論及問題的說法，將其後面出現的「不確定我能否準時完成」改成「沒有足夠的時間」來表達的(D)就是答案。 答案 (D)

**詞彙** **meeting room** 會議室 **available** 可用的 **attendance** 出席率 **attend** 參加 **due to** 由於… **affair** 某事件 **enough** 充分的 **prepare** 準備

## 64

明天的會議將會討論什麼？

(A) 新的廣告想法

(B) 一項預算計畫

(C) 商店的藍圖

(D) 管理員工的方式

**解說** 這是得聽完全部內容才能回答的問題。大致上是有關「明天的會議」的內容，而「想出一些概念」可視為討論「新的廣告想法」的意思。 答案 (A)

**詞彙** **discuss** 討論 **advertising** 廣告 **budget** 預算 **blueprint** 藍圖 **way** 方式 **manage** 管理 **employee** 員工

問題65～67，請參考以下對話。美M 澳W

M : [65]Hello, I heard from my friend that you carry hard-to-find books. He strongly recommended your bookstore for these books. Do you carry a copy of 'Secret' signed by the author?

W : Yes, I heard about the title, but [66]only an unsigned copy is available now. If you need it soon, I recommend buying that. Otherwise, I can do an online search to find an autographed copy. It could take some time though, and of course, it will cost more.

M : I understand that, but what really matters is the signature. [65]I'll give my father the book as a gift. [67]He was a friend of the author's.

W : I see. If you give me your phone number, I'll inform you when I find something.

男：你好，我從我的朋友那兒聽說你們引進很難找到的書籍。他強烈推薦你們書店的這些書籍。你們有一本作者簽名的「祕密」嗎？

女：是的，我聽過這個書名，但現在只供應沒有簽名的書本。如果您很快就要，我建議購買這種的。不然我可以上網搜尋來找一本有親筆簽名的。它可能需要一些時間，而且理所當然的，這將要更多花費。

男：我瞭解，但真正重要的是簽名。我將給我的父親這本書作為禮物。他是作者的朋友之一。

女：我明白了。若你給我你的電話號碼，當我找到時我會通知你。

**詞彙** **carry** 引進 **hard-to-find** 難以找到的 **strongly** 強烈地 **recommend** 薦 **copy** 薦 **author** 作者 **title** 書名 **available** 可用的 **otherwise** 要不然 **search** 搜尋 **autographed** 親筆簽名的 **cost** 需要(費用) **signature** 簽名

## 65

這個男人想要做什麼？

(A) 參加一本書的簽名會

(B) 買一份特別的禮物

(C) 退還一個有瑕疵的產品

(D) 上網搜尋一本書

**解說** 透過該男生的話語「有作者簽名的書」、「給父親當作禮物」，可以知道他在購買特別的禮物。 答案 (B)

**詞彙** **attend** 參加 **book signing** 書本簽名會 **special** 特別的 **present** 禮物 **return** 返回；退還 **defective** 有瑕疵的

## 66

這個女人建議了什麼？

(A) 買一本沒有簽名的書

(B) 打電話給特色商品店

(C) 購買同樣的幾本書

(D) 要求新的簽名

**解說** 考題裡的suggest的同義字recommend為核心語。錄音裡該詞附近出現購買unsigned copy，因此unsigned book為答案。 答案 (A)

**詞彙** **suggest** 建議 **purchase** 購買 **signature** 簽名

## 67

這個男人說了什麼有關於他的父親的事？

(A) 他是一位作者。

(B) 他銷售舊書。

(C) 他和該書的作者相熟識。

(D) 他曾有一間禮品店。

**解說** father為核心語。在錄音裡用he來指father，在he後面出現「作者的朋友之一」是指「和該書的作者相熟識」的意思。 答案 (C)

**詞彙** **sell** 賣 **be acquainted with** 與…相熟識 **used to** 曾經 **gift shop** 禮品店

問題68～70，請參考以下對話。美M 美W

M : We've got a lot of resumes for the accounting assistant position we posted last month. I've been trying to select several qualified applicants.

W : [68]We've been asked to hire someone for the accounting department. They are pretty shorthanded right now. When will the interview begin?

M : Well, [69]the interview is scheduled for the end of this week. [70]But I don't know if I can review all the applications in time because I'm also in the middle of working on other projects.

男：對於我們上個月刊登的會計助理職位，我們已經收到了很多履歷表。我試著挑出一些符合資格的應徵者。

女：我們被要求聘用某個人給會計部門。他們目前人力相當短缺。面試將會在什麼時後開始？

男：嗯，面試定在本週末的時候，但是我不知道我能否適時審閱完所有的履歷，因為我也工作於其他計畫中。

**詞彙** a lot of 很多的 resume 履歷表 accounting 會計 assistant 助理 position 職位 post 刊登 select 挑選 qualified 合格的 applicant 應徵者 hire 雇用 accounting department 會計部門 pretty 相當 shorthanded 人力短缺的 review 審閱 application 應徵函

## 68

這個女人建議了什麼有關於會計部門的事？

(A) 它需要更多資金。

(B) 它最近雇用了幾位員工。

(C) 它的辦公室正在被整修。

(D) 它人員不足。

**解說** accounting department為核心語，錄音裡在該核心語後面出現的shorthanded的同義字(D)為答案。答案 (D)

**詞彙** fund 資金 hire 雇用 renovate 整修 understaffed 人員不足

## 69

這星期末時將會發生什麼事？

(A) 應徵函將被收進來。

(B) 一場面試將會開始。

(C) 一張執照將被發出。

(D) 一個計畫案將開始。

**解說** 錄音裡的for the end of this week附近會出現答案。將「面試定在本週末的時候」做變化來做的(B)為答案。答案 (B)

**詞彙** receive 收 begin 開始 license 執照 issue 發給 launch 開始

## 70

這個男人為什麼擔憂？

(A) 這個計畫的預算有限。

(B) 他可能無法在截止日前完成。

(C) 有一些文件遺失了。

(D) 工作應徵者不具備所需的資格。

**解說** 在錄音裡可以聽到對於man concerned的答案線索I don't know。將其後面出現的「我能否適時審閱完」改成「可能無法在截止日前完成」來表達的(B)為答案。答案 (B)

**詞彙** budget 預算 limited 有限的 meet the deadline 在截止前完成 document 文件資料 missing 遺失的 necessary 需要的 qualification 資格

# Part 4

問題71～73，請參考以下電話留言。美W

Hi, this message is for Mr. Yanobe. My name is Sylvia Alexander. [72]I'm the personnel manager for MEXCOM International Corporation. [71]I'm calling about your recent application for the marketing position that I received early this week. I'd like to schedule an interview with you for sometime next week. [73]Please give me a call at 225-8649 and tell me when you will be available. I look forward to seeing you.

您好，這是給矢延先生的留言。我的名字是施維亞亞歷山大。我是墨西客國際公司的人事經理。我打電話來是有關我在本週初收到的您最近對於行銷職位的應徵函。我想安排下星期的某個時候與你面試。請撥225-8649給我電話，告訴我您可以的時間。我期待見到您。

**詞彙** personnel manager 人事經理 application 申請書；應徵函 position 職位 receive 職位 sometime next week 下星期某時間 available 有空的 look forward to –ing 期待⋯

## 71

這通電話的目的是什麼？

(A) 為了擬定預算計畫

(B) 為了討論調查結果

(C) 為了安排面試時間

(D) 為了應徵一個職位

**解說** 透過第一個考題，可以知道該錄音為「電話錄音」類型。I'm calling about為「電話錄音」的核心語，將其後面出現的「收到了應徵函，且想安排面試」以簡略表達的(C)為答案。答案 (C)

**詞彙** purpose 目的 draw up 擬定 budget 預算 discuss 討論 survey 調查 apply for 應徵⋯

## 72

說話者的職務是什麼？

(A) 人事部門經理

(B) 科學研究員

(C) 營運分析師

(D) 電子工程師

**解說** 這是詢問「電話錄音」的說話者為誰的考題。錄音前段部分裡，在I'm後面直接出現「人事部門經理」。答案 (A)

**詞彙** occupation 職務 analyst 分析師 engineer 工程師

## 73

說話者要求矢延先生做什麼？

(A) 順道來辦公室

(B) 上網填妥申請表

(C) 在不同的時間打來

(D) 打電話

**解說** 在「電話錄音」類型裡，要求事項總是在錄音後段部分出現，且大部分以「請回撥」、「請確認」來表達。錄音裡出現的please就是要求事項的線索，將其後面的give me a call做變化來表達的(D)為答案。 答案 (D)

**詞彙** **stop by** 順道到 **fill out** 填寫 **application form** 申請表 **different** 不同的

**問題74～76，請參考以下訊息。** 英M

Good morning! [74]I called this meeting to announce that next week new security software will be set up on all employees' computers. This software will help boost computer speed, increase stability, and protect confidential information from the unauthorized users much more efficiently. Now, to prepare you for this change, [75]our head technician will demonstrate how to use this software in the training session next Friday. [76]Please register for this session on our company web site by the end of this week. Do you have any questions?

早安！我召集這次會議是要宣布下週將安裝新的安全軟體於所有員工的電腦。這個軟體將有助於提高電腦的速度、增加穩定性，並且從未經授權用戶更有效地保護機密信息。現在為了讓你們對這樣的改變做好準備，在下星期五的訓練研習會，我們的首席技師將會示範如何使用這個軟體。請在這週結束前，上我們公司的網站登錄這場研習會。有沒有任何疑問呢？

**詞彙** **call a meeting** 召集會議 **announce** 公告 **security** 安全 **set up** 安裝 **boost** 提高 **increase** 增加 **stability** 穩定性 **protect** 保護 **confidential** 機密的 **unauthorized** 未經授權的 **efficiently** 有效地 **prepare** 準備 **head technician** 首席技師 **demonstrate** 示範 **training session** 訓練研習 **register for** 登錄…

## 74

什麼事情被公告了？

(A) 一項新的聘用程序

(B) 一項員工滿意度調查

(C) 一場會議日期

(D) 一套軟體的安裝

**解說** 透過這裡的三個考題，可以猜測該錄音為「公司內公告」或「會議上公告」類型。該考題是詢問主題的，在錄音的前段部分會出現答案線索。將「安裝新的安全軟體」以簡略表達的(D)為答案。 答案 (D)

**詞彙** **hiring procedure** 聘用程序 **survey** 調查 **satisfaction** 滿意 **installation** 安裝

## 75

下星期五將會發生什麼？

(A) 一件預算將被審閱。

(B) 調查結果將被公布。

(C) 電腦將被更換。

(D) 員工將被訓練。

**解說** 錄音裡提到的時間點附近會有答案線索。「首席技師將會示範」是「員工將被訓練」的意思。 答案 (D)

**詞彙** **budget** 預算 **review** 審閱 **survey** 調查 **replace** 替換 **train** 訓練

## 76

聽者們被要求在週末之前做什麼？

(A) 送出開銷報告

(B) 打電話給人事部門

(C) 與他們的經理見面

(D) 登錄訓練研習會

**解說** 這是詢問「要求事項」為何的考題，且有兩個答案線索。在Please和未來時間點之間出現的「登錄研習會」為答案。 答案 (D)

**詞彙** **submit** 送出 **expense** 花費 **personnel department** 人事部門

**問題77～79，請參考以下交通廣播。** 美M

Good morning. It's 9 o'clock and this is the latest Radio XKY traffic update. I'm Michael Walker. Well, it's not common that a traffic report can bring you good news but I'm pleased to announce that all highways are comparatively clear. [77]The expanded train service that was recently launched into operation has resulted in reduced traffic volume, so most drivers on the expressway will not be tied up in traffic. [78]There is about a 20-minute delay on Highway 100 toward the Oak Street bridge, though. A tractor-trailer is turned over on the left lane there. [79]I'll be back in 10 minutes with another traffic update, so keep listening.

早安。現在是九點鐘，這是XKY電台最新的交通更新。我是邁克沃克。很少有路況報導給您帶來好消息，但我很高興公布所有的高速公路都相對得通暢。最近開始運作的擴大的火車班次使得交通量減少，所以在快高速公路上大部分的駕駛人不會被困在交通中。不過，在一百號高速公路上往橡樹街橋方向有大約二十分鐘的延誤，一台拖車翻覆在左車道上了。我會在十分鐘之後回來做另一則路況報導，請繼續收聽。

**詞彙** **common** 平常的 **bring** 帶來 **be pleased to**

很樂於… highway 高速公路 comparatively 相對的 clear (道路)通暢 expanded 擴大的 launch 開始 operation 運作 result in 導致 reduced 降低的 expressway 快速道路 delay 延遲 though 雖然 turn over 翻覆 keep –ing 持續

## 77

(A) 近期的道路施工完成了。

(B) 天氣狀況不適宜。

(C) 市民在放假中。

(D) 火車服務改善了。

**解說** 該錄音裡沒有能直接聽到的核心語。「高速公路交通量降低」在錄音裡是以reduced traffic volume與expressway來表達的。目前情況的原因是expanded train service，將此做變化來表達的(D)為答案。 答案 (D)

**詞彙** decrease 降低 complete 完成 weather condition 天氣狀況 unfavorable 不適宜 citizen 市民 on holiday 在假期中

## 78

什麼事情造成了一百號高速公路上的延誤？

(A) 一台翻覆的卡車

(B) 一個故障的交通號誌

(C) 滑溜的道路狀況

(D) 道路維修

**解說** 數字為核心語，且也很容易記憶。將Highway 100附近的「一台拖車翻覆」改成「一台翻覆的卡車」來表達的(A)為答案。 答案 (A)

**詞彙** overturned 翻覆的 broken 故障的 traffic sign 交通號誌 slippery 滑的 condition 狀況 repair 修理

## 79

下一次的報導將會在什麼時候？

(A) 在五分鐘後

(B) 在十分鐘後

(C) 在十五分鐘後

(D) 在三十分鐘後

**解說** 這是詢問「廣播節目」的下一個時程的考題。在錄音最後出現的「十分鐘之後回來」就是提到下一次播放時間的線索。 答案 (B)

**詞彙** occur 發生

**問題80～82，請參考以下談話內容。** 澳W

Welcome everyone to the historic Kenwood Farm. I'm glad you could join us today on our tour. [71]I'm Sally, and I'll be your guide this morning. Kenwood Farm was actually started as a small vegetable farm by John Wilder, who eventually sold it to Kenwood. That venture lasted many decades, [72]but eventually ran bankrupt, and was purchased by the government. We'll spend an hour here, and during the tour, [73]please don't throw your garbage on the ground as we respect the environment. All right. Everyone's ready? Let's take a look at the farm house.

歡迎大家來到歷史上有名的肯木農場。我很高興你們能參加我們的觀光，我是莎莉，我將會是你們今天上午的導遊。肯木農場實際上是由約翰懷爾德從一塊小菜園開始，最後把它賣給了肯木。這項事業持續了幾十年，但最終破產了並由政府收購。在這裡我們會花一個小時，在遊覽期間，請不要把垃圾扔在地上，因為我們重視環境。好，所有人準備好了嗎？我們來看看這個農莊吧。

**詞彙** historic 具有歷史價值的 tour 觀光 actually 事實上 eventually 最後；終於 sell 賣 venture 企業；事業 last 持續 decade 十年 run bankrupt 破產 government 政府 throw 丟 garbage 垃圾 respect the environment 重視環境 ready 準備好 take a look at 看…

## 80

說話者很有可能是什麼人？

(A) 一位導遊

(B) 一位農夫

(C) 一位代言人

(D) 一位教授

**解說** 若選項裡有tour guide或tourist，其錄音很有可能為「參觀／觀光」類型。在該錄音前段部分出現tour。 答案 (A)

**詞彙** tour guide 導遊 farmer 農夫 spokesman 代言人 professor 教授

## 81

誰現在擁有這座農場？

(A) 懷爾德家族

(B) 肯木公司

(C) 一個地方財團

(D) 政府

**解說** 這是詢問具體人物為誰的考題。論及「由政府收購」了，所以(D)為答案。 答案 (D)

**詞彙** own 擁有 local consortium 地方財團

## 82

聽者們被要求做什麼？

(A) 不要丟垃圾在地上

(B) 保持安靜

(C) 自己帶食物

(D) 注意步伐

**解說** 「參觀／觀光」類錄音的後段部分，大部分會出現勸導以及禁止事項。錄音裡在please後面可以聽到「不要把垃圾扔在地上」，將此做變化來表達的(A)為答案。 答案 (A)

**詞彙** litter 亂丟（垃圾） silent 安靜的 bring 帶來

問題83～85，請參考以下電話留言。 美W

Hi, I'm calling from Anderson Realtor. [83]You called our office a few days ago and asked about an apartment. I remember you were interested in a two-bedroom apartment. Unfortunately, only one-bedroom apartments are available now. However, [84]if you're willing to wait, a two-bedroom apartment will be available next month; it is being renovated at the moment. If you'd like to see in advance what the renovated apartment would look like, [85]please call me to visit an occupied apartment with a similar floor plan.

您好，這是由安德森不動產經紀公司打來的。您前幾天致電到我們辦公室詢問有關一棟公寓。我記得你對兩房的公寓感興趣。很可惜，現在只有一房臥室的公寓可以提供。如果你願意等候，一間有兩房的公寓將於下個月可提供，它目前正在裝修。若您想提前看看這間裝修的公寓看起來如何，請打電話給我來參觀一間已被租用、但有類似平面佈置的公寓。

**詞彙** unfortunately 可惜；不幸的 available 可用的
be willing to 願意做… renovate 裝修
at the moment 此時；現在 in advance 提前 visit 參觀
occupied 被佔有的 floor plan 樓層平面圖

## 83

說話者打電話來要說什麼？

(A) 一個近期的詢問

(B) 一個新的規定

(C) 一個取消的預約

(D) 下降的租金

**解說** 這是詢問「電話錄音」的主題的考題。在錄音前段部分出現「前幾天致電、詢問有關一棟公寓」，所以可以瞭解該說話者要談「一個近期的詢問」。 答案 (A)

**詞彙** inquiry 詢問 regulation 規定 canceled 被取消的
reservation 預約 reduced 減少的

## 84

說話者說了什麼關於兩房公寓的事？

(A) 它已經被租用。

(B) 它非常昂貴。

(C) 它正在裝修當中。

(D) 它在老人當中很受歡迎。

**解說** 這是詢問意見為何的考題。透過在錄音裡two-bedroom apartment後面出現的「正在裝修」可以知道(C)為答案。 答案 (C)

**詞彙** expensive 貴的 undergo 經歷 senior citizen 老人

## 85

說話者建議聽者做什麼？

(A) 比較兩棟公寓的價錢

(B) 確認樓層平面圖

(C) 保留租賃合約

(D) 打電話聯繫看屋

**解說** 這是詢問建議事項為何的考題。錄音裡與suggest相關的說法，是在please後面出現的「打電話給我來參觀」，因此將這句做變化來表達的(D)為答案。 答案 (D)

**詞彙** compare 比較 price 價格 retain 保留 contract 合約
tour 參觀

問題86-88，請參考以下介紹內容。 美M

Welcome everyone to today's lecture. We're pleased to be hosting this lecture series on information security. To get more information on future talks, our schedule is available at the door. [86]Our featured speaker today is Mr. Steve Weir who worked as the president of a security company in San Francisco. [86]He is the author of a book entitled "Hacking Attack" which features discussions on computer security issues. Today, [87]he's going to talk about new advances in information technology and how they affect computer security. [88]After the lecture, there will be a question and answer session led by Mr. Weir at a reception downstairs. Now, let's give a warm welcome to Mr. Weir.

歡迎大家來到今天的演講。我們很高興舉辦資訊安全系列講座。為了得到更多後續演講的訊息，我們的時間表在門口可取。我們的特別演講者是在舊金山的一家電腦系統安全公司擔任過總裁的史蒂夫威爾先生。他是「駭客攻擊」一書的作者，此書特別討論電腦安全的問題。今天，他將談論有關資訊技術的新進展和它們如何影響電腦安全。在演講之後，在樓下的歡迎會上有一場由威爾先生引導的問答時間。現在，我們熱烈歡迎威爾先生吧。

**詞彙** lecture 演講 be pleased to 很高興於… host 舉辦 security 安全 available 可用的 featured speaker 特別演講者 president 總裁 author 作者 entitled 被取名為…
discussion 討論 issue 問題 advance 進步 affect 影響
a question and answer session 問答時間 lead
引導；帶領 reception 歡迎會 downstairs 樓下
give a warm welcome 熱烈的歡迎

## 86

威爾先生最近做了什麼？

(A) 舉辦了會議

(B) 在大學演講
(C) 寫了一本書
(D) 訓練了保全人員

**解說** 透過第三個考題，可以知道該錄音為「活動開始前公告」類型。該錄音裡出現「Mr. Weir是作者」，所以知道他寫了一本書。 答案 (C)

**詞彙** recently 最近 conference 會議 lecture 演講 write 寫 train 訓練 security guard 保全人員

## 87

威爾先生的演講主題是什麼？
(A) 資訊科學技術
(B) 工作場所的安全
(C) 醫學治療
(D) 國際法律

**解說** 將「他將談論有關資訊技術的新進展」以簡化來表達的(A)為答案。 答案 (A)

**詞彙** subject 主題 workplace 工作場所 safety 安全 treatment 治療 international 國際的 law 法律

## 88

說話者邀請聽者們在演講後做什麼？
(A) 參加歡迎會
(B) 建議會議議題
(C) 組成發表團隊
(D) 報名之後的演講

**解說** after the lecture也是一種時間點的說法，其附近會有答案線索。將「歡迎會上有一場問答時間」改成「參加招待會」來表達的(A)為答案。 答案 (A)

**詞彙** attend 參加 suggest 建議 agenda 議題 form 組成 presentation 發表 sign up for 報名

問題89-91，請參考以下廣播廣告。 英M

Good morning. [89]This is Victor with Perfect Cleaners. Over the last decade, we've provided the best dry cleaning service to the residents in our community. Due to the increase in popularity, [90]we've recently moved to a new location. Although our building has changed in appearance, our commitment to quality remains the same as usual. [91]We are celebrating our big move by offering a special 20% discount for all of our customers. This offer is only good for this month. This includes same-day service. We've also begun a free delivery service. For more information, including prices and hours, please call us at 555-2125.

早安，我是完美清潔的維多。過去十年當中，我們給社區的居民提供了最佳的乾洗服務。由於受歡迎度提高，我們最近搬到一個新的地點。雖然我們大樓的外觀改變了，但對品質的堅持仍就如同往常。我們正提供特別的八折優惠給我們所有的顧客來慶祝我們的搬遷。這項優惠只在這個月有效。這也包涵當日取件的服務。我們也開始了免費送貨服務。要得到包括價格和時間的更多訊息，請致電給我們555-2125。

**詞彙** decade 十年 provide A to B 提供A給B resident 居民 due to 由於 recently 最近 location 地點 in appearance 外觀上 commitment 堅持 the same as 與…相同 celebrate 慶祝 offer 提供 good 有效的 include 包含 same-day service 當日取件的快速服務

## 89

什麼東西被廣告？
(A) 訂做裝飾
(B) 房屋清掃
(C) 乾洗服務
(D) 配送服務

**解說** 這是「廣告」類型的錄音。廣告的商品在錄音前段部分常會和疑問句一起出現。「提供最佳的乾洗服務」作為答案線索。 答案 (C)

**詞彙** advertise 廣告 custom 訂製的 decoration 裝飾 cleaning 清掃 courier service 配送服務

## 90

這間公司最近做了什麼事？
(A) 擴大了員工數
(B) 搬到新地點了
(C) 不繼續供給某些產品了
(D) 辦了訓練課

**解說** 「廣告」錄音裡，說明特色的部分出現在錄音的中間。將「最近搬到一個新的地點」用類似的說法來表達的(B)為答案。 答案 (B)

**詞彙** expand 擴大 place 地點 discontinue 不繼續 supply 供應 product 產品 organize 舉辦 training session 訓練課

## 91

這家公司只有在這個月提供什麼？
(A) 禮券
(B) 接機服務
(C) 降低價格
(D) 免費安裝

**解說** 這是詢問「廣告」的優惠為何的考題。在錄音裡的優惠期間附近，可以聽到是折扣活動，將此做變化來表達的(C)為答案。 答案 (C)

**詞彙** gift certificate 禮券 pickup 領取 reduced price

降低價格 **installation** 安裝

問題92～94，請參考以下談話內容。 美W

Good afternoon everyone. Thanks for coming to this meeting on a short notice. The first agenda of this meeting: [92]I'd like to discuss a minor change in our technical support protocol. Previously, [93]if a problem cannot be resolved for a customer, we requested that the customer call us again later. From now on, [94]you'll need to give customers a reference number if they must call back. Also, you'll need to type in the computer what information you know about the situation, so that when the customer calls back, the problem can be solved more easily.

各位午安，感謝您前來在短時間內通知的本次會議。為這次會議的第一個議題，我想討論在我們的技術支援服務規定上的一個小小的改變。以前，如果無法為客戶解決問題，我們會要求客戶稍後再次打電話給我們。從現在開始，如果他們必須回撥，你將必需給客戶一個參考編號。而且，你也需要把有關這個狀況你所知的訊息輸入電腦，所以當顧客回電話來時，這個問題可以更容易的被解決。

**詞彙** **agenda** 議題 **discuss** 討論 **minor** 微小的 **protocol** 規定；程序 **resolve** 解決 **customer** 顧客 **request** 要求 **from now on** 從現在起 **reference number** 參考編號 **situation** 狀況 **solve** 解決 **easily** 容易地

## 92

這段談話的目地是什麼？

(A) 為了討論顧客的抱怨

(B) 為了公布政策改變

(C) 為了介紹新員工

(D) 為了腦力激盪而出新的廣告策略

**解說** 透過考題與選項可以猜測該錄音為「會議上的公告」。這是詢問主題的考題，所以答案線索在錄音的前段部分。將「想討論在技術支援服務規定上的一個小小的改變」以概括的說法來表達的(B)為答案。 答案 (B)

**詞彙** **purpose** 目地 **complaint** 抱怨 **policy** 政策 **brainstorm** 腦力激盪 **advertising** 廣告 **strategy** 策略

## 93

說話者很有可能是對什麼人談話？

(A) 會計人員

(B) 倉庫監督人員

(C) 客服專員

(D) 旅行社職員

**解說** 「會議上的公告」，這類型的說話者大部分為公司職員。「無法為客戶解決問題、要求客戶再次打電話」的人可以被視為「客服專員」。 答案 (C)

**詞彙** **accountant** 會計人員 **warehouse** 倉庫 **supervisor** 倉庫 **travel agent** 旅行社職員

## 94

說話者要求聽者做什麼？

(A) 經常打電話

(B) 提供參考編號

(C) 提出想法

(D) 紀錄來電

**解說** 這是詢問要求事項為何的考題。透過該錄音裡的you'll need to可以知道答案線索。將「給客戶一個參考編號」做變化來表達的(B)為答案。 答案 (B)

**詞彙** **ask** 要求 **frequently** 經常地 **provide** 提供 **come up with** 提出

問題95～97，請參考以下公告內容。 澳W

Welcome to the annual animation convention. I have a few reminders before we start today's programs. [95]During the convention, which will last for three days, please have your press pass properly displayed. [96]For those of you who want to be online by using laptops, we invite you to use the wireless service we have set up. To access the service, you need to input the password we provided in the registration packets. [97]Now you may find your places, and prepare for our first speaker, character designer Stan Lester, who will be presenting his idea on what the future's animation characters will be.

歡迎來到年度動畫大會。在我們開始今天的程序之前，我有幾項提醒。在這三天大會期間，請確實的出示您的記者證。需要使用筆記型電腦上網的人，我們邀請您使用我們已設置的無線服務。您需要輸入我們在報到資料袋裡提供的密碼來利用這項服務。現在請您找您的位置，並迎接我們的第一位演講者，人物設計師斯坦萊斯特。他將對於未來動畫人物會是如何發表他的觀點。

**詞彙** **convention** 大會；會議 **reminder** 提醒 **last** 持續 **press pass** 記者證 **properly** 適當的 **display** 出示 **set up** 設置 **access** 取得；利用 **input** 取得；利用 **provide** 提供 **registration** 登錄報到 **present** 發表

## 95

誰是聽眾？

(A) 電影導演

(B) 公司員工

(C) 報章雜誌記者

(D) 網路伺服器管理者

**解說** 在錄音前段部分聽到「出示您的記者證」，所以可以猜測聽眾為新聞業者。 答案 (C)

**詞彙** audience 聽眾 director 導演 journalist 報章雜誌記者 administrator 管理者

**96**

聽者們被邀請做什麼事？

(A) 提出問題

(B) 建立密碼

(C) 使用無線網路

(D) 參加晚餐

**解說** invite是「鄭重地邀請」的意思。該錄音裡出現核心語invite，在其後面可以聽到「我們已設置的無線服務」，所以是要求「使用無線網路」的。 答案 (C)

**詞彙** raise questions 提出問題 attend 參加

**97**

接下來將會發生什麼？

(A) 第一位演講者將會出現。

(B) 將有短暫的休息時間。

(C) 將分發傳單。

(D) 將供應茶點。

**解說** 這是詢問下一個行程為何的考題。「迎接我們的第一位演講者」是「第一位演講者將會出現」的意思。 答案 (A)

**詞彙** appear 出現 break 休息 handout 傳單 distribute 分發 refreshment 茶點 serve 供應

問題98～100，請參考以下新聞內容。 美W

Now for business news. Atlas Manufacturing announced that [98]they may not acquire GW Package, Inc. as early as they planned. [99]As Atlas' quarterly sales report released yesterday showed their first quarter's profits fell drastically to nearly 14 percent. According to the statement issued earlier today, [99, 100]Atlas' president, Larry King, acknowledged that this decision resulted from the concern over the company's recent financial condition.

現在是商業新聞時間。亞特拉斯製造公司宣布，他們可能無法如他們先前計畫的那麼早取得GW包裝公司。由於亞特拉斯昨天公佈的季度銷售報告結果顯示，其第一季度的利潤急劇下降了將近百分之十四。根據今天稍早發出的聲明，亞特拉斯的總裁賴瑞金承認，此一決定是由於擔心公司最近的財務狀況而做出的。

**詞彙** acquire 獲得；取得 profit 利潤 fall 下降 drastically 劇烈地 nearly 將近；接近 according to 根據 statement 聲明 issue 發表 decision 決定 result from由…產生的 concern 擔憂 financial 財務 condition 狀況

**98**

亞特拉斯製造公司打算要做什麼？

(A) 推出一項新產品

(B) 遷移它們的總辦公室

(C) 購入另一家公司

(D) 建立一個新品牌

**解說** 這是詢問具體內容為何的考題。「無法如他們先前計畫的那麼早取得」是指「打算購入另一家公司」的意思。 答案 (C)

**詞彙** intend 打算… launch 推出(新商品) relocate 遷移 head office 總辦公室 purchase 購買

**99**

什麼原因使這項計畫改變了？

(A) 利潤下降

(B) 不充分的工作場所

(C) 競爭對手公司的產品

(D) 法律上的衝突

**解說** 這是詢問具體內容的考題，但因沒有核心語，所以只能聽完全部錄音才能回答的。將「利潤劇降且財務狀況惡化，所以不要如預期併購」做變化來表達的(A)為答案。 答案 (A)

**詞彙** cause 致使…；使得… decline 下降 insufficient 不充分的 workplace 工作場所 legal 法律上的 conflict 衝突

**100**

誰是賴瑞金？

(A) 一位新聞記者

(B) 一位公司總裁

(C) 一位組織改革專家

(D) 一位副總裁

**解說** 該錄音裡的人名附近，出現了president，將此用相似說法來表達的(B)為答案。 答案 (B)

**詞彙** corporate head 總裁 restructuring specialist 組織改革專家 vice president 副總裁

只要7天，搞定英、日、韓單字

# 背1個，記10個
# 體驗「關鍵分類學習法」的魔力

| 短期開口說的江湖傳說，高效率學習的武林祕笈 |

WOW !!!

great !!!

〈 1書（軟精裝）＋1MP3
定價／280元 〉

**Fashion Recommended**

小開本＋MP3全收錄

站著 坐著 躺著→ 隨時記憶

# 用一本漫畫的時間，提升全球化英語能力！

所有的疑問，在《最後一次學英文》都可以找到最完美的答案！

《最後一次學英文－用一本漫畫的時間，提升全球化英語能力！》

定價／**320**元

## 學英文就靠這一本！
## 學好一次，受用一輩子！

＋ 生動比喻 ＋ 重點整理 讓你看一次就懂，看二次就精通！

# 歷史醞釀時代背景，戰爭決定弱肉強食！！

《畫給大人看的東方史－話說大河文明到帝國統一》

定價／**320**元

《畫給大人看的西方史－話說古希臘到二次大戰》

定價／**320**元

## 歷史課本變漫畫，一不小心就看完

### 6~66歲都看得懂，從早到晚都適合看！

小朋友看漫畫學歷史，考試融會貫通、一目瞭然。
大朋友看漫畫學歷史，精進事業發展的世界觀！

國家圖書館出版品預行編目(CIP)資料

50次新多益滿分的怪物講師NEW TOEIC新多益聽力攻略＋模擬試題＋解析 / 鄭相虎．金映權 合著；高俊江．賈蕙如 合譯. -- 初版. -- 臺北市：不求人文化, 2013.05 面； 公分
ISBN 978-986-89159-5-4（平裝附光碟）
1. 多益測驗
805.1895 102007284

書名 / 50 次新多益滿分的怪物講師 NEW TOEIC 新多益聽力攻略＋模擬試題＋解析
作者 / 鄭相虎．金映權
譯者 / 高俊江．賈蕙如
發行人 / 蔣敬祖
編輯顧問 / 常祈天
專案經理 / 廖晏婕
執行編輯 / 陳奕安．Jimmy Tsai
視覺指導 / 黃馨儀
內文排版 / 果實文化設計工作室
法律顧問 / 北辰著作權事務所蕭雄淋律師
印製 / 金灒印刷事業有限公司
初版 / 2013 年 05 月
出版 / 我識出版集團—不求人文化
電話 / (02) 2345-7222
傳真 / (02) 2345-5758
地址 / 台北市忠孝東路五段 372 巷 27 弄 78 之 1 號 1 樓
郵政劃撥 / 19793190
戶名 / 我識出版社
網址 / www.17buy.com.tw
E-mail / iam.group@17buy.com.tw
facebook 網址 / www.facebook.com/ImPublishing
定價 / 新台幣 599 元 / 港幣 200 元（附 1MP3 ＋ 防水書套）



台灣地區總經銷 / 易可數位行銷股份有限公司
地址 / 新北市新店區寶橋路 235 巷 6 弄 3 號 5 樓

港澳總經銷 / 和平圖書有限公司
地址 / 香港柴灣嘉業街 12 號百樂門大廈 17 樓
電話 / （852）2804-6687 傳真 / （852）2804-6409

不求人文化
Diy Culture Publishing

不求人文化
Diy Culture Publishing